I0730871

The Manson & Barbara Show

JAMES MURRAY

The Manson & Barbara Show by James Murray

ISBN 978-1-955136-18-1 (Paperback)
ISBN 978-1-955136-19-8 (Hardback)
ISBN 978-1-955136-20-4 (eBook)

This book is written to provide information and motivation to readers. Its purpose is not to render any type of psychological, legal, or professional advice of any kind. The content is the sole opinion and expression of the author, and not necessarily that of the publisher.

Copyright © 2021 by James Murray

All rights reserved. No part of this book may be reproduced, transmitted, or distributed in any form by any means, including, but not limited to, recording, photocopying, or taking screenshots of parts of the book, without prior written permission from the author or the publisher. Brief quotations for noncommercial purposes, such as book reviews, permitted by Fair Use of the U.S. Copyright Law, are allowed without written permissions, as long as such quotations do not cause damage to the book's commercial value. For permissions, write to the publisher, whose address is stated below.

Printed in the United States of America.

New Leaf Media, LLC
175 S. 3ʳᵈ Street, Suite 200
Columbus, OH 43215
www.thenewleafmedia.com

Chapter 1

Black Creek, New York
September 30, 1984
6:30 P.M.

Thunder roared as rain poured hard onto the street, with police cars surrounding the wreck that I stood in front of. A cold wind was lightly blowing. The dead driver's head was sticking halfway out of the car window, with some broken shards of glass embedded in it. An arm was hanging out. Blood, from both parts of the body, was dripping slowly down to the asphalt. I snapped a picture of this image with my camera, then examined the rest of the wrecked car. The driver had tried getting away from the cops. He thought he could lose them by going through a red light, which had ended his life. He was also not wearing his seatbelt.

Behind me was a wrecked Ford pickup truck. It had clipped the back bumper of the stolen car, causing it to spin and crashed head-on to a streetlight. I walked over to the front side of the stolen car and snapped one more picture, as I didn't need to waste all my film. Hunter walked in like a villain, trenched coat billowing from behind. His blonde hair and green eyes, the only colors, to break the black ensemble.

I was wearing a matching black trench coat, dark grey pants, boots, and leather gloves with finger openings. I had short black hair and dark blue eyes.

"We're done here, Hunter," I said. He had finished asking all the cops the questions we needed.

"This should do well in the paper."

"Sure. A short high-speed pursuit ends when the idiot drives through a red light. Gets clipped by a truck, drove head-on to a streetlight, killing himself, because of a beat-up V8 muscle car. Yeah, I bet it will be a real page turner." I turned and walked away, as Hunter followed me over towards my dark blue & silver '84 Honda CR-X. It had black tinted windows, a spoiler, and side skirts with dual side exhaust pipes.

"You know, Curtis, it's going to take time until we get a big story."

We both got inside my Honda. "I know that, but we're in New York. You'd think we would get something better than this! Sure, it might gain a few readers, but after they are done, they'll go read about sports, nuclear war, politics and all that other shit. I'd just like something better than this."

"Well, for now, it's what we got to work with." I nodded and stopped at a red light.

"What are you doing tonight," Hunter asked.

"I'll have a beer back home. Put something on to watch for a bit then go to bed."

"The single life, huh?" Hunter chuckled.

"So are you." I countered.

"Well, I'm trying to find me the right chick."

When the light turned green, I chose the quickest way to News 6. "Let me guess? You're looking for a hot sexy chick with really huge breasts, wide curvy hips and a big ass."

"You know me so well," Hunter grinned.

"You can find them dancing at any strip club. Those aren't the relationship kind, though."

"Well, you just have to know how to make them like you, over the other men they dance for."

"I'll tell you what. If you can do it without losing all your money, then I'll try it."

"Deal."

I got onto the highway. Traffic was pretty bad. I was in no rush to return to News 6 Studios, as they are always closed on Sundays. "I'm getting hungry! I think I'm going to order me a pizza and wings."

"I won't mind that, as well. Say wanna split dinner?"

"Sure."

When I got into the city, I drove through stop lights and slow-moving cars until I drove into the underground parking garage lot. We walked over to the elevator. I pressed the button to the film developing room.

"Here, I'll do the film while you write the story." Hunter suggested.

"Alright." I gave him my camera.

"Should take me no more than a few minutes."

"Okay, you know where to find me, when you're done."

When the elevator reached the right floor, Hunter walked out. I pressed the button to our office. It was quiet inside. I could hear the wheels moving while pulling on the cable. When the elevator came to a full stop the light above me flickered a bit, then the doors opened. I had to walk down the hallway, to get to my office. The door had my full name on it, Curtis Parker.

I pulled up my leather chair, sat down, and then turned on my computer. I turned on my desk lamp. I have one of the corner offices, over-looking Black Creek City. For a 20-year-old, this was the best view anybody could ask for. I had been working for News 6 for a year now and had been doing alright. Hunter, who was four years older than me, had been here for three years, and I had him to thank for getting me this job. I would have ended up flipping burgers at some local McDonald's or some other shitty job.

I turned back to my computer, opened my writing text program. I hope one day, Hunter and I, would have the biggest story ever. We could make a name for ourselves and get better ratings. I began typing the stolen V8 story. I added that the driver in the Ford pickup had walked away unharmed, however the car thief was killed in the crash. When I finished, I printed three sheets. They would all be edited into the newspaper to fit onto one page. I took the sheets from the printer and turned off my computer. I didn't hear any movement, so I knew Hunter was still working on the film.

I was glad I had finished high school, as I had a good-paying job and my own place. I felt proud, and so did my parents. Little brother, John, eight years old, was living with them. He was born in '76, and I was twelve years old when John came into this world. I was happy to have a brother. We fought like all siblings, but we like each other. I always let him go first in anything we did. I would call in on my parents, along with John, to see how everyone was doing. No bullies in my baby brother's life, yet. So far, so good. I had my fair share of them. I gave the last one a black eye, along with a broken nose, making him miss his high school graduation photo.

I was glad I had kept in shape and was able to handle myself. However, since then I had moved into my own apartment. John was getting older, and he needed more room. And Mom didn't like my choice of music. I also didn't want her knowing I liked buying porn videos, but I hated being single. There were some good-looking girls I could have hooked up with, if I only had the balls back then, but I was sure I'd eventually find the right woman, or hook up with a stripper, if Hunter's idea worked better than mine.

My wristwatch read 7:15 p.m. I turned back to the window. Rain was coming down harder, and lightning cracked the sky from time to time. I can hear Hunter coming my way. I stood up, holding onto the sheets of paper, and turned off my desk lamp, then walked out of my office and closed the door.

"Okay, got the photos done." Hunter had a stack of them in one hand.

"Here's our story." I handed the sheets to him.

"We'll just drop this off on Dan's desk and he'll take care of the rest for us."

We left our stuff on the layout guy's desk. He would be coming in at four in the morning to start getting the paper ready. Our story would be on Monday's paper. I was just glad I didn't have his job, as I hated getting up early in the morning.

We got back into the parking lot and headed to the best pizza place in Black Creek. We paid for our dinners. It only took around fifteen minutes. Once we had taken our food, I dropped Hunter off at his house. After his mother's death he now owned the place. It was a small house, so he didn't have much to look after.

"Alright Curtis, see you on Tuesday."

"Yep, see you on Tuesday."

Traffic was being a real bitch. I reached my apartment past eight. I was locking the door when I realized Hunter has my camera! Damn it. Oh well, I'll get it back on Tuesday.

I sat my pizza and wings onto the nightstand. I took off my boots and trench coat. Placed them into my closet. Carried my dinner into the kitchen. I placed five pizza slices and most of the wings on a plate. Grabbed a bottle of Dead Moon beer from the fridge and went back to the living room. I sat down on the sofa and set down my plate of food and my beer on the coffee table. I found the remote but had to get up, went back to the kitchen and opened the window. I felt the cool air blowing inside my apartment. I felt better already.

I turned the TV on and flipped through the channels. Most of the TV shows were boring soap operas, crappy late-night movies, game shows and religious bullshit.

I stopped on the weather report, and I heard a female voice, "Monday calls for more showers, along with overcast skies, however on Tuesday we should see some sunlight, but with cooler winds, as fall has finally come. But enjoy that sun while you can because we'll be getting another thunderstorm on Friday and Saturday. That's your weather forecast for this week. Good night, residents of Black Creek."

I grabbed the remote and flipped through a few more channels, but nothing was on. I pressed "input" and my screen went blank, and in white text it said in the right corner of the screen, "VIDEO ONE." I got up, walked over to my VHS shelf. I had a couple of movies, along with my collection of porn. I looked through them, then chose *"Hot Naked Chicks Gone Wild On The Beach."* The VHS player was set up on top of my TV. One smart move I did behind my landlord's back, is that I had sound-proofed the windows and the floor, so I would be able to enjoy my videos without anyone bitching that I was being too loud.

I reached over for a hot slice of pizza and took a bite, as I saw the title of the film come on the screen, and below it was a tropical island. The view then went onto the beach, as it showed ten very young and sexy looking women wearing very thin bras, bikinis and thongs, with huge breasts bouncing in slow-mo, wide sexy hips and nice round butt cheeks.

I grinned, eating my pizza, while the ladies ran towards the water. I saw their swimsuits were coming off, as the screen showed close-ups of the models and freeze frames showing their names. I wonder if I could hook up with any of them, if they are single, that is. When the names are done, they ran off into the water swimming. I reached for my cold beer and took a drink, as the camera, now under water, showed them swimming deeper. There were some colorful fish swimming with them, as the camera got close to their bodies, showing close-ups of their huge breasts bouncing freely in the water, then showing a view of their sexy asses.

I bet the cameraman got a boner from filming all of this! I ate some more and watched as they swam to the surface and went back to the island, where they posed for the camera and placed their hands on each other's huge breasts, playing with them. I felt my cock getting hard, watching this. I tried to keep myself relaxed, so I wouldn't cum in my underwear. Halfway through the video, I had to pause it so I could relieve myself. After I took care of that, I watched the rest of the video and went to bed.

Oct. 2 9:00 A.M.

I drove into the News 6 building with Hunter, and he remembered to give me back my camera.

"I got to stop doing that," Hunter said.

We pulled into my parking spot. Our story did well, as it was some nice action, however it wasn't a big story, so everyone forgot about it. Only a few that liked it, hung onto it.

I pressed the button as we waited for the elevator.

"Maybe today we'll get lucky." Hunter was always a hopeful guy.

"Maybe, but I'll bet on the 13th, on Saturday, we'll get something good."

"Aww yes, the 13th. If you really believe in that supernatural stuff."

"Well, there's things I believe, however the rest of this world doesn't, but when it's all about God and all that bullshit, everyone just accepts it."

"Well, I heard the boss was pleased with our work, and we'll be getting paid for that. However, he didn't use that closeup shot."

"I know, 'cause he doesn't have the balls to do it." Censure is ridiculous our news department isn't consistent in this stuff.

"You know everyone would throw a fit if they saw that in their morning paper," Hunter warned.

"I thought people pay to see violence?"

"True, but the other half doesn't want to see that."

"Yeah, all they want to see is the same old bullshit." I was checking the elevator's floor level indicator, it felt like it hadn't moved. I pressed the button a few more times.

"Don't tell me the elevators are out again," Hunter sighed.

"You'd think with the money they make, this place could get better stuff." I bet the bastards on News 18 have elevators that come when they want it.

"Oh, don't forget to say thanks to Dan, as he had a very rough morning on Monday."

"Let me guess? Him and his wife are splitting up?"

"Yep."

"I don't want to get married or have children. Just have a girlfriend. Keep life simple and easy."

"I wouldn't mind having a daughter, but I'll do that when I'm older." Hunter is on a wistful track this morning.

"Hope you have the money for it!" I teased him.

"Oh, I will! I won't just knock up some random chick and try to get more money from the tree, just keep all three of us with a roof over our heads."

The elevator doors opened, as we stepped inside and pressed the office floor.

When we got to our floor, everyone was working. We went to Dan's desk. He was Japanese, with short hair, glasses and light blue eyes. He was wearing a white sport coat, red tie, dark grey pants, and a black shirt with a silver watch.

"Morning, Dan." Dan lifted his eyes up at us.

"Hey Dan, thanks again."

"You're welcome, boys. The boss told me to tell you two he left some work for you to do."

"Alright, thanks again Dan." We walked away into our offices, where I saw a pile of notes. I pulled up my chair and looked through them. It was different stories our boss wanted me to do. While Hunter and I worked together, sometimes we did two different stories. However, since he didn't have a car, I would have to drive him. Hunter was saving up his money until he could afford his own ride.

My Honda had been tuned since I bought it because it was a slow car. Hunter wanted to get a Mustang or some other V8 muscle car, so he would be able to drive to any story he had to do on time, rather than having me drive him all over the place. He did own a car once, but it was a piece of shit, which ended up getting scrapped and he only got $800 dollars for it. I always wanted a big truck, but my Honda would have to do for now.

I heard a knock on my door. It was Hunter.

"Come in."

"So, our boss gave us some work to do?" Hunter opened the door and closed it.

"Yep, let's get started on that bank robbery, then we'll head over to South Side, where a murder happened."

"Shouldn't we go to the murder first," Hunter suggested.

"News 18 will be all over it and they won't allow us anywhere near it until they get what they need."

"Alright, let's get going then." We left my office and went to my boss' office, as we had to let him know what stories we would be reporting. Jake sat in his big leather chair wearing his brown suit. Dark black hair, brown eyes, and glasses. His desk was very wide, and he had a computer along with a phone beside him.

"Morning Jake. Hunter and I have picked these two stories here." I showed him.

"Do the murder one first. I heard News 18 isn't interested. They're too busy doing a story about some Christian thing." Jake spoke with a rough voice.

"Alright," Hunter agreed.

"After that we'll do the robbery report as well," I added.

"Don't be gone too long," Jake nodded and gestured for us to go.

Just as we were about to leave, Jake hailed my attention. "Oh Curtis, when you get back, I need to speak with you."

"Sure thing, boss." Leaving his office and got onto the elevator, and I made sure my camera was ready.

"I think I know what he wants to talk about, and I wish he wouldn't bust my balls over it."

"Maybe he won't?" Hunter pressed the button for the parking lot.

"I can see it on his face," I argued.

"Let's just get these two stories done, then worry about that later," Hunter advised. I didn't say anything as the elevator went down to the parking garage. We both got off and got into my Honda. I started it up and we sped off. When we reached the crime scene, the body was covered in a white blanket, which had the murder victim's blood on it. Police had taped off the scene, but allowed us to get the pictures I needed, while Hunter asked the questions. The cops told us the man had been shot five times in the back, with a 9MM pistol. After finishing his late shift at work. His wallet had been taken along with his keys. However, the killer didn't know the guy had parked his car a few blocks away. They found out from a co-worker of his when his car hasn't left its spot. So he was still on foot, or already had a ride.

Black Creek was no stranger to crime. This city has had its fair share of brutal murders and small-time gang fights that mostly happened in North Side, but that had died down after the crackdown back in '82. I finished getting the pictures I needed, and Hunter walked over to me, putting his note pad into his trench coat pocket.

"Alright, next story." I followed Hunter to my Honda.

"So, what did you get from them?" I asked.

"Not much," Hunter said. Apparently, the police don't know who the killer is. The murder happened around six or seven in the morning, and this is the dead section of this city.

"We'll keep our ears open about this, as this might lead to something good." We were on our way to the other side of town where the robbery took place. However, when we got to the scene, we saw the News 18 van parked in front of the bank, and that bastard, Ken Cage.

"What the hell?! I thought he was doing that Christian event!"

"Guess they changed their minds," Hunter deadpanned.

"Goddamn bastard! At least we got that murder story." I made a U-turn and drove back to News 6.

12:00 P.M.

I finished writing what Hunter had written down, and he came back with the developed photos, and we gave them to Dan to get tomorrow's paper ready. Since it was lunch time, Hunter and I could grab a bite, then I could speak to Jake, as he was a very busy man. It didn't take Hunter long to get us a couple of subs from the shop down the street, along with some cold cans of cola. We ate in the break room. The weather was a lot better than it was on Sunday. Once I finished my lunch, I left the break room and knocked on Jake's door.

"Aww Curtis, please come in."

I entered his office and closed the door and walked over to his desk and pulled up the chair.

"I heard that News 18 beat you two, to the robbery story?"

"Yeah, but we got the murder story, so that should pull in more readers."

"Yes, that's good, but that's the reason I brought you here. I saw the photo you wanted to use for that police chase."

"I knew it."

"Curtis, I know you're trying hard to get our name out there, but the public don't want to see the nasty stuff like that in their morning paper. It's too graphic."

I thought, *all talk, but no bark or bite.* "Well, the pictures I snapped of the murder victim wrapped in a white blanket, which is now blood red, will be in tomorrow's morning paper."

"At least that one is covered up, and the images are in black & white. Now, I don't want to make this a big deal. Just try to keep the violence toned down a bit, as words mean more than pictures."

I didn't agree with Jake, but I wasn't going to make a big deal over it. "Alright. I'll try not getting so graphic next time."

"Alright. You're free now. You guys are doing a good job. See if there's some extra work you and Hunter can do."

"On it." I got up and left Jake's office and checked the board and saw mostly boring stuff. I sighed and thought, might as well help Dan out, since I got nothing better to do.

5:00 P.M.

Hunter and I left the news studio, and I dropped him off at home after we cashed our paychecks. We would have Saturday and Sunday off, then back to work on Monday. I didn't feel like spending my days off alone in my apartment. I would see if my brother John wanted to go to the movies. When I pulled into my apartment parking lot, I went through the back and up the five flight of stairs and reached my room. I took off my boots, then went into the kitchen and grabbed the phone from the wall. I began dialing my parents' home number, and I put the phone to my ear and waited for the beeping to stop. However, when it stopped all, I got was the answering machine.

"Hey John, it's Curtis. I was calling to ask if you wanted to go see a show on Saturday? When you get this message give me a call back, OK? And oh, say hi to mom and dad. I'll talk to you later. Bye."

I hung the phone up and felt tired. Walked out of the kitchen, then went into my bedroom. I took most of my clothes off but left my underwear on and rested my back onto my bed. Closing my eyes to try and get some rest.

8:15 P.M.

I woke up when I heard phone ringing in the kitchen. I manage to get up and walk through the half-dark building and grabbed the phone. I almost bumped into the wall. I turned on the kitchen light and said, "Hello?"

"Hey Curtis!" John sounded so enthusiastic.

I yawned and said, "Hey John."

"You sound tired."

"Oh, you just woke me up. I felt tired after work, so I took a nap."

"So you wanna go to the movies on Saturday?"

"Sure."

"What's playing?"

"Hold on a second. I know I have the paper here somewhere." I it in the living room. I let the phone hang from its cord, then grabbed the paper and went back into the kitchen. I placed the phone back to my ear as I was going through it. "Okay, let's see."

"Any good horror movies? I like watching a good scary movie."

"Umm no, I don't see any. I know Halloween will have all the horror stuff." I laughed.

"What about action then?"

"Wait, how's "Big Mean Truckers" sound?"

"Anything else?"

I looked at the films and said, "No, unless you want to see the latest chick flick that's playing."

"Eww! No."

I chuckled and said, "OK, it's "Big Mean Truckers" on Saturday at 2 P.M."

"OK, we can grab lunch before the show." I said, "Alright, sounds good. Say, is mom or dad there?"

"No, dad's still at work, and mom stepped out to get something."

"Alright, let them know that I called, and we're going to the show this Saturday."

"Alright, see you soon Curtis."

"OK John, talk to you later."

"Alright. Bye Curtis."

He hung up as I placed the phone back onto its rack. I was glad I was able to hang out with my brother. However, my parents were a bit more difficult, as they had different shifts from me. But I would work something out, and I always got to see them on Halloween, Christmas and our birthdays. I checked the clock on the wall, I felt a bit hungry. I would make a little snack, then head off to bed. I had some things to do in the morning. I hope Hunter and I would have more to go on with that murder story, so we could get more people to read our paper. Sometimes I wish I had the reporter bonuses, but Jake let the other people handle that, as he didn't feel I was ready for it. Maybe if I did get my big story, I might just get that bonus.

Oct.6
11:00-AM

I drove through the neighborhood to pick up John I had Bathory self-titled tape playing 7th track Armageddon loudly. I was wearing my dark sunglasses with my trench coat, black shirt, dark blue jeans and boots and my leather gloves with finger openings. I was looking forward to having a good time as my murder story was cut short after the police got a lead and arrested the guy. Just another dumb shit, thought he could get away with murder. Hunter and I wrote our wrap up on that story. It was already forgotten, as the man he killed didn't have many family members left.

However, the bastards at News 18 got their big story about the robbery as the master minds had pulled off three more jobs across the states leading to New York. I really hated that Ken Cage guy. He was a fucking bloodhound that had his nose so far up this city's ass he could be the first to find anything good before anyone else did. One day I was going to get my big break with Hunter on my side and rub it all over Ken's face. For now, I would forget about it since it wasn't worth holding a grudge over. I had to keep my cool. If I let the pressure get to me, then I would lose it all.

I pulled up to my parents' house, it was very big. In the driveway was my father's 80 white Oldsmobile Custom Cruiser, it had wooden panels on its sides. I blew my horn. John wave his arm out of the living room window. He ran out the front door wearing his grey sweatpants, running shoes, dark red sweater with his favorite hockey team on it. He had the same hair and eye color as me.

"Hey Curtis."

"Hey John." Just as he got in, I saw my father coming out the front door speed walking towards us. I shifted the gear into park and roll down my driver side window.

Our father had grayish white hair, dark blue eyes. Wearing long sleeve sweater, jeans and leather slippers.

"Hey dad."

He smiled and said, "Hey Curtis I saw your stories this week."

"Not much but it gets me paid."

"You're doing great, Curtis. Your mother and I are very pleased."

"Thanks dad."

"Want to go out on Sunday for some beer and wings?"

"Sure."

"I'll pick you up at your place around 6-PM."

"OK sounds good."

"Alright, you two have a good time."

"Ok, dad see you later." John waved our father goodbye.

"See ya." I shifted the gear into reverse and slowly backed out as father waved at us.

"What song is this?"

"Oh I lost track, just picked it up yesterday."

John picked up the Bathory tape case and pressed the rewind button and got back onto the track I was on.

"Thanks, John." I smiled at him.

"I have my own collection of music which I only play when mom isn't around. She doesn't like it."

I laughed and said, "I know she doesn't listen to that."

"Always playing her Beatles or country."

"Well, John when your time comes, you'll get your own place like me and you can listen to your music whenever you want."

I came to a four way stop and John said, "I miss having you around."

"I do, too. Even mom and dad. But I need to work in order to get paid as money doesn't grow on trees."

"Well, if it does you just have to know how to get it."

"Kind of. But don't worry, when I get more time off, we'll hang out some more."

"Ok."

I was now driving through the city of Black Creek, I asked, "So John what's new?"

"Nothing much. School still the same. There's a big Halloween party coming up."

"Thinking about going?"

"Nah, I can't dance."

"You don't have to dance. You could find yourself a nice girlfriend."

"Girls…they seem too much."

I smiled and said, "You could just start out as friends. You know when I finished high school I never went to those parties. All the pretty girls we're taken by the guys who're mostly jerks. Only a few were good ones. And if I had gone, I might have gotten lucky."

"I'll think about it."

"Alright and if you need help, I'm always here for you, brother."

John nodded, a red light came up I stopped and asked, "What else?"

"Well, my friends and I played some street hockey a few days ago.

"During the rain?"

"Yeah, real men stand out in the rain."

I laughed and John said, "That's about it, I been watching a lot of cartoons lately."

The light turned green. I pressed my foot down and asked, "Like what?"

"My favorite is Transformers, He-Man and Scooby Doo."

"Oh, I've seen some of those. Yeah, those are some cool shows."

"I wish there was a horror one. I really don't like the new season of Scooby Doo, it isn't good as the previous seasons we're."

"Yeah. I wish they would give Scooby a girlfriend."

John turned his head and asked, "A girlfriend?"

"Yeah, a female dog. You'd think with all the cases he and the gang have solved, he deserves to have a reward."

"I think they would get him neutered."

"That isn't right!"

"Well, I guess he could. But it would take more than a new character to get me liking a series. It needs better writers."

"Yes, the story is more important than adding the love scenes."

John laughed.

We grabbed french fries with hot dogs and cold cans of Coke. I checked, it was 12:00-PM. We have enough time to make it to the show.

As we began eating John asked, "So, how have you been?"

"Alright. Very busy with work. Hunter and I continue trying to get our big story."

"Is that all you do?"

I looked at John and said, "Well, when I have free time, I like hanging out with you and our parents. Sometimes Hunter and hang out." I couldn't think what else to say. I wasn't going to tell John I watched porn. hat yet.

"Ever thought of being a writer?"

I took a bite out of my hot dog and after eating it and said, "No, I never thought of that. But I do read books, from time to time. Not really a big reader."

"I'm thinking of being an author. I'm saving up my money so I can get a typewriter and write down some story ideas."

"That's great, John. I would like to read them."

"I'll let you read them, when I finish them. As most of my ideas are just rough drafts."

"Alright."

"I'll tell you this, I have mostly dark fantasy and horror stuff planned with some sci-fi ideas."

"Well, if you want to be an author, I'll be willing to help you proofread your work for you."

"Thanks Curtis."

"Anything for you."

We finished our lunch and got back into my Honda and drove to the theatre, we got a good parking spot. We both got out and went inside where I saw the posters for the films. Big Mean Truckers had a buffed-up guy holding a pistol with a busty chick beside him. In the background was a truck jumping over a roadblock in a big explosion.

"This is going to be awesome!" John enthused.

I paid for our tickets and went to see the show. We had good seats as there wasn't that many people there. We won't have to worry about getting out after the show was over. It didn't take long for the show to get going.

4:15-PM

We left the theatre and John said, "Damn that was a good movie."

"Yep, it was." I grinned at John.

"I hope that gets a sequel."

"If they do it right, then I'll see it, too."

He turned to me and said, "Yeah, I know what you mean."

"Anything you want to do before I drop you off?"

John rested his arms on the hood of my Honda and said, "Umm no. But I wish we could do something else."

"Well, we'll hang out again."

"Yeah, okay."

"Alright, let's get you home."

Oct.7
6:00-PM

True to his word, my father pulled into the apartment parking lot in his Oldsmobile. It was lightly raining, and the sky was gray. I walked over and got into the passenger seat. I closed the door and said, "Hey dad."

"Hey Curtis. I heard you and John had a good time at the show."

"Yes, we did." My father backed the Oldsmobile out of the parking lot and drove out.

"It rained a lot last night."

"Yeah, it did. Glad I'm mostly an indoor person."

"Did John tell you about his writing?"

"Yes, he did. I told him if he wants to be an author, I would be willing to help proofread his work."

"Good. I'm glad you two kept in touch."

"I keep in touch with you and mom, too."

"I know, we're proud of you. We're planning on having a big dinner. I wanted to know if you would be able to come."

"I might be able to, if I'm not busy with work."

"Ever thought of working at another news studio?"

"I thought about it. But the rest are out of Black Creek area, which means I would have to move. I really don't have the money for that. I also don't want to work for News 18, I hate that Ken Cage guy."

My father chuckled and said, "I can't stand that guy either. I wonder how the hell he got where he is."

"Dirty luck that's how."

"Well, one day Curtis you'll get your big story. But I hope it doesn't involve a nice woman or child as I hate reading those type of stories. Or kidnappings! I heard some sicko tried to take this young girl and rape her while filming it."

"Oh yes, and News 18 got that story first."

"I don't get it, what goes through some of these people minds when they do sick shit like that. It isn't right."

"Yes, it's very messed up. If I do get a story like that, then I'll make sure I bring the bastard behind bars."

"Just be careful if you do. You'll never know what's waiting for you on the other side."

"I will." My father nodded and drove to the restaurant/bar parking lot.

We got the usual spot and waited for a waitress to come. It didn't take long. We both ordered our drinks and what we wanted, then she left us alone.

"So, how is mother doing?"

"She's doing alright. Been keeping busy, with work."

"That's good."

"Also goes out with her friends, too." I nodded my head and he continued, "I plan to go on vacation with, some friends by the end of October."

"What you plan on doing?"

"Camping."

"At River Point?"

My father nodded and said, "Yes I'll be spending about two weeks. John should be able to take care of your mother, while I'm gone."

"I remember that big bass I caught when we went up their back in '79."

"Oh yes, and it nearly caused you to fall into the water."

I laughed. "I still got the picture of me holding it. And that bass made a wonderful dinner."

My father laughed some more. Then the waitress came with our order, then set it down onto the table. She smiled and said, "Enjoy." She walked away and we began eating.

The storm grew worse outside. With thunder roaring, my father and I ate our chicken wings and French fries.

I finished my dinner I said, "That was good."

My father nodded. The waitress came over and asked, "Refills?"

My father shook his head and said, "We're ready for our bill."

She said, "Alright, I'll go get it."

"Here, I'll pay half with you."

"Alright." When the bill came, we split it then went outside and got into his Oldsmobile. He drove to my apartment and dropped me off.

"I'll call you if I'm able to come to the family dinner."

My father said, "Alright. And if you can't, don't worry about it."

"Alright see you later, Dad." I got out and closed the door and walked towards the back door.

I went up the five flights of stairs and unlocked my apartment room. I went inside and I took off my boots and jacket, then walked over to the kitchen. It was 8:00-PM, I went into my bedroom took off the rest of my clothes but left my underwear on and relaxed on the sofa. I turned on the TV, I flipped through channels 'til I found something to watch. It felt very cool inside my apartment, when I felt I was nodding off a bit. I reached for the remote turned off the TV and went to sleep.

Oct.8
9:00-AM

As I pulled into the parking lot of News 6 Studios, beside my parking spot Hunter was standing behind a black 83 Ford LTD sedan. He smiled as I shifted the gear into park then got out.

"So now you got a car."

"Bought it for $1500 dollars, and this car is in good shape."

"Nice deal." I nodded at him.

"Alright, let's get to work." We walked towards the elevator I press the button and saw it coming down.

Hunter turned to me and said, "I had some extra money, so I bought a CB radio. I can pick up police, big rig, or even other radio channels. So, if News 18 is on to something, we can jump in on them and get all the credit."

"Nice going." I chuckled

"Now, I'll I need is a black outfit and I'll look like I'm FBI."

I laughed as the elevator doors opened. I pressed the office button as the door closed, but the lights above us flickered a bit.

When the elevator reached the office floor we stepped out and walked towards our offices. When we got there, Jake walked in, and he called our attention.

"The mayor is giving a speech about gang violence. I want you two to cover it and interview the mayor."

"On it," I replied.

"Get going as most of the news studios will be showing up. And don't cause any trouble."

"You can trust us, Jake." I gave him a shit-eating smile. We left the news studio as we drive in Hunter Ford LTD sedan.

d weather was a lot nicer but still very cold. I sat in the passenger seat and saw Hunter set the radio up.

"Did it take long to set it up?" I asked him.

"Nope, it's very easy to set up." Hunter told me how it works. I turned the knob to see if we could pick up said radio channels.

"Damn this is great!" Suddenly I picked up News 18 channel as I heard Ken saying, *"Goddamn it, honey! How could you lose our house keys! How the hell am I going to get home after work!"* Hunter and I laughed, and we heard him say, *"Find the damn thing yourself! I gotta interview the mayor today and this goddamn traffic!"*

"We can beat that bastard to the mayor!" I exclaimed.

"Alright, we'll get our big break now." Hunter pressed his foot further onto the gas pedal driving through a yellow light before it turned red. He knows all the short cuts in the city of Black Creek.

We've beaten Ken Cage to the City Hall. As we walked over, we showed the officers standing by our ID cards, and they let us inside.

City hall had a very Gothic look to it. Built in the mid-1800s which most of the buildings still had that look while the rest of it had more of modern look to it. I opened the front doors as the floor was dark with bright white walls and ceiling with lights hanging above us. Large pictures showed Black Creek pass. Walking through it we came to the speech room as me and Hunter got front row seats with some other news reporters there. And that meant Ken Cage won't be able to get the good seats as we've beaten him for once and I've been waiting for pay back.

At 9:45-AM the mayor came out, I had my camera ready, while Hunter would ask the questions. I snapped a few pictures as the mayor held a sheet of paper and set it down onto stand.

"Good morning, everyone. I'm glad that you all can make it. B.C.P.D. Chief Frank West is unable to make it, so he asked me to tell you this. As police chief of Black Creek Police Department, he will clean up these filthy streets of crime. I will make it my mission to keep our people safe. Families can raise their children in a safe environment, so they can grow up and raise the next generations to come."

The crowd applauded. I snapped a picture of mayor smiling.

"The crime has risen too high in my city. I will not allow it to get any higher! I will have our fellow officers step up their game, to bring in these criminals who are harming our streets. We will try to bring them in but if they want to go down fighting, then we'll take them down, so they don't pose a threat to anyone who doesn't need to die."

The claps grew louder I snapped another picture with Hunter writing down everything the mayor was saying. The mayor looked at his sheet of paper. He flipped it to the next sheet and looked back at the crowd, while keeping his mouth not too far away from the microphone. He talked more about how crime was starting to make his city look bad, along with drugs. He was going to clear it up so the people will be proud to have a good mayor. He finished up by thanking the police officers for risking their lives to make this city safer and better.

"Now, I'll be taking questions." Hunter went first and knew what to ask him. I snapped a picture of him looking over at Hunter. As he got his questions answered, I heard a back door open. I knew who it was and could picture Ken Cage's face being late.

As the mayor answered more questions, Hunter and I got everything we needed. We got up and left. I turned to see Ken Cage looking pissed. I grinned at him, as we left city hall. We got into Hunter's Ford and drove back to News 6 Studio's. Jake was very happy with our work. For getting good coverage, we would be given a little bonus. This made me very happy. I felt more people would choose us over News 18. Dan took out the photos to be made, while Hunter and I we're writing out tomorrow's paper.

By 12:00-PM we we're all finished and went on a lunch break. I drove to Wendy's, as I felt like having a burger. Hunter and I grab our lunch and we got Dan his lunch, as well. Hunter drove back to the studio and went into the break room to eat. Dan thanked me.

"You're welcome, Dan. We got a great story for tomorrow's paper, and we'll have gained more views than News 18."

"I heard Ken was late," Dan chuckled.

"Yeah, his wife lost their house keys and was stuck in traffic," Hunter replied. We laughed some more as we finished our lunch and did what little work that had to be done until it was time to punch out.

Oct.9
9:00-AM

Hunter and I had our spirits up when we came in. We had made a big break for the news. Dan showed the News 6 paper with a picture of the mayor and text above it saying, "MAYOR WANTS GANG VIOLENCE TO END!"

"Very good work. We gained more views and now News 6 has topped News 18. Let's keep it up." Jake was saying during the morning staff meeting. Everyone clapped and then we were ordered to get back to work.

Hunter and I went to our respective offices. I saw sheets of stories to work on. I picked the ones that were good. We left our offices to go report on crimes.

I wrote down different crime stories. Some of them didn't tie in with the gang violence. I thought of stretching the truth just a bit so we could keep up higher ratings. People would buy it and won't think to ask twice about it. I knew if Jake found out what I was planning. I would get fired, but as long I didn't fuck it up, I would be fine. When I was done gathering details for the stories, I got into my Honda and drove back to News 6, writing the stories on my computer.

By 11:45-AM I had finished writing all the stories for tomorrow's paper. I took all the printed sheets and gave them to Dan for editing. I sat back in my office and looked out the window. It was very cloudy and windy. I could see lots of traffic on the streets below me.

I heard a knock on the door, I turned and saw Hunter. "d just finished getting the back stories. Dan got his hands full."

"Can't wait to see the look on Ken Cage's face when we make the bigger headlines."

"I heard he was pissed about us beating him so much, he had a breakdown at his office," Hunter laughed.

"Really?"

"Heard on it on the CB radio. The police had to come and take him in, until he cooled off."

Hunter and I laughed for a bit, "Let's get something to eat," I suggested.

"Yeah, all this work got me hungry."

I stood up and Hunter moved out of the way. We drove in my Honda, grabbed some burger and fries to eat. We took our lunch into the break room and ate with the rest of the staff.

"This mayor really is working his ass off to get rid of crime," Dan said with a tinge of admiration.

"The mayor isn't joking around. I heard already the police had arrested half of this city's gangs. With the rest getting killed during a shootout and our reporters we're the first to get this action," a colleague added.

"Just think by next year, we'll be the biggest news studio. We can finally have our own reporters with News 6 Studios' theme song."

"We should get a heavy metal band to make our theme song," I commented.

"I agree with you on that," Hunter pointed at me.

"You two are forgetting something else," Dan said mysteriously.

"Let me guess. A sexy reporter, right?" I joked. The others chuckled.

"Not just one, but two," Dan added. We all laughed. Finished our lunches and went back to work. I wrote down a few more stories that I thought were good for our paper, and had Dan edit them and relaxed in my chair. I thought about that family dinner. I haven't seen my mother for a while.

I reached over to my phone picked it up and dialed my parents' house number. After a few seconds, I heard my mother voice say, "Hello? Who is this?"

"Hi mom, it's me."

"Oh hi, Curtis. How are you doing?" I can hear her smile over the line.

"I'm doing alright, been busy working here."

"I've seen the stories you've done in the paper. I'm just glad we don't live near the city with all this crime going on."

"I'm sure things will quiet down over here. Say, I wanted to let you know that I would like to come over the family dinner."

"That's good news, sweetie. Okay, we're having it on this Saturday around 6-PM."

"Perfect. I'm off that day and I'll be able to come."

"Great, I look forward to seeing you again Curtis."

"Same here, mom." I'm looking forward for the week to end.

Oct.13
5:40-PM

It was a very cool evening, with thick fog and light rain fall. The sky was almost the same color as the fog. I had my wipers going. The street wasn't too busy, not many cars driving by, or people out walking. The stories Hunter and I have written we're doing very well. Jake plans on having our own big news team. If I was lucky Hunter and I could be part of it. The greatest news of the week though was Ken Cage has been fired. When I reached my parents' house, I saw in the driveway my mom's sisters 82 Chevrolet Malibu. Park next to it was a black 80 Cadillac Fleetwood Brougham. My father's brother's car. He lives out in Texas. I parked behind them just glad my Honda wasn't a big car.

I walked to the front door. Rang the bell but noticed there was something in the mailbox. I thought the post office doesn't deliver mail on Saturdays. Guess, it's one of those Jehovah's Witnesses assholes. I opened the mailbox and took out a thick black two-page booklet. On the front of it was old style fancy text in dark purple. It read, *"The Manson & Barbara Show"*. Under the text was an anthropomorphic white bat man wearing an old style dark purple suit, purple top hat, purple leather gloves, red bow tie, black boots. Manson was holding a purple cane with a golden handle on top. He had short white hair, red lips, red eyes and a big grin on his face.

Beside him was Barbara, a bunny woman. She too had white fur, long white hair, wearing a red suit, black leather gloves, black boots, black lips with dark purple eyes. Looking closely, I noticed Manson had a muscular body frame while Barbara had huge breasts, wide hips and big thick butt cheeks. She too had a muscular body. I rang the doorbell again while I opened the booklet. There were different images of Manson, his girlfriend Barbara and their five friends, fighting evil forces in The Dark Kingdom. From the clips, this show looked like it was drawn by a very talented artist. The next pages showed more information on the show, and it was coming out on Oct.31st I thought on Halloween. Might take a look at this. I looked at what time it would be on then I heard footsteps coming towards the front door. It was my mother. She was almost the same height as my father had light brown hair, wears glasses. She was wearing a dark reddish sweater, black pants with her long gray socks on.

"Hi mom." She smiled and had her arms out, I hugged her.

"Oh Curtis, I'm glad to see you again."

"Happy to see you too, mom." She moved back so I can enter the house.

"Very wet outside."

"Not too bad." I followed her inside.

She noticed I was holding something in my right hand. "What do you have there?"

"Oh, it's some flyer for some upcoming cartoon show called *The Manson & Barbara Show*. I bet John would like it."

"When did you find this?" She was flipping on the pages.

"It was in your mailbox. I just noticed it while I was waiting outside."

"I didn't hear anyone come to the door this morning. I was busy cleaning the whole house."

"Who knows when it came, but one thing I do know is how much I miss your cooking."

My mother chuckled and I heard John came over. "Hey Curtis!" Following John was my father's brother's two boys.

"Hey guys."

"Curtis, you remember Tom and Bill?" John introduced our cousins.

"Yeah, when they we're younger."

"Dinner should be ready soon, but I had lots of drinks in the fridge so help yourselves boys," I thanked mom for the offer. Tom and Bill walked over to me.

"Hey, what's that?" John reached over for the package booklet.

"Seems there's a new show coming out on Halloween."

"Wow this looks cool," Tom said.

"Yeah, I like the whole dark fantasy look to it," John agreed.

"I'll see if my friends have heard this," Bill added. They ran off while John and I went into the kitchen. The window was open so it was very cool in kitchen.

"Want a can of Coke, Curtis?"

"Please." John got me a cold can of Coke and another one for himself. "What time is that show on?"

"9:30PM," John said, after checking the sheet.

"That's a bit odd. Most cartoon shows are usually on around noon or before dinner time."

"Yeah, but I guess late night means it's going to be good. Best of all, I get to stay up late on days I don't have to go to school."

I chuckled then heard footsteps walking towards us. I lifted my head and saw my father's brother Harry. He has dark brown hair. He wore a denim jacket, black shirt, jeans, and cowboy boots. Harry spoke with a heavy Texas accent.

"Hey, Curtis. Glad to see you again."

"Hey, Harry." We heard his wife Lisa, calling after him to take his damn jacket off because it's very warm inside.

"Alright," Harry shouted back. John and I winced.

"Hey, Curtis. After dinner I want to show you some of my stories, I've been working on," John said excitedly.

"Sure thing," I replied.

We went into the kitchen as Harry removed his jacket. "Curtis, I heard you've been working your ass off at News 6."

"Yeah, Hunter's and my efforts have paid off."

Mom called that dinner was ready. We went to the formal dining area. I sat down at the table with Harry. On the other side was his wife Lisa and my mother's sister Trish, with her daughter. Trish almost looked like my mother except for their eye color and hair style. Trish's daughter Mary had golden hair. Currently, she had them tied into two pig tails. She had light blue eyes and was eight years old.

"Hey, Trish and Mary," I greeted them.

"Evening Curtis." Trish lowered her glass of wine to answer my greeting. Mary said hi shyly.

"Your father told me your news studio is getting a news team together." Harry continued his line of questioning.

"Yes, but it's going to take time and my boss already wants his own channel." I explained

"I see. Say, I always wanted to ask you this. Have you ever had any funny stories?"

"No. But if one did ever happen, I would put it in the paper."

"I read a funny story back in Houston."

"What was it about?"

"Some drunk guy thought he was riding a bull late at night. When the police showed up, the guy was still coaxing the bull to

move. He fell eventually. The bull was some restaurant's décor."
We both laughed loudly.

"So, I guess you heard that Ken Cage guy was fired," Trish
added to our conversation.

"Yes. News 6 will now have more listeners than News 18. I
heard from my friend Hunter they are trying to find someone with
more talent than Ken. They aren't having a lot of luck."

Trish thinks being a reporter is a lot of work. That young
people these days just want to do something for fun or just to make
some money.

"Well, I wanted something different. I don't want to be
working at some fast-food place or some other job that doesn't pay
well."

"I know some younger people in my town will get a job or go
out to form bands. Some of them do make it big," Harry observed.

"That or they go into politics," Lisa said.

"But who wants to do that? I bet it's boring as hell working
for the government," Harry argues.

"True but they make so much money they don't care," I
philosophized.

Mother made a lovely chicken dinner with grilled sandwiches,
salads, corn, cooked carrots and mash potatoes. Everyone was
eating away. I could hear the rain pouring harder outside, more
cold wind was blowing into the kitchen.

"Hey Harry, is it still warm in Texas?" I asked.

"Fall nights are a lot cooler, however when it's spring and
summer it's hot as hell."

"Everyone in Dallas has an AC if they don't, they would melt
into a puddle of goo," Lisa added.

"Well, it's either that or shoveling snow," I said.

"I got a snow blower, and it works well. It helps getting rid of
the snow and I also help some of the neighbors with it." Dad said.

"My landlord at the apartment has a few guys to handle
the parking lot and sidewalks. I'm glad I don't have to do it." I
pointed out.

Trish asked if I still live in the same apartment. I told her the
rent is good and that it's the close to my work.

"I just moved into my dream house back in Georgia. It's wonderful," Trish announced.

"And near Disney Land," Mary chirped in. Trish laughed. Apparently, they are going there next summer.

"I wish we could go," Bill looked at his mother.

"Why would we want to go there? I'd rather go to Super Action Park," Tom grumbled.

"I won't mind going to Florida for a nice vacation," Harry said.

"Same here. Relaxing on the beach while finding myself a lovely girl to take home." Harry laughed at me, while his two sons gagged.

"Or better yet move in with her," Harry suggested.

"Please finish up, don't want your dinner to get cold now," Mom admonished. We continued eating, it was getting very dark outside.

I finished my dinner and stood up. "That was very good mother, thank you."

"You're welcome, Curtis. I'm glad everyone enjoyed it, as well."

"Here, I'll help you with the dishes mother." John offered, while Tom and Bill we're still eating.

"I'll be back, Harry." Lisa left the kitchen and went upstairs to use the bathroom.

"I wish we could stay longer," Mary was bummed.

"We'll come and see you again soon, sister." Trish was holding on to mom's hands like she's not letting go.

"Next time we come back to Black Creek I want to check out the park," Mary declared.

"Yes, we'll do that." Trish promised her daughter.

When John was done helping mom with the dishes, John came over to me. He wanted to show me his stories. I followed him upstairs into his bedroom. There were a few changes since the last time I had seen it. Up against the wall, towards the back was the big bed. Infront of it, was a window. The wooden floor and the dark walls, courtesy of our father, stayed the same. Beside the bed was a closet I could see John's clothes hanging. Next to the window, was a big leather lazy boy chair with a table that had a lamp on it. Beside the chair was a tall bookshelf with a couple of books.

"I thought this room was smaller."

"Because your bed took up the most space," John laughed.

I went to inspect his bookshelf. "I see you are building up your book collection."

"Yep. Read most of them," John said proudly. He was rummaging through the drawers on his study table.

"Now, here's what I've been working on." He pulled out a thick notebook. *"John's Stories 82-84"* was written on the cover. There was a red book marker sticking out in the middle of it. As I took it John said he was just doing short stories right now. He was planning on turning them into full length novels. I flipped it open to the first page. It was an index, it showed all the stories that were written and what pages they were on.

"Which one do you want me to read first?" John looked at it and said, 7th story. The title said, *"The Dark City"*. I flipped through the pages until I reached the story and began reading it. It was about a massive medieval city attacked by monsters during a stormy night. There was a band of knights fighting them off.

"I love it!"

"I had some help from my history teacher," John had an ear-to-ear grin.

"Who?"

"Mr. Clark is a very nice guy. He told me what books about medieval era I should look up. The horror movies I watched, also gave me ideas."

"I would like to see this as a novel, too. I'll tell you what, I'll see if I can get you a typewriter so you can get working on these."

"Really?"

"Anything for my brother." I played with his hair to mess it up, and he kept moving away.

There was a knock on the door and Harry poked his head inside. We're going now. It was nice seeing you, Curtis and John."

"You have a safe trip back to Texas," John said.

Harry smiled and I said goodbye. He walked away and I turned back to John.

"What next?" John had me read a few of his other works which were really good. A few spelling errors but I could help him with that.

By 8:30-PM I had left my parents' house. I drove with rain still pouring. There was thick fog, too. I couldn't get that show, from the mailbox, out of my mind. There was something odd about it. I haven't seen any ads about it. None on TV, radio or even print ads around. It's even more odd to think that no one saw who dropped it in my mother's mailbox.

If it was dropped off while they we're out, then why didn't they see it? I saw it when I got up to the door. Did someone do it before I got to the door? Why didn't the others see or hear anything? I remembered the channel it would be and the time it would be aired. I didn't recall the booklet stating it was adult cartoon. It looked to be for teens judging from the way the characters, setting and mild violence. I also didn't see who the writers or the company were, that created it. I couldn't get this strange feeling off me. I shook my head and kept driving, knowing there were more important things than just cartoon shows.

Oct.15
9:00-AM

Hunter and I we're called into the meeting room where Jake would be picking who would be part of the News 6 team. I hoped we got picked. It would be more work, but our pay would double. Once we got in, Hunter and I pulled the chairs out. There was a lot of people. Jake in a suit, was drinking his coffee.

"Alright. Now, that everyone is here we can get this meeting started." Jake cleared his throat.

As most of you know, we now have become Black Creek's biggest news studio after News 18 lost its main star Ken Cage. While they are trying to find a new star, I want to use this to our advantage. We can give this city the best news team ever, and by the time News 18 has found its new star it would be too late." Jake took a drink of his coffee.

"Now, who is going to be our news team? I went through all your records. It wasn't easy, but the choices I made I think will give this city what it wants. A news cast that is honest, trustworthy and never afraid to show what the people need to see." Jake then picked up a sheet.

"The following people are going to become News 6 team. Camera crews will be Hunter, Sam and Hill. Reporters will be Tyler and Curtis." I said yes in my seat, barely keeping my voice down while Jake read the rest of the list.

"Tomorrow, you'll begin your first story. Our mayor is doing a speech about crime violence and other stuff. This should be a good test for you all. You'll get the feel of what it's like being part of a real news team. Now, one last thing, we only have one van that you'll be using and please take care of it. I have already spent a lot of money to make this the best news team. If we don't have our news van, then we can't give what the people want. Do I make myself clear?"

Everyone said, "Yes sir."

"Good. Now, let me show how this gear works."

Jake gave us a run down on the cameras we would be using. These things were a bit heavy, just glad I worked out so I would be able to hold them long enough. Once Jake showed everyone what we had to do he took us to the parking garage to show us the news van. It was a bright white 78 Ford Econoline Van with bright red text on both sides saying, "News 6".

"I had it tuned a bit just to give it some extra power under the hood. It has a CB radio. You'll be able to pick up other radio channels and call us back here to let our news anchors, do their part." Jake picked two women and two men to do it. They would take turns doing the news. I was happy to make it this far. Hunter and I would be getting the real action. I wasn't going to let all our hard work go to waste.

Oct.16
10:45-AM

Hunter and I we're in the back of the Ford Econoline Van while the driver was heading for city hall.

"Say, have you seen a booklet about some upcoming cartoon show?" I explained to him how I found it while visiting my parents over the weekend.

"No. What was it called?" He was busy making last minute checks on our gear.

"The Manson and Barbara Show. It's weird. John said that only the neighbors who has teenagers got the flyer. There's more, there is no info on who created it."

"That **is** weird." He stopped fidgeting with the tools and focused all his attention on me.

"Only thing the flyer had was the plot, cast and when it would be aired."

"When?"

"On Halloween at 9:30-PM. Whoever made the artwork, it looks great."

We we're getting close to city hall but we're waiting for the red light to change.

"And the place Manson, his girlfriend and friends live is called The Dark Kingdom."

"What other characters were there?"

The driver pulled into the parking lot. No more time to answer his question. Hunter picked up the camera, I picked up my microphone.

"Alright, let's do this."

"I'm glad we don't have to wear those suits. We look better in our trench coats." He was patting back the part of his coat that was snagged by all the tech he was carrying.

"As long as we look sharp, then people know we mean business." We both laughed as we got out of the van. That was how we started our first day as a real news team.

Hunter filmed the mayor talking while I moved as close as possible and held the microphone up. I noticed other news teams were there, too. News 18 wasn't here hogging up all the action. We don't work like that. When the mayor finished his speech, he took questions from every reporter, including me. When we're done, we left city hall and went back to News 6. I knew we would get more work and I was looking forward to it.

5:45-PM

I drove to the post office to see if I could find out where those booklets came from. It wasn't a busy day, I didn't have to wait in the queue for long. I went up to the front desk, a black man was doing paperwork.

"Excuse me. I saw a booklet for some upcoming show called The Manson and Barbara Show. Was wondering if you knew where these flyers came from."

"Can't say I remember. I don't think we delivered any of those."

"From what I heard from my brother, only people with children got them." The man finished writing his paperwork.

"Sorry, don't know what you're talking about. Now, I have work to do." He walked away. What a jerk! I left the post office and then tried the other post office.

When I got there, an older woman was at the window. I thought maybe she'll be a bit nicer than the other guy. I went up to her and told her the same thing I said to the other guy. But she too never heard of the show, or who sent out those booklets. She said if they did, they would have a record of it. It's getting weirder. I left the post office and drove to my parents' house. I wanted to get another look at that booklet, however, they weren't home. I did have a spare key. I went into John's room, I searched everywhere for it but couldn't find it. I tried everywhere else, but it wasn't there. I left John a note then head back to my apartment.

By then, it was 7-PM. I made a simple dinner and ate in the living room. I called Hunter.

"Hey, Curtis."

"Hey, man. I just finished checking out both post offices and they haven't heard about this show. They didn't send out the booklets either. And when I went to my parents' house, I couldn't find it."

"Dude, this is getting weirder. I looked into it, too. I tried looking up some of the cartoon studios, but they all act like this show isn't real. They also told me they'll be showing most of the Halloween stuff early, as adult programs will be on during night fall."

"Wait, that's around 11-PM to midnight."

"The only cartoons that are running are from 8 until 9-PM. After that it's mostly adult stuff. Something fishy is going on."

"You got that right. I'll be recording this show when it's aired on Halloween night."

"I don't think it's a prank. What's the joke, then?" Hunter was speculating.

"Maybe we'll learn more when it comes out...but I can't get over this strange feeling about it."

"That something bad is going to happen?"

"Yeah, that's what's what I'm thinking. I hope I'm wrong."

Oct.31
6:00-PM

I was wearing my tank top and underwear as I was lifting weights in my small gym. When John got back to me about the booklet, he told me everything that was on. However, when I went to ask him if I could borrow it he told me he lost it. I felt he was lying but why would he lie to me? I never once lied to him and got him the typewriter which he was very pleased to get. I felt like going to the houses that had kids and see if I could get the booklet from them, but Hunter tried around his area and pretty much got the same answer as I got. We both felt something wasn't right, but it seemed nobody else cared or had other things on their minds.

I set the weights down and wiped the sweat from my forehead with my arm then grabbed a cloth rubbing my face with it. I set the cloth down then grabbed a bottle of cold water and drank it. Outside was very overcast I had my windows open letting cool air inside my apartment. With crime rate now lowered as the remaining gangs had fled Black Creek with some hiding from the law the police have backed off. And so had our big stories as of now there wasn't much to report as Jake was being picky what he wanted us to show and some of the stories me and Hunter we're doing we're boring as hell. But it would only be a matter of time until another big story came our way again just had to wait.

I finished my work out then put all my gym equipment away then finished my water bottle I toss it into the recycling bin and sat on my sofa. I felt lonely and wanted to have a girlfriend but not just any girl I wanted to have the right one. I did have some extra money I could blow at a strip club but that won't mean some hot busty chick would come back to my place for have a good time. None of the women back at News 6 didn't interest me.

I reached for my TV remote press the on button and flipped through the channels. When I came to the weather report it called for more rain along with a thunderstorm tonight. I knew John was going to have a good time trick and treating tonight. I remember when we did it back when we we're younger. Well, I was in my teens but still it was fun dressing up and getting free candy as we always tried to see who could get the most candy and staying up late watching horror movies.

I then checked on index channel. It showed what was playing and I saw a few adult horror movies. But some of the titles looked goofy like The Mall of Hell, The Midnight Stalker, Night of The Dolls. You gotta be shitting me! I sighed, turned off the TV, and rested my head on the sofa. The phone rang, it was Hunter.

"Hey, Curtis. What's up?"

"Nothing much just lying around in my apartment, bored."

"Want to come to the strip club with me? We could try to pick up some chicks."

"No thanks. I don't feel like going out."

"You're not shy, are you?" I could hear Hunter's mocking smile through the telephone wire.

"Of course not. But if you do get yourself a girl, then I'll come next time."

"Alright, I'll let you know how it goes. Oh! Happy Halloween by the way."

"Hunter! Wait a minute!"

"Changed your mind?" Hunter laughed.

"No. It's about that show. I'm going to tape it and see what all the fuss is about it."

"Yes, that. Let me know if it's good."

"I will. By the way, weather reports call for thunderstorm tonight."

"Thanks for the update. I'll make sure me, and my girl are nice and dry when we get back to my place."

"Alright Hunter talk to you later."

"Ok bye." He hung up and I did the same. I set the phone back onto its rack. I went back into my living room and took out a blank tape. I placed it into the VHS player then I sat back on my sofa.

I checked the time it was still 6 clock I had three hours to wait until it was ready. I had laid off the junk food for a bit but didn't have much to eat. I would have to do some shopping later. Or I could do it right now to help pass the time. I went into my room to put on pants, socks, and a black shirt. Grabbed my wallet and key ring off my nightstand. I left my apartment and went down to the parking and drove to the grocery store.

When I got their it was 7:30-PM there wasn't that many vehicles in the parking lot. I would be able to get everything I needed, and not have to wait in line. Halloween themed music was playing inside. Guess for young kids. I knew what I needed and pulled my shopping cart as I toss everything into it then went to check out. It came to $90. I paid and got out. When I popped open the trunk of my car, I heard thunder roaring above me. I tossed everything in and drove back to my apartment.

By the time I arrived at my apartment, the rain was pouring very hard outside. There were occasional bright white flashes of lightning. I bet John was back home by now. Nobody would be trick or treating during a storm. I made myself a quick dinner and grabbed a cold bottle of Dead Moon beer. I parked myself in the living room again. When I checked the time, it was already 9-PM. I reached for the remote and realized I don't know what channel was *The Manson & Barbara Show* going to be on. I went to the index and went through the list. It was channel 13. There is no such thing. I tried pressing the 1 & 3 button but all I got was static. By then I was thinking I got the time slot wrong. Maybe the show will be at 9:30.

By the time I was done with my dinner, Channel 13 still had static. If I press the up or down button and tried going back to the channel it would skip the number. Just as 9:30 came around I quickly press the numbers in then hit enter as the TV static suddenly made a weird noise, I press the record button on my VHS. It wasn't working. I tried pressing it a few more times, then the static went away. The screen went blank. I press record and saw white text above the right corner, "RECORDING". I looked back at the screen, and it showed a massive castle with the front entrance shaped like a bat. It has dark gray brinks, tall thick guard towers painted red.

The sky was pitch black. The only illumination was from a large glowing moon above it. The ground was covered in thick fog. There were Gothic style lamp posts. A big black wooden sign said "Manson & Barbara Castle" written in red old English text. Then a voice spoke, electric guitars and bass strumming was the background sound.

"Welcome to The Dark Kingdom. I, Manson the bat and my lovely girlfriend Barbara, the bunny are the rulers of this wonderful land." The music grew louder.

"However, on the other side of this land is the evil rulers known as The White Order."

The scene changed into a city in a more modern setting city. In the middle of this city was a massive metal white castle. It had long white flags. The emblem on the flags was composed of a golden sword facing upside down with two crosses. It had an older style look to it. I saw the guards around the castle and notice they were all humans with blond or black hair. Inside The White Order castle was a round table with men and women sitting around it. They were wearing robes or outfits that were white, silver or black. However, the king had a golden outfit. Manson's voice came back.

"These evil people threaten my kingdom and my people. It's up to me and my gang to stop them from destroying my kingdom. It's time to begin the show."

The show's logo was then projected on the screen: a white bat head and a bunny head. Thrash metal music still played in the background. Then the scene changed to a Gothic-themed dining room with a massive fireplace. Standing in front of it was Manson, the bat, wearing the same clothes he had on the booklet. Beside him was Barbara the bunny along with five other anthropomorphic characters. All of them turned to the screen. I noticed Barbara's huge breasts bounced as she moved. I chuckled to myself.

Then they ran upstairs. There were other anthropomorphic beings running up with them. At the top of the castle, they all got onto a large airship. It had two balloon sacks and large fans spinning. Once they we're all onboard the fans lifted and moved the airship up. The animation was like nothing I've ever seen before. It was so detailed it was almost realistic. This must have taken months to make it look this good. As the ship moved through the sky, the screen changed to show Manson and his gang standing inside the cockpit with the other anthropomorphic characters.

First, was a muscular fox-man wearing a long jacket with a green cape while the inside was white, leather gloves and boots. On the right side was bright green while his left side was white. His eyes were light green, and he had short green hair. The screen went black. When it came back again, the fox lifted his cape to cover himself and was gone in a puff of smoke. A running text said: "Kane, The Magic Fox". Next, was a very tall, muscular hippo-man with a massive ten-pack on his belly. He wore a black sack over his head. His eyes appeared white but very bright. The sack didn't cover his muzzle and his ears were sticking out of the sack. He wore long black gloves, a pair of black pants, with a big thick belt and big buckle that had two hammers crossed on it. He then drew a very big hammer and slam down as the running text appeared: "George, The Hammer Hippo".

The third character was a muscular kangaroo-man, wearing an old-style hunting outfit. He had on a hat with a silver point on top, brown pants, brown hunting boots, brown leather gloves. He had goggles on his head, emphasizing his long dark brown hair. He then drew a very large crossbow, that had a magazine and a scope. The running text said: "Andrew, The Kangaroo".

The fourth person was a short, yet muscular raven-woman. Her feathers were jet black, eyes were dark blue, and her hair was long and black. She had huge breasts, wide hips and a big bubble butt. She wore a dark blue jacket and shirt, both having a black checker pattern. She lifted her arm, blue and white energy beams shot out. The running text said: "Sydney, The Raven".

The fifth character, to complete the team, was a very tall and very muscular bear-woman. She was almost as tall as George, The Hippo. She had reddish brown fur, long hair, light brown eyes, massive breasts, wide hips, and a very thick bubble butt. She wore a bright yellow jacket, yellow leather gloves, black pants, big yellow boots, long cape that was black inside and yellow on the outside. She had dual swords and a pistol holster belt. She drew her swords and swung them and her name popped up beside her: "Hellen, The Bear".

The screen changed showing Manson and Barbara in a pose. Manson took his cane. He pulled the golden handle part, revealing a very long and sharp sword. Barbara drew dual short swords from her holster belt then both their names were flashed on the screen beside each other. The screen cut to show airships, a bright white-and-gold spaceship-like crafts heading towards them. Hellen grabbed a radio and yelled with a Russian accent: "Fire at will!" Anthropomorphic people who were wearing sail outfits, armed with large double barrel cannons fired. The crafts, with the sword-and-double-cross logo, blew up. The thrash metal music was getting better along with the action.

The next scene showed "Kane, The Fox" chased by armored White Order guards. He was grinning the whole time. The guards aimed their laser rifles at him. He suddenly spun around, lift his cape, then threw a smoke ball. When it cleared, the wall was riddled with burning holes. The guards were left standing with a stupid look on their faces. Kane appeared from behind them. A guard turned towards Kane, but it was too late. He threw a big fuse bomb. The guards exploded, limbs flying. *This is a kid show?* I thought to myself. The scene continued. Kane caught one of the guards' head still inside it's helmet. He laughed and kicked it towards the screen. It went black, then switched to "George, The Hippo". He was inside some dungeon-like room. He swung and smashed his massive hammer into White Order guards. I felt my jaw dropped open. It was disturbingly graphic but well made.

When George was done swinging, he posed with his big hammer and laughed with a very deep voice. The scene changed into a dark, foggy forest. White Order soldiers were using flashlights. Above them Sydney was flying. She reached into a shoulder bag taking out some crystal gems. They glowed bright. She threw them to the soldiers below. Pointed crystal spikes stabbed them, then they all broke into tiny pieces. Sydney landed where the guards once stood. There was one soldier coming towards her.

"Nice try fools!" She laughed. She had an African American accent. She shot a blue energy beam at him. He melted in a matter of seconds.

The scene changed again, seen through a very detailed scope scanning. White Order members were travelling in large, bulky tanks through the desert. There were soldiers marching along, holding very large and high-tech laser rifles. Andrew was the user of the scope of his long rifle. He was grinning while pulling the trigger. He shot a group of guards in a row. The solder retaliated, firing their laser cannons, but missed. Andrew hopped on an old-style motorcycle, one hand was holding a large pistol. He fired rapid shots, killing more White Order soldiers. When he got closer to the bulky tanks, drove around them causing the tanks to fire and took each other out.

"Take that, you bloody wanker!" Andrew laughed. He spoke with an Australian accent.

The scene switch to Manson and Barbara fighting off White Order members while inside their enemy's castle. When they finished them off, Manson's whole gang arrived. A close up of Manson and Barbara, both grinning and looking into the camera, followed. The doors opened showing the leaders we're all scared. The screen showed the wall with the gang's shadows outlined getting closer to White Order leaders. A loud scream reverberated, the electric guitars roared over it, and a lightning strike hit the screen. Simultaneously, a loud boom of thunder crashed above me, made me jump before I remembered it was just the weather.

The screen went blank then I heard Manson's voice as text came on the screen, "Episode I The Beginning."

Then the screen showed the White Order city. No music was playing, just the sound of birds singing. People were walking around, while children were playing and laughing. I thought, where are the credits? Isn't the episode over yet?

The camera zoomed in on the metal castle. Inside was a round table where the king was presiding. This time, I got a better look on his face and I thought he looks like the pope. Does this whole White Order supposed to be based on a certain religion? The king was holding a thick leather-bound book with their logo. However, the text written on it was in a language I couldn't read. Guess it's a made-up language.

The other members of the White Order were looking at their king. He opened the book and with a powerful voice spoke.

"My fellow followers, the time has come to battle against the evil that threatens our great land!"

The king pressed a button on the round table. A screen popped up in the middle, a hologram of Manson & Barbara's castle with a big city in front of it. It was nighttime. While the king was talking, the screen showed anthropomorphic people walking through the streets. He said these beings were evil and needed to be destroyed. The king turned to a tall man with a beard.

"Mr. Sheppard, have your army assault the Dark Kingdom."

"Yes, my King." He stood up and left the round table.

The next scene showed him getting his men fully armed and ready. They walked out into a large hangar, got on their big spaceships and went into the sky. They we're heading for the Dark Kingdom.

The screen went black again and I thought a commercial would play. Instead, it showed a village of animal people working on the farm. I found it odd, how one side is night and the other is day. Does anybody sleep on this show?

The White Order spaceships flew through the dark sky. The animal people stopped what they were doing. The spaceships fired laser cannons down at them blowing up houses and destroying their crops. They ran, screamed in terror with a few of them getting hit. I thought, *this is too dark for a kids show. Showing scenes of death, destruction and war!* But I kept watching. This White Order group was killing every anthropomorphic person on sight. An otter woman yelled, "Someone call Manson and his friends! We need their help!" Suddenly she exploded, her small daughter cried. The older sister picked her up and they ran. The others we're yelling to get Manson and his friends.

If John's watching this, my parents won't like it, I thought. I turned to the clock on the wall, it was already 9:40-PM. I turned back to the TV. It showed Manson & Barbara's castle. Inside they were sitting at the fireplace. Manson was reading a big red leather book. Barbara was drinking from a tea mug. Then a black bat guard ran inside wearing a dark purple outfit.

"Manson! Barbara! Our village is under attack by the White Order! They're killing our people!" They looked startled.

"Barbara, my dear, get the others at once! I should have known this day would come!"

They went to the kitchen where the others were eating. They were shocked and angry when Barbara called them told them the news.

"I'm going to crush their king for this," George roared in a deep voice.

"Sick old man is gonna pay for this," Kane abandoned his dinner to get his weapons.

"Quickly, to my air ship!" Hellen was ushering them out of the kitchen.

"The king's head will be my next wall trophy," Andrew vowed.

They met up with Manson on the long flight of stairs. Hellen ordered her crew to get it moving. They quickly headed towards the village. Manson walked up to her.

"When this is over, send my men to help these poor people."

"Of course, Manson." Hellen replied.

When the airship got close enough to the White Order spaceships, Hellen ordered her crew to fire their double barrel cannons.

The spaceships exploded in a huge blaze. They all came crashing down to the ground. The animal people below, watching were cheering to their heroes. The spaceships fired back as the air ship got hit a few times but was still standing. *Shouldn't the laser beams be burning through the wooden ship?* I thought. *Oh, right this a cartoon. Not real.* The screen showed close ups of the double barrel cannons firing away taking out more spaceships. Then it showed Mr. Sheppard yelling in anger and ordering his men to retreat. However, Hellen's airship kept firing. It took out Mr. Sheppard's ship. He was screaming while he was burning, and his spaceship crashed to the ground in a huge explosion. Manson and his gang cheered at the death of Mr. Sheppard.

"Hellen, land the ship. We need to help our people."

"Right away, Manson."

The airship landed. The village was in ruins. Anthropomorphic people injured, hurt and crying. Manson and his gang were helping everyone they could. His men came to treat the injured.

The scene changed to a young otter girl looking for her mother. What she found was an empty house.

"MOMMY! MOMMY!" The girl cried. Manson walked over to her, he knelt and hugged her while she cried. The older sister and father came over.

"Why would they do this to us?" The father asked Manson.

"This is horrible! We didn't do anything to deserve this!" Barbara was almost crying.

The camera cut to a close-up shot of Manson, with an angry look on his face. He patted the otter girl's back.

"I will make them pay for this." He carried the otter girl to her father. Manson turned to a black bat and called him over.

"How bad is it?" Manson asked.

"Very bad sir. We lost a lot of people but thanks to you, we didn't lose any more."

"I fear war is coming." Barbara added.

"Yes, my dear, war is coming. When we get back, we plan our attack."

The screen went black then showed Manson and his gang sitting at a table. The walls have torches and large picture frames with paintings. The windows are Gothic. On the table was a big map, almost the length of the table itself. The camera zoomed in, and the map showed where these two kingdoms were.

"I made as many healing potions as I can but it wasn't enough." Sydney looked exhausted.

"Sydney, you did the best you can. Even with magic it isn't enough. This White Order thinks science and technology can do everything for them! We'll show them magic is stronger and better than they are!" Manson vowed,

"I'll be happy to show them a few of my magic tricks." Kane as always has cocky suggestions.

"I won't mind showing them our tricks, too." Manson smiled at Kane.

"We better get our ground forces ready. They'll be marching through our land while others will try to sneak in with their spaceships." Andrew is all about strategy.

"My air ship fleet can deal with them if they ever cross into our skies again." Hellen promised.

"While we're at it let's play some dirty games with our enemy just to keep them on edge." Manson smiled from ear to ear.

"Hehe. I can handle that." George grinned, bright teeth and all.

"Alright. You and Kane, cause some trouble for the White Order. Barbara, you'll be with Sydney to aid our ground forces, while I get my men ready for battle. I will NOT fail my people!" Manson sounds like a decent guy.

They left and the scene changed into the round table of the White Order. They all looked pissed, including the King.

"Get my men ready for war," he roared.

The screen went blank, Manson's voice came over: "Tune in next time for the next episode of The Manson & Barbara and we all hoped you enjoyed it."

Static came back on my TV. It sounded weird then I heard a loud cracking noise. I saw it was coming from my VHS. I quickly pressed the stop button and ejected the tape. I checked for scratch marks on it. *What the hell? No credits during the opening intro or ending? Graphic violence, basing the so-called villains of this show on religion, and making them look like cruel, careless murderers! Who the hell made this show anyway!*

I turned the TV off. There were so many questions running through my mind. I had to show this to Hunter, but first thing in the morning I have to know if John watched. If he did, I hoped he didn't like it. Or my parents stop him from seeing more of it. My VHS was damaged. *Damn it! I'll have to get new one!* I looked at the tape. I had a strange feeling about this. Like something bad was waiting for me on the other side.

Nov. 3
9:00-AM

I woke up early. I normally sleep in on my day off. The tape was still lying on my nightstand like I left it last night. And I could see the marks that my VHS somehow made. I knew what I saw happen last night I wasn't dreaming. It really happened. I took a shower. It woke me up some. I wiped the steam off my mirror and saw my reflection. *Nah I don't need a haircut yet.* I went into my bedroom grabbed some clean clothes and checked the time.

It was 9:40-AM. John should be up but I'm not sure about Hunter. I tried John first. I walked into the kitchen reached for the phone dialed my parents' number.

"Hello?"

"Morning, John."

"Oh, morning Curtis." He sounded surprise to hear from me.

"How was Halloween?"

"It was great! My friends and I got loads of candy! And just made it back in time before the storm came. It was so cool!"

He was rambling but he sounded okay. I was glad to hear he had a great night. I dreaded to ask him my next question.

"What did you do last night after you got back?"

"Well, mom and dad, went out for a late party so I had the whole house to myself! I made myself a big snack with lots of Coke to drink."

"Did you watch that show last night? The Manson & Barbara Show?"

"Yes, I did. Did you?"

"John, the show wasn't what I thought it was going to be. I..."

"Are you kidding me? It was awesome! The action was cool! The characters we're great and I really like the whole setting!"

"John it's too graphic for you. I...." John cut me off again.

"Curtis, you sound like mom. It's not real, besides it's just a cartoon."

"Did you see the scene where the otter mother gets blown up and the daughter is crying?"

"No, I didn't see that. It just showed The White Order attacking the town. Manson and his friends come in and save the day."

"Who were the villains then?"

"It wasn't shown. Their faces were hidden, but you could clearly hear them. Look I gotta go. I'll talk to you later, Curtis. Bye." I didn't get to say anything back, he hung up right away.

John has never done this before. He always let the other person say bye first before he hangs up. *Was he really telling the truth about what he saw?* I set the phone back onto the rack, nothing more I can do but shook my head. *John should have seen what I saw last night. There was no way he saw something different. Why would he lie about it?*

I sat at the kitchen table eating my breakfast. I was still contemplating on John's behavior. *John doesn't act like this. Sure, he would joke about our mother being too strict sometimes but this... this was never like him.*

I knew the show had something to do with it. I must find out what was really going on. I finished my breakfast and called Hunter. It was 10:30AM, he should be up by now. I took a quick look outside and saw the sun was coming out, although it was cloudy.

"Who the hell is this!" Someone's unlucky.

"Morning, Hunter." I added sweetness to my voice to piss him off some more.

"Oh, Curtis. Sorry about that. I didn't have a good night." *Aha!*

"Didn't work out at the strip club, last night?"

"Well, for starters all the good-looking chicks were with a bunch of bikers, so I couldn't get near them. Second, the remaining few chicks were mostly ugly-looking, and third it was pricey. I only had a few drinks. I'm not going back their again!"

"Better luck next time. Anyway, I watched that show last night and recorded it."

"The Manson & Barbara Show, right?"

"Yes, I recorded it from channel 13." Hunter was silent for a bit.

"Wait, is there a channel 13?"

"No, there isn't. When I tried it, at first, all I got was static. Then around 9:30-PM I went back to that channel. There was still static however, it was making strange noises. When I tried recording it, nothing happened. Then the screen went blank for a bit, I saw my VHS was recording.

Manson does the voice over thing, during the opening. There are two opposing sides in this cartoon world. Manson's Dark Kingdom versus the White Order Kingdom. And get this, Manson's side has animal people, while the White Order is composed of all humans."

"Ok, what else?"

"The White Order is the evil side. They are heavily based on religion. They are into science and technology, while Manson's side has a medieval setting. Yet their technology is somewhat like ours but from an older time. And they use magic."

"Sounds like a cool show."

"When I show you what I got, you won't be saying that. Oh, and get this, no credits during the opening or ending of the show."

"What? No credits? But by law they have to show that so nobody would copy someone else's idea."

"There are more issues than just no credits. I'll swing by your place in a few."

I bought me a new VHS player and hoped the next time I record the show, it won't break. When I pulled into Hunter's driveway I parked behind his Ford LTD and rang the doorbell. He answered the door right away. He was wearing a tank top and boxer shorts. I kept my trench coat on, it was chilly outside.

"Did John watch it too?"

"He did but said a few things that don't add up. I think he's being forced to lie to me."

"Forced? By whom?"

"I don't know, man. Maybe by whoever's behind this."

We stepped into Hunter's living room. He has a nice glass table, a big fancy jukebox in a corner, a shelf full of records, mostly heavy metal stuff. There was a big TV with two huge speakers next to it. Above the TV was a large picture frame with a photo of a tropical beach. In front of the TV were two big white leather chairs that looked soft. The walls and ceiling were painted white. The floor was dark and shiny.

"Also, after the show was over my VHS broke. The tape was all scratched up. Had to buy a new VHS player."

"Alright, let's see it."

I placed the VHS tape into the player then pressed the rewind button. When it stopped Hunter pressed the video input and play. I went over to sit beside Hunter on the sofa. The TV screen was blank for a few seconds. Then the opening scene started with Manson's voice over. It started off normal, but once the opening scene is over, Hunter would see what I was talking about.

"Whoa! The king looks like the pope and... doesn't that one guy over their kind of looks like our mayor?" Hunter paused the tape and stared dumbfounded.

"Holy shit. It does look like the mayor!" I felt my jaw dropped.

"Hey, that guy beside the king? Doesn't he look a bit like our President?"

"You gotta be fucking kidding me! That is the President!" Weird was all over the room but we got to continue. Hunter pressed the play button, and we watched the rest of the show.

I looked closely at hunter during village assault part. He looked as shocked as me I felt.

"This is fucked up!" I couldn't agree more.

We finally got to the brutal death of Mr. Sheppard. Manson was saying his lines and the screen went blank. We heard strange noises and thought someone was trying to speak. We tried listening in but couldn't make it out. The noise stopped when Hunter turned off the device. Hunter turned to me with a bewildered look on his face.

"Not so cool anymore, is it?"

"No, man! This is fucked up! No credits during the show. The villains are based on real people. I see your point about the setting with the two worlds." Hunter was clearly agitated.

"Don't you find it odd how one side is always night while the other is sunny?"

"Yes. Also, this order group is mostly adults. Why are there very few children?"

"We gotta find out what the hell is going on. Who made this show and where was it being broadcast from?" I suggested.

"Seeing how we're now a bigger news studio, I might be able to ask around. Some of the other stations might know."

"Also check with cartoon networks and see if they know anything."

"Do you think our boss Jake might let us make this our next big story?"

"Let's hold off on this. We need more evidence to go before we tell him anything. Besides, he might not believe us yet."

"Wait when is the next episode airing?"

"It didn't say. Shit! I don't know when to check. It could air anytime, even when we're at work."

"Or maybe every night from Monday till Friday at 9:30-PM." Hunter speculated.

"Ok. I can try that and see if I get the next episode."

"I want to make a copy of this, so I can show someone that might be able to help us."

"Good idea."

Hunter left the living room to grab a blank tape. I still couldn't get what happened to John. It felt like he suddenly changed after being exposed to this show. *Could the show brainwash him?* I didn't even want to think what horrors awaited Hunter and I, when this violent cartoon comes back. *What would the creators plan for the next episodes? What would they want the viewers to do?* I remember when religious groups strongly believed about heavy metal music. That if played backwards they would hear hidden messages that was meant to brainwash its listeners into doing violent crimes. But this felt like it was specially made to get its viewers, the children and young teens, to do whatever this show's creator wanted them to do. I can feel it now, this wasn't going to be good news for us.

Hunter came back into his living room with a blank tape began recording the first episode. I suddenly felt sick. It's too hot and too cold, at the same time.

"Curtis? You ok?"

"No, I don't feel too good." My head's about to explode.

"I got Advil in the bathroom." I stood up on shaky legs and went into the bathroom. I took one pill and went back to the living room.

"You should ask your parents if John was really acting strange after he watched the show."

"I will. When I called, he said they went out to some party, and he had the whole house to himself."

"Your parents left him alone?" Now that I think about it. My parents are good people, but maybe not all the time.

"They did, with me there. I was old enough to babysit him. Dad doesn't trust strangers." Hunter nodded.

"How are you feeling?" Hunter took out his blank tape, put the sticker and labeled it.

"A little better. I'll just rest here for a bit." I closed my eyes and got comfortable.

"Sure, no problem. I could grab us some lunch later."

"All right." I was getting ready to take a nap.

"Oh, almost forget. The booklet?"

"John won't give it to me. I tried searching for it three times and found nothing. I checked under John's bed, his closet, and other places. It's like the thing didn't exist."

"This shit just gets weirder and weirder by the minute."

"I got a bad feeling about this. I really do," I concurred.

"Funny, I was about to say the same thing." We stared at each other. It felt quiet inside the living room. I noticed there wasn't any birds singing. No noise coming from outside, just dead silence.

"Hungry?" Hunter broke the silence.

"Sure, I'm just going to make a phone call."

Hunter nodded and went into the kitchen. I grabbed the and dialed my parents' house. Nobody picked up. They should be home. They don't have work today. It's already eleven in the morning, they should be up by now. I thought about leaving a message, but I feared John might delete it. I hang up and set the phone back on the rack. At least, my headache is slowly going away.

By 11:25-AM Hunter had made sandwiches, two bowls of soup and big glasses of milk. He carried them on a tray. I thanked him. We ate, and I felt much better.

"Are you feeling sick?" I asked him.

"No, I'm fine. But I'll warn the person that will go over the tape, if I do." I nodded and went back eating.

By 12:45-PM I tried calling my parents' house again and nobody answered.

"I'm heading over there myself, to see what's going on," I told Hunter.

"Alright, I'll update you on the network stuff."

"See you later, Hunter." I took my tape and drove to my parents' house. When I got there, the station wagon wasn't in the driveway. I got out and looked inside the house, but I can't find my brother. I went over to the neighbor's house. They told me nobody's been home since last night.

Chapter 2

Nov.12
4:00-PM

For two weeks nothing was making any sense. When I did manage to get ahold of my parents on the 4th of November, they told me a different story of what happened last night. My father went out with John while my mother stayed at home handing out candy to the kids. When they got back the thunderstorm started. John took a shower, got dressed into his pajamas sneaked-watched some TV and went to bed. After school he was hanging out at his friend's house. Our parents, we're out doing some shopping. Dad went to help his friend repair an old truck.

I wasn't sure who was telling the truth at this point. I told my father about the cartoon. I asked if he could recall John saying he was going to watch it. Dad said he was upstairs reading a book with my mother, and they went to bed.

Later, when Dad confronted John about what I said, my baby brother lied again. Somehow, I have the shows mixed up. John was talking about another show. I asked Dad to keep an eye on him and to tell me if John starts acting differently. He said he would but found it a bit hard to believe that a kids show would show such violent content. I hoped my dad would do what he said. If it turns out both are lying to me, then I'll have to find another way of getting the truth out of them.

Hunter tried to contact different channels and networks along with some cartoon stations. He pretty much got the same answer. They never heard of *The Manson & Barbara Show* and told him they would never show anything like that. Hunter even told them he would send them a copy of his tape. They would refuse, hang up or act like Hunter is crazy. This wasn't going to stop us. Hunter knows someone with a background on how cartoon shows, how they're made and all that jazz. While we waited, we had to keep working on these stories our boss was assigning us. I tried not to think about it too hard, but sometimes I couldn't get the thoughts out of my mind. I feared something very bad was going to happen. We have no other option though but to wait and see what happens.

I finished typing out the latest stories Hunter and I did. I carried a big stack of paper to Dan to be released on tomorrow's paper. I rubbed my eyes, a bit tired today. I went to Hunter and see if he found anyone that would be able to help us on our own case. I knocked on his door he waved me in. I closed the door behind me.

"I know what you'll ask me, and I haven't had any luck." He was waving around sheets of paper with contact numbers.

"There has to be someone. Hell, maybe a person who used to work at Walt Disney could help us."

"Mmmm...I'll see what I can dig up. I'll even check out Hollywood, but it's going to take us a while until we find something."

"Here. I'll try one half while you do the other, so we can speed it up."

"Alright. I hope you have enough to pay for your phone bill."

"Yeah, I'm covered." Hunter gave me a list. A few of the numbers has been crossed out and below them were the company names and locations."

"There are more on the back." I turned it around. The day just got longer.

"Alright, I'll get started when I get home."

When we punched out, Hunter went off to use the washroom before leaving. I went down to the parking lot alone. It was very windy with lots of clouds covering up the sky, obscuring the sun. I came to a four way stop. I was going to drive through it, but I saw a cop car on the other side. I hit the brakes. "Goddamn it!" As I waited for traffic, I wondered if I would have any luck with getting the next episode of the show. I tried every night at 9:30, since. All I got was static and sometimes strange noises which didn't sound right. When the light turned green, I sped off to my apartment.

I pulled into the parking lot and carried the sheet with the numbers to call upstairs. I walked up the flight of stairs. Something was sticking out of the door panel. It was a dark purple envelope. It felt warm which meant it must have been placed here not too long ago. *How could this get in here? The mail is always brought up to the landlord and she brings it to the person when they're home.* I flipped it over, it said: "To Curtis Parker, from Manson." Below the words was a drawing of Manson's head, which was the same as the logo of the show.

I checked both ways of the hallway and heard nothing. I stepped inside and closed the door. I walked into the kitchen, turned on the light above the sink. The envelope had a strong flower-like smell, but I'm not able to identify it. The letter inside was handwritten.

"Curtis, I have become aware you and your friend are looking into matters you shouldn't be. Do you think I don't know what's going on in your world? I know you two are trying to watch more of my show, but it isn't meant for adults. You and your friend won't understand what I'm trying to tell the children.

I'm going to warn you only once. If I see you two are still sticking your noses where they shouldn't be, you'll wish you never met my angry side. Oh, and if you think this some sort of a joke look out of your kitchen window."

A chill ran up my spine. I almost didn't want to look. But there he is. Manson is standing outside my kitchen window. He grinned showing sharp teeth, bright red lips, and glowing red eyes.

"BOO!"

I jumped and fell backwards, landing on the kitchen table. I dropped the letter in my hand. He laughed, then pointed his finger at the letter. It burst into flames, and I scrambled to get away. When I looked back at the window, he was gone.

When I stood up, I looked where the letter fell. It was gone along with the dark purple envelope. My heart was beating fast. I took a few breaths to calm myself down then set my table back up. I heard a noise coming from my living room, and saw my TV was on. The screen was blank. I went over, grabbed the remote and press the power button, but nothing happened. I pressed the button a few times and my TV still wasn't turning off. I then tried changing the channel, but that didn't work. I walked over to my TV. As I knelt to press the power button, Manson and Barbara suddenly appeared. I jumped back falling on my ass. They laughed evilly and their red eyes glowed brightly. Then the TV turned off. *It's going to take more than some jump scares to make me back off!* My phone rang. I walked back into the kitchen to answer it.

"Curtis! You there?! I just had some crazy shit happen over at my place!" Hunter sounded frantic

"Let me guess. You got a letter from Manson himself, right?"

"Yeah! When I got home, I saw a dark purple envelope in my mailbox. I took it inside. It had my full name, and it was from Manson. It was a note warning about sticking our noses where they didn't belong. He was standing outside my living room window."

Hunter took a breath.

"He pointed at the note, it burst into flames, then was gone. Even the envelope was gone. Then, my TV was somehow turned on. The remote, didn't work. I reached for the power button and both Manson and Barbara yelled "BOO!" at me.

"Holy shit! That's what happened to me!"

"Did you check to see if the tape you brought over is still there?"

"Yes, I still have it."

"Ok, good. I have mine too. Just wanted to make sure." Hunter was breathing hard on the wire.

"We have to find out what Manson and his friends have planned for the children before it's too late. I'll get around calling those numbers."

"Same here. I'll let you know tomorrow if anything comes up."

"Ok, Hunter. Take care and watch yourself."

"Alright. Same to you, man."

"Ok, bye."

I sat the phone back on the rack. I went over to the fridge and grabbed a cold bottle of Dead Moon beer. I drank it then took a few breaths then sat down at the kitchen table. I grabbed the sheet with the phone numbers and looked at them. I won't tell anyone what happened to me or Hunter. I'll just say we we're looking into where The Manson & Barbara Show came from and who made it. I took another drink of my beer then set the bottle down. I reached for the phone again and began making the calls. I wasn't going to stop until I got to the bottom of this.

By 7:00-PM I had crossed off most of the numbers as they didn't take me seriously. I sat at the kitchen table with my dinner half eaten. I finished my 5th bottle of Dead Moon beer. I had my hand on my forehead covering up the right side of my face. *I don't get it. If nobody has heard or seen this show, then how the hell is it airing into millions of TV sets across America and only the children know about it?*

I still had three numbers I had to call. I sighed, then reached for my phone flipped it over, looked at the 1st number and began dialing it. I heard an auto female voice saying, "Hi you have reached California Cartoon Network unfortunately, we are unable to take your call. Our office hours are 9-AM to 6-PM from Monday to Friday." I dialed the second number. I waited for the beeping to stop but it didn't it kept beeping. I gave it about five minutes but got nothing. I hung up. *Give me a fucking break already!*

I looked at the last number on the list. I thought about waiting until morning. I would retry the other two numbers tomorrow when I get home from work. However, I would have only one hour before most of these places closed. *Fuck it.* I dialed the number and waited for the person on the other end to pick up. I closed my eyes, rubbed my face with my left hand and heard an older woman answer.

"Florida Cartoon Station. May I know who is calling?"
At last! I hope I have luck with this one!

"Hi, I'm Curtis Parker calling from News 6 in Black Creek. I'm calling to ask you if you've heard of a cartoon show called The Manson & Barbara Show?"

The woman was quiet for a bit.

"Could you please repeat that?"

I told her the name of the show, a bit slower this time.

"I...I think I heard of it somewhere before."

Please, I hope this woman isn't pulling my chain!

"Can you remember where you've heard of it?"

"You said your name was Curtis?"

"Yes, I'm Curtis Parker. I'm looking into this show. It seems nobody has heard of it, yet all the kids up here know about it than what they're letting their parents know."

"Yes, now I remember where I heard that name before. There was an artist I met back in '69 named Osborne Louis. He was working here during a Christmas party. He was working on this show since the mid-60s."

"Did he say what it was about?"

"Not much. He won't give us a lot of information about it but on the next day on December 25th he was killed in a car crash."

"What?! He died?"

"Yes, he was here on the 24th and the following night was killed. He went through a red light and a truck rammed into the driver side. It was horrible. His family was very upset when they heard the news."

"Is any of his family still alive?"

The woman was quiet for a bit.

"Ummm...I'm not sure where they went. They kept a low profile after the death of Osborne Louis."

"Ok. Can you tell me when Osborne was born and where he came from?"

"I think he said he was from New Orleans but that he hated it there when he was young. I'm trying to remember his age. Wait! Now, I remember he was 39 when he died. He lived both in Hollywood and Florida in his early 20s."

"This is great. Thank you so much for this information."

"I hope it helps you."

"Listen if you can dig anything else on Osborne Louis. Please call me back at 500-748-9966, that's my personal number."

"Ok, I'll write that down. I do find it odd that his show is airing when nobody knows what it was about." I

"Well, I hope to get to the bottom of this. Talk to you later... oh what's your name?"

"It's Dorothy."

"Thanks, Dorothy. Talk to you later, bye."

She didn't say anything back, but it didn't matter. I now had some data that Hunter and I could look into. Finally, a break in this case. If we got our hands on some real good information, then Jake would allow us to do a story about it. This might get people to open their eyes! I hang up the phone and yawned.

I would tell Hunter tomorrow, in person. I went into the bathroom and stepped into the shower. I brushed my teeth after. Tossed my dirty clothes onto the floor and quickly went to sleep.

That night I dreamed I was walking back home from school when I was 12 years old. I walked down the empty street. *I remember this day.* This was back in Oct.13, 1976 as John was born on April.1ˢᵗ I was born on Jan.20ᵗʰ" But as I walked further down the street, I remembered why I was going this way. So, that bully won't get back at me after I told the teacher on him. I stopped and saw an old run-down factory. *Wait, I could go through there to reach the other side of the street. That's a few blocks down where my house is.* I walked towards the factory and went inside.

It was very dark and creepy inside. I could hear thunder roaring above me and the rain was pouring harder outside now. When lightning flashed in the sky it would light up the factory for a bit, allowing me to see where I was going. I thought I heard noises behind me, but when I turned around to see what it was. I didn't see anything, I turned back where I was going and tried to move quickly. However, as I thought I was getting closer towards the exit I came to a dead end. I heard more noises I turned my around just then a lightning flash cracked the sky. It lit up the dark factory. Standing near the broken window was a tall dark person, his eyes were glowing bright red.

As thunder roared like a beast, my heart was beating fast. This person was running towards me. I ran and went through a doorway leading to another part of the factory. There were a lot of big machinery. I heard the person making loud noises. I ducked behind one of the machines. I could hear the person running past me. He glowed. I slowly moved, then tried to find the way I came. I kept bumping into the machinery. I stopped and thought I could hear the person breathing. I turned but I didn't see him behind me. When I turned back, I saw two bright red glowing eyes in front of me. I was then struck in the head with a sharp weapon. The pain was excruciating. I screamed, then woke up.

Nov. 13
7:00-AM

Sweat ran down my face when I woke up from that nightmare. I wiped my face and checked the time. I had two hours before I had to be at work. I slowly sat over the edge of my bed, took a few breaths, and stood up. I went into the bathroom, might as well take a shower. I rested my head against the shower wall. I was unable to keep the memories at bay. I got lost inside a factory back in '76. I could hear someone following me. At first, I thought it was the school bully. It turned out to be some crazed homeless person, that nearly killed me with a fire axe. I didn't tell my parents about what happened. I went home the long way after that. I hadn't thought of that day for several years now. Why would I suddenly have a nightmare about it? This was all Manson. He was trying to scare me off, but I wasn't going to quit!

I made myself breakfast and poured myself a glass of milk. I sat at the kitchen table. I must tell Hunter about what Dorothy told me before we went into work. Halfway through breakfast, I was beginning to feel sick it. I put my fork down and placed my hand over my forehead. I remember feeling like this after the 2nd time I watched the recorded tape of that show. This felt worse, thought. I felt like puking. I ran to the bathroom and emptied my stomach with what little breakfast I got into me. I coughed and felt another bout of vomiting coming. I felt warm and cold at the same time. I reached for the sink, pulled myself up on shaky legs and grabbed a facecloth. I got it wet with warm water and wiped my face. On the mirror I looked exactly like how I felt. I turned the knob on the sink, drank some of the water, and spit it out to clean my mouth. I took two Advil to kill the raging headache.

It was 8:35am by the time I cleaned up my mess. I must leave if I want to get to work on time. I don't feel well, though. *Should I call in sick? Or should I go?* My body decided for me. I found myself slumped on the bathroom floor. I was so weak, I couldn't stand. I wasn't going to risk it. I mustered the remaining strength I had and called News 6. It didn't take long for Becky to answer. She handles most of the calls at the news station.

"Hi, Becky. This is Curtis Parker I'm calling in sick today. I just threw up this morning. Not feeling good."

"Ok, I'll let Jake know you're not coming, too."

"Wait, who else is sick?"

"Hunter called in a few minutes ago. He too is feeling sick. Guess a bug is going around."

"Guess so."

"You get well soon, Curtis. Make sure to call in tomorrow if you're feeling better."

"Alright, thanks again Becky. Bye." I hung up then dialed Hunter's number. I sat down. My legs can barely carry me. I got Hunter's machine. Guess he's too sick, he can't even get to the phone. I left him a message that I got our first break on the case. I hang up, went to the living room, and laid down on the sofa. I felt very warm. I rested my head on the pillow and closed my eyes.

2:00-PM

I woke up feeling lightheaded, but my headache was gone. I rubbed my eyes, they felt gritty. My mouth felt very dry. I reached for the top of the sofa and pulled myself up. It was dark inside my apartment. I reached over for the lamp on the nightstand and grabbed the TV remote. The screen lit up the dark living room.

I flipped through some channels then stopped. I needed a drink. I slowly stood up, shuffled over to the fridge, and poured myself a glass of milk. I walked back the sofa and drank my glass slowly.

I flipped through a few channels then stopped on a cooking show hosted by a sexy woman and a blond guy.

"Everyone, it's me, Cindy and Peter. Today we're here to show you the new Super Blender 9000!" The camera zoomed in on a big white blender, with a round glass case above it and lead. I took another drink, as Cindy went on how great this blender was. I didn't feel lightheaded anymore.

"Alright, let's show what the Super Blender 9000 can do." Peter was saying, when suddenly my TV had a bit of static, but it quickly went back to normal.

Cindy opened the blender lead then went to grab some fruit. Suddenly Peter grabbed her arm, then using his left hand turned on the blender. I couldn't have moved even if I wanted to help Cindy. Peter forced Cindy's hand into the blender. The sharp blades tore through her hands and quickly sliced off her fingers. Blood splattered everywhere. Cindy screamed while Peter grinned.

Then Peter grabbed a knife from the kitchen counter and slit her throat. Blood poured out but the camera man continued showing everything. Peter then pulled her destroyed arm out. Forced her face into the blender. As it was being shredded to pieces, the camera zoomed in on this. I could hear the sharp blades ripping through the flesh and bone. I felt my jaw hanging open. The scene changed instead of Cindy there was Manson. He was grinning, his red eyes glowing. He took the blender top, drank Cindy's blood then faced the audience.

"Quite refreshing, isn't it?"

I shook my head. When I looked back at the TV, it was normal again. I reached for the remote and shut it off.

My heart was beating fast. I jumped when I heard my phone ringing. I nearly spilled my glass of milk. I set it on the nightstand and picked up the phone.

"Hello?"

"Hey Curtis, I just got your message. I was resting up on the sofa for a while." I was quiet for a bit. I don't even know where to begin.

"Curtis? You, ok?" Hunter sounded scared, maybe worried.

"I just had some weird shit happened. Manson was playing with my mind!"

"He gave you a nightmare?"

"Ummm...I had a nightmare when I went through that factory back in '76. I was chased by some dark person with red glowing eyes. When I woke up, I was sweaty. It seems to fade away. When I started eating breakfast though, I got sick and was unable to go to work."

"Damn! I had the same thing last night. I had no luck with the phone calls. When I went to bed, I had a nightmare. I was at my mother's house, I heard someone break in and someone was chasing me. I only woke up after they caught me. I felt sick after that and puked all over my bed. After I cleaned up, I called in sick then passed out on the sofa and... what time is it?"

I looked at the clock.

"2-PM."

"Anyway, this weird shit you saw?"

"After I woke up on the sofa, I got myself a glass of milk. I was watching this cooking show on TV." Hunter was horrified with the whole thing, too.

"Fuck man. This shit is getting serious."

"We're not backing off. I got a lead to go on."

"Oh yes, please tell me." Hunter's voice brightened a little.

"I spoke with a woman in Florida named Dorothy who works at a cartoon studio."

"Ok, so we just find him." Hunter said after I filled him in.

"Here's the catch, he's dead."

"You're shitting me, right?"

"I wish I was." I told him what happened on that Christmas day.

"Wait, if he's dead, then who's running the show?"

"I don't know but we're going to find out." I told Hunter the rest of the detail.

"Sounds like he came from a well-off family."

"I think you're right about that because after Osborne's death, every member of his family has kept a low profile."

"I wonder why."

"We'll find out and see if Dorothy has any more leads for us."

"Ok. I'll do some research. I feel like I'm able to move now."

"Alright, let me know what you find."

"Ok, and to be safe, I'm not turning on the TV for a bit."

"Yeah, that's a good idea. We don't want Manson fucking around with our heads."

I got dressed and went to Subway, then drove to the gas station. I didn't realize my Honda had a nearly empty tank. It was getting colder with weather reports saying we might get early snow fall by end of this week. I remember back in '79 Black Creek got hit with a nasty snowstorm. I was trapped in my apartment for five days. Just glad I had enough food to last me and all those books I owned helped to pass the time.

I knew I would have to pull my winter clothes and I hated winter weather. I specially hate Christmas music. I could never understand why people like that kind of music, and why December and October are the only two months with their own theme music. I have thought of moving somewhere warmer but that would mean I would have to work at a different news studio. I might not have a good partner and friend like Hunter. And I would need a lot of money to travel. I knew this city very well, I lived here for 20 years, but it doesn't have everything I want.

I then heard the pump nuzzle stop I looked at the screen and saw I had filled my tank up. I went inside the gas station, paid the guy and drove back to my apartment. I placed my subs onto a plate, grabbed a bottle of Dead Moon beer from the fridge and began eating my lunch.

4:00-PM

I counted my money making sure I had enough for shopping and to pay the landlord by the end of the month. I put the money for rent pay in my nightstand drawer. I always kept it there. This is how I do my budgeting. I put the rest of my money back into my wallet. I checked the time and thought of giving Dorothy a follow up call. Or call Hunter, but he might be still busy. I wanted to check on John by calling dad. My phone bill was going to skyrocket but if I was going to look further into this show. We still have to check on the remaining family members of Osborne Louis. Maybe I should use a payphone.

I knew a few places where I could find payphones that anyone hardly use. I would tell Hunter this as well so we could make long distance calls without having to burn through our money. I went over to the phone to call Hunter and give Dorothy a call tomorrow with the payphone. I picked up my phone but as I went to dial, I thought of checking on John first then Hunter. So, I called my parents' house.

"Hello?" Mom picked up and after the greetings she wondered why I was home early.

"No. I was sick this morning, so I didn't go in but I'm feeling better now."

"Are you sure you're alright?"

"Yes, I'm fine now I think my dinner didn't sit well with my stomach last night. Anyway, is dad there?"

"No, he's out right now with his friends. John is over at a friend's house."

"Do you know what John and his friend is up to?" My mother was quiet for a bit.

"Oh, I just remembered I have something cooking in the stove. I'll call you later Curtis, bye."

"Mom, wait!" But she hung up. She's never done that before! Something is going on over there. If I can't get the answers, I want from any of them, then I'll get those myself!

I hung up then dialed Hunter's number.

"Oh hey, Curtis. I was about to call you."

"What do you have?"

"Oh, I was going to ask if you had any more luck. I can't seem to find anything on Osborne Louis."

"No, I haven't but been thinking we should use payphones to keep our phone bills from getting any higher. I'll try reaching Dorothy tomorrow. However, I do think something is going on at my parents' house. I was just asking my mother how John was, and she had told me he was at his friend's house. When I asked what they we're doing up there, suddenly she told me she had the stove on and hang up on me."

"That's rude."

"I know! She's lying. She never cooks anything around 4 o'clock, it's always been 6 o'clock. I'm starting to think Manson isn't just brainwashing children. Now he's forcing parents to keep their silence on whatever the children are doing."

"What do you have in mind?"

"I'm thinking of getting some cameras and placing them inside my parents' house."

"Isn't that illegal?"

"What choice do I have? I need to know what's really going on."

"How are you going to pull it off?"

"Simple. The attic. My parents did some work on it, but nobody uses it. It's more of like an extra room, we practically have forgotten about it."

"Ok, but still security cameras aren't cheap."

"Who sells them?"

"Umm…I think you would have to order them. I can't think of any electric store that sells them here."

"I'll look into it. For all I know Manson and his friends are brainwashing John into doing something bad."

"I agree with you on that part. By the way, I just noticed there is no channel 13 anymore."

"What?!"

"Yeah, if you try putting in that number on your TV it won't show up anymore. Not even the channel index shows what channel has the Manson show."

"Ok, let's park that one for now. When we get back to work tomorrow, we'll see if we can dig more up on Osborne Louis. Then I look into some security cameras. You know what, I might have some, set up here, just in case."

"I really hope it doesn't come to that but then I might do the same too. Alright, see you tomorrow, Curtis."

"Ok Hunter. Talk to you later, bye."

I went into my living room and turned on my TV. I got "NO SIGNAL" on the screen when pressed the 1 & 3 buttons on the remote. *What if the show wasn't coming from a normal network station, then it would mean someone found a way to broadcast a show while keeping a low profile? Maybe Osborne's family members we're the ones behind it, but why would they do this? If it's revenge, it's over the top. There has to be something more to it. I just don't know yet, but I'll find out.*

Nov. 14
9:00-AM

I told Hunter my theory at work, the next day. He agreed with my theory, that somehow the people behind it found a different way to broadcast the show. He too was stumped on why Manson was targeting adults and how he was able to get a way with the things we saw so far.

"Magic then. There is no other explanation. We aren't seeing things."

"I guess, but if that is true, then why not just kill us. If Manson doesn't want us sticking our noses in?"

"Hopefully he doesn't have enough. Because I don't really like the other option."

"What do you mean?" I can't think straight anymore.

"That he enjoys fucking around with us first, before going in for the kill."

"I fear you're right about the 2nd theory."

"Hey, Jake wants to see you two in his office." Dan met us right after we both walked out of the elevator.

"Thanks, Dan." I replied.

We walked over to Jake's office. He answered right away when I knocked. I closed the door behind us. Looking through Jake's office window, I saw an overcast sky and the wind was blowing loudly.

"Morning you two. Glad to see our top news team members are back in action."

We smiled and pulled up chairs.

"Now that you're both back, I got a story I want you to film and write. This is going to make the headlines." We just stared at out boss.

"B.C.P.D. made a major drug bust. The police chief personally took part, a few gang members were shot. They're allowing us to do an interview, so everybody can see how well our police force fights crime.

"Where did this happen?" Hunter asked.

"Near the harbor. Around five in the morning, we got the call on our radio. Since the mayor is so pleased with our work, he's going to let us report it. Channel 18 lost a lot of its viewers. Ha-ha!"

"Alright, let's get started then." I smiled at our boss.

"That's the spirit you two. Make this city proud of its police force and it's news team."

Hunter had the camera ready and I had my microphone set up. I heard one of crew members asked if the police are getting too extreme.

"No, besides I don't want crime in our city." I replied.

"If the police and their actions are causing a panic, I'm sure our mayor is open to feedback from his people." Hunter suggested.

"It just seems they are more violent than before. They'd rather shoot than bring them in." The crew guy continued saying.

"Keep your mind on your work. As long we're getting paid for this, that's all I care about." Our driver shut the guy down and stopped the van in front of a house that looked worse for wear.

"Alright, let's do it." Hunter said. The Ford's back doors opened, and we got. Our boss wasn't kidding about the shootout.

The living room window was broken. I could see a few bullet holes through the wooden frame under it. The front deck of the house was a bit damaged. Shotgun shells were lying on the ground. Parked beside the house were two squad cars. The gang members might have let loose with their fire power as both cars were covered in bullet holes.

"Alright Curtis, ready when you are." I nodded and stood in front of Hunter. "Ok live, in 3...2...1"

"Curtis Parker here with our breaking news. At 5AM Black Creek police have busted a major drug den which led into a deadly shootout. Not one single officer was lost in the incident. All gang members were killed during the shootout. Let's go inside and speak with the chief of police himself." Hunter stopped recording as we went inside the house.

I stood beside the police chief, a every tall well-build man with short dark hair and he was wearing glasses. d had the camera pointed at us. I held the microphone close and asked him the questions that Jake would want to hear. He gave a lot of details on how the whole operation went done. He said the shootout happened because this gang was packed with serious fire power, from Uzi's to sawed off pump shotguns. The chief told me if they had bigger guns than they would have been in trouble. Luckily, none of them had assault rifles. I finished up with the questions. When we had everything we needed, Hunter put down the camera.

"Alright, got what we came for." Hunter said.

"Ok, let's get back to the studio." I suggested, but before I can get out of the room the police chief called my attention.

"Curtis, can I ask you something?"

"What is it?" I asked.

"Have you heard of a cartoon show called The Manson & Barbara Show?" I saw out of the corner of my eye Hunter abandoned what he was doing and came over to us.

"I heard a few kids talking about it, but I can't seem to find anything more about the show." I hedged.

"I manage to see bits of it, but my two sons won't tell me much. I was curious, just wanted to ask if you heard anything about it."

"No problem. If something more comes of it, I'll make sure to make it our next big story." The police chief chuckled. We walked out of the house. On our way to the car, we met a few reporters coming in.

dBack at the studio, our boss was very pleased with our work. I went into my office to type up my conversation with the police chief. I was now wondering who else have heard of the show. His two sons were also keeping it a secret from their father. *Maybe older people are not susceptible to Manson's powers. Younger people are easier to control. However, Manson can still fuck with adult's minds.* I finished writing my report but saw my printer needed more paper and ink. I carried the sheet of paper to Dan to have in tomorrow's paper while I went to the storage room to get the supplies I needed.

Hunter knocked on my door when I finished putting in fresh paper and a full cartridge of ink.

"So, we're not the only one who's wondering what the children are hiding." I let Hunter in and he sat down on the extra chair in front of my worktable.

"I wonder how many parents are seeing this show." Hunter looked downtrodden.

"For all we know it could be the whole goddamn country. But if something does happen, knowing our boss, he'll want us to look into it."

"Any luck with Dorothy?"

"Aww shit! I'll try after we're done today." I had forgotten about her.

"John and your parents?" I shook my head.

"I think Manson found a way to air his show without us seeing what he's showing."

"Let me know what Dorothy has for us." Hunter left my office. I turned to my window looking down at the city of Black Creek.

When Hunter and I punched out at 5-PM, I drove to the payphone. It was over by an old train bridge that wasn't being used anymore. I put in a quarter and pressed the numbers. I heard a male voice.

"Florida Cartoon Station, Dale speaking."

"Hi, my name is Curtis Parker. I spoke to Dorothy two days ago, she had information for me. Could I please speak with her?"

"Oh Dorothy. I'm sorry to say this. She had heart attack, she passed away last night."

"Really?" Poor lady. I can't get out the nagging feeling though, the heart attack may not be just a natural occurrence.

"Yes, and for a woman to live up to 69 she had a good life."

Maybe this guy would know something. Here goes nothing.

"Maybe you can help me out here, Dale. I'm looking into a cartoon show called The Manson & Barbara Show. Dorothy had information on its creator, Osborne Louis. Would you know anything?"

"Ummm…I'm afraid not. I've been working here for ten years, so anything before that I won't know. Sorry Curtis. Is there anything else I can do for you?"

"Yeah, where is this carton station at?"

"Miami."

"Thanks, Dale. Have a good day, bye."

d was wondering if the show's characters were behind it. Or it could be someone else. I would need more information to prove which theory of mine was right. I got back into my Honda and drove to get some groceries then head back to my apartment.

It was passed 6PM. I made sure the dead bolt was engaged on my way to the kitchen. I took off my trench coat and boots. I put the groceries away, then opened my window just a crack. It felt very warm inside. I would tell Hunter the bad news tomorrow. I didn't feel like calling him, I felt tired to the bones.

I relaxed on my sofa for a bit and thought on how to go about setting up hidden cameras in my parents' house. I yawned. If I don't want to wake up later hungry, I have to make myself dinner now.

Nov. 15
9:00-AM

Hunter and I stood in the elevator. It seemed to be moving slowly up the shaft.

"Dorothy died of a heart attack, but I don't think that was the reason for her death. "So, all we got to go on now is that Osborne Louis might have a house somewhere in Miami." I appraised Hunter of what I got so far.

"I hope that guy you were speaking to was telling the truth." Hunter replied.

"I'm sure if we looked up birth date and death records in New Orleans and Florida we'll find more on Osborne."

"What if Osborne is still alive and he faked his death?" Hunter speculated.

"If so, the question is why?"

"Maybe Manson and his friends have something to do with it. After everything that we know so far, it's not a stretch."

"This shit just gets weirder and weirder." I shook my head, bewildered.

When the elevator came to a full stop the doors didn't open. The light above us flickered for a bit, then the light came on as the doors opened. We stepped out into the elevator just glad it was nice and warm inside. Outside it was getting colder which meant it would begin snowing if not tonight, the next the day.

The story was a big hit. The mayor of course was happy to see his fellow police officers doing their job and keeping the public safe. However, I did notice something odd. It seemed everyone was so happy with how the police have quickly cleaned up crime. Why haven't I heard sirens going off regularly or other shootings for that matter? Hunter agreed. We heard a few police cars and some ambulances, a couple of fire trucks here and there. On the days these raids happened thought, I hardly heard anything.

I wasn't sure if something was up, or I just haven't been in touched with the rest of the city. I couldn't stop thinking about that goddamn show and what it has done to my little brother including my parents. My father phoned me this morning stating John was alright and would like to hang out with me on Saturday. Dad told me that he saw an episode of The Manson & Barbara Show. It has been going since the 31st of October, and it was on channel 13. *What?! That does it!* I needed to get those video cameras set up. I knew I had to be careful. My family won't be pleased to find out I've been monitoring them through hidden cameras. I needed to know what the hell was going on and why children were keeping this show a goddamn secret.

By the end of the month, I'll have enough money to get what I need and see how I can pull this off. I knew every inch of my parents' house, where some good hiding spots were, along with which part off the floorboards could be pulled out. Dad hid his Playboy Magazines under those loose floorboards.

Jake came into my office letting me know that the mayor was holding a special event for the brave police officers of Black Creek. Hunter and I should be there before 11AM. So, we had everything ready to go. Half past 10AM, we left News 6 and drove to city hall. Cold wind was blowing hard outside. Dark heavy clouds loomed all over the city.

"Here it comes. I really hope we don't get a blizzard like in '79." The driver commented.

"If we do, it will be our next breaking story." One of the crew members replied.

"Tag line for the paper: *Black Creek hit with massive snowstorm; weather reporter tells everyone to chill out.*" I joked. Everyone laughed, as our driver reached city hall.

I saw a few other news reporters were there, but it didn't matter. Everyone would be tuning into our station. As we enter inside city hall, Hunter had the video camera all set. I went closer to the front so everybody watching would be able to hear the mayor. When everyone was seated the mayor came out and stood in front of the platform. He adjusted the microphone closer to his mouth. Hunter signaled me through the earpiece that he began recording.

"Good morning, everyone. I'm happy to say that our great police force has once again removed unwanted criminals in our city and not one brave officer was lost yesterday. Today, we honor Black Creek's finest, including the police chief himself." The crowd clapped their hands. Camera flashes went off.

Black Creek officers came out followed by their police chief. The mayor walked over to them while his assistant held a fancy wooden box. The mayor began pinning medals onto the police uniforms. Hunter continued filming. Camera flashes were going off, the crowd was cheering, and everyone was clapping away.

I noticed something out of the corner of my eye. When I turned my head, I saw two boys around 9 or 10 with guns on their arms. One kid with black hair was holding a Ruger Mini-14, while the 2nd kid with blond hair had an M1 Garand with a bayonet attached to it. I manage to yell before hell broke loose.

"LOOKOUT! THEY GOT GUNS!"

The crowd screamed. The kids shoot all the police officers, the chief was hit on one shoulder and the chest. The mayor and his assistant were also shot in the head. Blood splattered all over the place. One wounded officer managed to fire a few shots back but didn't hit the kids. He was shot dead by the 2nd kid.

They turned towards us and began firing again. Hunter dropped the camera. I had already let go of the microphone. We quickly ran up the stage with bullets nearly hitting us. I could hear those two coming after us. We ran to the back door, but it had no lock.

"Shit!" Hunter sounded frustrated and scared.

"Come on!" I dragged him with me, and we ran down the hallway. We could hear more gun fire behind us. Then the door opened, I turned to check and see the blonde kid holding the M1 Garand aimed and squeezed away at the trigger. Hunter and both nearly got shot.

We continued running downstairs towards the back exit. I could hear sirens coming towards city hall. Guess one of the officers manage to call for help. Suddenly, I felt a searing pain in the back of my left leg, and I fell. This time it was Hunter who dragged me through the exit door. I have never been happier to see police officers.

"DON'T SHOOT. THEY'RE ARMED! THEY'RE RIGHT BEHIND US!" Hunter yelled and we ran behind the police cars.

When the back door opened and both kids came out. The officers were dumbstruck.

"Shit. Isn't that the chief's sons?" One of the officers commented. I felt a chill ran up my spine when I heard that. Without warning, both boys opened fire on the officers. A few bullets zoomed above us. Windows exploded and shards of glass flew into the air. One officer fired his pistol hitting the black-haired kid in his chest. The blond kid turned to where the bullet that killed his brother was shot from. The officer's head exploded, blood and brain matter flying everywhere. The blond kid was now getting closer, and the officers are unable to put down these kids.

"Fuck it!" I crawled towards a dead officer grabbed his S&W 659 pistol. The blond kid fired a few shots where Hunter was. He jumped over the truck of the squad car for cover. I crawled some more to get a better aim. The kid turned to look at me with emotionless eyes.

"Manson and his friends are going to get you and your friend Curtis! You'll wish you never made him angry!"

He gripped the M1 Garand more firmly, but I quickly pulled the trigger. I watched his upper body jerked with the impact. His body dropped to the cold ground while more sirens roared in the background. Hunter came over to me, as I stood frozen. I can't believe I was holding a pistol. I can't believe I just shot a kid.

Paramedics came along, with more officers but they we're in shock when they saw who was killed and by whom. Luckily the one son fired his last round from the Ruger Mini-14, if he had more ammo I would have been wasted. I was lying in the back of the ambulance after having my wounded leg wrapped in bandage. I was given pain killers to help with the pain, after having a .223 removed from my left leg. Hunter was sitting beside me, white as a ghost. He couldn't believe what happened. I saw the other reporters filming us. I told Hunter to close the ambulance's back door, so they won't see us.

An officer came into the ambulance to fill us in. He introduced himself as Officer Smith. He was a tall black man with short hair.

"How are you feeling, Curtis?"

"A bit shaken up but...but the hell is going on?"

"The two boys were in fact the chief's two sons Bobby and Robert. We checked their house to find that both boys have murdered their own mother and grandfather."

I felt my jaw dropped open.

"How did they get in here then?" Hunter asked.

"They took their mother's car and their father's rifles. They killed 15 people, including your news crew."

"What?!" Hunter shouted.

"After you two ran they shot your crew members along with the camera. Then they reloaded their weapons and continued the rampage." Officer Smith was shaking his head, as confused as we were of the situation.

"How much ammo did they have on them?" I asked.

"A lot, and they also had pistols with them, as well. I'm still scratching my head trying to figure out why these two boys, whom I've met in person, both nice and very friendly suddenly turned into killers."

"I think we might know the reason." I replied.

"Yesterday, when Hunter and I we're reporting that drug bust, he asked me if I heard of a cartoon called The Manson & Barbara Show. I told him that I have heard of it and did in fact see the first episode of it. He told me that he saw bits of the show and his two sons won't talk to him about it."

"Never heard of that show what channel is it on?" The officer was looking at me speculatively.

"Well, it was on channel 13. It isn't there any more though. I've been looking into it, trying to find out where it's being aired."

"Well, I'm sure there is more to it than just a cartoon. I have to add that to my report." The officer got up and was about to leave.

"Wait, there's one more thing I have to know. When Robert stood in front of me with his rifle, was it still loaded when I shot him?"

"No, he wasted his last shot trying to hit your friend. You had no choice, no one blames you."

"How can two sons easily get their hands on weapons like that?" Hunter asked.

"Their father along with his sons we're hunters. We don't know the answer to that question thought because the chief always kept the guns in a safe. I guess they saw what the code was to open it. Anyway, I got to report this whole goddamn mess."

12:35-PM

Hunter went with me to the hospital, to make sure my injury wasn't too serious. When I got the x-rays back, the bullet missed the main bone. It would take two or three weeks to fully heal and was told not to put too much pressure on it. They gave me a bottle of pain killers. Hunter had to call a cab to take us back to the news studio. I'm sure our boss knew the massacre that happened today. Everyone would be in shock to hear the deaths of those they once knew.

The cab drove through the city. The radio was on, we heard female voice saying: *In our breaking story the mayor of Black Creek along with the police chief and several officers and civilians were killed during an honoring event at the city hall. Bobby and Robert, the police chief's sons opened fire with weapons they took from their father's gun safe and killed over fifteen people. It was also reported they murdered their own mother and grandfather. It's unknown why both boys would do this, but police are looking into this event. The whole city is in shock. Both boys were shot by the police while attempting to escape.*"

When the cab reached News 6, Hunter paid the driver.

"Feeling alright?" Hunter asked me.

"Yeah, I'm fine. Look we're going to start looking for Osborne Louis, no matter what it takes!"

"Alright we'll make some calls to New Orleans and Florida and see what we can dig up."

"Ok, sounds good. And remember to use payphones."

Hunter nodded and we went to use the elevator. We saw a sign on it: "OUT OF ORDER" I sighed.

"You gotta be kidding me!" Hunter and I took the stairs slowly. I didn't want to push my left leg.

d we made it to the main floor I checked the time on my watch it was already 1:45-PM.

"Curtis! Hunter! I can't believe what I heard on the radio! A massacre!?" Dan met us right on the doorway. The rest of the news team was behind him.

"I know Dan. One minute it was just another story and the next, shit hits the fan."

Jake was walking towards where we converged.

"I'm glad to see you two made it but goddamn! Losing half of team by the police chief's own sons?!"

"I know Jake, it's really fucked up." Hunter replied.

"Curtis, how are you? I heard you were shot. Do you want to leave early?" Jake turned to me.

"No, I'll be fine. I just want to get back to work."

"You're sure?"

"Yeah, I'm sure."

"Alright, you two. Get to work with this story while I make some phone calls."

We dispersed. Hunter and I walked over to our offices.

"Well, if we find more clues pointing to that show as the cause of the massacre, then we'll be able to crack this case open." I whispered to Hunter.

"Somehow, I don't think it's going to be that easy. Then again maybe it's the only way we can make parents to ban that show."

"Let's get to work then." I nodded.

I went into my office and looked over the window. Snow was falling much thicker now. I could hear the wind blowing loudly outside. I turned back to my computer, opened my writing text program, and began writing what happened. I stuck with the police report that both boys were shot by them. The reason for committing these murders was they we're told by Manson the Bat from the cartoon show, The Manson & Barbara Show. When I finished my report, I printed it out then took the sheet of paper to Dan to have it printed into the paper. I was going to get this story blown wide open, so I could make parents stop their children from watching the show before it does anything worse.

5:00-PM

We punched out, I shuffled downstairs. My left leg wasn't bothering me that much anymore. Maybe the painkillers are working their magic.

"Take it easy, Curtis." I heard Hunter say from my back.

"Alright, as soon as we get those numbers, we'll start making phone calls." I replied.

"Yep, and I'll watch my back just in case."

"Good idea, man." I got into my Honda and drove to McDonald's for dinner. When I got to my apartment it was almost 6PM. Half of the parking lot in our apartment building was covered in snow. I opened the door and grab my dinner.

I saw the janitor cleaning the wet floors as I went upstairs. Taking my time, I reached the 5th floor and went inside my door. I took off my boots and trench coat. I carried my dinner into the kitchen, grabbed a bottle of ketchup from the cupboard and a large coke from the fridge.

I felt the heat blowing through the vents, soon I felt someone was watching me. I looked around and that's when I noticed my TV was on. *Oh, no. Not tonight, assholes. I'm not playing your fucking games!* I said aloud. I tried the remote, it didn't work. I went over to the TV to pull the plug when I heard Manson's voice behind me.

"Who said I wanted to play your games!"

I spun around, there was no one. He suddenly appeared in front of me with his glowing red eyes. I jumped and he went to grab me. I fell onto the floor nearly hitting the coffee table. Manson grinned.

"You may have escaped death this time. You won't be so lucky next time, nor your friend." He disappeared and the TV turned off. I got up and pulled the plug. I went back to the kitchen table but found I lost my appetite.

It was so damn quiet. I opened my window a bit to allow outside noises. I kept looking over at the living room. Scared Manson was going to keep messing around with me. I rubbed my forehead. I put the remains of my dinner into the trash, then my phone rang. It was mom.

"Curtis? Is that you?" She sounded upset.

"Yes, mom it's me."

"Oh, I'm so glad to hear you're ok. I heard on the news about the horrible shooting at city hall. I can't believe it."

"I know, it was...horrible."

"Were you hurt?"

"No, Hunter and I managed to get out of the building in time. The police to handle the killers." I lied.

"Was it true? The police chief's sons did this?"

"Yes. I couldn't believe what I saw but it's true. By the way, I'll still be able to hang out with John on Saturday." My mother went silent for a bit.

"Ok, I'll let him know. Come after lunch."

"At 1-PM?" I asked her.

"Yes, he has to study up on a history test that's coming next week."

"That's good. Say, has he been using the typewriter I gave him?"

"Not sure, you'll have to ask him that. Alright, bye now." She hung up before I could say anything back. I was annoyed by her behavior. Something's not right. I really needed to place those video cameras inside my parents' house. I would be able to see what the hell was really going on over there.

Nov. 16
9:00-AM

I pulled into the parking lot and stepped out now wearing my winter clothes. My left leg was a bit sore, but I wasn't going to let it stop me from doing my work. A car horn blew behind me I turned and see Hunter's black Ford LTD. When Hunter got out, I noticed he was livid.

"Curtis, get a load of this bullshit!" Hunter shoved the newspaper to me. The headline said: "CITY HALL MASSACRE! POLICE CHIEF'S SONS SECRETLY WORSHIPPED CHARLES MANSON!"

"I didn't write that!" I couldn't have lowered my voice even if I wanted to.

"Look at the rest of it!" Hunter was yelling, too.

I read the rest of the story. It said that both boys had kept books about serial killers such as Charles Manson. Many believed that this and listening to heavy metal tapes was the reason those boys turned into murderers. It was insinuated that they had a fight over getting a low report on their homework.

"This is bullshit! I didn't fucking write this!"

"Let's go find out why Dan changed it."

"It might have been Jake, as well." I countered.

We climbed upstairs and when we got to the main floor, we saw our boss waiting for us.

"Just the man I wanted to see!" I can barely contain my anger.

"I want to talk with you in my office." Jake said gravely.

"Fine. As long as I'll know why you had Dan change my story."

We went into Jake's office, he closed the door behind us, and went over to his desk.

"As you have seen on the paper the police found the real reason behind this massacre."

"Bullshit! It wasn't a goddamn serial killer!" I exploded.

"Curtis, you should know that cartoons don't cause children to kill people. And if you swear at me again consider yourself fired."

I shot him a look of anger but kept my mouth shut.

"Now, I hope I make it clear if I see this type of garbage, I'll have both of you fired. I have just formed a new team. When the time comes for you two to do your work, all I want to know is I can count on you two to bring me what I want. Is that clear?" Jake continued.

We both said, "yes sir" and Jake replied with a terse "good". We left his office. *Fucking prick!*

"The hell?!" Inside my office Hunter exploded.

"I know it's bullshit, but I guess the only way we're going to prove him wrong is find what information we can from the police."

"The police won't give us anything, Curtis. And if our boss finds out, we're fired."

"I'm sure the police won't mind if just asked them about a few things." I sighed.

"I'll see if Dan was forced to change our story or if Jake did it."

I nodded and Hunter left my office. Staying angry wasn't going to help me get the answers I wanted. I looked at the stories Jake wanted me to do, usual stories. Some were related to heavy metal and other bullshit that religious groups strongly believed turns children and teens into evil. I took the latter and dumped them into the trash bin and stuck with the other stories. I got back up and saw Hunter was walking over to me.

"Got some stories to do." I told Hunter.

"Alright, let's get going."

Hunter and I went downstairs. He told me Dan didn't rewrite our story it was Scott who did rewrites.

"I hate that guy!"

"Yeah, me too. But how did Jake manage to change the story so fast? It takes hours to set up the printing press. It would cost him a lot of money to have the whole thing changed."

I stopped and stared at each other.

"Do you think Manson is controlling them, as well? Yesterday he tried scaring me off."

"Yesterday? What time?" Hunter looked startled.

"Around at 6-PM."

"His girlfriend Barbara jumped at me when I got out of the shower yesterday. I almost shit myself."

I turned my head up the stairs, I thought someone was coming down but there was no one. We kept walking.

"She warned me that we won't escape death next time." Hunter continued.

"We're going have to be very careful with this case." I warned Hunter.

"Think we should get guns?" Hunter asked and I agreed. We got into Hunter's Ford LTD we had people to interview. He asked how my leg was and I told him it was a bit sore.

I wrote down everything I got from the interviews. When we finished, Hunter drove back to News 6. The elevator was still out of order.

"What's the story with the elevator?" I asked no one.

"It seems it broke last night, that's all I got." Hunter replied, anyway. We walked up stairs into our offices to begin writing our stories.

4:00-PM

Snow was coming down harder. I could barely see the city from my office. I had finished writing all the reports and had them taken to Dan. I wonder who was going to be part of the news team now that the others were murdered. I'm sure Jake would choose the right people, hopefully. However, that wasn't on my mind's forefront. I was trying to think if Osborne Louis or Manson were behind this. If it's one of them, why the strong hatred towards adults? Was it one person or both behind this? If Osborne was dead, then how would a cartoon character be able to do this?

Magic was the only thing I could think of. There was no other way around it. I remember reading horror stories and comics about people using black magic to summon demons, monsters, or to curse someone. *Could you really use something out of fiction, like a cartoon character to become real?* There was a knock on my door and Jake came in.

"Curtis, I got word from city hall. They will vote for a new mayor tomorrow. I want you and Hunter to film it with the new team I have formed."

"Sure thing." I said unenthusiastically.

"I noticed you didn't pick some of the other stories I had for you." Jake ignored my sarcastic tone.

"I don't go for garbage like that. I listen to heavy metal music and watch horror movies and I can tell you, that stuff doesn't turn people into killers."

"I just did it to see if you can tell the difference from real stories to garbage." Jake grinned and left.

I'd like to blow your fucking brains out you, fucking prick!

Hunter gave me a list of numbers to call in New Orleans while he would handle the Florida calls. Since I would be busy on Saturday with John my only free day to do most of this was Monday. Hunter was taking Friday off so he would be able to make the calls and would let me know on Monday. I hope we found some clues. I really wanted my boss to open his goddamn eyes and the parents too. The other option is to wait for something big to happen. I hate the waiting game.

Nov. 17
1:20-PM

I drove to my parents' house still feeling unhappy with the choice of mayor this city picked. There were six people. Only two of them were the right choice but for some odd reason the city picked the least qualified of the bunch. It seemed this fat prick only cared about business, money and looking good. He is not into public safety or it's people like our last mayor. I guess he had a way of charming people, but his words didn't fool me. Even Hunter was pissed off about our new mayor. I knew if I wrote what I thought it would get me fired. I made it short and simple for our paper, while Hunter filmed everything that Jake wanted.

I saw a few cars driving by the neighborhood. There were mostly older people shoveling the snow and they weren't enjoying it. When I came to a four way stop, I noticed the public park was empty. I didn't see one kid playing out there. *Sure, it's cold but the kids didn't care.* I remember John and I would play there. Not seeing one kid, felt wrong. As I drove on, I began to see there wasn't any snowman out, no snowball fights. *Are kids spending more time watching that goddamn show?* I had a gut feeling I was right. There was one house, when I drove by, I saw the whole living room. A little girl was watching TV and it was that show. I went to look closer. I heard a car horn blew behind me. I jumped and looked up at my rearview mirror. A station wagon was behind me. I pressed my foot onto the gas and drove to my parents' house.

I pulled into the driveway. Both of my parents' cars were in and the window lights were on. I remember I would try to make the biggest snowman with John back in the day. He kept on doing it even after I moved out but not seeing one today made me feel unhappier. I blew my horn and after waiting five minutes, I saw John waving at me through the window. He ran to the front door and out, wearing his winter clothes. I looked at the attic. I had to find the right day to set up the whole video camera thing. The only time would be late at night or when nobody was in the house. The neighbors were always watching out for each other, so if one of them saw me wearing all black, they'll think I'm a thief and will call the cops.

Day time was way too risky. However, during school hours both my parents were out of the house and won't return until after. They don't rush things so I could take my time to set up the cameras. I would have to plan it carefully so I would be in and out before anyone noticed me. I looked down and John was about to enter my car. *Let's see how much you changed in a short period of time.* John opened the passenger door.

"Hey Curtis."

"Hey John, glad we could hang out again." I smiled at him.

"Yeah sorry, I didn't get back to you. I have been very busy with schoolwork, hanging out with my other friends and doing some early Christmas shopping."

"No worries. I've been busy with work myself."

I shifted the gear into reverse, and we went on our way.

"So how are those stories coming along?" I asked John after a bit.

"I've been working on the one I told you about."

"The dark fantasy one?" My heart stuttered a bit.

"Yes, I manage to write up to150 pages this week."

"That's good. I'll have to take a look at it some time." I hope I was able to keep my voice lighthearted. John was silent. When we came to a four-way stop. He talked again.

"I rather show you when it's finished."

"Alright. So, what do you want to do today?"

"Well, I already had lunch so I'm not hungry. Why don't we go to the arcade for a bit?"

"Sure, why not? Haven't been there in a while."

"I'll beat you like last time."

"Oh, we'll see about that." I smiled at him.

I drove to the arcade called "Gamer Zone". Its sign has an UFO shooting lasers out of it and around the sign was bright neon colors. The building had dark tinted windows so the neon lights could be seen. The walls were painted dark with a red outline. I pulled into the parking lot and saw few cars and a van in the parking lot.

"Doesn't look like they're not that many people here." John commented.

"And that means only one thing." John turned to me, and I knew what he was going to say. He just looked at me though, so I continued. "It means we don't have to wait in line for any of the games."

"Oh, right." He eventually replied. I killed the engine and we both got out of my car.

d paid the guy, took the game tokens and I walked over to where John was waiting for me. I looked around and didn't see that many people.

"Guess it's the weather. But that doesn't matter we have pretty much everything to ourselves." I told him.

"Yep. Let's start off with that one." John pointed to an arcade game called *"Attack of The Invaders"*.

"Aww my favorite." We sat down onto the short stools as I put the token. I asked him if he was ready.

"You bet." He replied.

I pressed the start button. The big screen showed John and I as soldiers holding what was supposed to be our laser rifle. We ran back and forth on the screen shooting the UFOs shooting at us. We did well and got a high score. *When should I ask him about that show? Maybe I'll ask him on our way home.* But I noticed his eyes were looking at me the same way Robert did during the city hall massacre. I almost lost my concentration. I tried to keep calm and glued my eyes to the screen. John ended up winning the game.

"Alright, nice job."

"At least we stopped the aliens from invading earth, right?" He laughed.

"Yep. Let's go do another game." I suggested.

"Alright. After that I want to eat."

"Sure, I feel like having pizza and cold a can of Coke."

"Mmmm…sounds good."

So far, he's acting himself. But let's see if he remembers the show or tries changing the subject.

After a few more games it was 3-PM. I ordered John and myself four slices of pizza and two cold cans of Coke. We sat down at the dining area of Gamer Zone. I looked over and there were hardly any people left and noticed how quiet it was inside. John thanked me for the food, and I told him it was nothing. We began eating our pizza and John looked at me.

"So, how are you?" He asked.

"Not too well. Don't like the new mayor we got and the news stories I've been working with aren't the kind I want."

"Is it true that you killed that boy during city hall massacre?" John asked innocently enough that I was startled.

"Who told you that?" John stared at me but didn't say anything.

The hell? I didn't tell my parents or John this!

"I know you were there on that day." John replied eventually. I suddenly felt lightheaded. I didn't know what I should say. John didn't seem worried or shocked.

"Who told you this? That's a lie John." I said asked him again.

"You and Hunter were lucky to have escaped that event. It's a shame those two boys had to die but what else were you going to do?"

I felt the hairs on my neck standing up. John finished his pizza. Once again I didn't know what to say.

"After we're done eating you can drop me off and we'll hang out again some time." He said matter of fact.

I reached for my Coke can drank it.

"Alright. And yes, I was lucky. I don't want to die or lose my friend." John just stared at me.

"However, you two might not be so lucky next time."

I ate in silence. I couldn't believe what I was hearing.

When I took John home, he was quite throughout the whole ride, and I was still in shock. When I pulled into the driveway, I saw the house lights were on inside.

"Ok John, see you next time." He looked at me and took his seat belt off.

"Maybe." He got out and walked towards our parents' house looking unhappy. *Manson I'm going to stop whatever the hell you are doing to my little brother!*

Nov. 18
9:00-AM

I got up early putting on my winter clothes and driving towards the payphone by the old train bridge. I had already gone to the bank and exchanged a $20 bill for quarters. I took out the sheet of numbers I picked up the phone, placed a quarter into it and began dialing the numbers Hunter had written down. I knew he would be shocked at what John said to me on Saturday.

When I heard the beeping stop a deep male voice said, "New Orleans Birth & Death Records."

"Hi, I'm looking for records for an Osborne Louis born sometime during the 30s and died in Miami on Dec.25th, 1969."

The line was quiet for a bit.

"Could you please state the name of the person you are looking for?"

I spoke a bit louder and said, "Osborne Louis."

"We don't have anyone with that name."

"Ok, how many people with the name Osborne then?"

He hung up. I took a marker out of my winter coat and crossed out the number then tried the next one.

As I tried asking the people on the other line of the phone the same question, I was still getting the same answer back. Not even telling them the name of his cartoon show wasn't helping at all. It seems there was never a person named Osborne Louis or the crash in Miami never happened. How did one person know him then? I wished I contacted her when I had the chance. Now, I'm not getting anywhere. The last call didn't give the answer I wanted I hung up. I used up all my quarters, I put the sheet of paper into my coat got back into my Honda and drove back home and hoped Hunter had better luck than I did.

5:30-PM

When Hunter did call he only had bad news. He too had no luck finding any information on Osborne Louis. He couldn't even get the address from Dorothy, the woman who told me who made this show.

"We're back at fucking square one all over again!"

"I think the only way we can know where Dorothy lives is by breaking into that cartoon network and see what their records have."

"Ok. The only problem is we don't have the money to get there."

I sighed and said, "Well, we'll have to come up with some way of getting the money. We're going to need it as those video cameras I was looking into you weren't kidding they aren't fucking cheap!"

"What about John? How was he?"

"When I picked him up, he was acting fine at first but when we went to Gamer Zone. There wasn't that many people and I said you know what the this means. He always told me less people means no waiting in line ups. And he didn't say it I had to say it for him to understand. So, we played some games, and he was acting himself again. When I was wondering when to ask him about the show, I noticed out of the corner of my eye he was staring back at me the same way Robert was."

"Ok what else?" I told Hunter the rest.

"Wait, he never met me before."

"I know. It's Manson. No other way around it. He told John about that massacre. I didn't tell our parents what I was forced to do."

"I agree but there is no other option now. We just have to wait what happens next." I sighed.

"I hate waiting but you're right."

"Alright, I see you tomorrow." We both hang up. I went to bed right away.

Dec.13
3:30-PM

Nothing else happened in November and now it was the 2nd week of December. Lots of snow fall with the sky so white you couldn't even see the sun. The wind howled loudly outside of my office as I sat there with my right hand into a fist pressing against my cheek. I wasn't happy how the mayor was slowly turning this city back to its older ways. Crime had return and now the police force isn't good as it once was. I wanted to break out of this silence and say something to get the people to do something about it. Jake seemed to like the new mayor way too much and the stories Hunter and I had been doing were nothing but bullshit!

I strongly felt our ratings had gone down after that day at city hall and News 18 would work its way back to the top again. Not only was my job now leaving a bad taste in my mouth, but things with my family wasn't also any better. My parents now hardly call me. I would ring them up only to get the answering machine. When I left a message, they never called me back. Not even John has spoken to me. Every time I drive by my parents' house no car is in the driveway, neither morning, noon, evening or nights. I strongly felt Manson was brainwashing my family. He didn't want me or Hunter knowing his big secret.

I was hoping that when I saved up on the video cameras, I could find out what the hell was really going on. The knock on my door made me jump. It was Hunter.

"Jake wants us to check out a church burning!"

I had a gut feeling who was behind it. We and our news team got into our Ford Econoline drove through the freezing weather. We could hear roaring sirens. We left the city and drove into the town area of Black Creek and what awaited us was horrible.

The church had been burned to the ground. Fire trucks and a few police cars are everywhere. There were a few people watching from their homes. One officer was hugging a woman who was crying in his arms. We opened the back doors to our van and Hunter carried the video camera. I held onto the microphone I stood in front of the burned church.

"Ok. I'm all set here, Hunter." I nodded looking at the camera while keeping calm. Hunter did the number count with his hand, and I we started filming.

"Curtis Parker with News 6 on our breaking story! Behind me was once the church of Black Creek which has been burned down to the ground! We're about to ask the police chief if anyone survived this horrible event."

Hunter stopped recording and went to speak with the police chief and he filmed the officers carrying stretchers with blankets over them. When the police chief was available, Hunter trained the camera to him. I stood in front of the chief with my microphone.

"Sir, could you please tell us what happened here? Who burned down the town's church?"

"We...we have captured the criminal behind this." Police chief cleared his throat looking up at me.

"It was Sam Cunningham. A 7-year-old boy who did this."

"A 7-year-old boy?" I asked, I couldn't even managed wit neutral tone.

"Yes, he...he had killed his whole family then attacked the church, killing everyone inside then setting it on fire. We found him sitting at the front. He was crying. He told us that he was forced to do it."

It's Manson alright. I know it!

Police chief rubbed his eyes.

"He took his father's pistol and shot everyone!"

"Who forced Sam to do this?" I can barely contain my anticipation. Finally, a break on this case.

"He just kept saying "He". That's all we got out of him, but it seems he has gone insane. We will take care of him. That's all I got to say." The chief looked forlorn. I felt the same but for a different reason.

d turned around and walked away before I could ask any more questions. I turned back to the camera and said, "Back to you, Shelly."

Hunter lowered the video camera and we both stared at the burned church. There will be more of these events to come. The distraught boy was driven inside a van by police officers.

"Let's see if we can get inside the police station and record what he has to say." Hunter suggested.

"Good idea. Let's follow that van!" I told the driver.

We followed it to the police station. Jake called wondering why we haven't returned yet. but I told him the police we're going to allow us to record what the boy had to say. Since it means more footage to this breaking story, he allowed us to continue. I hoped that prick would open his goddamn eyes and see that Hunter and I we're on to something with this cartoon show.

When we got out of the van, one officer noticed us.

"Hey, what do you think you're doing?"

"We're here to film that boy who was just taken in after murdering his family, members of a church and burning it. Everyone would like to hear some answers." I used my matter-of-fact tone, hoping the officer would take it.

"I can't allow any of you inside." I had an idea. I looked at him with a straight face.

"Alright then, we'll tell the other reporters where the boy is so you can deal with them. Or if you let us in, we'll have them, go to the wrong police station. Your call." The officer sighed.

"Alright but make it quick." We went inside the police station. Hunter and I fist bumped.

Hunter had the video camera aimed at me while I stood outside of the interrogation room. I held the microphone and said, "Curtis Parker live inside the police station where the officers are about to interview Sam Cunningham. We will find out his reasons for committing this crime."

We heard the door opened behind us. I turned around and had the microphone turned off. Hunter would be able to pick up what the officers and Sam were saying.

Sam and three officers walked into the room. Sam was wearing a white shirt which had blood splattered on it, winter pants, boots and had hand cuffs with both of his arms were resting against his blood-stained shirt. He sat down and the police chief turned to the others.

"Wait outside for me." d both left, and the police chief looked at Sam. Hunter was zooming in with the video camera.

"So, are you ready to talk now?" Sam was quiet. So, the chief continued.

"Was it something your parents did to you?" Sam shook his head.

"Was it anyone from the church that made you, do it?" Again, Sam shook his head, but this time showed us his face. He had a confused look.

"He made me do it! I...I...I didn't want to hurt anyone but he made me do it! And threaten to hurt me if I didn't do it!"

Come on! Say his name! I urged him with my thoughts.

Sam's eyes were watery. He started to sob.

"I can't help you Sam, if you don't tell me anything." Sam suddenly lifted his head up and raised his voice.

"Help me how?! It's already begun! There is nothing that can stop what he has planned, and you'll think that I'm insane! He and his friends are going to round up all the children and every adult will die from the flames of hell!" Sam cried more and the police chief shook his head. He stood up and walked over to the door to let the other officers in. I noticed Sam had reached into his pants and took out small knife. I tried to warn them, but they can't hear me.

The police chief turned and saw what Sam was holding. He went to stop him, but it was too late. Sam slit his own throat. Blood poured all over the table and his clothes. His lifeless body fell to the floor. Hunter recorded all it. Sorrow and anger warred inside me. Then two officers came in and told us to leave at once.

On our way back to the studio, I told Hunter to make us a copy of what happened.

"Round up all the children and every adult will die from the flames of hell. What did Manson show that poor kid before he committed these horrible crimes?" I was wondering aloud. I also suggested we find the boy's address. Maybe we can get more information. Hunter nodded and we returned to News 6.

Jake was disturbed by what we had recorded inside the police station. He refused to air it and stated that we'll go with the police report that Sam Cunningham went insane. Once again, my hope of that kid spilling the beans failed. That didn't mean that my case was over.

Hunter got the address where Sam lived. He found out the police had searched through it already. Whatever they had found they would have put it into their records room.

I've been in police stations before. I knew where to find what I was looking for. I planned to break into that station tonight and find what Sam won't tell us. Hunter made a copy of the tape and hid it on his way out after we left. I got into my Honda with Hunter wishing me luck with my plan. I knew if I screwed this up, I would get fired from my job and spend a few days in jail. I wasn't going to fail. I will find the answers I'm looking for!

11:45-PM

Snow fell hard and thick. Streetlights shined brightly and the streets were deserted at this hour. Wind blew at my face as I walked through the back parking lot of the police station. It was closed with only a couple of squad cars buried under a layer of snow. I had my big gym bag around my shoulder. I wore my black winter jacket, black pants, boots with plastic bags tied around them, black ski mask and leather gloves. I went over to the back window and used a crowbar to open a window. I sat on the window ledge, took off both plastic bags from my boots and crawled inside. I closed the window and went to unlock the door. I walked upstairs into the main office area.

I went into police chief office and to my surprise he left his door unlocked. I was able to find the spare keys in his desk along with a sheet of what locker had the evidence I was looking for. I went there and at the lockers until I found the number I was looking for, No.13. I searched through it. I found a sketch book. I flipped through the pages and saw mostly kid drawings. The top corner of each page was dated. I flipped through them leading up to Dec.13th and saw that the drawings changed. The whole look, the mood of it, and the feeling it, changed. From mommy and daddy's birthday to Manson and his friends. I looked at one drawing which showed Sam standing in the night world from Manson & Barbara Show. Something seemed off about it. There we're other kids with Sam and in front of them was the castle but it had a sinister look to it.

I flipped the pages and saw the kids looking scared. There was Manson pointing at them, a dead child stabbed by his own cane sword. There was a wall with images on the wall. There were small images, I had to looked closely. It seems to show five things. The first image was a cross with a stick man drawn on it that meant Religion. Second image showed a man wearing a white suit and holding a flask. Science? Third image showed tanks and soldiers fighting each other, and above them were fighter jets shooting missiles. That one's crystal clear. Fourth image showed a man wearing a suit with a tie and behind him was the dollar sign. Money? Power? The government? The fifth image showed two sick figures and two children standing above them but both adults we're crossed out with bright red X's. This meant no adults. I thought, "Religion, Science, War, Government and Adults. What does Manson have against these five things?" I went to turn the next page but saw it was torn out, and the rest of the pages were blank.

I checked the rest of the evidence but there weren't any missing pages. I took some VHS tapes and locked the thing, shut off the light, put the keys back into the chief's desk, and went out the way I came. I picked up the plastic bags and ran over a few blocks to my Honda. I checked around me before I left, making sure nobody saw me. There wasn't a soul out here. I started up my car and sped off heading back to my apartment. I was going to be tired as hell when I went to work, but this evidence I had would be all worth it.

Dec. 14
9:30-AM

I was thirty minutes late. I had slept in a bit, but Jake would brush it off as I was rarely late for work. When I went into my office, I saw my boss had left me stories to write to go through them. When I was done, I threw all of them into the trash. This wasn't the work I wanted to do when I became a journalist. These shitty stories were a waste of my time! If this is the shit Jake wants, then he needs to get someone else to do it. I stood up, left my office and went over to Hunter's office.

I knocked on the door and he waved me in.

"So, what did you find?" He was whispering.

"A drawing book with some sketches made before Sam was told by Manson to carry out his attack."

"That's it?" He sounded unbelieving.

"Nope, it gets better. I've also gotten ahold of six VHS tapes with all of them having episodes of The Manson & Barbara Show."

"How many episodes?"

"Not sure, but it's written on the tapes."

"Alright, we'll have to watch them when we're off from work." Hunter sounded hopeful.

"Do you have any spare stories I could do?"

"Let me guess. You didn't like what Jake had out."

"I swear if this keeps up, I'm leaving."

"Same here, man. We might have a better chance at one of the bigger news studios."

We were interrupted by a loud knock. Jake was on the other side, and he didn't look happy. He opened the door and told us to come to his office at once. We followed him and waiting for us inside Jake's office was two Black Creek officers

Shit! I'm busted! Jake closed the door.

"Officer, which one of these two men said that we're allowed to film the interview of Sam?"

"Curtis Parker." The officer with light brown hair said. Jake turned to me with barely contained anger.

"What we're you thinking?"

"My job, what's else." Jake looked annoyed. "Curtis, I already told you what we want and yet you did it again. We go with facts not fiction! And yet you still believe this so-called cartoon show is what drove this boy and the other two from the city hall massacre into murder! And now you went into a station and recorded something that has nothing to do with our main story.

"That you're a total prick and I'm done working with assholes like you!" I shouted at him, too.

"I came here to do real breaking stories not this bullshit!" Hunter added.

Jake was pissed but there was nothing he could do about it we both left his office. We chose not to take the elevator and walk downstairs instead.

"Now that we're done working here, I guess we could try to get a job at News 18?" I asked Hunter.

"Nah I got a better idea. We could work as underground journalists. It pays better and best of all we'll be able to investigate that show more that way." I nodded.

"Alright, that's what we'll do."

"Just have to make a few calls, then we should be set up. First, let's go over those tapes you found." Hunter suggested.

"Ok, where do you want to watch it?"

"Might as well be my place. We won't have to worry about anyone in the other apartments hearing what we're watching."

"Alright, I'll grab the tapes and bring the sketch book."

We got into our cars and drove off separately. I drove to my apartment, picked up the tapes and sketches placed them inside my gym bag. I was glad the police didn't ask if we had anything to do with the missing evidence. Then again it seemed they didn't want anybody knowing about it, and I guess if someone showed it to another person, they would think they we're crazy.

I reach Hunter's house and saw his car in the driveway. I grabbed my gym bag and walked to Hunter's front door. When he let me inside, I took off my boots and walked into the living room.

"Alright, let's see what we got here." First, I handed him the sketch book and we sat down on the sofa. Hunter went through it and told me what I already know. There were from Oct 31st through November. As he got further through it, he saw the pictures had changed.

"Whoa I see what you mean."

"Keep going until the last picture." Hunter flipped through the pages and saw the last one. "The five images on the wall?" I told him what I think they mean.

"Which Manson and his friends are strongly against." Hunter replied. He noticed the page that was torn out and looked at me.

"I looked for the last page but couldn't find it. Maybe Sam tore it out himself and destroyed it or Manson might have."

"Say when he said the flames of hell what do you think it means?"

"Could it mean d itself or something else?" I countered.

"I'm sure we'll find more answers as we go on. Now, let's see those tapes." I took them out of my gym d and gave them to Hunter. He checked the stickers placed on the VHS tape.

"Ok, 6 tapes with 79 episodes in total." Hunter announced.

"Shit, that's a lot."

"So, Sam recorded this show every week until Manson forced him to attack his whole family and the church." Hunter theorized.

"Did the same thing to Bobby and Robert back in November."

"Do you think we'll get brainwashed by this?" Hunter looked nervous.

"No, it seems Manson goes for younger and weaker minds. We should be able to handle it and seeing how he hates adults we won't become his next victims."

"Alright then, let's put some cartoons on."

Hunter put in the 1st VHS tape which had 15 episodes with the last tape having only four episodes. Hunter and I watched the first episode, and it was just like how we first saw it. However, this recording was much cleaner than mine. I guess since a kid was watching Manson won't give his younger viewers a hard time. Also, no commercials play every time it faded black. It just went back to the show to the show right away. The first episode ended, it continued to the second episode right away. However as it started the intro, it suddenly cut out making a lot of strange noises then came back with Manson voice saying, "Episode 2 Roar of Thunder."

The screen faded black then showed tall mountains covered by thick forests. The moon glowed brightly, not many clouds in the sky. Then the camera zoomed out a bit. A tall handsome blonde man holding a scope and was wearing a robe of The White Order.

"Manson and his friends won't see this sneak attack coming! And once we clear through these forests, we'll be in his Dark Kingdom knocking at his door. Get my men moving now." The guy said to a soldier.

"Yes, Mr. Van Herbert." The soldier replied.

Large bulky tanks were moving through the forest. Some running over trees destroying them.

"Those tree lovers won't like this." Hunter commented.

I didn't say anything I kept watching and wonder if the Van guy was based on a real person. I tried to see if this new character is based on real life. The previous mayor was a White Order character, too. Before he died, that is.

"I wonder how many episodes until it shows the mayor's death?" I asked. Hunter pressed the pause button on the remote

"So far there doesn't seem to be any date. Unless it's hidden within the background."

"That could be true." Hunter turned to me.

"Feeling anything so far?" He asked.

"No, let's keep going." d pressed play again. I felt antsy. I checked out the living room window, just quick. I was glad nobody was watching us, but I couldn't shake the feeling off though.

As the White Order were destroying half of the forest, then Manson soldiers spotted them. They were shooting cross bows with glowing arrow heads. The tanks fired their laser cannons, but the arrow heads had already done the damage.

"Say, doesn't this remind you of the Soviet invasion? The Afghanistan wars?" I thought about it for a bit but found it hard to say anything back as the battle went on, the worse the violence became.

Hunter and I couldn't turn away from the screen. The airships showed up and fired their double cannons blowing up the rest of the tanks. The screen switched to show Van Herbert standing in front of a short round table with a hologram screen in front of him. The image was of the king of the White Order.

"My King! I need more support! Manson's air ships are preventing me from moving further!" Herbert was frantic.

"No! You will continue with what you got. I have an even bigger surprise for Manson." Van's face turned a bit red.

"I'm not requesting a whole fleet. I'm just asking for some support." The king shook his head.

"I will contact you with further instructions after you clear a path for my army." The hologram went blank, and Van Herbert looked pissed. He turned around and went over to his guard.

"Send the rest of my tanks to the other side of the mountain, so we can deal with those damn airships!"

"Right away, sir." The screen faded black. Hunter paused the video.

"Shit! My head hurts!" Hunter was holding his head with both hands.

I felt a headache coming on, as well. I looked at the screen, it was still blank. Hunter pressed the play button. It showed Manson looking down a map showing the two kingdoms.

"It seems The White Order can cut through my forest to reach my castle. Hellen will be able to hold them off, but I feel that evil king is trying something else."

"Let me handle them Manson. I'll be able to take care of those bloody tanks. Hellen can send her airships, if there any problems." Andre offered. Manson turned with a grin.

"Alright, but would you like someone else to help you out?" Andrew rubbed his chin.

"As a matter of fact, I'll take Kane with me."

"Alright, go get him. I hope Barbara and Sydney return soon. We'll need everyone if the king strikes our kingdom."

"Oh, I'm sure they'll be back soon. I'll see you later Manson."

Andrew walked away. The scene switched to a dungeon-like garage. He was getting on his motorcycle and putting on his goggles.

"Alright, friend let's go show these White Order guys who they are messing with!" Kane said enthusiastically.

Andrew revved his motorcycle with Kane on the back. A draw door opened, Andrew kept going. They flew through the air before landing on the ground. Andrew was grinning the whole as they sped off into the forest.

The screen went to the tanks now getting further through the destroyed forest. There were many dead bodies, both sides taking heavy loses. The tanks were now using flame throwers to clear their way through Manson's soldiers.

I felt the headache was getting worse. I rubbed my forehead as Hunter paused the video again.

"How the hell do the kids watch this without getting any headaches?" Hunter complained.

"There has to be some way around it. We'll never be able to watch the rest of these. We need to find more clues."

Hunter and I waited a bit then continued after the pain went away.

Andrew and Kane reached the forest. Manson's soldiers trying their best to hold off the enemy tanks but they we're getting burned away.

"Let's help our friends out." Kane suggested.

Andrew pulled out his laser pistol and fired it at the tanks blowing them up. Kane threw big fuse bombs. Andrew drove past the trees. The tanks switched their firing mode to their laser cannons and fired but they all missed. Andrew then drove in front of two tanks. They went to fire and ended up destroying each other.

Manson's soldiers joined in, using the destroyed tanks as cover. They we're able to take out the rest. Andrew looked up and could see a White Order ship on the top of the mountain.

"Looks like their leader is about run off like a chicken!" Andrew observed.

"Let's get him!" Andrew sped up the path towards the mountain.

The screen switched to Van, now angry.

"DAMN YOU ALL! RETREAT AT ONCE!" Van yelled.

However, just as he and his men we're about to get onto the White Order ship it was destroyed by an airship. Van grabbed his large laser rifle firing it into the air. His guards we're shooting, as well. When Andrew reach the top of the mountain he drove around them making circles, making themselves a difficult target. Kane threw a fuse bomb at Van's face knocking him flat off his feet. He added some smoke grenades, so Van and his soldiers will be blind.

Van tried to pick up the fuse bomb but couldn't. It was too heavy. He turned and ran. He got a few inches away. It exploded and blew off his legs. He landed on the ground face first and he tried to get up.

"Need a hand mate?" Van looked up and there was Andrew grinning above him.

"You and your rotten friends will pay for this!" Van growled.

"d mate, that's where you're wrong. You don't have any friends. Without any you don't have the most important thing."

Kane placed his boot beside Van's body, rolled him. The screen switch to a close up of Kane's face.

"And that's teamwork." Kane grinned. He pressed his boot down on Van's throat. There was bone crushing sounds. Hunter and I were shocked.

When Kane had killed Van, the screen showed him looking up and Andrew said directly to the screen: "Now he's taken care of, Hellen will be able to deal with the rest of the White Order ships." They both looked up and there were airships moving through the sky.

Screen faded then showed the king slamming his fist on the table.

"Damn them! They'll be able to hold us off, but not forever! Make sure my ships push through Manson's forces. I will not let their kingdom stand for as long as I live!" The king yelled. He pressed a button on his table. It showed different images of the Dark Kingdom, then zeroed in on Barbara and Sydney walking through a foggy forest. The king grinned.

"Mary, send your highly trained spies to take care of them." The camera panned to a beautiful woman, with long bright red hair and dark blue eyes.

"Yes, my king." She stood up and left the round table.

I noticed something.

"Hunter, pause it! Look behind the king's head." Hunter looked and we saw a date which read November 1st .

"Ok, now we know when these episodes came out. I bet on each day that Manson has someone killed it will be marked different." Hunter observed.

"We'll just have to watch all of them until we find it."

"Yep, even if it gives us headaches." Hunter grumbled.

Hunter pressed the play button for the 3rd episode. Again no intro. The title showed but it was Barbara's voice who spoke this time: "Episode 3 Hunting Witches."

Barbara and Sydney were walking through the thick foggy forest with pumpkins lying all over the ground. They we're both carrying baskets filled with flowers.

"These should be enough to make more healing potions," Sydney said.

"Yes, this will have to do. If only we saw them before they came," Barbara replied.

"I know the pain sugar, but we'll make that evil king and his White Order pay for what they did." Barbara nodded.

"We should head back to the castle now."

The two turned back. We noticed in the background they we're being watched by Mary's spies. The two anthropomorphic women walked through the forest. The screen showed different views, Mary's spies were getting closer to them. The screen switched again to show the back of the women. Barbara's ears twitched a bit.

"We're being followed." Barbara whispered.

"Yes, I know." Sydney replied.

"Nothing like a nice warm up." Barbara grinned.

"Yes, we need to keep our skills sharp!" Sydney answered with a grin of her own.

As they both dropped their baskets the spies came out of the thick fog holding swords and double-bladed axes. They we're wearing dark robes with the hoods up and long leather gloves, boots and dark pants. The closest spies we're about to swing them but Barbara and Sydney quickly dodged their attacks and kicked them. Barbara drew both her short blade swords as she swung them fast slashing out the spies' throats. As a group of spies came at Sydney both her hands glowed a bright blue and she lifted up her arms and fired blue beams and when they hit the spies, they turned into ice Sydney laughed as she swung her arms at them and smashed into a thousand pieces.

Suddenly a spy came behind Sydney and went to swing his axe at her, but she quickly turned her head back and jumped into the air just barely missing her. She laughed and said, "Nice try, fool! You'll have to do better than that!" Sydney opened up her wings and sharp crystals flew towards the spy as they all hit him Sydney then air-kicked him in the head. Once back on the ground she fought off the other spies with her magic. The screen showed Barbara using a mixture of kicking moves and her short swords and it was hard to not stare at her sexy body. A few spies would be able to get close enough to her but when they did, they would end up dead.

A spy yelled in anger as he went to swing his axe. Barbara dodged it and he struck a tree. The screen showed at close up on the blond spy as Barbara stabbed both her short swords into his head killing him then pulled them out. Barbara holstered both her short swords then took the spy's axe and swung it at the remaining spies, but Sydney finished off the last few. Barbara said, "Aww already over? I was having a blast." Sydney giggled and said, "Come, we better hurry back to the castle before more shows up." They picked up their baskets and ran off.

As the screen faded black Hunter paused it and said, "I'm getting Advil. It feels like a knife is twisting inside my skull." I said, "Yeah same here." Hunter left the living room as I checked the time on my watch it was 11:35-AM. When he came back with the Advil and two bottles of water. We took the pills and drank the water as Hunter said, "After this I'll make us some lunch." I said, "Alright sounds good." Once our headaches were gone, we continue to watch as the screen came back it showed Manson standing by a fireplace with a large clock hanging above it as it was raining outside with lightning flashing in the background as thunder roared.

The screen then showed Manson's face as he looked up at the clock then looked over at the window. Then heavy footsteps came over as it showed George walking over to Manson. When he turned his head over to him Manson said, "They've been gone for too long." George asked, "When have they gone out?" Manson said, "Barbara went with Sydney to get flowers to make healing potions, but I get the feeling the evil king is trying something." George asked, "Want me to go out and find them?" Manson said, "Alright Andrew and Kane should be back soon." George said, "I'll be back with them as it's going to take more than the king's men to beat me." The screen showed George leaving as he grabbed his big hammer and left the castle.

The screen faded black again then it showed George walking through the foggy forest while lightning flashed above him with roaring thunder. He turned his head looking around I thought, "Are his eyes always white or is it just with that sack over his head?" Just then he heard the sounds of fighting. George turned his head where the sounds were coming from had his big hammer ready and ran towards it. When he got closer, he saw more spies now, soldiers were fighting against Barbara and Sydney. George growled with steam blowing out of his nose he held up his big hammer and ran towards them.

As the screen showed the soldiers were about to be outnumbered, Barbara and Sydney without a warning they are knocked down by George's hammer. We could hear their bones snapping and cracking with each strike of George's hammer. The soldiers yelled and screamed in pain. The spies tried getting around him, but he saw them coming and swung his hammer at them sending bodies flying into the air as some hit the trees which were killed on impact.

One soldier went to thrust his sword into George's chest, but it didn't go through his skin, it broke in half. The soldier looked dumbfounded by this. George lifted his hammer with both hands and slammed it down, turning the soldier into a pancake. The scene switched to Barbara and Sydney fighting off the last of the soldiers and spies. Then just as they we're finished it showed Mary watching in horror as her highly trained spies and soldiers had failed.

Mary took her laser rifle from its shoulder strap and flicked the safety switch off and aimed through the scope as it showed it on TV. Mary was going for a head shot on Barbara. Mary grinned as she slowly wrapped her finger around it's trigger about to pull it as the screen faded black.

When the screen showed the same scene of Mary aiming her laser rifle at Barbara then a close up of her finger about to pull back on the trigger. Just then Sydney saw Mary and said, "Oh no you don't!" Sydney quickly shot a white pointed crystal at Mary's rifle. When the white crystal hit the barrel of the laser rifle it exploded before Mary could fire her shot. Mary dropped her useless weapon she turned around and tried running but George yelled, "NOT SO

FAST!" George threw his big hammer spinning through the air. It showed Mary running with the hammer spinning behind her.

The hammer whacked her from the back. Mary fell headfirst into the ground. The impact of the spinning hammer had snapped her spine, she couldn't get up. George, Sydney and Barbara walked over to Mary as George picked up hammer then lifted Mary up by her long hair. Barbara said, "So your king sends you on a witch hunt while we're trying to help the people you have harmed and badly injured!" Sydney said, "And trying to kill my friend in cold blood is so unkind." George said, "Well then why should we leave her like this after what her people have done to ours." Barbara said, "Let's treat her like a witch and see how it feels. George, tie her up." I thought, "Are they are going to do what I think they are going to do!?"

It then showed George took a chain and wrapped it around a thick dead tree. Mary begged but there's no stopping George. He tightened the chain around her. Then Sydney and Barbara walked over holding two thick sticks as Sydney said, "Let's burn her!" It did a close up of the two women touching their sticks together as the tips suddenly burst into flames. Mary begged louder as it showed from their view as both women toss their burning sticks onto Mary the flames licked her robe as it bursts into flames Mary screamed as the fire rise up towards her face. I suddenly felt sick watching this as I looked over at Hunter and notice he was turning green.

Hunter hit the pause button and said, "Fuck! I feel sick!" I said, "Same here." Hunter went to the upstairs bathroom. I went downstairs bathroom. I dropped onto my knees and puked into the toilet. I suddenly felt my brain was burning with my skull becoming smaller. I threw up again and coughed a bit then reached the handle and flushed the toilet. I grabbed some toilet paper to whip my mouth then threw it out into the garbage then slowly walked upstairs. I rubbed my head as this feeling got worse. I then heard upstairs toilet flush as Hunter came out.

Hunter said, "Fuck! My head feels like it's burning!" I coughed a bit and said, "So does mine." We went back into the living room and drank some water as it took a few minutes for this feeling to go away. When I looked at the screen it was paused on the horrible image of the woman burning. Hunter said, "How do parents even not see this sick shit?!" I said, "Yeah a helpless woman burning to death as she screams! How do they not even see this!?" When Hunter picked up the remote, he pressed play but hit the fast forward button to speed it up but I noticed it didn't work Hunter press the button a few more times and said, "What the hell?"

Hunter couldn't get the VHS player to skip over this footage or mute it out as we forced ourselves to watch as hearing Mary's scream felt horrible it made me think it came from a real person. The flames ate away at her flesh as it quickly burned away showing damaged muscle tissue then some of her bones. Then it showed George, Barbara and Sydney standing with big grins on their faces. George said, "All this fighting has gotten me hungry." Sydney said, "Yes burning humans is making me want to have sausage right now." Barbara said, "Yes let's eat and not keep my loving Manson waiting." They walked away as the screen faded black, I said, "Please this is the end of this episode!"

Hunter placed his hand over his forehead as the screen came back showing Manson and the others eating at the very long dining table as Manson said, "Very good work with the healing potions." Sydney said, "Thanks, I'm glad we got it to all those who needed it badly." Hellen said, "My airships are patrolling the skies so those damn White Order ships can't harm our people again." Manson said, "We'll all doing well but we'll need to start pushing back against them. I'll make sure my men do their best to defend this city from any future threats when we go to crush the White Order kingdom." Manson turned to George and said, "And George thanks again for helping Barbara and Sydney."

George smiled with his big teeth and said, "You're welcome, my friend, I always help out anyway I can." Barbara said, "Aww George you're too kind." George chuckled and they went back to eating. The screen changed as it showed the burned body of Mary still tried to the tree with White Order soldiers standing looking in shook the king in the middle of them said, "They will pay for this. Let's go." They left and got onto a small ship and flew through the sky. I thought, "After this that's enough! I can't stand any more of this sick shit and my goddamn brain is going to explode!" Just as the screen faded black, I thought this would be the end of it but as I went to stand up suddenly the screens showed George standing in a dungeon room with torches with a table that had some tools on it as he was cleaning his big hammer.

There were no windows in this room and as the screen showed a closer shot of George behind him, we could see an makeshift gym and another table for black smith work in the background. As George finished cleaning his hammer, he set it down as the light from the torches showed the outline of George's massive muscles. Hunter asked, "There more to this?" Suddenly we saw on the TV the screen had a bit of static then it went back to normal as the door opened it was Barbara.

George turned his head over and said, "Oh hi Barbara." Barbara lightly smiled and said, "Hey George I thought I would just stop by to see you." As she walked closer to him, I thought, "What's going on? Shouldn't this episode be over already?" Hunter said, "At least my brain isn't burning anymore." George looked down at Barbara and asked, "Ummm…is there something I could do for you?" Barbara grinned and she said, "Oh nothing I can think of, but I wanted to reward you for helping us back there and saving my lovely face from being hit by a nasty laser beam." I suddenly knew where this was going it then showed a close up of George's crotch as Barbara placed her hands onto it as she was stroking his big dick.

Hunter said, "Wait…am I thinking what she's doing?" George just looked down at her as Barbara keeled down and said, "You want a reward for your bravery? I'm sure Sydney would be happy to give you one, as well." George begun to moan as his big dick was pressing against his pants. I didn't want to watch this. I said, "Hunter please stop this!" Hunter tried press the stop button but nothing was happening he said, "I…I can't stop it nor get up!" Suddenly I too felt I couldn't move my body like an invisible force was holding us down.

Barbara grinned as her hands began loosening George's pants then pulled them down and making a goofy sound effect as his massive 14-inch dick popped up from George's pants. Barbara giggled as she placed her hand under George's big ball sack as his balls were the size of bowling balls. Barbara said, "You're so tense, let me help you with that." Barbara stroked his massive dick with George smiling. Barbara rubbed her hands a bit faster while George took off his gloves and gripped the edge of the table behind him.

George moaned more as Barbara giggled and said, "Come on give me your sweet sugar. You don't have to hold it back." Then at the tip of his massive dick precum was leaking out Barbara said, "Good boy." We watched as using her left hand Barbara began unbuttoning her suit it quickly showed George looking down then it showed what he was seeing then showed Barbara's huge breasts pop out of her suit as she took it off and could see the thick pink nipples were fully hard.

Barbara then placed her huge breasts in between George's massive dick then wrapped her arms around it so her breasts were pressed firmly against his dick then kissed the tip of it and began rubbing them while sucking on it. Hunter asked, "This can't be in the show, right?" I said, "No I think it's Manson or Barbara messing with our heads again!" The screen showed Barbara sucking harder while moaning as George had his hand on top of Barbara's head lightly stroking her long white hair.

I couldn't believe she was taking it like it was nothing but then again this was a fucked-up cartoon! Barbara grabbed George's huge balls stroking them trying to get him to cum as more precum was leaking down onto his massive dick. George moaned louder and moved his legs out more getting himself more comfortable. Then George moaned louder as he chuckled then his massive thick dick burst cum into Barbara's face as she sucked every drop of it.

George blew some steam out of his nose as Barbara giggled and licked her lips and asked, "There. Doesn't that feel better?" George chuckled and said, "Yeah...thanks." Barbara giggled and said, "Oh I'm not done with you yet. I can tell, you want more, big boy." The screen then showed behind Barbara as she stood up taking off her boots then unbuckle her belt and letting her tight pants fall down to show her sexy thick bubble butt cheeks. George grinned as she hopped onto the table then had his arms out. Barbara took them she crawled up top of his muscular chest. The two lean in and began kissing with George playing with Barbara's hair. Then the screen showed behind view with his hands running down her muscular back.

Barbara spread her legs open allowing us to see her big pussy hidden under those long muscular legs. After the two were done kissing each other George held onto Barbara with one arm while using his left hand to have his massive dick go into her big pussy. Barbara said, "Yes ram your hammer into me." George did as he thrust his dick up and down then grabbed onto Barbara's huge breasts as she moaned with the screen now showing from George's point of view.

I kept looking around to see if Manson or one of his friends would pop up to screw with us but nothing else was happening, I also checked outside the living room window and notice not a signal car or person has passed by ever since we began watching this tape. When my eyes turned back to the screen Barbara moaned louder as George was ramming his dick into her pussy very hard as George had now placed his hands onto her thighs with her huge breasts bouncing faster.

Then after a while George released his 2nd burst of cum as Barbara moaned loudly then wrapped her arms around him tightly it showed an under shot of cum dripping down George's long thick shaft then it went back to Barbara as she and George began kissing again. I felt I was getting lightheaded from watching this then suddenly more static came on the TV as Barbara stopped kissing and turned to the TV screen as we could feel her dark purple eyes staring back into ours. She giggled with a big grin and asked, "What's wrong fellas? This hot steamy sex doesn't turn you two on?"

I felt my jaw drop open as Hunter was trying to press the stop button Barbara said, "If you like I could put that lovely clip of that ugly bitch burning on the tree if you two like." I manage to say, "No! Don't!" Barbara giggled and said, "I thought so, but our time is over. But we'll get play with you two again soon. Bye now." Then the screen faded black as the feeling from our bodies as now gone Hunter press the stop button and we both tried to stand up but we both fell onto the floor as I nearly landed on his glass table.

Hunter said, "Aww fuck my head hurts like hell!" I sat up and asked, "How can they do that over a recorded tape?" Hunter said, "I guess every time that show is on, they know who's watching it and it seems it doesn't matter if it's live or recorded they'll still fuck with our heads." I said, "I aren't waving the white flag." Hunter said, "Me neither. Let's take a break from this shit and I need to make those phone calls." I said, "Yeah good idea." We both got up and slowly went into the kitchen to eat.

1:00-PM

After eating lunch, we felt much better but still shaken up from what we saw. I felt my body wanted me to stop seeing this, but I wasn't going to quit. Hunter made a few phone calls for an underground journalism work and luckily, we got a job for magazine that does the kind of stories we we're looking for and if we got the right information we could blow this cartoon case into the public view and make people wake up to what's happening on their TV's and what it's doing to their children.

Hunter said, "Ok, an old friend of mine is going to let us work for him and we don't have go through any interviews or to proof ourselves as their boss knows our work." I asked, "That's good. When do we start?" Hunter said, "Monday on the 17th as my friend Tony will get us an office for us to share and work in. And we get paid every two weeks." I said, "Ok." But I knew what I wanted to ask him but Hunter knew as he said, "I...I'm not feeling in the mood to continue getting back to those." I said, "I'll do it. I go through as many as I can and write down anything that I see." Hunter asked, "Are you sure?" I said, "Yeah, I'm sure. If I find anything you need to see, I'll show you." Hunter said, "Alright I'm going to lay down for a bit." I said, "Ok see you later."

I woke up after taking a nap around 4-PM and have slept in and felt very warm as my mouth was dry. I rubbed my eyes while my brain had a strange feeling inside of it. As I slowly stood up I thought last night I had a dream but couldn't remember it I wasn't sure if it was a good or bad, but I didn't feel like lying in bed to remember what it was about. I stood up naked and walked into my bathroom I turned on the shower then stepped into my shower feeling hot water waking my body up. I rubbed my hands through my hair now waking up but when I grabbed the soap bar and began washing my back, I suddenly felt something. I stopped and placed my hand over what felt like scratch marks. Touching my chest, I felt more I looked down to see them.

Red marks that looked like it came from sharp claw nails I said, "The hell?!" I knew no cat could have done this nor myself. I suddenly felt a chill ran up my spine thinking my dream had something to do with it. After I washed up, I got dressed in clean clothes and went into the kitchen. Cooking myself lunch. I thought, "I wonder if Hunter had the same thing happen last night?" As I had my lunch ready, I set it onto the kitchen table and was about to eat when I heard a knock at my door. I turned my head over as another knock came, I asked, "Who is it?" I then heard a voice say, "Got a package for you." It sounded similar but couldn't think of who it was. I quickly ran over and looked through the peephole but didn't say anything I thought, "I'm not falling for this." I went to turn around when the knocking came again.

I spun around unlocked the door then opened it to see no one standing in front of me. I looked both ends of the hallway, but d was there. I looked down to see a purple box with a note attached to it. My heart was beating faster I looked again at the hallways nobody was here. I slowly bend down and picked up the purple box which had some weight to it. I went inside my apartment closing the door and locking it. I could feel the hairs standing up along my arms and back. I looked at the note it read,

"A lovely gift you for Curtis Parker. From Barbara, The Bunny." Under the writing was a logo of her head with a heart drawn beside it. I felt scared of what was in the package but knew I had to see what it was. I walked back to the kitchen table to eat first with my brain feeling like it had bugs crawling around I guess this was one of side effects from watching this cartoon show for too long I worried if watching too much would these side effects get worse.

I finished my lunch and felt butterflies in my stomach I knew whatever was inside this box wasn't going to be nice. I took off the note then opened up the purple box to find a purple VHS tape. It had no title on it nor anything written on it. However, I could smell that strong flower scent on it as my stomach pain was getting worse, I took a few breaths then went into the living room to see what Barbara had for me. I turned on the TV then placed the purple tape into the VHS player, and I thought, "I hope it doesn't wreck it." I took a big breath then press the play button and walked backwards to my sofa looking at the screen. I suddenly felt the living room was dark I went to turn on my lamp but saw static on the TV screen then an image was starting to show.

I stared at the screen waiting to see what the distorted image was then as it began to clear up my eyes open wide as it was showing my bedroom. I then heard noises which was of me getting back from Hunter's place. I could hear the lights turning on with me making sighing noises then turning off the lights as I enter my bedroom. The lights came on as it showed me getting undress then me entering my bed naked. I thought, "Wait. Is this of yesterday?" The screen suddenly had static as I couldn't see anything on the screen again, but it went away. On the screen it showed me now lying in a different position now and thought I could hear old music playing in the background.

I tried to listen in so I could hear it better, but it stopped, and I could hear someone walking towards my bedroom. Then the screen changed its view now showing where the bedroom door was and standing in the doorway was Barbara wearing a bright red & black outfit. I notice behind her was nothing but darkness, but I knew there should be a short hallway that leads into the living room and kitchen. Barbara smirked and she entered my bedroom then went over to the right side of my bed and began undressing. When she was fully naked the view changed again this time now showing behind my head. Barbara crawled onto my bed then went over to me pulling the blanket off then she touched me I suddenly could feel her soft hands against my skin.

I then felt her hands were touching my face then the screen showed what Barbara was seeing. She sat on top of my chest while rubbing my chest. When my eyes opened Barbara giggled and said, "Hey handsome thought I come by and say hi." I thought, "Why am I acting so calm? I won't act like this!" On the screen it showed me smiling and my arms wrapped around her body, she giggled then leaned in towards me.

The view changed again now showing the left side of the bed as it was much closer to us. I felt weird watching this as I don't remember dreaming about this. When our lips touched, we began kissing each other her soft body was now lying on top of mine. Barbara moaned as it showed on screen my hands reaching towards her thick bubble butt cheeks, I gave them a firm squeeze. I looked down at my hands I felt what Barbara's soft bunny butt felt like. Lifting my head back at the screen and it showed me spreading her cheeks open showing off her big pink pussy while her cute bunny tail was wagging.

The view changed again as our slow kisses were becoming harder and faster. Then Barbara touched my dick. I suddenly felt this and thought, "Am I'm dreaming?! Is this all in my head or I'm really seeing this freaky shit!?" Barbara giggled and said, "My! Such a big boy, you are!" I then felt her claw nails lightly brush my ball sack then touching my big dick as I felt it getting hard. Barbara began stroking my dick as I moaned on the TV. Barbara broke away as she lay down on my chest then made her way to my big dick she giggled and licked it.

I moaned more on TV it showed a close up of Barbara now sucking on my dick I looked for the remote but didn't see it and suddenly felt I couldn't move again. Suddenly my eyes were locked on the TV screen I couldn't move. When I saw Barbara getting a burst of cum onto her face, I felt it as she licked her lips giggled then crawled up to me and asked, "Ready for more?" On the TV I said, "Yeah." Barbara grinned as she slid her pussy into my dick and thrust her waist up and down while it showed me holding her huge breasts and squeezing them while Barbara was making my bed bounce.

The view changed, now showing Barbara's thick bubble butt cheeks bouncing while she thrust her body harder and moaning louder. While watching this I felt the sex, yet I didn't feel warm cum in my underwear. Then another burst of cum came with Barbara said, "Awww yes!" Then she lifted me up and kissed me. Suddenly static came on the TV with the image becoming hard to see now. I felt a bad headache coming as I closed my eyes and rubbed my forehead, I heard the static getting louder than it stopped. I opened my eyes, but I saw I wasn't sitting in the living room I was lying on my bed.

I looked around, then heard Barbara giggling loudly when I turned my head, I suddenly felt her arms around me and asked, "Looking for me handsome?" Suddenly I felt sharp pain across my back as Barbara scratched up my back felt blood dripping down. Then I saw her in front of me her eyes were glowing bright red, and her face was so fucking creepy! The fur now looked old, rotten as sharp teeth were sticking out her mouth. She scratched my chest it burned and when she spoke her voice sounded like a demon, "YOU HAVE SUCH PRETTY EYES!" Barbara tore out my eyes as I screamed.

Dec. 14
9:00-AM

I woke up, jumped out of bed, sweaty and heart racing. I placed both my hands onto my face then rubbed my eyes. I felt my chest and back and didn't feel any of the scratch marks. My heart rate was starting to slow down I lowered my head and had my hand covering my face I said under my breath, "Fucking hell!" Slowly I got out bed and went into the bathroom as I took a hot shower. I washed my body and didn't feel the marks nor was my brain feeling strange. I guess when Manson or Barbara is messing around in my head I'll know it when my brain feels like it's got bugs crawling around it.

After my shower I went back into my room as I put my dirty clothes into a basket as I would take them downstairs into the laundry room. When I was done, I put on some clean clothes and stopped. They were the same ones from the dream I checked if I had anything else to wear but I didn't. I checked the time then went into the kitchen while holding the basket. I looked out the window as it was pouring thick snow fall outside. I left my apartment and locked the door and walked down the flight of stairs into the laundry room.

I was only the one in there I sat on the chair listening to the washing and drying machines while wondering if I would get the same package today or not. I thought Hunter might have the same fucked up dream I had as well. I knew I had to go through those tapes, but I wish there was a way around the headaches or feeling sick. But I hope there wasn't no deadline but if there was then I won't know what to do when Manson reached the goal of his plan whatever it was.

When my clothes were done, I walked upstairs to my apartment room and saw no package in front of my door I was relieved, it wasn't there. I unlocked my door and entered inside then closed it and locked it. I carried my clean clothes to my room. I sat the basket down onto the bed and heard the phone ringing I turned around and walked into the kitchen to answer it. When I picked up the phone, I placed it to my ear and said, "Hello?" Hunter said, "Curtis... it's me." I could tell he was shaken up and disturbed I asked, "Let me guess you had a very bad dream, right?" Hunter said, "Yeah a very fucked up dream."

I said, "I had one too. I thought I got up and when I did, I got a package from Barbara. When I opened it inside the purple box was a purple VHS sex tape." Hunter said, "Same with me but it was that raven woman." I said, "That's Sydney." Hunter said, "Yeah anyway I...I got the same package with a note as it had my full name and it was from her along with a logo. I put it on, and it showed me lying in my bed after you left yesterday then...the TV had some static with some old music playing in the background."

I said, "I had the same thing too." Hunter said, "Then once the static was gone, Sydney entered my room wearing her blue & black outfit she didn't waste any time getting her clothes off and... well if that were me on the video I would never have sex with an bird woman or any other animal person for that fact!" I said, "I get it in the video it made it look like you enjoyed but the real you didn't. And while she touched you during the sex tape you could feel it."

Hunter was silent for a bit and said, "Damn it this is really getting fucking weird! After I fucked her hard suddenly, I was now in the bedroom as she...she looked so fucking creepy with her rotting flesh, grinning with blue glowing eyes and sounding like goddamn demon she tore my eyes out and holy shit did it fucking hurt like hell! When I woke up, I was just glad it was just a fucked-up dream." I said, "Same here. I'll be going through the rest of the tapes today as I don't have anything better to do and I'll need to save up money if I want those video cameras." Hunter said, "Don't watch too many at once." I said, "Don't worry I'll get through them as we might be able to stop one of murders from happening in the real world." Hunter said, "If we're lucky enough." I said, "I'm sure we'll be able to. All we have to do is stop the person and catch them in the act and they'll believe us." Hunter asked, "And if they don't?"

I said, "They'll believe us as why would stop a murder and know all the information about it. Say while we're saving up on money see what you can dig up for TV stations and cartoon networks as there more to this case and having an 3rd person to help would be great." Hunter said, "Alright I'll see what I can do. I'll pick you up on Monday at 11-AM we don't start work until 1-PM so we'll grab lunch, and you can fill me in on what you learn from those tapes." I said, "Alright sounds good. I'll see you on Monday Hunter." Hunter said, "Ok Curtis take care. Bye." I said, "Bye." I set the phone onto the rack.

I spend the whole day going through those tapes as I had a notebook and wrote everything that happened and which of the White Order members were killed on the show so far. I would play each tape for ten minutes then take breaks before getting back at it which helped a bit but still had that strange feeling in my brain. I only managed to get through about 15 episodes on the 1st tape and after that I felt very sick. My whole body felt so hot I puked twice in the bathroom. I then opened all my windows letting freezing cold wind to cool me down.

I wiped my head with a wet face cloth when it felt like my brain is about to boil. I checked the time on the clock it was 8:00-PM I thought, "I should get some sleep." However, I feared what my next nightmare would be as I worried would Manson or his friends try killing me in my sleep or would he do it through the real world? I now felt very cold but only left my kitchen and bedroom window opened and closed the rest. I felt better, but my brain still had that strange feeling I decide to go to sleep I turn off the lights and went into my bedroom. As I felt my body slowly shutting down, I hoped our boss won't be anything like Jake was I didn't want to work for a prick like that ever again. I slowly closed my eyes and had my bedroom door closed to feel safer I had placed a heavy thick object against the door, so it won't be opened easily. I had a bit of trouble falling asleep at first. When I was able to sleep though, my worst fears nightmare came alive.

I dreamed that I was standing in the neighborhood where I grew up, but it was now in flames with warm air blowing against my face. All the trees were rotten and dead with hanging corpses from them and when I looked closer, I could see they were police officers, priests, nuns, teachers and a few government members. I turned to the sound of screams. I saw a gang of children, young and old chasing after their own parents. They were armed with knives, baseballs bats, hammers, meat cleavers, shovels or pitch forks. They chased them until they gave up and were beaten to death. I felt shocked at what I was seeing. I thought, "Is this what Sam meant was going to happen?" Suddenly I heard a kid yell, "HEY, THERE'S ANOTHER ONE! KILL HIM!" I turned my head to see John pointing at me with a blood-stained meat cleaver in his hand. The children were now running towards me I said, "Oh shit!" I began running down the street I could hear them yelling and calling me.

I felt my heart beating faster as this felt so goddamn real! I kept running but suddenly I came to a dead end I knew there wasn't one on my street. I went to run but stopped when I saw my dead parents nailed to dead tree with their house up in flames.

The children were in front of me, and I could feel their anger and hatred. John whacked the meat cleaver into my neck. Powerless to stop him or the gang as they hacked me to death.

Dec.15
10:00-AM

I woke up in cold sweat and jumped out of bed I looked at my body and was shocked what I saw. My tank top and underwear were ripped and torn like I was attacked in my nightmare. I removed the heavy object and took off my clothes and went into the bathroom to take a hot shower. I felt better as I stepped out then walked into my bedroom and changed into clean clothes. I looked out the window. It was thick snow fall outside I felt cold air blowing against my face as I could see some steam coming off of my body.

I closed the window just a crack, so it won't be too cold in my apartment. I picked up the notebook as I would do what I did yesterday I wasn't going to let these fucked up nightmares stop me! I will stop Manson and his friends from whatever they are planning! I cooked breakfast on the stove but could still remember the smell of those burning houses along with the corpses. I would sometimes zone out if I thought about it too much and nearly burned my breakfast. When I finished, I sat at my kitchen table and began eating it.

Around 11-AM my brain felt better as I didn't have that strange feeling anymore. I went over to my gym and began working out. I knew if I was out of shape, it would make me weaker, and I wasn't going to be. I spent 2 hours working out then stood up from my long workout. I looked where I left the VHS tapes, I sighed knowing the sickening feeling I would get but if I was going to stop Manson I had to keep watching. I took the notebook and pencil along with my sharpener and placed 2nd tape into the VHS player sat down on the sofa and watched it. I was starting off episode 16 and this time I heard Hellen's voice she said, "Episode 16 War in The Skies."

As the screen faded black it then showed The Dark Kingdom with Hellen's air ships as they were being repaired from the battles they had with the White Order. I notice a few of the so-called villains won't be risking their lives now as Manson along with his gang we're kicking their asses for good. It then showed Hellen working on her ship with George helping her. Hellen rubbed her forehead and said, "Those bloody White Order laser cannons are a pain to repair the damage they caused!" George turned his head over to her and said, "I bet, my hammer to their heads would help them think better."

Hellen lightly laughed and said, "Yes that and my double cannons would take good care of them." I thought, "Her Russian accent is so strong it's like they really got a woman from the Soviet Union and hired her to act for this show but most people who come here from that country try to keep a low profile since Americans are hostile towards Russians. But if those characters were real then it won't be a problem but where the hell was this show coming from?

Hellen and George finished repairing the air ship Hellen said, "That should do it for the next battle." George said, "That won't be long knowing those evil idiots will strike again soon." Hellen said, "Da, very true. Alright George, I'll be at Manson castle tomorrow as I'm going to rest up after a long day of work." George said, "Alright Hellen see you tomorrow." It showed Hellen getting on board her air ship and walked through the wooden hallway as it showed different picture frames which had paintings of mostly night scenery with a few pictures different bear people I guess it was Hellen's family members. When Hellen reached her captain's quarters, she ran her hands through her long hair then walked over into her bedroom and next to it was a big bathroom.

I suddenly saw static on the screen again which I haven't seen after the witch hunt episode but knew what was coming when I saw static. The screen showed in front of Hellen taking off her yellow gloves then unbuttoning her yellow jacket. I thought, "Was the episode original like this or is it being edited because I'm watching it?" As Hellen took off her yellow jacket letting it fall to the floor showing her massive breasts with black shot glass size nipples.

Hellen placed her hands under her breasts lightly messaging them as she moaned. She took off her boots then began removing her pants I press the pause button as my mind would need some time before it could handle what I was seeing.

When I was ready, I pressed the play button Hellen stripped out of her pants as the screen showed behind shot of her huge wide hips and thick bubble butt cheeks along with a big black pussy. I couldn't help but stare at her beauty. Hellen moaned more and said, "Aww much better." Hellen reached for her bathtub turned the knob as hot water poured into it. Once it was filled up, she got into the tub and rested her head against the wall while closing her eyes. It then showed a close up at her face and I could hear a younger voice that was Hellen's saying, "Mommy! Daddy! Come play with me!"

There was close up shot of Hellen followed by a younger version of her running through a field with her parents beside her. And I could hear old music playing I thought, "That's the same music I heard during that fucked up dream I had!" I paused the video then grabbed my notebook and picked up the pencil and wrote down the name of the episode and what I heard on it. As I set both these things down and turn back to the screen, I nearly had a heart attack. The screen showed Hellen looking at me with an annoyed look on her face and felt her light brown eyes staring back at mine. I quickly turned my head away then grabbed the remote and press the play button as it went back showing Hellen's flashback.

As Hellen stopped with her parents holding both of her arms it showed a very big town below them while standing on top of a hill. They looked happy, suddenly the clouds above the sky moved as White Order spaceships were above the town and began firing their lasers at them Hellen screamed then she woke up. She looked at the wall as it had a clock and had been sleep for an hour. She sat up from her tub as she looked worried and said, "My town! I think it might be in danger!" Hellen hopped out of the bathtub and quickly grabbed a towel then dried herself. Putting her clothes on, she ran into the control room of the air ship.

"Dmitry! Come in, its Hellen!"

"Aww, Hellen! What's up? I heard you and your bat friend have been fighting the White Order forces."

"Da, we did." Hellen smiled. "But how is my town doing?"

"All right, we have been guarding it since the war. Don't worry Hellen, we'll fight to the death if the White Order comes by."

Hellen was silent.

"Hellen, you still there?"

"Yes, I'm still here. Glad to hear it. If anything happens, please call me at once."

"Da I'll do that you take it easy old friend." Hellen said, "You too. Bye." Hellen turned her head looking out the window of her air ship to where her town was looking worried. The screen faded black then when it came back it showed Manson and Barbara looking over a big very detailed map of The Dark Kingdom. A black bat standing beside them said, "As you can see Manson the White Order have taken over small areas south of the mountains and have destroyed much of the forests clearing their way to set up factories so they can build more battle tanks and other weapons."

Manson crossed his arms and sighed then asked, "What else?" black bat said, "We sent our soldiers to watch them closely so we can plan a sneak attack on them and capture their leader and see what secrets he or she is hiding from us." Manson said, "I don't like this at all. I want my men to destroy all factories at once but do capture their leader." Black bat man said, "Yes Manson." Barbara had an annoyed look on her face and asked, "How much more land do they have to destroy?" Manson looked at Barbara and said, "They'll pay for this Barbara as I too had enough of the White Order destroying my land."

Kane, George, Sydney and Andrew walked in as both Manson and Barbara looked over. Manson said, "Good your all here. But where is Hellen?" George said, "Last I saw her was at the docks repairing her air ship yesterday." Manson turned his head over to Barbara and said, "Barbara try calling her as I'm going to need her air support for the next attack." She said, "Alright." Barbara walked away as Manson said, "Once we have Hellen here

I will tell you all about my attack plan."

It showed Barbara walking through the castle hallway and stairs I paused the video as I felt a light headache coming, I felt my mouth was dry I stood up and kept my eyes locked onto the TV and grabbed a bottle of cold water from the fridge. I walked back into the living room drank it then reached for the remote and press the play button as it showed Barbara entering into a large room with a gothic style looking mirror. Barbara placed her hands onto two crystal balls and the mirror suddenly changed color. Barbara stared into and said, "Hellen." It then showed Hellen standing in front of the mirror and behind Hellen was her bedroom.

Hellen said, "Aww Barbara sorry I'm unable to reach Manson's castle I've been busy repairing my air ships." Barbara said, "Manson wants you here as we'll need your airships for a fight with the White Order that have taken over small areas of mountains in the south." Hellen said, "Alright I'll be there. Oh, Barbara could you do me a favor?" Barbara looked at Hellen and asked, "Sure, what's that?" Hellen said, "Could you have Manson send extra forces to my town in Zelenyy Vesna." I thought, "That's very Russian." I wrote down the name as Barbara said, "Sure thing Hellen I'll tell Manson that you'll be here shortly." Hellen said, "Thanks friend. See you in a few minutes." The mirror went blank as Barbara let go of the crystal balls and the mirror turned back to its normal self as she left the room then the screen faded black. I drank some water then set the bottle down it showed the White Order factories with lots of workers and big trucks moving around with heavy armed guards patrolling the area.

When it showed inside the factory as machines were building many different weapons from firearms to battle tanks and other deadly machines. Then as the screen moved from one side of the factory to the other it showed an office with a big window and behind it was a shadow outline of a very big man standing as the screen zoomed onto the shadow it then showed on the other side a very big man with a grin on his face. He had his arms behind his back, wearing a white-and-black robe on with white pants and black boots.

He laughed maniacally and said, "I can't wait to see the look on Manson's face when I drive my unstoppable war machines to his castle! Once I'm finish building everything then I will unleash the White Orders wrath on Manson and his friends!" Then he turned over to a large screen as he typed away on the keyboard and said, "But first to keep those air ships busy I'll have them somewhere else." The screen showed the name of the area he wanted to attack it was Hellen's town. As he hit the enter key it showed White Order ships heading towards Zelenyy Vesna. The screen showed a close up of his face showed half of it in shadows.

The screen faded black and when the picture came back it showed a very big town and in front of it were bright green hills. When it showed the town's people mostly bears with a few other anthros walking by as air ships flew towards it as it was Manson. The air ships landed by the docks black, white and a few grey bat soldiers stepped out as bear soldiers came over with one wearing an officer uniform greeted by a black bat wearing a purple and black uniform and said, "Evening sir I was sent by Manson to send extra forces here in case of an sudden attack."

The bear officer said, "I guess it won't hurt having some extra help here after all it has been very quiet after those attacks by the White Order." The black bat said, "Also I have a message for Dmitry to have his air ships standing by as well." The bear officer said, "Alright, I'll go tell him. Do your men need any help with the weaponry?" The black bat man said, "No thanks we're good here." I reached the remote and pressed the pause button and finished my water bottle but as I turned back to the screen, I saw the two characters that were talking to each other were now looking at me with a very annoyed look on their faces.

I quickly reached for the remote and pressed the play button, static came over the screen, I couldn't see the image suddenly I thought I saw a face looking at me, but it flashed so fast on the screen I didn't have time to make it out then it went back to normal showing the two anthro men walking away with the soldiers being told to stand on guard. When the bear officer went over to Zelenyy Vesna it showed a very large airport like building with more air ships that were bigger than Hellen's and had steam stacks on the back of them.

As the bear officer walked towards one of these steam airships it showed a muscular bear man wearing overalls, pants and work boots as he had short hair and dark brown fur color. He was working on some engine parts when the bear officer said, "Hey Dmitry!" When he turned his head over, he said, "Hey Boris what's up?" Boris the officer said, "Hellen sent a message for you."

Dmitry asked, "What's that?" Boris said, "She wants you to have your air ships ready as she'll be busy fighting White Order members that have taken over small areas in the mountains." Dmitry said, "Alright I'm almost finish repairing this engine and I'll have them ready." Boris said, "Manson also sent some of his men to aid us in case anything happens during this battle." Dmitry said, "Gotta love Hellen, she is a very kind woman." Boris lightly smiled and said, "Yes, she is and... Suddenly a bear guard yelled, "White Order ships are heading this way! Sound the alarm at once!"

As Dmitry looked up into the sky it showed the big spaceships as they were getting closer to Zelenyy Vesna. I paused the video and rubbed my eyes but when I looked back at the screen it showed Dmitry with a very angry look on his face, I suddenly felt my heart was beating faster and could feel his hatred towards me I quickly pressed the play button, but nothing was happening I kept looking at the screen fearing if I moved away it would show something worse but the play button wasn't working. I quickly look down to see if my thumb was pressing it and sure enough it was when I looked up at the screen Dmitry's face looked more sister and evil-looking as I felt the hairs on the back of neck standing up and giving me chills.

When I press the play button the screen had some static, but it quickly went away as it showed the White Order ships firing their laser cannons at the town. A few buildings were hit and exploded Dmitry ran into his steam air ship with crew members rushing on board as thick smoke came out the stacks and quickly lifted into the air then moved towards the White Order ships along with Manson's air ships. As they fired their double barrel cannons or rocket launchers hitting the first row of White Order ships as they came crashing down onto the ground. There are ground forces shooting at the White Order ships as well.

It then showed Dmitry moving his steam air ship he press the speak button on the speaker beside him and said, "Fire the cannons at the closest enemy ships!" It then showed the double cannons firing away at the White Order ships as they took out 4 of them. Suddenly laser shots hit Dmitry's ship the blast took out a good chunk of his ship he gripped the wheel tightly and said, "It's going to take more than one shot to bring us down!" He pressed the button and yelled into the speaker, "FIRE AGAIN!" They fired their cannons hitting the White Order ship that shot at them as it blew up. Dmitry's crew cheered but suddenly they were shot as the steam air ship was heading towards the ground the screen showed a below shot of the steam air ship coming down in flames as it crashed into the ground the screen went blank and I could see the reflection. Suddenly I notice a shadow figure standing behind me I quickly spun my head around but saw nothing I turned back to the screen, and it was gone.

When the screen came back on it showed Manson men moving through the forest along with air ships above them heading towards where the White Order had set up their factories. It then showed Hellen holding onto her wheel as she heard Manson's voice on the speaker, "Alright Hellen as soon as my men take out their aircraft guns, I'll give you and your air ships the order to assault the factories below." Hellen pressed the speaker button and said, "Da Manson, understood." As Hellen pulled a lever as her and the other air ships hold their position, she turned her head over to the cockpit window and far off in the distance she could see explosions and gasped knowing her town was under attack.

The screen then showed Manson soldiers slowly moving up towards the factory as they quickly ran over to a building wall. A bat solider peeked his head over to see two guards walking on the other side he looked back at the bat soldiers beside him. Nodding his head as the two quickly sneaked behind the guards and covered their mouths and slid their throats then slowly rested bodies down as more soldiers were making their way towards the aircraft guns. With lightning speed, they killed all the soldiers without making too much noise until one White Order soldier saw them and went to sound the alarm but was shot in the neck by a cross bow as it showed Andrew who killed him.

I paused the video the screen showed a background of dead bodies I felt my head was feeling strange again, but it felt much worse this time I felt I had bugs crawling both on the outside and inside of my brain and swear I could hear them as well. I closed my eyes and lightly growled as this feeling felt horrible. I shook my head for a bit then turned to the TV screen and suddenly saw what looked like eyes pressed against the other side of the screen looking back at me. It quickly then moved away.

I quickly press the play button and felt my heart was racing I took slow breaths to calm myself down as Manson grinned while standing beside Andrew as he took out his radio and said, "Alright Hellen attack the factories!" It showed the air ships moving in firing their double cannons or dropped bombs onto the factories blowing them up as White Order guards and soldiers came rushing out but were greeted by Manson's soldiers as they quickly fired at them.

White Order soldier fired their laser rifles but were overpowered by Manson's forces as the factories were all quickly destroyed. The man in white and black robes yelled in anger as he ran out of his office when Kane the fox came behind him and asked, "Going somewhere?" He turned around; Kane threw a smoke bomb. The man went to draw out his laser pistol. Kane was too fast. Before he can draw, Kane had disarmed him breaking his right arm in the process. There was a loud crack and the man howled in pain while Kane grinned.

Barbara came in and said, "You got a lot of talking to do fat man!" The White Order man said, "I NOT telling you anything!" Barbara grinned and said, "Oh we'll see about that." They carried him towards Manson with Andrew, George and Sydney stood waiting for them as Kane lightly laughed and said, "We got our fat criminal!" Manson crossed his arms and said, "You're going to pay for the damage you caused to my land, you scum!" The White Order member said, "I won't tell the King's enemy anything!"

Sydney grinned and said, "Sure a fool like you won't talk but I know how. Allow me." As Kane and Barbara let go of him Sydney opened up her arms as she had two glowing yellow orbs in her hands the White Order man said, "It's going to take more than magic to make me talk!" Sydney then shot the two yellow orbs at him as they went inside his body. He looked where they went. Sydney giggled and said, "Look into my eyes fat man." He did as the screen showed what he was seeing. He was unable to look away as he kept staring into Sydney's pretty blue eyes. I could hear strange music with suddenly images popping up which showed what he had been doing along with speaking with the King. Then the music grew stronger while the screen was zooming into Sydney's eyes.

More images flashed and I swear some of them looked like real-life stuff, but it was going so fast I couldn't make out much and feared if I paused the video too much something bad would happen. When he gave all the information Manson wanted Sydney giggled and said, "See that wasn't so hard was it?" The White Order man looked shock as Manson said, "Thanks Sydney, now it's my turn." Manson then placed both of his hands onto his shoulder. Manson raised his voice and said, "Look into my eyes!" Again, it showed what he was seeing I felt sweat running down my body however this time it wasn't so nice. As he stared into Manson's bright red eyes loud screams could be heard as I saw images of people being burned along with getting beaten to death as these flashed quickly on the screen, I felt my brain was now burning along with butterflies in my stomach. The sounds grew worse with the screams turned into loud yelling along with bones being broken, flesh being torn to pieces and the sickening sound of limbs being chopped off. I felt I was going puke from this as I tried to fight off.

Then suddenly a loud howl was heard as it showed the White Order man screaming in pain as he fell onto the ground yelling, "MAKE IT STOP! PLEASE, MAKE IT STOP!" Manson then waved his soldiers over as the White Order man had pissed himself Manson said, "Beat them scum to death!" His soldiers took out big wooden clubs as they walked over to him and began beating him to death. The man begged and cried but Manson's men didn't stop they kept hitting him breaking more bones until he gave in. When Manson soldiers walked away his clothes were torn and his face was covered in bruises and blood.

The screen showed Manson and his gang as he said, "Alright now that we're done here let's go check on Zelenyy Vesna and see if they held off the White Order sneak attack." The screen faded black I grabbed the remote and paused it not caring this time, but I had to throw up. I ran towards the bathroom and puked my lunch out and coughed hard. I gagged for a bit then reached the handle and flushed the toilet I slowly stood up then grabbed a face cloth got it wet then wiped my face got it wet again and rubbed my forehead. I thought, "Those images I saw...were those real? If so where were are those scenes supposed to be from?"

As I thought about it more some of those images looked like they were taken from a war. I then noticed that in all of them had one thing in common the ground was covered in snow. I then thought one of the images I saw was my father standing behind his F-86 Sabre which were used during the Korean War. I remember when I was young before John was born my father would tell me some of his dog fights, he had back in the Korean War and after he return back to America, he met my mother and the two got married. I then thought, "Did my father have something to do with Osborne Louis family? Or was Manson fucking with my head again?" When the sick feeling had finally left, I slowly went back into the living room and sat down onto the sofa and saw on the screen it was the same as I last saw it. I took a big breath and reached for the VHS remote and pressed the play button.

The screen showed some damaged buildings along with destroyed steam air ships with both bear and bat people helping the injured. As it zoomed in on this it showed Hellen along with Manson and his gang moving towards one wrecked steam air ship that Dmitry was in. It then showed Boris as he was looking in anger of what the White Order has done. Hellen yelled, "Boris! Boris!" As he turned around Hellen asked, "How bad is it?" Boris said, "Well if it wasn't for Manson's extra support, we might have lost more men along with people, but we still took some heavy losses and...

The screen showed Hellen's eyes watery as she said, "Dmitry... no!" Hellen ran towards Dimitry's body, but Boris intercepted. She cried into Boris' chest.

Boris said, "Dmitry was more than a soldier. He was a good friend always looking out for everyone." Hellen moved her head away and wiped the tears as Boris said, "He thanked you for telling him that the enemy would come." Hellen said, "At least he put up a fight and I would have done the same." Boris said, "We'll be aiding you Hellen, in the battle against the White Order."

Manson said, "We'll all make them pay for this. I think it's time we give them a taste of their own medicine." Kane grinned and said, "I like the sound of that." George said, "Yeah, let's teach those idiots a lesson!" Hellen said, "For Dmitry and our fallen comrades, let's do it." The screen went blank as Manson said, "Tune in next time on The Manson & Barbara Show." I press the stop button I picked up the notebook and pencil writing down what happened and what I saw during those images that were flashed onto the screen along with the war photos of my father in the Korean War.

When I was finished writing I got up walked into the kitchen then opened the fridge grabbed another water bottle opened it then drank down the cold water. I wiped my lips and took another breath and thought, "One more. Just one more and that's it. Too much of this fucking shit is going to kill me." I went back into the living room and sat down onto my sofa and reached for the VHS remote and press the play button.

The screen showed the next episode as it was Manson's voice, "Episode 17 Revenge." It then showed Manson's castle as it was pouring rain with roaring thunder and bright flashes of lightning. It then zoomed into a window as it showed Manson and the gang standing in the dining room with the long-detailed map but this time it was a different kingdom. Then the screen showed Manson along with his friends standing next to each other. Manson said, "Alright if we're going to make the White Order get the message, we aren't messing around anymore we're going to attack one of their towns and kill as many people as we can to see how they like it. And while we're at it let's destroy everything on sight." Hellen grinned and said, "My air ships will hit every building until there's nothing left!" Manson looked at the map and said, "We'll start with this town here, then work our way up."

As the screen showed a close up of the town, he was pointing town I saw its name "White Creek" I thought, "Wait that's my town's name but it's Black Creek." I kept watching as Manson told his friends what area to attack and where Hellen could send her air ships. Once they had their plan together Manson said, "Alright, let's go." The screen faded black I quickly paused the video grabbed my notebook and pencil wrote this down then grabbed the remote and press the play button.

When the screen came back it showed the King of the White Order standing in front of two men both wearing white and sliver outfits as the King said, "I have chosen you two on an important mission. We are starting to lose support from our people and if this continues then Manson and friends will attack our kingdom and destroy our way of life. We cannot allow that to happen. I want you two to travel through the land and tell everyone who the real enemy is." Then the screen showed who the King was looking at. I said, "No fucking way!"

I quickly grabbed the VHS remote and paused it. When I looked at the screen it was still the same image. Standing in the white and sliver outfits was me and Hunter the faces matched what we really looked like even our height, hair, eye color everything else matched. I felt a chill ran down my spine fearing the next thing I would see and when I pressed the play button I was damn right. On the TV screen I spoke first and said, "We won't let you down King." Hunter spoke next, "Anything for the White Order." The King then gave us handheld computers and said, "This will show what Manson and his friends have been doing. When you reach each town show everyone what's really going on. With their support we will double our numbers against Manson's forces. When I need you two again, I will call you. Good luck and may the Lord guide you."

I watched as the two of us walked onto a hover ship like vehicle as the small ladder platform closed along with the door and it sped off. The screen showed a close up of the King. I didn't recognize the face but felt I saw it somewhere long ago. I paused the video and wrote down in the notebook what I saw I thought, "When I tell Hunter this, he isn't going to be happy about." I set down the notebook and grabbed the VHS remote and press the play button as it showed the hover ship speeding through an open field. It then went inside with Hunter driving while I was sitting beside him.

Hunter asked, "So what's the first town we're going to?" It then showed me as I looked at the handheld computer, I typed for a bit then turned my head over and said, "Lakeview mostly black people but they'll be dumb enough to fool." Hunter grinned and said, "We'll easily trick these people." We both laughed but I thought, "Me and Hunter aren't evil! We would never do that!" I quickly paused and thought, "Dorothy told me Osborne Louis was born in New Orleans! Lakeview is a town that's there!" I grabbed the notebook and wrote this down and thought, "Ok. Now, were starting to get somewhere now that I know town Osborne was in me and Hunter should be able to find a birth certificate then we'll be able to track down his family members...if their still alive that is."

Pressing the play button, it showed the hover ship heading towards Lakeview as the screen faded black. When it came back, it showed air ships heading towards White Creek. I saw some of the buildings were almost like the ones here in Black Creek. Only difference was that everything was high-tech and hover vehicles were driving around the streets with people wearing older style outfits. When they saw the air ships coming in, they fired their double cannons at the buildings blowing them up and taking out a few people as well. They ran and screamed in horror. White Order guards came in and fired their laser rifles at the air ships but were killed my Manson's ground forces.

Next, it showed George running after the scared civilians and swung his hammer at them knocking them down as I could hear bones breaking and backs cracking as one woman holding an newborn baby fell onto the sidewalk she turned around it showed George lifting up his hammer she screamed as the screen showed behind the woman as George slammed his hammer down onto the woman and the newborn killing them both. I felt sick.

Next it showed Andrew riding on his motorcycle as he fired his laser pistols at the running civilians and White Order guards. Then it showed a young man running down the street turning his head to see Andrew was heading towards him. Andrew grinned as he turned the handlebars gaining more speed and ran over the man I watched as the tires drove over the helpless body along with the motorcycle weight crushing his bones, as well. Next it showed Manson and Barbara fighting with swords against the White Order guards they hacked and slash their way through them.

Kane came in and threw a bomb at a guard post as it exploded with some of the guards running out while on fire. They screamed in pain while Manson's soldiers fired their cross bows pumping their bodies full of arrows. One guard had both of his eyes shot full of arrows as he fell onto the ground as Manson's soldiers stumped him to death. I felt sicker as I quickly paused the video I thought, "How the hell does a kid watch this sick shit and not realize it's wrong?! Or their parents for that fact? They always check to see what their children are watching as they won't allow them to see such graphic violence or sex!" When the sickening feeling went away, I grabbed the remote and press the play button.

As Hellen's air ships destroyed more of White Creek; thick black smoke rose into the sky along with bright flames. It then showed Manson and Barbara looking over at the destruction they had caused they both smiled. His girlfriend asked, "Isn't this a beautiful sight?" Manson turned over to Barbara with a grin and said, "Yes, it is." The two began kissing in front of the bright flames, as the screen slowly darkens.

When it came back it showed me and Hunter had reached Lakeview the town it showed had an older style to it I wasn't really sure what the real Lakeview looked like, but I'll find out about that later. As the hover ship came to a full stop the door opened with me and Hunter getting out as all the town's people came towards us. I said, "I have a message from the King of the White Order!"

As more black people came over, I said, "We have a hostile enemy that wishes to harm everyone. This enemy is Manson, The bat, along with his gang of cold-blooded killers! Hunter, show them."

Hunter pressed a few buttons on the handheld computer then hologram like screen came up and showed images of Manson and his friends attacking other towns and villages killing people. The people looked shocked and angry what they were seeing I then said, "The King wants all of you to join against Manson and his friends to stop them and to destroy the evil Dark Kingdom for good." The people clapped as I said, "Spread the word to everyone that Manson and his Dark Kingdom is a threat to everyone!" A loud cheer came as it showed me and Hunter getting back into the hover ship. Hunter grinned and said, "Told you these people would be easy to fool."

I laughed, interrupted by a loud beeping noise. I pressed a button on the dashboard. The Mayor of White Creek came on.

"Help! If anyone can hear this message, please help us! We're under attack by Manson's forces!" I said, "Copy that, we're on our way!" The screen then showed the hover ship turning around and speeding over the fields heading towards White Creek. I grabbed the notebook writing down that the mayor was it which meant this episode aired before Nov.13th when that massacre happened. When it showed the hover ship reaching what looked very much like Black Creek's city hall. Me and Hunter got out of the hover vehicle as we ran up the steps inside armed with our laser pistols.

Once inside we ran through the building until we reached the meeting room. Inside was the mayor along with other White Order guards that were in fact the police officers including the police chief that were killed. As it showed us running towards them, I yelled, "QUICKLY! FOLLOW US, WE'LL GET YOU OUT OF HERE!" Then it showed Manson's soldiers bursting through the front door and firing their cross bows killing the mayor along with the guards as we ran over to the stage and nearly got hit by the arrows while guards came in firing their laser pistols or rifles at them. I couldn't believe what I was seeing the events that me and Hunter went through were preconditioned just what happened only of course it was shown in the cartoon that me,

Hunter along with those who were killed were really the villains and Manson, his friends and soldiers were the heroes.

It then showed me and Hunter shooting at Manson's soldiers as we ran out of city hall and down into an alleyway with more soldiers firing their cross bows at us but missed. Manson soldiers looked annoyed as one said, "We'll get them next time, come on." They left as it then showed the King along with other members of the White Order, they were watching White Creek being destroyed he yelled in anger and said, "That bat is going to pay in blood for what he did!" He smashed his fist onto the table and seem to have caused it to crack." The screen faded to dark, and Manson's recorded voice said: *Tune in next time for The Manson & Barbara Show.*

I had so many questions running through my mind I knew I couldn't answer them all at once me and Hunter will find the answers we are looking for. These tapes are paying off however the side effects from watching them too long was the only problem. If there is a way around it me and Hunter could find more clues and maybe stop one of these massacres from happening or future murders of parents and children.

But first, I had to check out my father's war photos to ensure what I saw on the screen was the photos he had taken during his time in Korean. But I also wanted to set up the video cameras as well and for that I was going to need money I knew the waiting would pay off however the more time we wasted by during work Manson and his friends were getting slowly closer to whatever the hell they got planned but I will stop them!"

10:50-PM

I finished writing down everything I needed to show Hunter on Monday I knew he was going to be thrilled about finding more clues but when I tell him that we we're on the show it was going make the both of us worried. If what the show said, was coming true, would there be a way to change it or stop it? I was also worrying what was going to happen to John and my parents. I couldn't get the horrible thoughts out of my mind that Manson would brainwash John into killing my parents in a graphic way then hunt me down. I didn't know much about Hunter's parents as he wasn't that open about them, and I felt it was rude to bring it up. However, we would need help with this bizarre case as the two us have barely made any breakthrough. If we could find someone who knew more about cartoons and how they are made and aired. We could try tracking down wherever this show was coming from along with digging more background on its creator Osborne Louis.

But there was something that was bothering me I thought, "What would my father and the Korean war have to do with this and why was there some Russian names being used? Was Osborne's father in the Korean war and if so, was he half Russian and American? Or pure Russian? And if true then...then did my father kill Osborne's father?" I felt very tired and went to sleep.

Dec.16
11:00-AM

I woke up feeling lightheaded but had no nightmare I blew some air out then slowly stood up as it felt very warm inside my bedroom. I stripped out of my clothes and put clean ones on. I removed the heavy object from by bedroom door and opened it then stepped into the small hallway and walked towards the kitchen. I opened the fridge and saw there wasn't much to eat. I thought, "I'll step out and grab a bite and get some air." I closed the fridge door went over to the front door and stood in front of my closet as I put my winter jacket, boots and gloves on then grabbed my apartment & car keys then wallet which I nearly forgot and left. When I got outside it was very cold with a thick snow fall, I didn't see many people out driving I walked over to my Honda and brushed off all the snow got into my Honda started it up and drove off.

Went to McDonald's and got two burgers, large fries and a big Coke. As I drove back, I saw more cars running than people walking. When I got back to my apartment, I went upstairs until I reached the 5th floor and when I got there I stopped as I saw dark purple envelope sticking in between my door I thought, "Oh shit!" When I went inside my apartment, I locked the door and put the chain and dead bolt on as well then took off my winter clothes and went into the kitchen. I set the McDonald's paper back down along with my drink holding the dark purple envelope as on it said, "To Curtis Parker, from Manson the Bat." Beside the writing was his logo, but this time I wasn't going to stand near the kitchen window.

I sat down at my sofa I could smell the stronger flower like smell from it I took a breath then opened it having a good idea what it was going to say. When I opened it up the letter inside it was much longer but the minute, I lay my eyes on the message I felt nothing more than hate, anger and fear. Manson wrote,

"So, Curtis you didn't listen to my warning. Very well then you and Hunter have crossed the line and there is no going back. As you saw last night the two of are in fact on my show but not for long as I will get rid of you two and anyone else you bring into this matter. You can watch what you got but mark my words you can NOT change what is going to happen next year or the year after that! The further you two go on with this...FUCKING

BULLSHIT I WILL RIP EVERY FUCKING BODY PART OUT UNTIL YOU ARE NOTHING MORE THAN A ROTTING CORPSE HANGING ON A FUCKING TREE!"

I looked away from the letter as I thought I could hear his voice yelling inside of my head. My heart was beating fast I knew I was in deep shit. So deep in fact that this was going to get me, and Hunter killed if we won't be careful of what we do next. I took a few breaths and said, "I can beat him. He's just a cartoon character! I'm real, he's not!" I felt I wasn't alone, and I looked back at the note then noticed there was something else written on it, it said, "Look up." The feeling of someone standing right behind me along with their eyes looking down at me was the worst feeling ever. My heart felt like it was going to explode.

Suddenly I felt two hands touching my shoulder tops and when I looked at them, they were Manson's purple leather gloves I suddenly felt his warm breath on the top of my head. I manage to say, "You're not real! You're just in my head trying to fuck with me!" Manson's hands were now moving towards my neck I wanted to stand up, but I couldn't, and my heart was racing. His hands then gripped by throat I felt they were slowly starting to squeeze. I couldn't fight anymore I turned my head to where Manson was and gasped.

Manson's head was nothing more than a rotting skull with bright red, glowing eyes with the smell of burning flesh and death blew into my face. Blood oozed out of his skull. I could hear a loud demon-like growl. He opened his mouth full of fangs and I screamed. He squeezed my throat so tight, I passed out.

When I woke up I saw I was lying on my sofa breathing heavily I rubbed my throat and still remembered the feeling of his purple leather gloves touching my cold skin. I slowly stood up and saw that the tapes and notebook were still here, however, the letter and envelope were gone. I turned to where I left my lunch. It was still there. I quickly walked over, the burgers and fries were still hot. I checked the time I was only out for few minutes I turned my head away and thought, "Did I really scream of was just in my mind?"

I rubbed my forehead then my eyes as I hated being alone more than ever. I got a plate out ate my lunch and planned to call Hunter as I wanted someone over here right now, I didn't want to feel alone in my apartment. After lunch I picked up the phone called his number but there was no answer, I felt my heart had sunk I thought, "Shit! Did Manson get Hunter already or is he out doing something!?" I tried a few more times but got nothing.

However, by 6:30-PM Hunter called me and said he was out making calls. I told him that I had both good and bad news.

Dec. 17
10:00-AM

I asked Hunter to come early, as I would need time to tell him what happened to me, and the danger we were in. Hunter sat down at the kitchen table. The wind was howling outside. I had the notebook as Hunter rubbed his eyes and drank coffee, I made for him. He asked, "So what first? Good or bad news?" I drank my coffee and said, "The good. While watching episodes 16 and 17 there were names of people and places that were said which might lead us in a direction to go in." Hunter asked, "What is it?" I said, "Ok first Lakeview that's in New Orleans and the woman I spoke to in Miami told me that Osborne Louis was born there."

Hunter nodded his head and asked, "What else?" I said pointed on the notebook and said, "Next these Russian names were said." Hunter looked at them and asked, "What does Zelenyy Vesna mean?" I said, "Not sure might be a place or something but we'll get it translated for us. And last the massacre that happened on Nov.13th was aired the day before the event I saw the date behind the King's head when I was watching it yesterday. So, the more we watch these tapes, the more we can learn of future events that Manson plans to happen next year. We'll have a chance to stop him."

Hunter looked at me asked, "Ok now onto the bad news." I sighed and said, "Very well...we're on the 17th episode and I'm not kidding we looked, acted and sounded the same on the goddamn TV however Manson shows us as being evil."

Hunter's eyes widened.

"In the episode I watched, the town we lived in was called, White Creek. The King ordered us to spread lies about Manson and his forces. We went to a town called Lakeview, told a bunch of black people that we're the good guys and Manson and his friends are evil. You showed them on a handheld computer all the violent acts and lies, they have done.

When the mayor of our city and on the show was killed the same way as we both ran out however it changed it showing us running through an alleyway escaping as I bet its going to show us getting more people to believe our lies and join the King so his White Order can double its numbers against Manson."

When I notice Hunter almost looked white as a ghost, he looked at me and said, "I can't believe what I saw! I would never do that!" Hunter covered his mouth and started saying, "No! No, it can't be true!" I asked, "What can't be true?" Hunter looked at me and sighed and said, "My...my father was racist he tried to get me and my mother not to like other people. Strongly against blacks. When I was 8 my parents had a big fight, and my mother took me, and we left that asshole as we didn't want to be part of his world. I remember when I started my new life in school, some of the kids would pick on them which pissed me off. This...this one girl I liked I wanted to ask her out, but her parents didn't like white people and when I tried to reason with them. I ended up getting my ass kicked around. I didn't tell my mother what happened to me. I tried to brush it off but...I didn't understand it."

I notice his eyes were getting watery as he wiped them and said, "Well, I kept to myself and once I got into high school, I avoid them.. I never hated them, but I just never understood why they hated me." I said, "Manson is just fucking with our heads he's trying to get us scared." Hunter looked at me and said, "I am getting scared by this shit, man! How the hell does he know about our past, along with our worst nightmares! I've been having the same goddamn dream over and over again with some nights I'm unable to fucking sleep without pissing myself!" Hunter took a few breathes then drank his coffee then asked, "What about you?" I said, "Well...during the 16th episode there was scene were both Sydney and Manson are using magic to get the information out of this guy. When it was Manson's turn, he made the poor bastard feel pain as disturbing images of people being burned, beaten and chopped along with screams in pain and terror could be heard then I saw images flashing on the screen which some of them look very much like my father when he was in the Korean war."

Hunter looked at me as he finished his coffee I said, "My theory is that somehow my father might have killed Osborne Louis's father during the Korean war, and he might not even be

American he could be half or pure Russian because why would a show use Russian names unless it's part of Osborne's life." Hunter said, "If that's true, then maybe Osborne Louis isn't his real name. Might have made it up so he could travel freely through US because if kept his Russian name would be looked down on like a cockroach." I said, "Yes that could be true as well, but I also fear that we might be part of Osborne's life and if our parents did something to damage or ruin him, I won't be surprised if he wanted to take his anger out on us." Hunter said, "You know the more I think about. How much Sydney sounded like that black girl I liked? But I never got the chance to go out with her so how would that affect me?" I said, "Not sure but we'll find out. Let's do what we can and once we have enough money saved up, we can go further with this as Manson is now pissed with us." Hunter said, "Fuck him. Nothing is going to make us stop." I said, "Goddamn right about that."

Hunter drove his Ford LTD working our first day as underground journalists while we both sat in silence. I guess what I learned so far, spooked us. When we came to a red light, Hunter turned his head over and asked, "Did the *me*, in the show say anything about my parents?" I said, "No." Hunter lightly shook his head I said, "Hey let's worry about that later, as we got work to do today." Hunter sighed and said, "True."

Once the light turned green Hunter drove to other side of Black Creek and we pulled into a parking lot of a building that looked like a small apartment. I asked, "This is it?" Hunter said, "Yep, it used to be an office from the early 70s. When the company went broke it was bought by Richard that's the guy, we're working for by the way he turned it into his underground magazine company back in 81 and has been doing very well."

Hunter locked the car doors and we walked towards the door of the building. Hunter knocked and a hidden panel on the door moved. We saw a face on the other side.

"Hey, I'm here with my good friend, Curtis. We're here to see Richard." Hunter explained.

The person on the other side said, "Aww yes he's waiting for you." The panel closed and we heard unlocking, then the door opened. We both stepped inside and followed the man upstairs, into the office area.

After going up some stairs we entered into the office area and saw Richard reading over the newspaper. He had dark brown hair, glasses, light blue eyes and wearing a sweater, black pants and black shoes.

When Richard lifted up his head he said, "Aww Hunter, please come in." He looked over to me and said, "You must be Curtis." I said, "Yes."

Richard said, "Well I'm glad you two are here. as the latest from News 6 is nothing but horse shit." He put the paper down showing an image of Scott standing with the new mayor I said, "I know what you mean by that."

Richard smiled and said, "Good now let's get you two started I have some addresses written down for you to ask questions and once you get everything you need come back and write it all down. We do have computers, so you won't have to use typewriters."

Richard gave Hunter the notebook with the addresses as Richard went over some more details about the job and we would be paid by the end of every week which was fine. We left and drove around the city. I handled the questions while Hunter wrote everything down, but both agreed we would take turns, so it wasn't always one person doing everything, but I was wondering something, "Was John still using that typewriter I bought him?"

Dec. 24
2:00-PM

Work had been going well. It was what Hunter and I were looking for. Sure, it was more work, but the pay was worth it. I would be able to save extra money. But first, I had to check with my parents and John. They always call me before Christmas day and I would come by to see them, bring gifts and they would always have something for me. But since I haven't heard a word from them, I wanted to know what the hell was really going on. When I pulled into the driveway, I saw my father's Oldsmobile and my mother's station wagon. I shifted the gear into Park then killed the engine as I got out seeing the living room light was on. I was about to walk in, I noticed that the trash bins were out. I just remembered that Tuesday was garbage day.

I had a sudden urge to look into the trash bins. When I walked over the leads were cover both of them. First one I opened was nothing but empty beer cans, Coke cans and milk bottles. I put the lead back on and went over to the 2nd trash bin and when I opened it, I saw the typewriter along with some of the books John had written in. I felt furies when I saw this I thought, "Who threw this out?! Was it my parents or John?!" When I picked up the typewriter, I notice most of the keys were damaged and when I checked the books the pages had been torn out. I dropped them and walked towards the front door and knocked loudly.

When the front door opened it was my father, he looked surprised to see me. His jaw opened a bit as I said with an annoyed tune, "Hello dad! Don't you remember your son, Curtis Parker?!" He said, "Umm Curtis I...I was about to call you." I said, "Sure you were! After the number of messages, I left on the phone." I saw his arm reaching for the door I grabbed him and pushed him out of the way as looked at him I asked raising my voice a bit, "Who the hell threw out John's typewriter and his books?!" My father stared at me, not saying anything I was tired of his bullshit. I slapped him hard across the face and yelled, "WHO!? He nearly fell over as I heard my mother getting up from the living room, I turned to her as seemed unhappy to see me.

I said, "Answer my goddamn question! Who threw out John's typewriter!? You know how much I spent on it!?" My mother raised her voice a bit and said, "Curtis, John isn't interested in writing anymore." I said, "Bullshit! He enjoyed writing!" My mother said, "Curtis, I think you should leave!" I asked, "Where is my brother then? I want to speak with him. Maybe all three of you have been lying to me. My father grabbed my arms and said, "Leave now!" Without thinking I punched him so hard in the face he fell down my mother looked shocked as I pushed her out of the way and stormed upstairs into John's room and when I opened the door, I was shocked what I saw.

His whole room had changed the wall had posters of The Manson & Barbara Show along with some fan drawings as well. His bookshelf now had different books and when I saw some of the titles, they were all about dark events of human history and war. I turned my head over as there was a very big TV on a fancy stand with another shelf that had VHS tapes and when I looked closer, they were all of that goddamn cartoon show! I felt so pissed off Manson and his fucking friends had ruined my little brother and my parents I turned around and walked out of the house as they didn't stop me. As I got into my Honda I started up and backed out of the driveway. When I turned my head, I saw John's face looking out the window from the bathroom he looked angry that I was here I turned my head away and drove off.

On my way back to my apartment I thought, "I'm going to make Manson and his friends pay for this! Turning my life upside down and ruining it! And if he dares to ruin Hunter's life any further, I won't stop until I find Manson or whoever the hell is behind this!" I saw a yellow light about to turn red I floored and sped through the four way stop as a car nearly hit me it blew it's horn, I stuck out my finger at them and kept speeding.

When I reached my apartment parking lot, I shifted the gear into park then killed the engine and sighed. I got out of my Honda locked the door and went inside the apartment I slowly walked up the five flights of stairs went towards my apartment door. As I pulled out my keyring, I suddenly notice a purple envelope on the floor I said, "Not in the mood for your fucking games." I kicked it and entered my apartment and locked the door. I took off my boots and winter coat as I walked towards the kitchen and grabbed myself a cold bottle of Dead Moon beer. I got the lid off and took a drink of it. When I stopped, I took a few breaths knowing after this month I would have enough money saved up for my plan to see what was really going on at my parents' house.

I thought about calling Harry and Trish to see how their children were and if they too are being brainwashed by that goddamn cartoon. I walked over to the living room sat down and turned on the TV. I haven't watched it in a while as I been watching more of those tapes as it showed more of us spreading lies to other groups of people while Manson and his gang were slowly taking back his land. As the TV came on, I held the remote in my right hand while the bottle of Dead Moon bear was in my left. I flipped through channels but some of the channels were out then I got nothing but static.

I tossed the remote away and went to drink my beer suddenly I heard Manson voice ask, "Nothing on TV?" When I looked back at the TV screen, I saw Manson looking at me while wearing his dark purple outfit.

I stared at him as he reached for his red bow tie fixed then said, "Seems your holidays aren't going too well. I thought a nice Christmas card would make you feel better." I said, "Fuck you, Manson!" He said, "Oh you think it's my fault that your parents stopped calling you or making your little brother John from writing. The truth is Curtis they chose not to, because of me." I said, "You're so full of shit!" Suddenly Manson's faced changed. It looked more sinister. He yelled loudly and his voice echoed around my room. "I AM FULL OF SHIT!? AM I?!" I jumped and nearly dropped my beer bottle as Manson face was very close to the screen as he spoke with a demonic voice, "IF YOU HARM JOHN OR TRY ANYTHING WITH HIM I WILL TEAR YOUR FUCKING EYES OUT!"

I yelled, "I would never harm my little brother but if you do!" Manson eyes glowed bright red and said, "ME?! YOU THINK I'M THAT CRUEL TO CHILDREN!? YOU HAVE SO MUCH TO LEARN CURTIS BECAUSE ADULTS LIKE YOU!" Suddenly he appeared standing in front of me as I could feel his strong hatred and his warm breath and yelled, "BECAUSE ADULTS LIKE YOU ARE SO FUCKING STUIPID!" He screamed as I swung my beer bottle at his head it smashed as he growled then punched me in the face I went flying over my sofa and landed onto the kitchen table it broke. My heart was racing, and my nose was broken.

As I began to calm down, I notice it was very quiet inside my apartment. I slowly stood up and felt blood I reached for a paper towel wiped it then turned to the TV as it was turn off. I went into the bathroom and bandaged my nose as I would have to get it checked out with the doctor and if he asked, I would just say I nearly got mugged. I got a face cloth and ran it under warm water I wiped my face and eyes then walked back into the living room to see the beer bottle I had smashed over Manson face was broken with some of the beer spilled onto the floor. I clean the mess up and got another bottle and I sat on my sofa.

Once me and Hunter had enough money, we would look further into this cartoon show as I wasn't going to let Manson get away whatever he was planning. He could try all he wants with his fucking tricks and scaring the living shit out of me, but it wasn't going to stop me or Hunter! I turned my head around and saw the broken table and thought, "I don't need it anyway I'll just use my coffee table then." I drank my beer feeling my heart rate starting to slow down but I still feared what Manson and his gang had planned for us next year.

Chapter 3

Jan.1.1985
9:00-AM

I sat in the living room eating breakfast with the TV on showing the weather forecast that we were still going to get hit hard with snow and it won't warm up until halfway through February. I was glad my nose had healed as the doctor believed my story. I found a magazine that talked about video cameras for setting up home security and a way to watch it in another room while not in the same place. It would use a dish that sends radio signals back to the other dish and shows what the video cameras were seeing. However, the cameras won't be able to turn so I would have to set them up in a way that would allow me to see what was going on and make sure nobody saw them.

I had read over how to set it up and planned to place an order for it but this video camera set up wasn't going to be cheap and even with the extra money I was making at work it wasn't enough so I would steal to get this video camera gear. Luckily, I lived here long enough to know where the rich live. As I finished my breakfast, I looked up at the TV showing the weather report again I reached for the remove and changed the channel when static came on but the program came back on.

It was an ad for gardening tools as it showed a couple wearing spring wear with the man said, "Aww glad that winter weather is over but we're going have to clean up the yard." The woman said, "Yes and to help us we have new gardening kit from Home

Depot." First it should some old dead trees as the man holding an axe said, "Only $25 dollars for our heavy-duty axes that are great for...chopping up limbs." Suddenly static came on the screen and it showed the man chopping off his wife with the axe then beheading her on top of a tree stump with blood poured out of her headless d. I stare in horror at the TV then more static came as it went back to normal.

It then showed the woman holding a pair of hedge clippers and said, "Make sure you trim those hedges as they...they can be a real bitch to cut." More static came and when it was it gone it showed the woman now covered in blood as she was cutting off fingers with arms sticking out of a wall. I could hear the sound of the fingers being sliced off followed by the screams of both men and women as she did this. I grabbed the remote and tried changing the channel, but it wasn't working, and I felt powerless to move.

Then it showed the man holding a hammer with a set of nails as he said, "The new hammers are built to last along with the toughest steel made nails that will last a lifetime." More static came and showed the man hammering nails into people placed on upside down crosses they howled in pain as blood poured and hear the bones cracking. Then the screen showed the naked bodies being placed along where the fence was supposed to be, but it was upside down crosses as the people who were nailed to it tried moving and moaned in pain.

Then it went back to the man now sitting on a riding lawn mower and said, "And get a load of the new 9000 model mowers." As he began moving it more static came on the screen as he looked at the camera and said while blood covered his face, "It's perfect for chopping up these motherfuckers." The screen then showed heads buried under the ground as it did a close up of the lawn mower running over the heads I could the people screaming followed by the sound of its spinning blades slicing off heads as splatter of blood, bones and other bits such as eyes, tongues or teeth would spit out of the lawn mower. More static came as I could hear what sounded like two people laughing and listening closely it was Manson and Barbara I thought, "Those sick bastards!"

Then it showed the woman holding a pile of sticks and said, "Honey, I got more to chop up here." He walked over and said, "We also have a stock full of chainsaws for only $195." As he pulled the cord with the chainsaw revving up more static came and attacked the woman she screamed and chopped her up with blood splattered all over his clothes along with the grass. When he turned to the camera he said, "So hurry up assholes and don't miss this fucking spring deal before it's too late." Suddenly he was whacked in the back of his head with an axe as it showed his blood-stained wife now chopping his body. I grabbed the remote and press the power button turning it off.

My brain was burning what I saw and feeling sick I looked at the time and thought, "Better place that order now." I got up went into the kitchen and called the security company and told them what I wanted. They told me I would have it by Friday this week and I would pay for the order with cash. I didn't have a credit card and knew those could be traced and didn't want the cops getting in the way.

I turned to where my kitchen table was and forgot it was damaged as I threw it out, I thought, "I can't stand this I need to get one." After I was done talking with the man, I hung up walked over to my closet grabbed my winter jacket then put my boots on then reached for my gloves I took my key ring out and left my apartment I needed to get out and clear my head. As I drove through the city feeling better, I went to a store where people would bring in stuff they didn't want and would sell them for a lower price.

I enter the store and heard old Christmas music playing as I walked past the shelves of books and went over to where the furniture was and overheard two women talking. One said, "I can't believe how many toys have come in since the first of January. Half of them won't even take out of the boxes." I stopped and listened in as the 2nd woman said, "It seems all the kids are talking about this cartoon show that's going around." The 1st woman asked, "What's it called?" The 2nd woman said, "The Manson & Barbara Show. I try to ask my children if they heard of it but they say they haven't. From the children that have seen it told me it's about a gang of animal people fighting against an evil kingdom, but I won't allow my children to watch such garbage as it's silly." 1st woman said, "I know what you mean cartoon violence is bad for the children." They went on I kept walking and looked at the tables and found one that would work as I would be able to take it apart and put it back together. I turned to see if there an employee to help me I saw where the toys were, and those women won't kidding.

It seem all the kids were getting hocked onto this cartoon, but I wondered if there any children that won't interested. When an employee came over, I asked a hand with the table and we carried it and had it taken apart so I could put it into my car I paid for it then checked the time. It was 10:45-AM I wasn't hungry yet so I would make lunch at my place later. I drove back to my apartment and took the table parts and carried it to my apartment room.

d didn't take me long to set up my new table and when I was done, I made myself two sandwiches along with a hot cup of coffee. I sat away from the living room and looked out the window. Sun light was shining through with light snow fall outside. I thought, "Which house should I rob in Black Hill Side?" The mayor's house was my first choice but heard he has guard dogs along with some weapons, so I won't be able to sneak in so easily despite the fact I hated him. I choice to pick a house that was empty to break in to. Once I had the gear, I would need to set it up in my parents' house but would need to do it while they were gone and had to make sure nobody saw me or Hunter. If everyone is glued to their TV screens, then I won't have any problems with this then.

I asked Hunter to keep his ears open if any more murders happen so we could get our hands on the evidence before the police did since it seemed they wanted to hide the truth from everyone. But that made me wonder, "If more children watch this cartoon will they talk about it more or act like it isn't real?" That was the 2nd time I heard someone else talking about the show. Maybe those who had stronger minds couldn't easily be brainwashed.

On the days I wasn't working I tried watching the tapes, but it took so long to get through the episodes as sometimes I was unable to watch anymore with my headaches would get worse. From what was going on it showed more of White Order and less of me and Hunter I guess Manson had a big nasty surprise waiting to show us. I turned my head over where I had left the tapes and had two more to go through then that would be it until Hunter and I found more to watch as I couldn't find the channel, they were airing them on.

1:00-AM

It was very foggy, cold and dead quiet in Black Hill Side. I was wearing all black along with my ski mask and leather gloves. I had parked my Honda up on the hills and won't have to worry about anyone seeing my car since who would be up at this hour. I had scanned the area and found a few large houses and mansions that looked empty with no cars in the driveway and were fully dark inside. I carefully went down the hill then walked towards the backyard and climbed over the gothic style iron fence. Once I was over it, I reached into my gym bag and took out the crowbar. I pried open a window and crawled inside. Slowly walking through the house, I went upstairs and went into the master bedroom. I turned on the lights since nobody was up. I searched through the dressers and closets until I found a safe.

It was an older style with a big knob along with a keyhole I knew this would take hours to open and finding the key which might not be even here. However, I had a faster way around it. I took a power drill then attached a large drill head to it that was covered in diamond dust. I stole this from a hardware store before I came here since I wasn't paying $300 bucks for it. I set the drill to full power then began drilling out keyhole. Judging the age of this safe I would say it was from the 30s or 40s that meant it would easily crack open.

It took about 5 minutes but I drilled through the keyhole and drilled out where the main lock was which didn't take that long. Once I broke through, I opened the safe. Inside were stacks of money I lightly grinned and took a plastic bag and toss it all inside.

But as I cleared out the money, I then saw a pistol along with some magazines and 5 boxes of ammo.

When I reached for the gun and pulled a CZ-75 pistol it had a jet-black finish with a dark wooden handle. I thought, "Should I take it? If I run into trouble, it would be smart to arm myself with a gun." I toss the gun along with the magazines and ammo then put everything away in my gym bag then stood up shut off the lights and went out the way I came. I climbed up the hill and nearly fell twice but was able to grab a tree branch and pull myself up. Once I got to my Honda, I unlocked the door got inside toss my gym back in the passenger seat started it up then sped off.

Jan. 4
11:30-AM

I stood in front of the booth that had thick glass with a speaker and an opening that could be only opened from the other side. I told the man my name and the order number as he typed it up on his computer and said, "Alright I'll go get it." He walked away I already had my wallet out with the money I stole from that house scoring myself $90.00 more than enough to continue this case as me and Hunter would be able to look further with this. As the man came with my order he said, "Ok that's $5.95 please." I said, "Sure thing." I started counting the money I felt the man was looking at me then asked, "Say, didn't you use to work for News 6?" I lifted my head up and asked, "Yes I use to?" The man said, "Use to watch you on News 6." I said, "Last I heard about that place they won't doing so well with that new guy." The man said, "Yeah so I'm stuck with News 18."

When I had the money, I paid him as he took it counted it quickly then passed me the box and asked, "Anything else?" I lightly smiled and said, "Nope this well do." I took the box as the man said, "Have a good day, Curtis." I said, "Thanks." It didn't take me long to drive back to my apartment I took out the manual and read through the pages as this was going to take me 3 or 4 hours to set up then I would have to test and if anything wasn't working that meant I would have to go back and fix it and try again. d knew there wasn't room for error I would have to get this right on the first try. I then remembered that on Sundays my parents would take John to church and do shopping. If I was lucky, they won't be home until after lunch as one way they would reward him for going was getting him McDonald's or pizza. This would be only day I could pull this off. I stood up and called him and he answered but sounded shaken up and said, "Oh Curtis it's getting worse! Every time I turn the TV on any commercial, news or late-night films it's always fucked up and violent!"

I said, "I been having the same thing too. Listen I'll need your help on Sunday." Hunter asked, "Alright what time do you need me at?" I said, "Early in the morning I'll come and get you." Hunter said, "Ok see you later." I said, "Ok Hunter bye."

Jan. 6
9:00-AM

Just as I thought my parents were leaving and they were taking mother's station wagon this would double our luck since that thing was slow. Once they were gone, I pulled into the driveway as we both got out. I had gym bag with the camera gear along with power tools. We wore plastic bags over our boots, so we won't bring snow inside the house. As I took my spare key, I suddenly notice the lock was different I said, "What the hell?" Hunter looked over and asked, "What?" I tried the key, but it didn't fit I said, "Shit! They must have changed the lock." Hunter said, "Here I'll handle that." I then saw Hunter take out a lock pick I asked, "Where did you get that?" Hunter said, "Got it from a friend." He quickly got the front door unlocked I quickly checked around and saw nobody was out.

It inside we took off the plastic bags and said, "Ok let's get started." I had already told Hunter the instructions, so he knew where he had to go. I went up into the attic and like I thought nothing had changed. I began setting up the radio dish as I would have set it in an area that would be able to pick up the signal. I saw a small circle shaped window that was in front of the house it had always been closed. I opened it just enough that would allow the dish to pick up the signal I then set the radio dish up then finished with the other electric stuff. Once that was done me and Hunter used power drills making big enough holes and placing the cameras in the two bedrooms, kitchen, living room and dining room. As Hunter finished up, I checked for the war photos and when I did find them, I couldn't believe it was the same photos that I saw during the Manson & Barbara Show. I had to leave them since if I took them my father might catch on that I broke into his house.

We left around 11:00-AM and drove back to my apartment and set up the 2nd half of this security gear. When I had set up the other radio dish, I had hocked up a keyboard to my TV and now I would be able to watch all the cameras through this but only one at a time. I said, "Alright let's see if it works." I flicked a switch on the radio dish then set my TV to video one and saw in color was the living room. Hunter said, "Alright." I said, "Ok next room." I typed on the keys and flipped through all 5 rooms and saw the cameras were working and I could hear every sound.

Hunter asked, "So you'll be able to record this as well?" I said, "Yes I got some blank tapes I'll be using." Hunter asked, "So how much did this thing cost?" I knew it was safe telling him since he wasn't going to rat me out. I said, "$5.95 which I borrowed." Hunter looked at me and asked, "Borrowed?" I said, "You know what I mean." Hunter said, "Oh so you visit Black Hill Side for some cash." I said, "Yeah it was only way besides we're going have to break the law here and there if we're going to stop Manson."

Hunter said, "If so, we should pick some fire power just in case." I said, "I also borrowed a pistol from the same place as well." Hunter asked, "Really?" I said, "Yeah got my hands on a CZ-75 pistol." Hunter said, "Good choice. I know a contact that can help us with guns if we need them." I said, "I also have extra cash which means we can use to help our investigate further with this." Hunter said, "d going to New Orleans?" I said, "Yes and Florida as we got find that cartoon network and see what they have as well." Hunter said, "Ok this all sounds good but who is going to watch John along with your parents?"

I thought, "Shit I forgot about that." I checked the cameras again as they won't home yet I said, "I wonder if someone else is looking into this matter as well. We can't be the only two investigating a cartoon show." Hunter said, "If there is, then how would we know. Hardly anyone is talking about this show to begin with as only the kids talk about it." I said, "I heard two women talking about when I went to get a new kitchen table." Hunter turned his head and notice I had a different table and turned back to me I said, "It was Manson he punched me out of my sofa, and I landed on the table with such force it broke it and my nose."

Hunter said, "Shit man! Did anyone else hear it?" I said, "No since my walls and flooring are soundproof but it seems when Manson or his friends are talking with someone, they seem to be able to block out any noises, so they won't be interrupted." Hunter said, "I guess so. But after that fucked up shit, I been having I now hardly watch the TV." I said, "Same here. When I was finished watching a weather report a nice commercial about gardening tools turned into a fucked-up torture/snuff film while hearing Manson and Barbara getting a kick out of it."

Hunter said, "Anyway we'll have to find a way around it unless one of us goes while the other stays." I said, "I would rather have you come along in case anything happens." Hunter said, "Let's see. How many more tapes do you have left to watch?" I said, "Only two and like I said before we haven't been shown that much." Hunter sighed and said, "Damn we're running out of options here. We can't just up and leave now."

I said, "Hang on I might be able to ask some of John's teachers if they have been noticing anything different about their students." Hunter said, "Good idea but you'll have to wait a bit since the heavy snow fall schools are still closed, I haven't seen any school buses driving at all." I said, "Great and with all this goddamn snow it seems it will never stop until spring comes around." I checked the cameras again I could hear a car pulling up in the driveway from the kitchen. I said, "That's my parents." Hunter and I watched on the TV screen we could hear them walking through the front door as they had bought lunch. However, as they took out the plates for them John got his lunch set and walked upstairs, I said, "He normally asks before going to eat in his room."

I changed camera now showed his bedroom as he sat in front of his big TV then turned it on. I said, "Hunter put in a blank tape." He did, placing it into the VHS I watched John flipping through channels backwards until he was on channel 13 I said, "The only channel that children can get." I press the record button and zoomed in so I could see what John was watching and sure enough it was The Manson & Barbara Show. We watched him eat as the show now had a new intro along with higher detail in the animation. Hunter said, "Guess we're on season 2 now." I said, "He has all the tapes to season 1." Hunter asked, "Where did he get it? I never seen the show for sale anywhere." I said, "From Manson who else."

When the show was finished it's intro, we heard Barbara voice say, "Episode 110 The Return Of The Tricksters." Hunter said, "Is that what their calling us?" As the John's TV screen faded to black for a few seconds then an image came up as it showed us standing in front of a large keyboard with a big screen and on it was the King. Hunter said, "It's creepy seeing our faces in this fucked up cartoon!" On John's screen the King said, "Very good work Curtis and Hunter we have gained more support which has doubled our numbers and plan on using them for small attacks that way we can weaker Manson's smaller areas then send our soldiers to the larger areas."

It then showed a close up of our faces on the show as the King said, "However I need to ask you two for a very risky mission." On the show I asked, "What's that?" The King said, "Our spy satellite shows Manson is having families leaving on this big ship." It then showed the screen showing a very large fancy looking steam ship. The King then said, "I want you two to sneak on board and sink it."

The screen then showed a map of where the ship would be going as the King said, "Once it reaches this area sink it and Manson will be force to send help and while he does this, we'll be able to gain more land from him. d and one last thing make sure to cover your tracks as I can't risk Manson and his gang finding this base." On the show I said, "We won't fail you King."

Just as the King went off screen, we saw a number flash on the screen, but it was too fast we didn't see it. I said, "Good thing

I am recording this as I'll be able to see what that number was." Hunter asked as it showed us on the TV show gearing up, "Do you think Manson is going to try and trick the kids that we're really evil?" I said, "I had bad feeling your right about that, but this is bullshit! We won't do something like this!" I then saw John turning his head over to the bed like someone was talking to him, but we didn't see anything then noticed on the screen more words flashed then John turn back at the screen faded black and went back showing the steam ship as anthro families were getting on board.

Hunter said, "I think I know what those words were?" I asked, "What?" Hunter said, "On John's screen it said, "Were watching you" so they can see anything that happens through the TV." I said, "So that adds more proof that Manson and his friends are in another world." It then showed Manson standing with Barbara, Sydney and Kane as it went closer to them. Manson said, "I want you three to watch this ship closely as I don't want to lose any more of my people."

Kane said, "We'll keep a close on everyone making sure there are no strangers on board." Barbara said, "You be careful Manson I sense things are going to start heating up." Manson lightly smiled and said, "I will, and I'll see you soon." They kissed for a bit then a black bat guard said, "Sir, we're ready to head out." Manson turned his head said, "Ok let's go." Manson and the black bat guard walked away as Kane asked, "So how many more families on coming on board?" Sydney said, "A lot more. I wish we could use an air ship as it would be faster." Barbara said, "We could have but the bloody White Order ships are forcing Hellen to use more air ships to keep them out of our land." Sydney crossed her arms and said, "Once we get these families to safety then we'll be able to deal with the White Order fools." Barbara turned her head to the families she said, "I can't wait until this war is over." Sydney said, "Same here." Kane looked up at the sky and d, "Looks like it's going to rain better get inside."

Then the screen faded to black and when it came back it showed the town with one building as it was very dark inside but as the screen zoomed in it showed me holding a high-tech binocular with Hunter in the background setting up the bombs. I said, "There still loading. We'll sneak on board just before the ship leaves then place the bombs in the lower deck then make our escape and have a boat come pick us up since the lifeboats will be all destroyed." It then showed Hunter finishing the bombs and said, "Good as I hate swimming." Hunter jaw dropped open I notice as he said, "That fucking bat! How the hell does he know I hate swimming?!"

I said, "I didn't know that." Hunter said, "How the hell did he know? I never told anyone that!" We saw on the TV screen the two characters leaving the building while wearing black robes and they turned invisible it followed the footsteps leading towards the ship. As the two characters got closer to the steam ship, they slowly walked around the bat guards and went on board the ship as it began to rain. Hunter on the TV said, "Hurry!" Once the two of us we're on the ship it then showed the last remaining families getting on board. Two bat guards followed them and closed the door as a loud horn blew letting everyone know that the ship was about to leave.

It then showed Barbara, Sydney and Kane checking with the families and guards making sure everyone was on board and no intruders. The screen showed different scenes of the steam ship, it then showed the lower level which was the engine room. Then the two of us placing bombs all over the ship while still wearing the black robes. Hunter on the TV said, "Almost done here." I said, "Same here." Just as went to place the next bomb suddenly a guard walked in and saw us. As the guard went to draw his side arm, I quickly punched him in the head then went to disarm as Hunter quickly came behind him and slid his throat with a knife.

I said, "Good timing. Quick hide the body." As it showed both of us hiding the body then setting up the bombs. Then it showed Kane walking towards the kitchen of the ship as picked up a bright green apple and ate it. Kane stopped to look out the window looking at the sea suddenly as a bright flash of lightning lit up the sky, he then saw boat speeding away from the steam ship his jaw dropped open and said, "Oh no! It's the Tricksters!" Kane turned to a guard and told them to get d, Sydney and the rest of the guards to lower levels.

It then showed us and, on the boat, as I looked back with the high-tech binoculars and zoomed on the steam ship I grinned and said, "Soon it's going to be kaboom time!" As it showed what I was seeing I d, "I use to say that!" Hunter turned to me know I was wondering how Manson knew so much about us. The screen faded black as John finish his lunch then when he turned to the screen drinking his Coke it came back as it showed Kane, Barbara and Sydney and the guards entering the engine room and saw all the workers had been killed along with the guard then notice the bombs on the wall.

Kane said, "Damn it! We have to disable these bombs before they go off!" Barbara looked at them but saw on the screen the timer was running closer to detection she turned her head back and said, "We won't have time!" Sydney said, "I'll handle this." Sydney lifted up arms then they glowed bright yellow as beams of light went all onto the bombs which caused the timer to stop as Sydney turned her head over where the boat was and opened a portal. She then lifted them up and threw them through it the portal closed.

d the screen went back to us I asked, "Where the hell is the kaboom?" Suddenly the yellow portal opened in front of us and out came the bombs. Hunter said, "Oh no!" Hunter sped away as the bombs crashed into the sea and exploded nearly hitting us, but one bomb caused the boat to flip. Hunter went underwater then showed me holding onto the boat looking for him then saw he went under. When I looked over at Hunter his face had turned white as a ghost with his jaw dropped open. I quickly looked back at the screen as it showed me saving him as we swam back to the surface and coming towards us was Manson guards. I turned to Hunter said, "I got an idea."

It then showed d guards armed with crossbows or short laser rifles which had Manson bat head logo on the stocks. As they aimed their weapons, they saw the boat flipped over and two black figures were seen standing on top as the boat sped towards them. I knew what was going to happen and I was right as Manson's guards were shooting at the two black cloaked figures, they saw their shots won't doing anything as it was a hologram. But before they could turn away the bomb blew up taking half of the guards out while the rest were knocked into the sea by the blast wave.

It then showed me swimming while Hunter was hanging on and looked a bit sick. When we made it to shore Hunter let go and lay on his back and coughed as I turned my head back to the steam ship moving away with the few guards returning. I looked at Hunter said, "We better leave before enforcements show up." Hunter slowly got up as we ran off then it went back to the steam ship as Kane, Barbara and Sydney standing in the bridge with Barbara holding onto two crystal balls as a mirror came out of the ceiling and it showed Manson face as he asked, "Barbara is something wrong?"

Barbara said, "Yes the Tricksters tried bombing the steam ship if it wasn't for Kane spotting them and Sydney getting rid of the bombs this ship and everyone on board would have been killed." Manson showed an annoyed look then asked, "And they escaped, didn't they?" Barbara said, "Yes they escaped by placing a bomb on their boat and send it back to the guards and swam towards shore." Manson said, "They might have gotten lucky this time but next time they won't be. I'll make sure to put up wanted posters so if anyone sees them, we can capture them and make them pay for their crimes." Kane said, "I sure like to get my hands on them and show them my tricks." Manson said, "We will for now just guard the ship until it reaches to safety as I'll make sure none of my people are harmed by the evil King." Barbara said, "Yes Manson."

It went back to us as we fled the town on our hover vehicle as I said, "We'll get them next time." Hunter said, "And hopefully not near the damn sea!" It showed the hover vehicle speeding off as the screen faded black as Barbara said, "Tune in next time for another exciting episode of The Manson & Barbara Show."

As it ended it showed John changing the channel but couldn't see the number it just looked like static, I then thought I could hear him speaking to someone but was talking in such a low voice I couldn't make out what he was saying. When John was finished, he turned off the TV then left the room. I changed the cameras following John was took his plate into the kitchen to wash it off. I quickly checked to see what my parents were doing but didn't see them. I then as I tried the next camera, I saw them in their bedroom having sex. I gasped and quickly changed the camera and said, "Didn't need to see that!"

I reached up and press the stop button and went to check on John but now I couldn't find him. Hunter said, "Damn this is really getting stranger by the minute." I said, "Where is John?" As I went through the cameras while skipping my parents' room Hunter asked, "Say is there anything in the basement?" I stopped and thought about it and said, "No, just the washer and dryer. Oh, my father has a work bench but what would John need it for." Hunter said, "He must be down there." I said, "I swear if this shit gets worse than we're going after Manson or whoever the hell is behind this."

Hunter asked, "Do you think that we saw is going to happen on the 13th?" I thought about it and said, "We don't have any cruise ships that take people from the docks mostly fishing and shipping stuff. Unless it's going to happen somewhere else." I checked the time it was 1:00-PM. Hunter said, "Ok I'm going to head back home I'll see you tomorrow for work." I said, "Ok Hunter." As Hunter went to leave the living room, he turned to me and said, "I'll call you if I hear anything happens so we can get more clues about this show." I said, "Alright...I feel that won't be long." Hunter lightly nodded his head and said, "I knew you were going to say that."

Feb. 11
11:45-AM

I watched John through the video cameras and saw whenever he was home the show would start so it seemed Manson wasn't running his cartoon on normal broadcasting time. And when John was watching, my parents never bothered him or called him downstairs if he went into his room to watch that damn show.

The episodes now showed the people that were tricked by us were fighting alongside The White Order which Manson and his gang weren't going down easily. I wondered what Manson was going to throw at us next but knew when me and Hunter found it, it wasn't going to be nice.

When I pulled into the parking lot, I saw Hunter's Ford LTD, and he stood behind the driver side door holding a newspaper. When I stopped my car and shifted the gear into Park then killed the engine I got out and walked over to him as Hunter said, "Shit has hit the fan again." When he handed me the newspaper, I saw on the front page it showed house in flames with police cars and fire trucks parked around it. I read the text belong as it stated that between Feb 3rd until today over 115 fires have happened across North America and even Canada as houses, churches, schools and day care centers have burned down with dozens of children have gone missing while some of the children have killed themselves from their crimes as not one was brought in alive.

I said, "Shit!" Hunter sighed and said, "Yeah it's fucked up but not one of these crimes has happened here yet. But I think the 13th there is going to be." I asked, "Did you look into anything that could match what we saw?" Hunter said, "I have looked every cruise ship, but Black Creek doesn't have anything that matches that." I said, "Wait a minute! Down south they use steam ships." Hunter said, "And New Orleans is in the southern area of the states." I said, "I think that's where that event is going to happen, but it doesn't happen it might be Manson trying to mess with our minds." Hunter said, "I don't know I think it might happen." I knew he was right as much I didn't want to believe it was going to happen but what could we do? It could be any steam ship and who would believe us that a cartoon show warned us of this event.

I gave Hunter back the newspaper as he tossed it into his car. We both locked the doors and went inside to work knowing our boss had stories for us to do. After going through the stories Richard gave us, I was sitting at my desk typing away at the computer I was now worried if John would be taken next and would he murder my parents? They haven't spoken to me ever since that day back in December, but I saw they haven't thrown out the pictures with me in it. I knew deep down inside they still cared for me, but Manson was trying to keep them away from me. I really felt this work wasn't imported anymore and I was wasting time just doing work to get paid. I wanted to go to Florida and New Orleans to see what me and Hunter could dig up as if we found a clue that led to Osborne Louis or one of his remaining family members or even the person behind this whole thing but every time, I thought of that one person came to my mind and that was Manson. If Osborne was really dead, then how would a cartoon character be doing all of this? I rubbed my eyes and thought, "I'll wait to the schools are opened then try to talk with Mr. Clark and see what he or the other teachers know what the hell is going on.

Feb.13
11:00-AM

It was very sunny outside and heard on the radio that the schools would be opened tomorrow after being closed for two weeks in a row. However, I won't be able to ask the teachers any questions since Monday meant they were going to be busy as hell. I would go on Tuesday and a bet a few of them won't mind if I ask them questions about their students specially John.

I felt sick from finishing those last two tapes. In the end it didn't show much of us, but I bet this season two would. As I finished my mug of coffee and egg sandwiches, I was about to get up to put plates into the dishwasher when I heard my phone ringing, I stood up reached for it and picked it up then said, "Hello?" I then heard Hunter said, "Put channel news 18 on!" I went into the living room and picked up the TV remote I press the power button and flipped through the channels then I felt my jaw dropped open as my eyes open wide. On the TV screen it showed a news helicopter filming an steam ship burning away as people were force to jumped off into the water. I said, "Oh shit!"

Hunter said, "I know man it's fucking bad!" I asked, "When did they start filming this?" Hunter said, "Just a few minutes ago." I had a bad feeling this would happen and knew things were only to get worse. Hunter said, "They haven't said anything else just that the steam ship suddenly burst into flames but shit man." I said, "Look on Tuesday I'm going to pay John's school a visit and ask his history teacher and see if he has notice anything different with the students along with the other teachers." Hunter asked, "Ok but if things get worse then what?" I was quite for a bit then said, "We'll go after whoever is behind this." Hunter said, "Ok that case I'm going to look into buying a gun just in case." I said, "Ok see you tomorrow, Hunter." Hunter said, "Alright see you tomorrow." We both hanged up as I looked at the screen and thought, "Wait if Manson showed that his gang stopped us then why did this happen?" I feared that we might be framed for a crime we didn't do.

Feb. 15
2:30-PM

I had parked my car a few blocks away as I knew if John saw my Honda it might cause to think I'm coming after him and didn't want my parents sending the cops over to my place as I felt they would search it. All the school buses pulled up as both young and young teens getting on board. But from where I was standing every signal one was talking about the fucking cartoon! I couldn't believe it. It was like everyone was on drugs and though it was the best goddamn thing in the world. I overheard some of them talking about the Tricksters had sunk a different steam ship which I didn't see on the show guess Manson added that off screen so he could make everyone watching show believe every word he said it was like those goddamn Christians trying to get millions of people to pay them money so god will keep them safe from harm.

I stood against a brick wall wearing my black winter coat, dark grey pants, boots, leather gloves and black sunglasses. Once all the kids got onto the bus, I didn't see John but knew had been going to school. When the buses left, I began walking towards the school. I went inside and went into the office I asked the woman behind the desk if I could speak with Mr. Clark and said I would find him in his history class on the 2nd floor in room 052. I went upstairs and when I saw the classroom the door was left open, I walked halfway inside and knocked on the door.

I then heard Mr. Clark asked, "Yes who is it?" I turned my head and saw him sitting at the desk. He had dark grey hair, thick glasses, wearing white button long sleeve shirt, jeans and brown shoes. I said, "Hi I'm Curtis Parker. I'm John's older brother mind if I ask you some questions?" Mr. Clark said, "Well...as a matter fact I have some questions to ask you since his parents aren't being helpful." I thought, "Just as I feared." I walked over towards him and took off my sunglasses and said, "Sure." Mr. Clark said, "Ok first of I have notice John and pretty much all of my students are acting strange. I gave them a test about history but instant of putting the right questions they all choice to name dark moments from the pass and when I ask them where they got these answers, they just kept on going that adults are a mistake."

I said, "That is strange." Mr. Clark said, "Also a few others have refused to do study and told me that learning about our past won't teach us anything and if we did, we would just repeat it." I asked, "So all the students are acting like this?" Mr. Clark looked up at me with a serious look I said, "You gotta be kidding me. It seems they all care about is that goddamn cartoon show."

Mr. Clark said, "Yes that as well. During lunch break all the teachers talked about this cartoon show the Manson & Barbara Show as Mrs. Red stated that science isn't learning the human race to success it will only lead to our downfall." I said, "It seems like their parents are leading them read books about doomsday events. I tried speaking with my parents but both them and John won't talk to me. Hell, they don't even act the same as I once knew them." Mr. Clark sighed and said, "I tried talking with most of my student parents and don't believe the cartoon show isn't real or act like I'm not doing my job right. We'll getting fed up and our principal is planning on having a speech about this cartoon as we can't teach the students right then we'll have to action against this show."

I said, "I tried looking into it on the day it came out but so far I don't have much to go on and was hoping you might have something that would help me." Mr. Clark said, "Sadly I don't." I asked, "Anything else strange with the students?" Mr. Clark said, "Yes. I notice some of them haven't shown up and when we tried phoning their parents, we had no luck." I asked, "Would I be able to see numbers? I'm reporter." Mr. Clark said, "Sorry the principal has that list, and he won't allow anyone to have them." I knew there was nothing else to go on here I said, "Ok but do me a flavor Mr. Clark." I grabbed a scrap piece of paper from the trash bin took a pen from his desk and wrote my apartment number and said, "If you find anything else going on call me as you can trust me."

Mr. Clark looked at my number then back at me and said, "Alright just between us." I said, "Works fine with me. Thanks for your time." I left the classroom and walked out of the school putting my sunglasses back on. Walking towards my Honda I saw a ticket under my wiper blade I sighed and thought, "Their no law of parking here!" Just as I went to look at it, I heard a deep voice behind me, "Hey you." When I turned my head halfway around, I saw a big fist ram into my face as I was knocked out cold.

When I woke up, I felt a sharp stinging pain in my nose and my vision was burly I took off my broken sunglasses when my sight came back and saw my Honda was gone, I looked around as it was very foggy with thick snow fall, I moaned then slowly stood up. When I looked where I was knocked out, I didn't see any foot prints I thought, "This isn't good at all." I began walking down the sidewalk then waved down a taxi to take me back to my apartment.

As I sat waiting to get back home, I was trying to think what hell to do, "Should I call the police and tell them someone stole my car? Or not say anything about it?" I feared if I went to the cops, they might take me in with evidence against me and Hunter for a crime that we didn't do. When I got home, I paid the cab driver and got out then went inside and walked upstairs and reached my room.

Once I entered my room I locked by door and walked into the kitchen I picked up the phone and looked at the time. It was 6:15-PM I had been out for 3 hours and nobody had notice me? I called Hunter to see if he was alright when he answered I heard him yang and asked, "Hello?" I said, "Hunter it's me." Hunter said, "Oh hey Curtis what's up?" I sighed and said, "Not good man." Hunter said, "Let me guess the teachers won't that much help." I said, "Well I only spoke to one Mr. Clark and told me he and the other teachers had notice both their students and parents are acting different and can't get a straight answer out of them."

Hunter said, "So they all know about the cartoon show then." I said, "Yes and their principal wants to make a speech about it, but he isn't going to get any luck with that." Hunter asked, "And what else?" I said, "Someone stole my car." Hunter asked, "What? Someone stole your car?" I said, "Yes when I finish talking with Mr. Clark, I walked back to my Honda to find a ticket on it when I went to look at it someone came up behind and I was knocked out for 3 hours. I just got home from a taxi." Hunter asked, "Who the hell would steal your car?!" I said, "I have a gut feeling it's going to be used for that steam ship thing I just know it." Hunter said, "Damn. Alright I'll have to pick you up for work then but are you sure you can't call the cops?" I said, "No I bet if I called them and if they find my car there will be something in it that will make them ask a dozen questions for a crime that I didn't do."

Hunter asked, "Ok I'll keep my eyes for any trouble and listen to the radio just in case. Say anything going on the show?" I said, "No that's what worries me." Hunter and I were quiet for a bit then he said, "Ok update me if anything happens." I said, "You do the same and watch your back." Hunter said, "I will. Ok talk to you later." I said, "Alright see you later." We both hanged up as I felt sweat running down my forehead, I feared that me and Hunter were in deep shit now and there was no turning back from it.

Feb. 17
10:00-AM

I woke up and heard the phone ringing I got up only wearing my boxer shorts. I left my bedroom and into the kitchen and answered the phone. I rubbed my eyes and asked, "Hello?" I then heard Mr. Clark voice, "Ummm…Curtis, is that you?" I asked, "Mr. Clark?"

He said, "Yes it's me. My wife found a notebook and I looked over it last night and what I found it quite shocking." I asked, "What's on it?" Mr. Clark said, "I don't wish to speak about it over the phone. Can you meet me in person?" I said, "Sure." Mr. Clark said, "Meet me at the parking lot at the downtown mall at 11:30 don't be late." He hung up before I could ask anything else. I looked at the time and knew I would have to get there right away. I quickly got dress then hopped on a city bus as it would save me some time.

d I got the downtown mall, it was empty as the place was always closed on Sundays. I was about 10 minutes early so I sat in a bus stop and waited for Mr. Clark to show up. And when he did, I saw a silver 83 Jaguar XJ6 Vanden Plas pull up into the parking lot. I knew it had to be Mr. Clark I stood up and began walking towards the Jaguar as he made a U-turn then killed the engine as I walked over to the passenger side of the Jaguar. I got inside as he asked, "Did anyone follow you?" I said, "No I haven't seen anyone follow me." Mr. Clark asked, "Where is your car?" Knowing he would get nervous if I told him, so I said, "I parked it somewhere else, so I just walked over here." I turned to him and asked, "No school today?" Mr. Clark sighed and said, "Not a single student has shown up today. We tried contacting them and haven't gotten a call back."

Mr. Clark shook his head and said, "Open the glove box." I looked over to it and opened it and inside was a black notebook I took it out and closed glove box then took off my one glove so I could flip through the pages and inside was handwritten plans for all the children of Black Creek for burning buildings. I few more pages I flipped and stated which adults needed to be taken out and at the top spot was me and Hunter. It had our full names I turned to Mr. Clark with a shock look as he said, "My wife thought about going to the police when she saw this, but I wanted you to see it first since I heard that one of the French teachers tried talking to the police about this and they didn't believe his story." I said, "Just as I thought."

Mr. Clark asked, "So, this Manson & Barbara Show. What is it about?" I closed d notebook turned my head over to him and said, "It's about... Suddenly I heard a loud smack then watched as Mr. Clark's face exploded with blood splattered onto me followed by shards of broken glass which flew passed my face. I yelled, "SHIT!" When I turn my head to the front windshield, I saw dark purple 85 Chevrolet Astro Van's with dark tinted windows then speeding pass them were 5 dark purple Dodge Diplomat speeding towards me.

I notice beside the two dark purple Astro Vans were two figures wearing dark purple or black suits with big fedora hats with cloths covering up their faces and dark sunglasses and were holding rifles. They fired more shots as I quickly ducked my head hearing the speeding bullets above my head, I quickly opened up Mr. Clark driver side door pushed his body out then closed the door. I heard the 5 Dodge Diplomat getting closer to me. I quickly turned the key and heard the V12 engine roar to life I quickly shifted the gear back then press my foot down hard onto the gas pedal burning rubber I peeked my head and saw the leading Dodge Diplomat getting closer to me. I quickly turned the steering wheel then shifted the gear into Drive and press my foot down hard as I tried to get out of the parking lot.

I breathed, "Shit! Shit! SHIT! I should have brought my fucking gun with me!" As I got back onto the main street, I saw the 4-way stop had turned red I blew my horn which was very loud as I nearly got hit by a truck, but the speeding Dodge Diplomats were keeping up with me. I felt whoever was driving those cars would kill me if they caught me. I made a sharp right turn and slid sideways into a car as I turned back onto the road then made a hard left. I drove pass the slow cars with a few blowing their horns at us. Suddenly I saw a figure sticking his body halfway out the passenger window holding a machine gun that looked like from the 30s with a big drum magazine my eyes open wide as he was about to fire it. I quickly slammed on the brakes the dark purple Dodge Diplomat rammed into me but caused the gunner to get thrown out of the car and crash into a power pole I quickly press my foot back onto the gas pedal speeding away.

I looked up in the view mirror and saw he got back up and ran into the car with the other 4 Dodge Diplomats were chasing me.

When I looked ahead of me suddenly saw a row of cars blocking the way with the stop light red. There was heavy traffic on the other side. I quickly drove onto the sidewalk and blew the horn forcing people to run out of the way I slowed down a bit then made a right turn speeding off with a car nearly hitting me. I looked up in the view mirror and saw the dark purple Dodge Diplomats were speeding after me. Then out of the corner of my left eye the dark purple Chevrolet Astro Van rammed into the left side causing the Jaguar to spin out and hit a parked sedan. My neck felt liked it got thrashed around I quickly press my foot onto the gas pedal and sped off before they could get close to me. I made a hard left speeding down a narrow street.

Speeding up alongside me was that Dodge Diplomat I turned my head and saw the gunner who was a bat man he was just like Manson's guards from the show, but he was fucking real!" He grinned and was about to fire when I saw a parked car. I ducked as a row of bullets nearly hit me, but I rammed the dark purple Dodge Diplomat into the parked car as it crashed head on and flipped through the air and landed inside a jewelry store.

Suddenly two dark purple Chevrolet Astro Vans blocked my way as the sliding doors opened with 6 bat men wearing purple or black suits and holding those machine guns. I yelled, "GOTTA BE FUCKING KIDDING ME!" I then saw an alley way on my right side I made a hard right and ducked my head as bullets went through the back door and rear window. The alleyway was tight I could hear the walls touching the Jaguar as the 4 dark purple Dodges were still chasing me. I kept going fast and prayed that a car won't hit me when I got out. When I did a black pickup truck crashed into the dark purple Dodge Diplomat blocking the rest. I made a left turn and kept speeding.

My heart was racing with my eyes looking everywhere for any more of Manson goons. I thought, "If I take the highway I can quickly get to my apartment and warn Hunter what's going on." Just as I was about to do that suddenly the dark purple Dodges were back, and they were shooting at me. I could hear those bullets tearing through the metal and seats I made a sharp left turn and drove onto a road which I drove through roadblock signs as thick bright yellow wooden boards went flying in the air.

Suddenly ahead of me was a big bulldozer I wasn't going have time to stop. I grabbed the notebook opened the driver side door and jumped out of the Jaguar rolling on the hard cold ground but landed in a ditch. I watched the dark purple Dodges speeding after the Jaguar as it crashed into the bulldozer they stopped and waited for a bit. I quickly fled the scene before they realized I jumped out of the car. I ran down the sidewalk with a few people looking at me as I didn't stop, I kept running and running until I got to my apartment. I quickly entered the number on the keypad and opened the door and rushed to my apartment room.

Once inside I locked the door and felt my heart was going to explode from my chest. I took heavy breathes as I thought, "I can't fucking believe it! One minute I'm talking with a teacher in his car suddenly I'm in a goddamn car chase and nearly get killed! Shit has really hit the fucking fan!" I ran into my kitchen and picked up the phone, but the line was dead. I said, "No! This can't be fucking happening!" I tried again but it wasn't working then suddenly I heard Manson say, "Phone trouble?" d quickly turned my head to see Manson on my TV wearing his purple suit as he grinned at me.

I went into the living room and said, "You motherfucker!" Manson lightly laughed and said, "I'll hand it to you Curtis you can really drive. Maybe you should have went with that racing career as that might have kept you alive long enough but sadly d game of ours has to come to an end. I'm sure the children will love the chase I'll have to recreate for them as they'll see you pushed your luck too far." I said, "Whatever the hell you are planning I will stop you!" Manson laughed as his eyes glowed a bit bright red and said, "Oh Curtis when you understand you cannot beat me as I have already won." I raised an eyebrow and asked, "Already won what!?" Manson lightly laughed and said, "I know you been watching them Curtis through those video cameras. At first, I was very annoyed as you found a way around the tapes you have been watching as I specially made sure only children can watch it. Not adults but then I had idea how to get rid of you for good. Now sit down and relax for a bit you'll pass out if you don't rest."

I felt his eyes staring into mine as I suddenly felt weak and fell onto the sofa Manson d, "Good now relax and enjoy this special picture I made just for you." Suddenly the TV screen had static then when it came back it showed my parents' house through the video cameras then it showed me entering the house as I went into the kitchen then grabbed sharp knives, wooden rolling pin, meat cleaver and a cheese grater. I then saw myself looking up at the camera with a grin then suddenly static came and it showed Manson holding it he laughed as the camera went out. But when it came back it showed my mother tied up in her bed fully naked with myself standing next to her body as I looked up the camera static came now it was Manson, he said, "Curtis, you'll wish you took my warning serious but since you haven't you must be punished."

My heart was beating fast with my eyes locked onto the TV screen I feared what was about to happen I couldn't move nor speak I felt helpless and powerless to do anything that was about to happen. Manson picked up the rolling pin, but I notice attached to it was razor blades the camera zoomed in on my mother's pussy as static came now showed me forcing the rolling pin into as I could hear screaming in pain. I tried to close my eyes, but couldn't I then saw blood oozing out of her and screamed louder. Then it showed me stabbing her arms, legs and upper chest area with the knifes. Screams into loud howls of pain. I felt sick to my stomach watching this. Then the camera zoomed on my mother's face with a bit of static now showing Manson holding the cheese grater he grinned at the camera then turned back to my mother's face and began rubbing it with such hard force her flesh was being sliced off as blood poured down from her face and onto the bed. My eyes were getting watery and felt I was going to cry I wanted to scream to make this shit stop but couldn't do anything!

When Manson was done, he lifted up the cheese grater and my mother's face was badly damaged I start to sob and manage to say, "Please, stop this!" Manson looked at the camera as it zoomed out and said, "Were not done yet Curtis." Static came as it showed my father tied up in the living room with rope and he too was naked. Manson looked up at the camera now holding my baseball bat and said, "I'm glad to see you understand the anger I feel but maybe after this you'll learn to not stick your nose where it shouldn't be." He turned to my father as static went over the screen now showed me as I began beating my father to death with the bat. I could hear the sickening sounds of his bones breaking, his cries of pain.

Then it showed me picking up two forks and stabbed out both of my father's eyes and tore them out. I felt my face was turning green with my eyes so watery I was going to break down in tears. Then I saw myself picking up a pair of scissors as I cut off his dick and ball sack then forced it down his throat and sliced off his fingers and toes. I yelled, "FUCKING STOP IT!" I cried as it showed me finishing off my father as I slid his throat with blood spraying onto me. The screen went blank as I cried then rubbed out my eyes and when I looked up Manson stood in front of and said, "There now that you have finished watching my picture, I made for you I thought the locate police would love to see it as well. However, when they watch it they won't see me but... Manson changed into me pointed at the screen and said, "But you instead." He laughed like me then changed back into himself and said, "So enjoy the rest of your life in an insane asylum as the world won't be able to look at you the same again and for you little brother John." Manson grinned with his eyes glowing bright red he laughed with a demonic voice and said, "He'll always be with me." He laughed then the screen faded black I covered my eyes fearing that my parents were dead, John had been taken by Manson and now framed me for murder!

I thought, "What about Hunter? Did Manson and his other sick friends get to him too or did the police already got him?" Suddenly I heard sirens coming here I knew I had two choices now. Be thrown away for the rest of my life for things I didn't do or go after Manson and stop him! I remembered the good times I had with my parents and John. I wanted those moments to come back again. I quickly got grabbed my gym bag put in all the tapes I had, the sketch book, money, my CZ-75 with all the magazines, wallet and notebook. I zipped it up and ran into my bedroom window I opened the window fully then crawled out and quickly ran down the narrow alleyway. As I was about exit suddenly 3 black helicopters came flying, I stopped myself in time and pressed my back against the wooden fence and waited them to fly over then ran over to the next alley way and just in time. An armored SWAT truck along with black sedans which I knew were the FBI. Me and Hunter were really in deep shit now!

I avoided being out in the public too long and made my way to Hunter's house and saw his car was still there. I checked the time it as already 1-PM we had to get the hell out of Black Creek fast! I went to the front to door to knock but suddenly it opened as it was Hunter he said, "Oh Curtis it's you. Quickly get inside!" As I went inside Hunter told the bad news I knew that was coming. He said, "It's all over the fucking news! They claim that you brutally murdered your parents while recording the whole thing and have kidnapped your little brother." I said, "Bullshit! I didn't fucking do it! It was that motherfucker Manson!" Hunter said, "I know but there more. The police found your car loaded with C4, pipe bombs and enough shit to get the fucking feds after us as they also linked me to that steam ship bombing!"

I said, "You know what that means we got to get the hell out of here!" Hunter said, "Damn right but if we're going to stop Manson, we have to be careful as one mistake and we're dead. I know a route we can take but we better hurry before the feds block out ways in and out of Black Creek. Just let me get a few things." I asked, "Hunter did you get a gun?" Hunter said, "No but I'll get one later." Hunter quickly got his things as we ran back outside into his black Ford LTD, he started it up and drove off and turned on his CB radio as we heard both the cops and FBI looking for us. Hunter said, "Shit! They know what car I'm driving! I know a short cut I get out of here in time." Hunter made a sharp left turn going over 60 MPH I said, "I went to speak with Mr. Clark today he gave me note book his wife found during her class it has names of buildings to be burned and people mostly adults to be killed and we're at the top spot."

Hunter looked worried I added, "And just when I was about to tell him what the show was about, he was shot and I was chased by Manson's goons in dark purple cars and vans and nearly got killed by them." Hunter asked, "Manson guards those black bats?" I said, "Yeah! They looked just like from the show but fucking real." Hunter turned his head and said, "Shit man! This is really not good!" Then we heard police radio, "All units! All units Hunter's black Ford LTD is not in the driveway be on the lookout for a black 83 Ford LTD." I said, "If we stay on the roads too long, they'll find us!" Hunter said, "Wait! I know a way out of here it will take longer but it will throw them off." I asked, "Where?" Hunter asked, "Remember the old stone bridge that leads into the forest?" I said, "Yeah." Hunter said, "We'll ditch my car their and travel on foot if we're lucky enough we can grab some wheels are make our way to Florida then head to New Orleans and see what we can find on Osborne Louis."

d the time we got the bridge it was a 3:00-PM I couldn't believe nobody thought of checking here then again Black Creek has a lot of ground to cover. We took all that we could carry and walked together on the stone bridge as cold wind blew against us. Sure, we would freeze our asses off but won't have to worry about the cops finding us.

No trains passed by as we walked with heavy snow fall coming down it would help cover our tracks and I bet Hunter's car was already covered up by the snow. I did hear helicopters flying far off in the distance, but they won't find us. We were quiet since we didn't want anyone to hear us, we also knew that hunters would go deep into the forest to hunt which it was against the law, but the hard-core type didn't give a shit. We came to a stone tunnel with a light above it that was glowing brightly while making a loud buzzing noise. Hunter said, "I need to rest up for bit." We entered inside the tunnel and sat down I sighed then said, "Once we're out of Black Creek we have to change our looks since the feds are going to be putting wanted posters everywhere."

d lightly nodded his head and said, "We'll also need to make fake ID's and get our hands on some CB radios since knowing where the heat is first will keep us a step ahead of them. Also we'll need guns as we don't know who we'll be going up against." I said, "Hunter. If we get the cops or feds after us, they'll shoot first and won't ask any questions of their orders. If it comes between us and them, I'm not going to be taken alive." Hunter said, "Same here man nothing is going to stop us."

I turned my head looking down both ends of the tunnel then rubbing my eyes Hunter said, "Alright let's get going." We stood up and continued our long walk down the tunnel but as we walked, I pulled my gym out and pulled the zipper opening it then reached in and took out the CZ-75 then the five magazines and placed them into my jacket pocket. I then took out my wallet which had $195 dollars in it and placed it into my left pocket then closed the gym back and placed the strap over my shoulder. I flicked the safety off so if I had to use it, I would be ready.

Deeper into the forest with the sky starting to get dark I thought, "Damn it! Wish I grabbed my flashlight before I left." I turn to Hunter and asked, "Say, do you have your lock pick?" Hunter looked over at me and said, "Yeah didn't forget that." I said, "Good." Hunter said, "There will be another bridge just a few miles up, but we don't wanna go near a city. As soon as we reach the end of the next tunnel we'll begin cutting through the forest and should be able to find a truck stop that's close by to the highway we'll use that to make our way towards Florida."

I said, "I know that truck stop they also have a gun shop as. Always closed on after 7-PM." Hunter said, "Great we'll be able to pick up some extra fire power and maybe a truck or a 4-door car but something fast." When we walked through the thick forest it was very dark with only the bright moon light above us as our only source of light.

The ground was hard, very cold and covered in thick fog while heavy snow fall kept coming down on us. We haven't heard any helicopters or seen anyone else I guess the cops and feds were too busy searching around Black Creek thinking we were dumb enough to try hiding it out in the city or taking a different route.

But once covered every inch of Black Creek they would start looking into the nearby forests for us and they would be armed as well. My face felt cold as I would wipe my nose and kept my ears open for any sudden noises, but it was dead quiet and didn't like it. I held my CZ-75 tightly in my right hand but knew when the time came to use it, I would have to make my shots count I didn't want to waste ammo.

Suddenly we both stopped when we heard a loud thumping noise Hunter said, "Shit! It's a helicopter!" We looked for cover and found a big think tree we ran over to it and got low to the ground as we could hear a helicopter flying over with a bright spotlight. It moved all over the place but when the light shined on the tree that we were hiding behind it, it didn't move for a minute I thought it found us, but it moved and flew over us. I blew out air and waited for a bit then stood up and began walking again Hunter whispered, "That was too fucking close." I said, "No shit."

Hunter checked the time as I forgot my watch he said, "It's already 8:30-PM. It will take us an hour or two to reach the truck stop and get something to eat." I asked, "That helicopter do you think they found your car?" Hunter looked up at the sky and said, "No if they did, they would have been already crawling all over this place. But I bet by morning they'll find it we better keep moving." We walked on with my legs feeling cold along with my eyes as I would rub them bit to keep them warm.

10:00-PM

We reached the truck stop its big empty parking lot was lit up by the 4 street light poles. The gas station was closed but a few of its neon lights were still on inside. The gun shop along with the big cafe had also closed me and Hunter checked both ends of the street twice so the minute we crossed the road no cars were driving by. Once we saw the coast was clear I climbed over the hill followed by Hunter and ran across the street. First, we went over to the gun store as Hunter took out his pick lock while I watched over him and didn't see any head lights coming down the end of the streets or helicopters. I then heard Hunter said, "I got it." He opened the door and we both went inside.

Hunter said, "Holy shit! Enough weapons in here to last a small war." I said, "Remember we're only taking what we need." Hunter said, "Yeah, yeah I know but we still need good stopping power when we come up against the heat or Manson." Hunter went behind the desk and using his lock pick got the glass case sliding door opened and reached for the first pistol he could grab his hands on. It was an SIG Sauer P226 he looked at it and said, "Very nice." Then took magazines for it and asked, "Say your gun is 9MM right?" I said, "Yeah." Hunter knelled down and picked up ammo boxes for it and said, "One half for you the other half for me."

Next gun Hunter picked out was a Mossberg 500 Cruiser shotgun which had a shoulder strap attached to it. Hunter said, "This should work for us." I said, "Not bad but since I been hunting before I like something with more kick to it." I went over and grabbed Remington 870 Marine Magnum and said, "Grab some metal slug that stuff packs one hell of a punch when it hits its target." Hunter looked through the shotgun shells and grabbed a couple boxes which showed the image of blue shells on them.

I then saw two Colt M1911's I turned to Hunter and asked,

"Say should we take two extra pistols just in case?" Hunter said, "Sure, why." I grabbed them and took the ammo for them which was .45 Hunter grabbed a duffel bag and we put the weapons we were taking along with the ammo. Hunter said, "Still got room for more if we want to take anything outs." I looked on the gun rack and most bolt action rifles and shotguns then saw two Ruger Mini-14's with wooden stocks I said, "We'll take those." Hunter looked at the two semi-auto rifles I pointed at he and took them off the rack I asked, "What ammo does it take?" Hunter looked at the magazine and said, "Remington .223" I found the ammo and grabbed all of it. Once we had it into a duffel bag, I grabbed one for myself as we left the gun shop then looked around for any parked vehicles but saw none.

Hunter sighed and said, "I guess we're still walking at this point." Suddenly we heard a truck coming we turned our heads, and it was coming behind us. We quickly ran over to the gas station and saw a dark green 81 Ford Bronco with dark tinted windows, fog lights, heavy duty tires. When it came to a full stop a big man came out as he said, "Son of a bitch! I wish I had a someone to guard the damn place!" As he came into view, we saw the big man wearing winter clothing and holding a revolver in his right hand. Hunter turned to me and whispered, "This is our chance let's sneak up on him and take his truck." I knew it would be walking but we had to be careful as this guy wasn't going to screw around with us.

Me and Hunter slowly went over to the gun shop as we could hear him swearing his mouth knowing his weapons were stolen. Hunter was holding his SIG Sauer P226 while I aimed my CZ-75 just we got close to the door I peeked through the window as he was standing at the front of his desk about to pick up the phone, I quickly opened the door he lifted up his and went to pick up his gun but I shot the phone destroying and raised my voice and said, "Don't move!" Hunter came in grabbed his gun a Smith & Wesson Model 60 with an 5-inch barrel.

I moved closer to him and said, "Give me the keys to your truck." He did what I asked as he said, "You won't get away for the horrible things you did." Hunter went behind him as I said, "Said who?" Hunter punched him in the head knocking him out cold and pulled his body into the back and closed the door. We ran off and hopped into his Ford Bronco and drove off. Before going onto the highway Hunter pulled into a McDonald's drive through as the guy working was too busy to notice that we were wanted or maybe didn't hear it yet.

Hunter drove onto the highway as we ate our late dinner, but we had the radio on and when I found the news station we heard, "Continuing our breaking story the FBI is on the lookout for two men Curtis Parker and Hunter Cunningham believe to be responsible for the New Orleans steam ship bombing as it was reported to have a history against non-white people." Hunter said, "Bullshit!" Then we heard, "It's also reported that Curtis and Hunter have suffered stress and anger from being fired from their news network station taking part in mass murder, arson and kidnapping as the latest was John Curtis his younger brother and had filmed himself killing his parents in a very graphic murder. Police found hidden cameras in the house and contacted to it was a camera control setup in Curtis apartment. FBI and police ask everyone to keep a look out for these two wanted criminals as they are reported to be armed and extremely dangerous. They were last seen in Black Creek and have disappeared from the area which it's strongly believe they are trying to escape."

The person then went to another story Hunter shook his head and said, "How is any of this possible!? How the hell does a cartoon character know so much about us, yet we know hardly anything about them!" I thought about what he said, and each time Manson or Barbara were playing tricks on us or trying to scare us they always came from the TV. That boy Sam stated they were being watched through the TV. I said, "I guess we really are dealing with a bunch of cartoon characters." Hunter turned his head over at me and asked, "What?" I said, "I get it now. Manson his girlfriend Barbara and their friends are the ones who are behind this. And they living inside the TV world or the Dark Kingdom and have the power to control and brainwash anyone to do their bidding."

Hunter turned his to face the road and said, "As crazy as that sounds it's the truth after all we saw both Manson in person while only those two female characters in our dreams. d me think of black magic or some alternate dimension." I said, "I'm sure we'll find the answers were looking for but my idea is that they been watching us through TV and maybe are family tree might be linked with Osborne Louis as well." Hunter said, "We'll see about that. Remember where that cartoon network was in Miami?" I said, "Yeah shouldn't be too hard finding that place."

Hunter said, "But first before we go, we have to come up with fake ID's and change our looks." I asked, "What do you got in mind?" Hunter said, "First we'll shave off our hair then grab wigs, glasses and anything else so people won't know it's us." I said, "I'm also going to have to talk with a different voice since people know me from my News 6 days." Hunter said, "Yeah that too. But we won't be able to drive this Bronco for long. We'll have to change vehicles to keep heat off our tracks." I said, "We should only spend one night at cheap a hotel and avoid spending too much time in the public." Hunter nodded his head and said, "But first let's get far away from Black Creek as possible."

We finished our dinner then a few miles into the drive we pulled over to relieve ourselves then got back into the Ford Bronco, luckily for us the weather was getting nasty so there won't be that many police cars out. Those that we saw didn't know what vehicle we were in yet. By 2 in the morning we we're now out of the Black Creek area and got off the highway driving through North Carolina. Hunter pulled over into a small hotel and we were the only ones there. He paid for one room and took our luck no TV. We both passed out on the bed from the long drive but knew we still had a ways to go.

Feb.18
11:00-AM

I woke up then heard the shower going I rubbed my eyes then slowly stood up in the bed which I didn't find that comfortable I stand up then raised my arms and cracked my neck. My mouth felt very dry I then heard the bathroom door open as Hunter wearing the same clothes, he had yesterday he said, "Morning." I asked, "Sleep well?" Hunter said, "Yeah. Need to take a shower before we go?" I said, "No but could use something to eat." Hunter said, "Same here. We'll grab something to eat then get what we need to change our looks then ditch the Bronco." I said, "Alright, let's get going then."

We left the hotel and this time I drove while Hunter pulled out a map, he found in the glove book. He said, "If we stick to this road, we avoid the heat as they'll be busy checking highways then we'll drive through South Carolina to Georgia then we'll be in Florida." As I went to talk suddenly, I notice ahead of us were a bunch of cars stopped when I slowed down a bit, I saw in front of the cars were two police cars with state troopers. I said under my breath, "Oh shit!" Hunter said, "Quick, make a U-turn before... It was too late behind us was another car and was so close to us I didn't have enough room. Hunter said, "Fuck! Now what!?" I sighed and said, "Tighten your seat belt." As I adjusted mine Hunter knew we were about to get into a chase. As the row of cars slowly got closer to the state troopers, they were looking at us I saw the one on the right each for his walkie-talkie and lifted it up to his mouth I took a slow breath and once the car ahead of us moved I pressed my foot down hard onto the gas pedal and drove around the head car as both officers yelled at us but ran back their squad cars.

I was going over 100 MPH down the road, and it didn't take long for the loud sirens and flashing lights to catch up to us. I saw a sign pointing to two streets Hunter said, "Stay on the right side we don't want to go towards the city." I made a hard right turn with the police cars catching up. Suddenly as I looked up in the view mirror the leading squad car passenger window was opened as the state trooper came out holding a shotgun. I yelled, "DUCK!" We both ducked as the shotgun blast blew out the rear and passenger window. Another shotgun fire went off this time taking out window behind my head.

Hunter pulled out his SIG Sauer P226 he quickly turned his body now facing where the state trooper was and pulled the trigger shooting him in the head. His body hanged halfway out of the car while he dropped his shotgun. Hunter let off a few more shots hitting the police car windshield forcing it off the road while the other was catching up. I yelled, "SHOOT THEM!" Hunter fired his SIG Sauer P226 through the broke rear window shooting the police car windshield then shot the driver as the squad car made a violent turn into forest area and crashed into a tree.

Hunter turned back and reloaded his pistol then we heard a loud thumping noise I turned my head over to the left and saw a helicopter coming I said, "Shit!" The sliding door opened as an officer holding Heckler & Koch HK94A3. Without warning began firing at us. Hunter opened his side window and took off his seat belt then put half of his body out of the passenger door window and fired his pistol at the officer. He fell out of the helicopter then Hunter aimed at the pilot and squeezed off a few shots and scored a shot on him. I watched as the helicopter flew away but behind us were more squad cars. I quickly looked up at the view mirror then back at the road and saw a roadblock.

The officers were now holding M-16 assault rifles along with shotguns I yelled, "HUNTER GET DOWN!" Hunter turned his head and quickly got back inside as I pressed my foot down while lowering my head as bullets zoomed above us and hitting the Ford Bronco. I kept going then I quickly turned to the front side of the police car and rammed through it but kept our heads low as more bullets zoomed above us and a few shots nearly hit me. We raised our heads as Hunter said, "Motherfuckers! Their hellbent of taking us down!" I said, "Get the Ruger Mini-14! They'll be coming after us!"

Hunter took crawled into the back seat and opened the duffel bag and took out the semi-auto rifle then loaded a magazine into it. He pressed the wooden stock firmly against his right shoulder then adjusted the sights as the police cars were catching up behind us. Hunter squeezed off the trigger shooting at the police cars as I kept my foot down going faster. I could hear the bullets hitting the back of the Ford Bronco and zooming by us. I saw Hunter took out a few cops then suddenly on our left side a police car was driving up the side of the road with an officer holding a shotgun I grabbed my CZ-75 smashed out my driver side window and quickly fired away shooting at the officer then rammed the police car off the road as it crashed into a ditch. I saw another turn coming I quickly made a hard left.

Suddenly another helicopter came above us Hunter reloaded the Ruger Mini-14 and waited it to move away then fired at it. A few shots hit the hood as I saw smoke I said, "Oh shit! Not fucking good!" Hunter took out the pilot as the helicopter crashed into the ground. Suddenly the Ford Bronco was starting to slow down with more smoke coming out of the hood Hunter turned over to me and said, "Shit! We're going have to make a mad dash to the forest!" I pulled over stopped the Bronco as we grabbed out duffel bags and my gym bag and ran for it while sirens were roaring behind us.

Running faster while my heart was racing, I kept turning my head to see if there were any officers running after us. As we ran, we happen to come across another road we ran onto the forest next to it. I heard yelling behind us followed by more helicopters coming. I then heard the sound of a few police cars stopping on the road we had ran pass with doors opening and the sound of boots stumping quickly across the road with guns being armed coming after us. I knew if we tried fighting them off, they would kill us.

However, the trees were so close to each other the helicopters won't be able for the snipers to get a clean shot on us. I then noticed Hunter was slowing down I knew we weren't going to last much longer running. Then I saw two officers in front of us I quickly aimed my CZ-75 and pulled the trigger shooting both of them. We kept running and saw their Chevrolet Caprice Classic police car. I ran into the driver side door while Hunter fired off a few more shots then got in as I floored it.

I drove down a dirt road the lead away from the city taking us back to the highway. My lungs felt they were burning as Hunter said, "Fucking hell! That was too fucking close!" I asked, "Did you bring the map with you?" Hunter said, "Shit! I forgot back in the Bronco!" I said, "Ok we'll go to a small down get what we need then find a safe place where we can change our looks then ditch this car."

d we heard a male voice on the CB radio, "Curtis Parker! Hunter Cunningham! If you can hear this answer me now!" Hunter looked over at me and asked, "Should we answer it?" I said, "They'll just try to make us give up. Save your breath." The officer called our names again, but I refused to answer back then he said, "If you two can hear me I just to let you know we haven't forgotten what you did to our fellow officers, and I swear to bring you two back alive to face punishment for your crimes. I'm giving you one last chance to surrender now." I turned off the radio as Hunter said, "Wait! We can use it to hear where they'll be." I said, "I bet they have already thought that up sadly." Hunter said, "Oh right." I saw a sign pointing to a town coming up I sighed and said, "Let's make this quick and find something else."

When we reached the town, I pulled into a hardware store I shifted the gear into Park then killed the engine as we got out. Hunter went over to me and said, "Helped myself with the spare handcuffs." I saw an dark blue 79 Chevrolet Blazer I checked inside the driver side window and saw the keys were still in the ignition switch I turn my head over to Hunter waved him over as we quickly got inside I started it up and drove off and just in time too as a few minutes later I saw police cars pulling into the parking lot but by the time they finished searching the whole area we were already long gone.

2:00-PM

We reached the town of Greenville in South Carolina once there we grabbed some lunch to eat and ate it in the back parking lot as we had our windows halfway opened letting some cool air. Once we finished our lunch Hunter drove off as we stopped at a store were we grabbed the wigs, hair clippers and different clothes to wear and the other stuff we needed then went into a rest stop. We shaved our hair off then tried the different wigs and picked the ones that felt right and a pair of glasses. We changed and threw our clothes out then to make it harder for the police to find us we changed the Blazer license plate. Hunter got into the driver side while I hopped into the passenger side, and we were off again.

The route we were taking would lead us to Atlanta, George we planned to make the full drive there to cover much ground as possible if we were going to solve this bizarre case, we gotten ourselves into. I had the radio on and sure enough we made the headlines again, "The two wanted suspects have been last seen in North Carolina after leaving police in a deadly car chase and shootout. It's reported that 14 officers were killed during this chase as the FBI will be stepping up its search for them." Hunter said, "What other bad fucking news is next for us?"

We then heard, "In other news more schools, churches, houses and even some city halls are destroyed by arson followed by murder with more children gone missing. Police are trying to get the bottom of this with no clues pointing out who is behind these horrible acts." I said, "Are these people really that blind!? This fucking cartoon show is behind it! It's being aired through North American and Canada, yet everyone acts like it doesn't exist!" Hunter said, "It seems those who do know about it up dead or the on the wrong side of the law." I hated Manson even more I didn't care what pissed him off from the start I just wanted to get my little brother back and bring an end to whatever he is planning!

By 6:00-PM we had entered into Georgia, but we won't be going to Atlanta knowing the city was going to be crawling with cops. Hunter was heading for Florida but we didn't plan on driving through the night we needed to rest but first we bought some food and drinks so we could have breakfast in the morning. Hunter found a cheap hotel as I paid for it and acted like I was from Texas. The man bought it and gave us a room to spend the night in. Once we got in, I started cooking dinner while Hunter worked on the fake IDs for us.

It didn't take him long to get them done nor our dinner. We sat in the small kitchen as we began to eat, I happen to notice there was a TV in the living room. Looking at it made me feel uneasy. I stood up and walked over to it as I unplugged then turned it around, so I won't see its screen. I went back into the kitchen to eat. Hunter said, "The one thing I'm looking forward to once we get into Florida we can ditch those winter clothes were carrying." I said, "When we do get there, we'll have to find a good hotel and a map of Miami so we can find this cartoon network station and see what data it has on Dorothy. Find her place or find what information we can get on Osborne Louis."

Hunter said, "And if no luck then it's Lakeview in New Orleans." I said, "We'll find what we're looking for. I know it." We finished our dinner as I went to use the shower first. When I was done, I changed and went to bed to get some rest. Hunter later fell asleep on his bed as I had our bedroom door locked and our duffel bags close by just in case.

Feb. 19
10:00-AM

We both woke up at the same time but felt very warm inside our room. I got up and unlocked the door then we both stepped out carrying our duffel bags into the kitchen. Hunter said, "I'll get started on breakfast check outside." I rubbed my eyes then looked out the hotel living room and saw the Blazer was still in the same spot and no other cars were in the parking lot. I turned around and said, "We're ok no... Suddenly I notice Hunter wasn't looking at me he was where the TV was. I thought, "No! It can't be!" But when I turned, I saw the TV had been plugged back in and was now facing us.

It turned on as I felt the whole living room was darken then Manson came on the screen and boy, did he look pissed off. When Manson looked at us his eyes were bright red he yelled in rage and felt the building was shaking violently. I covered my ears, but I could still hear Manson's anger. When he stopped yelling, he grabbed the TV screen and smacked his head hard against the screen a few times and it cracked. When he moved his head away, I saw blood was now pouring down his forehead. He sighed and said, "Look what you two made me do. I was so happy to finally get rid of you two but instead of accepting defeat you two choice to run away and now I have to change what you two did on my show!"

I couldn't help but laugh Manson turned to face me with a very annoyed look on his face he yelled, "YOU THINK THIS IS FUCKING FUNNY!?" Manson grabbed his right arm and bit into it as he growled loudly then tore a good chunk of his arm off with more blood pouring out of it. Then I notice it was now pouring out of the cracked TV screen. As Manson spit out the piece of his purple suit, he looked at us and asked, "I want to know what you two are trying to find so badly that you would cause me so much pain and anger." I wanted to know if he knew his creator and if so, would he say something that might help us. I knew if I yelled back, he would just leave us or try scaring the shit out of us. I said, "We're looking for your creator. Osborne Louis."

Manson looked at me and said, "That's who you're trying to find?" He was quiet for a bit and as I said, "Yes, him." Manson held his bleeding arm and said, "You won't find anything of HIM! I'll make sure of it and as for my show I'm going to make sure the children fear you and the adults hate you forever!" He then yelled and punched out the screen as the TV exploded. Me and Hunter were silent and saw that Manson did destroy the TV and we pissed him off. Hunter broke the silence and said, "I'll get started on breakfast now."

11:00-AM

We changed our clothes and ate breakfast then left fearing if the hotel owner heard the noise but a theory, I had about Manson was true he hated his creator as much as he hated adults. I drove while Hunter sat beside me. Hunter said, "Damn we really pissed him off." I said, "Yes and I can't imagination what he'll do to us if we ever do that again." Hunter said, "I don't get it. If he wants us dead so badly why not just kill us now?" I said, "I bet it has to do with magic he doesn't have enough to be in our world long enough. Sure, he killed my parents, but it seems he's toying with us and is waiting for something then maybe he'll come after us later and I'm not looking forward to that."

Hunter turned his head over to me said, "Wait if his characters won't release to the public in 84 then how did he end up on TV? And what did Osborne do to his characters to make them hate their own creator so much?" I thought about as I saw the signs showing that I was getting closer to Florida. I said, "You know I heard an story about a thrash band that was around for a few years before it's lead singer was died of drug overdose." Hunter asked, "The Rotting Corpses?" I nodded my head and said, "Yeah those guys." Hunter said, "Never liked them I thought their singer wasn't that good." I said, "Anyway I heard a rumor that before they went to play for their opening show the lead singer used black magic to sabotage the other band allowing them to gain frame while the other band just flat out quit."

Hunter asked, "What's the point to this?" I said, "The point is that I think it's true. He used black magic to gain his fame but got reckless and ended up getting killed by the Satan for not doing what he wanted in return so my theory is that Osborne Louis made a deal with the Satan to gain his drawing skills however before he could create his show back in 69 was killed in a car crash. My guess is that Satan killed Louis because did something against

Satan's deal. Or maybe his characters had something to do with and wanted more then what Louis planned to do with them."

Hunter was quiet for a bit and said, "So you think Osborne idea was that Manson and his gang were the villains, and the White Order group was the heroes and each one of Manson and his friends is based on Osborne's view of the world he doesn't like." I said, "Yes that's what I'm thinking and if that were me, I too would hate my creator specially his goal is to make his characters feel nothing but his hatred, anger and abuse he went through. And in Osborne mind his charterers are only real in his mind but to Manson and his gang there are more than just cartoon charterers their people just like us." Hunter said, "I hope we find a spell or some black magic shit to destroy them." I said, "I have a bad feeling it isn't going to be that easy, but we aren't quitting until I get my little brother back."

Chapter 4

Jacksonville, Florida
5:30-PM

We both felt very tired, but we reached Florida. The border guards bought our fake ID's and my Texas accent. I had the AC on while driving along side road with the beaches on our left side. As I looked over at the view mirror the border guards didn't look at us, they went back talking to each other. But I was wondering if Harry or Trish were still alive. I thought about calling them. I won't know who's side they were on until I spoke with them.

Hunter said, "We still got a long way to Miami and if we don't find what we're looking for then we'll have gone to New Orleans." I said, "Yeah and we'll have to ditch this Blazer when it's reported stolen." Hunter said, "And if things get worse, we could always take a boat and reach New Orleans." I said, "That sounds like a better idea with Florida being around an open sea that will make it harder for the feds to find us." Hunter then said, "Shit. I gotta take a piss." I saw a restaurant and said, "Let's get something to eat then find a hotel for the night." I pulled into the parking lot shifted the gear into Park then killed the engine as we both stepped out and went inside.

After we used the men's room, we got ourselves some dinner and sat next to the window and ate with only a few people inside. There was a radio playing thrash metal which felt like ages I haven't heard in a long time. I bet my apartment had been cleared out for someone else to live in and all my stuff was thrown out or maybe the feds helped themselves with it. While we ate, we scanned the restaurant to see if anyone was looking at us but nobody was. By the time we we're done eating we left got back into the Blazer. I started it up and drove off looking for a hotel to spend the night and didn't take me long to find one.

I paid for the room as me and Hunter carried our stuff into the hotel room as we locked the door. There was a small kitchen with a very roomy living room. A small bathroom and two bedrooms. Me and Hunter saw the living room had a big TV I asked, "Mind helping me with this?" Hunter said, "Yeah not having the same thing happen again." As we walked over to it suddenly it turned on and looking at us was Barbara.

Barbara was wearing her bright red and black outfit with red leather gloves, red lips. Her ears were halfway bent down which meant she was pissed. The whole room suddenly felt silent then could hear a demonic growl as Barbara raised her voice and said, "I never thought anyone could cause my lovely husband so much anger! So much pain!" Suddenly her face changed into a horrify demonic face as her fresh looked rotten with blood oozing out as she screamed, "SO MUCH SUFFERING!"

The TV had static while making strange noises, but it quickly stopped and showed Barbara back to normal and said, "Hmmm! And I even had sex with you." I said rising my voice a bit, "I didn't fucking ask for it!" Barbara said, "Really? You enjoyed fucking a bunny didn't you Curtis as much as your friend enjoyed fucking a bird." Hunter asked, "What do you want with us?" Barbara said, "Just to let you two know how much trouble you're in. My husband came up with a nasty surprise for you two and when our sweet children see it, they'll point you to anyone after what you did to my husband." Suddenly the screen went blank then the intro for the second season of The Manson & Barbara Show was playing I really didn't want to watch it but knew we couldn't stop it.

Barbara voice spoke as the text came up and said, "Episode 143 Manhunt Part 1" As the screen fade to black it then showed Manson walking down a dark foggy street with a few street lights were on. I noticed on the stone buildings were wanted posters of us. The screen then showed a close up of Manson face as he had a very angry look with his ears bend down. It then showed flash backs of the lost battles along with the steam ship bombing with dead families floating in the water. He growled and we heard his thoughts as he said, "I'm going to make the Tricksters pay for this!"

Just as he came to end of the street and went to turn suddenly an older man asked, "Sir. Would you please spare me some coins?" Manson turned to look at the old man who was wearing dirty clothes and had a hood on so you couldn't see his face but was holding out an empty mug Manson went to reach into his pocket suddenly the screen showed someone sneaking up behind him and the right arm raised up with a large wine bottle. It struck Manson hard over his head knocking him down onto the ground but before he could get up the old man holding the mug changed into a dagger and it stabbed Manson under his right arm.

When both attackers got closer into the light, it was revealed to us that was a disguise. We grinned then it showed us beating Manson to death. Stumping and kicked him around. He tried to get up but wasn't able to we both started taunting him. When it showed beaten up Manson, we both drew out our laser pistols aiming at him ready to fire while we laughed with Manson looking at us with anger then the screen faded black. I notice Hunter had a disturbed look on his face.

When the screen came back on it showed a close up of our laser pistols as I said, "Say your prayers Manson!" Just as we we're about to squeeze the triggers suddenly we heard a male voice yell, "HEY! STOP RIGHT THERE!" When we turned our heads, it was guards and they knew who we were. Before they could fire Hunter turned around fired off his laser pistol shooting them as a few manage to fire back their cross bows, but we ran into an alleyway.

The guards ran towards Manson lying injured on the ground and helped him up. Another guard said, "Quickly! We have to get him back to the castle." Then it showed the guards carrying Manson onto a small air ship but as they got on board a disc shaped tracker was thrown onto it, it lifted up into the air then showed us while I was holding a handheld computer showing where that air ship was going. Hunter on TV said, "Alright, let's cause some trouble." We both laughed ran into the darkness." The screen faded black and when it came back it showed Manson lying on a bed and covered with a blanket while Sydney had her arms over him as her hands were glowing bright green.

Watching them was Barbara, Kane, George, Andrew and Hellen and they were not happy at all. Kane said, "I knew I should have gone with him knowing how dangerous the streets have been ever since the Tricksters!" Andrew said, "Manson was just caught off guard, but I won't mind getting my hands on them!" Barbara with her arms crossed and said, "I'll give those Tricksters a good beating!" Hellen turned her head and said, "We'll make them pay for this Barbara, but I get the feeling this cruel act is part of their plan."

Kane said, "That's what I think. They want us somewhere else but when we leave, they'll come back to finish off Manson but we're not going to fall for it." Andrew turned his head over to Kane and asked, "What makes you sure that they'll be able to sneak inside this castle it's heavily guarded." Kane said, "They won't call us the Tricksters, for nothing. If they do, try we'll have Manson forces handle them while we watch our friend." Barbara said, "I agree with Kane and Hellen on this one. If the White Order or the Tricksters try anything we'll let our forces handle them, but it won't hurt to have air ships patrolling the area." Hellen said, "Good idea I'll radio a few to watch over the Kingdom and our castle as well."

As Hellen left Sydney walked over to the others and said, "Those two beat him badly and since we'll limited to magic, I'm force to use a slow healing spell. By the time Manson wakes up he'll feel better but it's going to take time until my spell fully heals his body." Barbara said, "Which means we'll have to guard him as nobody is going to harm my husband again." Hellen came back and said, "My ships are watching this area and the town so if the White Order is dumb enough to send any of their forces here, they won't be getting close to the castle."

Andrew said, "Well I guess we better patrol the castle as well." Barbara said, "No, I want all of us here. If the Tricksters show up, they'll have more to deal with then just a few people." Barbara walked over to Manson and placed her hand over his head lightly rubbing it then turned over to the window as it zoomed it then showed further away into a scope. Then on the TV it showed Hunter watching Barbara with me standing next to him Hunter said, "There guarding their leader and have a lot of air ships in the area." The screen showed a close up of my face as I had annoyed expression and said, "We should have killed him when we had our chance!"

Hunter said, "Our King won't like that we missed our chance." I didn't say anything then Hunter turned to face me and asked, "Curtis? Did you hear what I said?" I said, "Yes but quite frankly I'm getting tired of working for the King." The screen showed a close up of my face and I felt the cartoon version of me looked more sinister. I then said, "We risked our lives and nearly died and for what. The King's gory?" I looked over at Hunter and said, "Think about it friend we could have it all to ourselves and why take orders when we can be the ones telling others what to do. I got bigger plans then what the King has for us." Hunter on the TV was quiet for a bit and asked, "What are your plans?" The screen went back to me and said, "Seeing how Manson can't move and his friends won't leave him alone this will give us a chance to weaken the White Order enough then make it look like the King did this take to get rid of half of his members allowing him more control. And once we tell those survivors about what the King was doing behind their backs we'll have our own army and our own kingdom."

Hunter grinned and said, "Alright! I'm with you on it." The screen went back to me as I grinned with lightning flashing in the background I said, "Tell the King the good news and while all the action is happening let's make our fellow White Order soldiers work much harder." We both did an evil laugh as the screen went back to Manson lying on the pillow then it faded black.

Suddenly I felt a sickening feeling and that horrible thought of bugs crawling around my brain from watching this I had almost forgot the side effect that his messed-up cartoon does to adults. Hunter placed his hands over his forehead I heard him ask,

"Curtis? Did we bring Advil with us?" I said, "I think so!" Then the screen came back on now showing White Order ships heading towards Manson's castle. The storm was getting worse and felt the whole room around us was getting dark, cold and swear I would see things moving around in the corner of my eyes.

Then the screen showed the inside of the leading White Order ship with a man wearing a white suit with medals on it. When we got a good look at his face, I knew who it was – the President of the United States. Just then a number flashed, and I saw it, it was number 31 as a hologram screen came up in front of him it was the King he said, "Mr. Nicolas I want you and your ships to launch full assault against the castle as this will be our only change to take out the leader and his gang while there all together." Mr. Nicolas said, "We shall not fail my King. We will crush the enemy while their guard is down." The King lightly grinned and said, "I been looking forward to this victory for such a long time."

The screen showed Mr. Nicolas as I remembered the speech he made about fighting against the Soviets in Afghanistan and wasn't scared of the Russian army which the media dubbed him "The President with An Iron Will" I thought, "He's going to be the next person to be killed by Manson. How is Manson going to pull that off?" The screen showed the White Order ships getting closer to Manson's castle with Hellen air ships waiting to open fire. Just then it showed on the roof tops of some ruin buildings me and Hunter holding large laser cannons with high tech scopes. It showed me aiming at the White Order ships it then showed what my cartoon version of me was seeing through the scope.

On the scope I saw it had locked onto the lead White Order ship then heard myself on the TV say, "Wait until they warm up a bit then take out the lead ship. Without their leader we just have to pick off a few more ships so this whole attack looks like an ambush, and we'll spare...Frank he'll be dumb enough to believe our story." Hunter said, "Never liked him anyway." I lightly laughed and said, "Which makes even better once we're in charge, he'll be easily removed from our kingdom." We both lightly laughed while Hunter and I were feeling our headaches getting worse.

The screen showed Hellen's air ships getting ready to attack and it didn't take long. Laser beams and double cannons fired at each other with big explosions in the air with a few ships quickly taken out. The screen then showed the cartoon version of me say, "Alright, take Nicolas out!" A close up of the finger pulling back against the trigger as two dark blue laser beams shot straight up into Nicolas's ship followed by two big explosions it showed the inside of Nicolas ship as the blast knocked him down from the bridge and smacked his head hard against the floor breaking his nose.

It then showed his White Order ship burning straight towards the ground. My cartoon version grinned as Hunter and I we're shooting more White Order ships down then it showed Hunter aiming for Frank's ship and shot his engines as it was quickly descending towards the ground, I turned to Hunter said, "Quickly let's warn Frank about the bad news." It showed us running off the rooftop then hopping down into an alleyway and threw out the large laser cannons as we ran into the thick dark fog with the screen faded black.

When it came back it showed badly damaged White Order ship with the remaining crew members and captain crawling out of the wreck. It showed a close up of Frank as I knew who he was the Vice President for President Nicolas. He asked, "Who else was shooting at us? Manson forces didn't have any ground forces!" A White Order crew member said, "We didn't pick up any on the scanner!" Then I heard my voice in the background say, "Frank!" The White Order members turned around to see me and Hunter came out of the darkness as I said, "Frank we just learned the King has betrayed us!"

Frank looked shocked and asked, "What? Betray us?! Why?!" I said, "Hunter picked up a secret radio message and wants to remove half of his order so he can full control of everything." Frank looked at us along with the crew members I said, "Why else didn't you pick up Manson ground forces as only our scanners can pick them up not our men."

Frank didn't seem to trust me and said, "I don't buy it. Why would our fellow King betray us?" I said, "Look he set this whole thing up and right now as I speak, he is going to kill off more members of the White Order. Our King just wants to take all the credit as he's tired of having others take it and wants to learn how to use magic." Frank and the crew members stared at us then Frank moved his left arm slowly towards his hostler and said, "I don't trust you, Curtis." I said, "Well...I never liked you either." Just as he went to draw his laser pistol Hunter shot him in the head. I drew my laser pistol out and said, "Your choice everyone! Die here, get captured by Manson forces or join me." The crew members looked nervous but each one nodded their heads the screen went back to me I grinned and said, "Good now follow us."

It went back to Manson still lying in the bed as Barbara and the others were looking over at him then Hellen entered the room and said, "Something strange is going on!" Everyone turned around as Kane asked, "What's that?" Hellen said, "Someone else attacked the White Order ships but it wasn't us." Everyone looked at each other confused as the screen went to Barbara and said, "I know who did it. The Tricksters." George turned his big head and asked, "Wait aren't they working for the King?" Barbara said, "Guess they had a falling out with him." Sydney crossed his arms and said, "Hmmm! Nothing but greed that's gotten to those fools."

George said, "I can't wait to smash them to dust with my hammer!" Kane turned to George and said, "We'll get our chance big guy but first we need our friend Manson on our side. Without him we won't haven't made it this far." As the screen turned back to Manson face it slowly zoomed in then began fade black. But when it fully back we heard Barbara voice say, "Tune in next time to see what the evil Tricksters are planning, and will our hero Manson fully regain his strength to fight evil again? Stay tuned or...Suddenly Barbara's face popped on the screen as it was demonic looking with bright red glowing eyes, sharp teeth with rotten flesh and blood oozing out of her body with her ears bend down as she screamed, "OR ELSE!!!"

I felt my heart rate was rising and suddenly we saw the big TV was coming straight for us. Me and Hunter manage to move just in time as the big TV crashed into the wall behind us and smashed as Barbara loud screams caused the whole hotel room to shake violently. The living room didn't feel dark or cold but both me and Hunter felt very sick I stood up and ran into the bathroom and felt I was going to puke with my brain burning. Hunter ran into the kitchen and vomited all over the sink.

This sickening feeling was the goddamn worse I ever felt my whole body was burning with my brain had tiny bugs crawling around inside as I placed my hands onto my wig, I pulled it off then scratched my head and fell onto the bathroom floor feeling like I was going to vomit again. Hunter gagged as he went into the bedroom to grab us Advil I slowly stood up as Hunter came in with the Advil, we both took it however I began to feel lightheaded as me and Hunter passed out on the living room sofa.

I woke up but everything felt dark around me then I slowly started to hear what sounded like old classic music playing behind me. I lifted up my head but couldn't see much but the sounds around me were growing louder then I started to see bright flashes of light. My sight was starting to come back as the music was becoming clearer now, I thought, "Wait. That sounds like... carnival!" Suddenly I saw people walking around me as there were tents, rides and a big Ferris wheel with bright lights running along it.

I thought, "Wait! This is when I went to the carnival in Oct.13, 1979 with my father." Then I remembered this was the time I almost got lost but found him as we had a lot of fun here. I remember taking John here in Oct.13,1982... I felt my eyes open wide and my heart beating faster I thought, "No! It can't be on the same day!" Suddenly I felt someone was watching me I turned around and as crowds of people were walking by standing there was Manson wearing his dark purple suit and matching top hat. When I saw his face, he grinned those bright white fangs and his red eyes glowed I quickly turned my head and started running as I could hear his black leather boots touching the ground following me.

I looked everywhere for my father but didn't see him. I could hear Manson getting closer to me I ran faster and was trying to find a place where I could hide. I turned to the right and saw more tents but couldn't see what was inside of them with the crowd of people not looking at me or Manson. However, they were slowing me down and could hear those boots walking closer towards me followed by Manson's crane touching the ground. I pushed my way through the crowd then I saw a big purple tent I ran inside and was running through a long tunnel with soft grass now turned into stone floor. I kept running but felt Manson was still keeping up with me. Then I saw lights at the end of the tunnel and in front of me was a roller coaster.

My heart was beating so fast I remember my first time getting on one of these things and I hated it! So much so I ruined my nice shirt and swore to never get on one of these things again! The leading car had its safety bars up as I felt it was waiting for me to get on board. I could hear the footsteps getting closer and when I turned my head back to the dark entrance, I could see Manson's red glowing eyes and his sharp bright white fangs grinning at me. I feared the only way out was to get onto the roller coaster. I got on it as I sat down on it suddenly the safety bar came down and heard loud clicking noise, I gripped it tightly and turned to see Manson now standing in the tunnel and heard him lightly laughing as the roller coaster began moving, I turned my head back however in front of me was a dark tunnel. It was now pitch black I couldn't see anything however the cool air suddenly felt very warm. I then felt the roller coaster picking up speed I could hear Manson laughing loudly as it was getting faster and faster until I woke up screaming after it crashed.

Feb. 20
7:00-AM

I opened my eyes feeling my head was boiling and slowly stood up. I had fallen out of the sofa and was lying on the flood. I rubbed my eyes and saw Hunter lying on his back on the other side of the sofa. Suddenly I jumped when Hunter screamed and nearly fell out of the sofa then saw I was up. I breath, "Fucking Manson!" Hunter rubbed his forehead and said, "I feel like I went to hell and came back while still burning." I said, "Goddamn it! I had another nightmare about my past at the carnival." Hunter said, "Same shit, man. First off that beating scene from the show...I saw a poor man getting beaten to death when I was teenager, and I didn't do anything to stop the attackers or help him after. Second nightmare I had was when I was shopping with my mother and saw Barbara following me and felt she was trying to kill me as...as I remember this creepy woman who I thought was going to kidnap me. That's what my nightmare was based on."

I sighed and said, "It's just them fucking around with our heads! Let's change our clothes then leave and try to get closer to Miami and later on we'll have lunch." Hunter turned his head over and said, "I hope nobody heard the TV getting smashed." I had forgotten about that as I looked over by the wall lying there was a broken TV as I said, "Shit, we better get going."

We fled the hotel as Hunter was driving this time. I was wearing light button jacket with a dark green shirt under it, blank pants with my boots on. Hunter was wearing light red shirt, dark grey pants and boots. We both had our wigs on along with sunglasses. I looked at the map of Florida as we we're driving around route 95 if we kept going straight, we would reach Miami however it was going to take us a while to get there. I said, "Hunter last night when President Nicolas was shown I saw the number flash on the screen 31st which means he'll die on that day along with the Vice President Frank."

Hunter turned his head over and asked, "Do you think we could stop that?" I thought about as we came to a red light, Hunter stopped the Blazer and said, "I don't know if we can or not. Since we're wanted by the law if we get close to any government places, they'll be all over us." Hunter said, "If we caught them red handed in the act, they'll have to believe us." I said, "They'll still take us in as crazed terrorists and after the things we we're force to do they won't put us away for life. They'll give us the death penalty." The light turned green as Hunter pressed his foot onto the gas, I checked the view mirror and saw a police car a few cars behind us but it turned at stop lights I said, "After we have lunch let's find something else to drive in."

12:00-PM

We ditched the Blazer in an underground parking lot and cleaned it up then picked a bright orange 85 Ford Mustang GT with black tinted windows. I changed license plates on it then stopped for lunch and quickly got back onto the road. We we're now in West Palm Beach I knew in a few hours we would reach Miami and to find this cartoon network I would check the payphone book and look up the number I still remembered it, so it won't take me long to find it. I also remembered I haven't called Harry, or Trish I would do that after if I had time.

Hunter drove while I had the radio on turning the knob trying to find some heavy metal music however, I stopped when heard this. A male voice said, "In our breaking story a mess murder that has caused the state of Alabama full shock." I reached over the volume knob turned up a bit and heard, "It first started when a man found brutally murdered inside a house with his hands chopped off and his face stabbed a dozen times. Police are unable to identify the man as no wallet, ID or damaged body are able to give them any DNA." Hunter turned his head over and said, "Bullshit." We then heard, "Then a series of murders hit Alabama and Georgia from churches, schools, city halls and even a KKK protest was turned into a massacre with a few officers killed during the shooting as this happened yesterday."

I said, "Shit! We we're nearby Georgia, when we reached Florida." As the man finished the breaking story Hunter said, "How the hell can't the police identity the man unless... I said, "Manson and his fucking magic bullshit." Hunter said, "Only thing that makes sense. Let's just find what we're looking for then get out of here." Then we heard the voice on the radio talking about the two wanted criminals the FBI was looking for which were us and stated how dangerous we we're which the media had dubbed us as "The Tricksters" with the FBI stepping up their search fearing the two terrorists are planning on fleeing the country or their next attack." I heard enough and changed the station and found the heavy metal channel as we heard Killers by Iron Maiden.

Miami, Florida
3:30-PM

After a long drive we made it, Hunter pulled over into a gas station to refuel the car while I went over to a payphone and opened the phone book. As I began looking for through it, I heard the corner store front doors open with young teens buying snacks along with packs of Coke cans and heard one of them saying, "Did you see what those damn Tricksters did to Manson?!" A teenage girl said, "Yeah they beat him to death!" Another teenager said, "I can't wait until Manson and his gang captures the Tricksters." The girl said, "Knowing the Tricksters are trying to form their own army it just goes to show how bad greed is."

But just as they left, they stopped talking and felt their eyes were looking at me. I didn't look at them I kept turning the pages until I saw what I was looking for. Miami Cartoon Network Station I saw the address I took out a note pad and pen writing down the address and still felt those teenagers staring at me. I took a quick glance at the corner store window and in the reflection, I saw their faces with angry expressions on them. I noticed in the background Hunter had finished pumping the Mustang full of gas and looked worried I thought, "Shit! What the hell am I going to do? There just teens it's not like their carrying guns on them.

What if they reported me to the police?"

I then thought about scaring them off then looked over and noticed there was a video camera inside the corner store. I then heard a car pulling in I quickly looked over at it was black 80 Mercedes Benz SL R107 pulled in then the teenagers turned their heads away and left but not before staring down Hunter. I blew some air out and walked back to the Mustang. I went up to Hunter and whispered, "There's a video camera inside don't raise your head." He nodded his head and went inside the corner store to pay for the gas I went over to the passenger door got inside the Mustang waiting for Hunter which didn't take him long.

Once Hunter got in, he asked, "What the hell was that all about?" I said, "Those kids knew we we're the Tricksters as we're the villains on that show." Hunter said, "Damn I hope they don't report us." I said, "I don't think they won't but let's hit that cartoon network station I got the address written down." I showed Hunter as we took a quick at the map then drove off.

When we saw it, it looked more like an office building then a cartoon station however we won't be able to look around as we saw video cameras around the place. Next to it was an underground parking lot with a guard booth Hunter had picked on the opposite side so we could have a good look at it. I said, "Looks like the only way we're getting in is by night." Hunter said, "We'll have to sneak through the parking garage and work our way up." I said, "Their computers or files should have Dorothy record and maybe Osborne Louis as well." Hunter asked, "And if they don't?" I said, "We'll try city hall then. They always keep records of people."

We then saw a guard walking over to the booth we book looked at him I said, "He got an .38 revolver not really a powerful gun but at close range a chest of head shot is fatal." Hunter said, "We should still bring ours just in case." I lightly nodded my head and said, "Let's return here at 1 in the morning when everyone is asleep." Hunter started up the Mustang and drove off to a cheap hotel and lucky it had no TV in it. We paid for two nights so we would be able to check city hall if the cartoon network didn't have what we we're looking for. I knew this was risky, but we had to take a chance as I wasn't going to get beaten by a cartoon character.

12:50-AM

We returned to the cartoon network and saw only one guard in the booth. Me and Hunter had put on black clothing and using ski masks to cover our faces. We had our pistols and shotguns just in case. As we got closer to the guard booth, we could see the guard a big man holding a Playboy magazine he grinned at it. I held my CZ-75 sneaked up beside him and whacked my pistol above his head knocking him out cold. I quickly grabbed his walkie-talkie; .38 revolver then took his backup revolver from his right ankle holster. I then grabbed his hand cuffs and opened them as I cuffed his right arm to his heavy chair then me and Hunter entered the parking lot garage and found the stairs we ran upstairs.

Using the walkie-talkie, the guards were busy patrolling the building and would know if anything was up. When we reached the main floor, I slowly opened the door peeked my head out and saw it was empty with only a few lights on. Me and Hunter went to the main desk it was a large round shape with two big black computers I pulled up a chair sat down. I rested my CZ-75 on the desk and turned on the computer. It didn't take long for main menu to pop up I began typing away on the keyboard while Hunter watched over me.

I found the file I was looking for clicking on it as it uploaded a list of the employees here. As I looked through it, I didn't see anyone with the name Dorothy I then tried a few other files but wasn't getting anything, I said under my breath, "Shit!" I was now trying to think what else I could try then I saw an folder which said, "RECORDS 60-69" I clicked on it and there was a shit load of information I read through it quickly then I saw near the end of the list was "DECEMBER CHIRSTMAS PARTY 1969" I clicked on it then I saw a list of people who were going to be their along with guests and sure enough found what I was looking for. I turned my head to Hunter said, "Got it!" Hunter looked over as on the screen and saw the name we been after.

Special Guest-Osborne Louis
Address-Fort Lauderdale, Paradise Drive-8080 Phone Number-600-4499-000
Vehicle-Dark Purple 69 Ferrari Dino 246 GT

Hunter said, "Seems Osborne and Manson have the same taste in color." I took out my note pad and wrote down this information suddenly we heard the walkie-talkie go off as a male voice said, "Has anyone heard from Nelson? He hasn't reported in 15 minutes." Another male voice said, "This is Joe I'll go check on him." Hunter said, "Shit we better get out of here." I said, "Hang on let me write this down first." I wrote down the address then shut off the computer grabbed my pistol and said, "Let's leave."

We went out the back exit as Hunter ditched the walkie-talkie since we won't need it running back into the Ford Mustang GT, I got in started up and just I did we heard sirens coming we quickly left and checked the time it was only 1:15-AM I turned to Hunter and said, "Next stop Osborne's house." Hunter said, "Alright let's go." I sped down the empty road hoping we won't get pulled over by any cops.

When we reached Paradise Drive the house, we saw looked much older than the others however we saw two parked vehicles in the driveway. Dark blue 85 Porsche 959 and a silver 64 Aston Martin DB5. Hunter said, "Damn it! Now what?" I wasn't going to call it quits here I turned over to Hunter and said, "Wait here I'm going inside." Hunter grabbed my shoulder and asked, "Are you crazy? They might have guard dogs in there." I said, "I'm not leaving until I find what I'm looking for." Hunter asked, "How do you know that house will have anything that Osborne have lived there. I bet the people here threw it out in the garbage."

I said, "Unless Osborne was smart enough to put it into the attic." Hunter looked up at the roof then at me and said, "Here I'll unlock the door." I killed the engine as we both got out and slowly closed our Mustang doors and climbed over the iron fence and went over to the front door. Hunter got it unlocked as he whispered, "Don't take too long." I lightly nodded my head and went inside as Hunter slowly closed the door and went back into the Mustang.

I slowly walked through the hallway looking at the ceiling but didn't see an attic opening. I knew the only places left were the bedrooms I checked into the guest room but saw nothing I then knew where it would be in the master bedroom. The door was left open I slowly walked inside and lying on the king-sized bed was a big man with a very sexy looking woman. She had long golden hair, wide hips, a thick bubble butt and large breasts that were pressed against the man's chest I thought, "Lucky bastard."

I turned to the closest then slowly opened and sure enough above my head was the attic entrance however it was going to be a tight fit. I closed the closest door then took out a small flashlight turned it open then got the attic entrance open as I grabbed it and pulled myself up and slowly walked across the attic, I aimed the flashlight around and didn't see much until I saw a big old trunk against the attic wall. I slowly walked towards it I knelt as I removed the latch and opened and when I did something swung at my face I jumped and saw it was a toy bat hanging inside the trunk lead. I lightly shook my head and shined the flashlight inside and saw big leather-bound book I reached and pulled it up.

I wiped off the dust and saw it was a fancy note book I opened it and inside were title text of The Manson & Barbara Show I flipped a few pages and saw Osborne had been writing this series since the mid-60s. I closed it and set it beside me then looked inside the trunk again to see another leather bound book inside I reached in and pulled it out I flipped it open and on the first page it said, "Arkard Glukhovsky Diary" I thought, "So Osborne isn't American after all he's Russian." I closed it and placed it on top of the photo book and took one more look inside the trunk and saw nothing suddenly the toy bat fell on my head as it made me jump and whack my head into the trunk which caused it to slam down hard. I thought, "SHIT!"

I turned my head over where the bedroom was and feared the couple woke up to the loud noises however it was quiet, I waited a bit and thought they didn't hear it I wiped my forehead then heard the closet door opening I knew that the man might have a gun on him I turned to where the guest bedroom was, I quickly grabbed the two books got up ran over to it and jumped.

My body weight caused the ceiling to break I landed on my feet and quickly ran out the room and into the hallway I could hear the man coming. I quickly opened the front door and towards the iron fence. Hunter started up the Mustang I climbed up got into the passenger side and just as I got in, I turned to see the big man wearing a housecoat and holding a small pistol in his right hand Hunter burned rubber and sped off. The man didn't see our license plate. Hunter said, "Please tell me you found what you we're looking for." I showed him the books.

Feb.21
9:00-AM

It was pouring rain outside as Hunter got us breakfast, we both sat in the living room with the lamp on next to us while we went through the two leather bounds, I found. I was reading over Arkard Glukhovsky's diary while Hunter went over other book. I said, "Dorothy wasn't lying Arkard came to New Orleans in Oct.13.1922 at the age of 4 so that means he was born in 1918." Hunter said with a disgust tune, "It seems Arkard isn't a people person. His version of the show is just downright racist!" I turned my head over to Hunter and said, "Mmmm might explain why Manson hates his creator so much." Hunter said, "See for yourself and what did you find out in his diary so far?" I said, "Arkard and his whole family went under the alias as Osborne and get this he had an older brother named Dmitry as the two were very close to each other."

Hunter said, "That other Russian bear from the show was him." I said, "Yeah and he states he wonders what his hometown is like as his mother told him that Zelenyy Vesna is Russian for Green Springs." Hunter closed the 2nd leather bound book and set it down beside me and asked, "How long is that diary?" I said, "Over 500 pages and I'm not anywhere near the middle of this thing." Hunter said, "Take a look how messed up his cartoon ideas were." I placed a book marker so I would read more of the diary later and picked up The Manson & Barbara Show novel as the text was the same one used during the first season of it.

Before the first chapter it said, "Written by Osborne Louis, Dated Oct.31,1966" Hunter said, "I read a few parts of it but near the end is one month before he died in a car crash." I nodded my head and began reading what he written down however I saw what Hunter was talking about. The White Order were the heroes while Manson and his gang were the villains and Manson had a different suit as it was heavily based off of Uncle Sam's patriot suit and was a master card player, scammer and trickster yet was an alcoholic. The other characters were all based on other races of people. George & Sydney were based on black people, Andrew was based on a very cruel Australian hunter, Kane a cold stoned killer, Barbara was Manson's girlfriend however he abused her, and Hellen was a female version of Joseph Stalin.

Another difference was the White Order had more of a modern city as Manson lived in a dark gothic fantasy town. But as I read more it, I saw this was never meant to be a kids show it was for adults only and Arkard seem to have a strong hate towards other races. And it showed even more when the White Order poked fun against Manson, his gang, and the animal people. The more pages I turned and read the dark and racist detail in the story the more uncomfortable I got with it. Hunter said, "Is it just me or Arkard doesn't like people at all." I said, "There is no way a show like this would ever be made...unless Arkard made a deal with Satan." Hunter said, "I can see why Manson hates his creator so much but seems to take some things from Arkard and used it against him."

I said, "I'll have to read more of that diary and see what drove Arkard to create this." Hunter asked, "So I'm guessing we'll check out city hall tonight?" I said, "Yeah as we'll be able to find what we're looking for since nobody is going to give us a straight answer." I closed the novel and would read it later. Hunter took a look outside and saw that only out Mustang and two other cars were in the parking lot and no police cars were nearby. Hunter asked, "So after city hall we just go to New Orleans?" I said, "Yes and thanks to the diary, Arkard was kind enough to tell us what his mother house address was." Hunter asked, "He also lived in Hollywood too?" I nodded my head and said, "His diary should cover that as well."

Hunter said, "Well while we wait for night fall might as well read more of it." I yawned and asked, "Alright say mind making me some coffee?" Hunter said, "Sure I could use some myself." When Hunter made us coffee, I picked up the diary again and opened it where I left off and waited for Hunter to return, I looked out the window again and didn't see any vehicles passing by. I turned my head back and didn't take long for Hunter to make the coffee I said, "Thanks." I drank it and read more pages through the diary while Hunter looked over.

So, for starters Arkard Glukhovsky under the alias Osborne Louis born in Russia on Oct.31, 1918 in town known as Green Springs. His brother Dmitry was born 5 years ahead of him but doesn't say what month or date it was, but I knew the year would be 1913. Arkard's father is written as an outdoors man who enjoyed the cold weather and loved hunting showing no care for wildlife, yet he did like his wife and two sons. However, Arkard didn't like his lifestyle or what his father's pass times. Arkard and Dmitry would play games in the forests and pretend they we're on another world. But as time went on their father begin to show his darker side and wanted his boys to act like grown adults and made them read the bible, go to church on Sundays and making sure he never missed school.

By 1921 things in Russia aren't going so well a power struggle happen after the fall of The Russian Empire in 1917. At the age of four Arkard is forced to watch his father kill a wolf which he writes he felt horrible about it. When Joseph Stalin is gaining more power, trust and control Arkard's father helps his wife, two children and their mother's sister into American as his wife is Jewish and states he'll join the army to when things have changed for the better, they can return to the motherland, but Arkard isn't interested in coming back.

I drank more coffee along with Hunter I turned to the page as Arkard writes his he had to sleep on a cargo ship filled with other people hoping that American will give them work. Arkard writes how he hates how poor people smell and carrying the damn bible is a waste of space for his backpack and time. It takes them 4 days to reach New Orleans and before they get their Arkard throws his bible into the sea and states he will never believe in God. Once in New Orleans things just wend from bad to worse the house, they've been given is small rundown and in disrepair. There were cockroaches, rats and muggers around every corner.

Arkard and Dmitry learn to speak English through their mother however, both women are forced into prostitution in order to make ends meet and to give their children a chance for school.

I lightly shook my head and said, "Talk about having a shitty life." Hunter said, "No kidding." I read more and by 1929 Arkard now 11 and his brother Dmitry 16 look out for each other as they both learn every person is hostile to other races especially those that aren't from American. Arkard writes detailed hatred towards other races believe that if nobody else like different color races then why are they even created in the first place.

While during small jobs to earn money Arkard states he loves art and seeing cartoon characters. However, his school doesn't have an art class, so Arkard teaches himself how to draw while at home. By the '30s times grow harder with many people jobless and prohibition taking a full effect against alcohol Arkard hates the world even more than ever before. Me and Hunter we're shocked by the level of anger, violence and language on everything he saw around him and wished it was all destroyed. Not only that Dmitry was starting to grow apart with Arkard actions but their mother or her sister wan't at home that much there wasn't anything to stop Arkard from what he was doing. Arkard stole a .22 lever action rifle and would sneak out at night shooting small animals or street light poles for fun I read his following words, "If animals are weak, so are colored people and the other races that see themselves as powerful. No, the only ones in power our like me pure white. And someone strong like me needs to clear them out."

I looked at Hunter with a disturbed look as he drank his coffee and said, "This is just sick reading this. It's like that fucked up racist novel The Turner Diary." I asked, "You read that shit?" Hunter said, "My...my father had it and he tried forcing me to read that bullshit. I don't know what gets in people's mind on this so-called perfect race it's just a bullshit." I said, "I can guess things just keep getting bad for...

When I turned back to the diary turning the page, I was unable to finish my sentence as Arkard wrote down a very dark event in his life. His mother's sister was killed by a tall black man and Arkard witness the whole event he wrote down in detail what this person did to his mother's sister and got a kick out of it seeing a weak person being killed by a stronger person however he despised the person. He writes how he followed the black man to his house and poured rat poison into his liquor and enjoyed watching him die in front of his eyes. By 1935 prohibition is now over and Arkard managed to talk his way making comics for the locate newspaper and does a strong satire on everyday life and to his luck it earns him money.

His mother and Dmitry dislike it but have no control over him as Arkard has been working out ever since coming to American and can easily beat up his older brother and mother. As we reached 38-39 Arkard writes he feelings for nature and wishes he could be part of it and his other feelings Arkard dark desires on destroying it. However almost every night Arkard has nightmares of being attacked by a gang of anthropomorphic animal people with leader of this group being a white bat and a white rabbit. On some mornings he would break down and cry for harming animals and others he would want to kill more of them.

Hunter said, "I think he is suffering from split personality disorder." I said, "Like Dr. Jekyll and Mr. Hyde." By the early 40s WWII has begun and Arkard mother has quit prostitution and found a job in a factory where Dmitry works as well however Arkard on the other hand is making more money by writing racist, satire comics for an small publishing company and this sparks interest in Hollywood. I said, "You gotta be fucking kidding me. He's getting paid for this shit." Hunter said, "Look at the asshole who wrote The Turner Diary all the racist dick heads bought it."

In 1944 in early spring Arkard is contacted by a studio called Knight Studios to work as an animation artist and agrees to it leaving his older brother and mother behind with not a care in the world for them only for himself. Hunter said, "I wonder if this studio is still running or under a different name now." I said, "We'll see." I turned the page and kept reading more of Arkard's diary.

When Arkard reaches Hollywood, he quickly works his way through Knight Studios making satire cartoons which are only shown to adult theatres, and they earn a lot of money on them. By 50-57 Arkard now using his American name Osborne Louis is living the American dream he buys two houses one in Hollywood and on in Florida however didn't write down the address on the

1st house but might have written down later. Arkard is able to buy anything he wants from sharpest suits, fancy cars, women and travel the world to enjoy its beauty and find anything else he hates to make a joke out of it.

However, things take a turn for the worst on April1, 1959 when Knight Studios is destroyed in a fire which is strongly believe to be an attack from protesters. Arkard takes his anger out on different races of people by going every night and kill them with his silenced pistol or hunting rifle. But killing isn't going to solve all of his problems as he writes down, he is running out of money and is being targeted by a group that dislikes his racist satire cartoons. By 1962 Arkard joins a Satanic cult known as "The Followers of Lucifer" there he takes part in black magic rituals and burning down churches.

I was now near the end of this diary and couldn't wait for the end because I couldn't stand Arkard anymore. He prays to Lucifer asking to remove his nightmares and to punish those that have harmed him and in return will kill people who desire to die. From 63-65 Arkard has killed over 175 people of different color in the name of Lucifer and his old friends from Knight Studios have reformed a new company believing that his wishes has been granted. However, he misses his brother and mother and wonders if they are still alive or dead.

On September1,1966 Arkard begins work on his greatest creation of all The Manson & Barbara Show believing this cartoon will wake up American and the rest of the world of the problems he sees and by getting Children to watch it they'll learn the true meaning of being an adult. But just as things were moving forward with Arkard he learns his brother Dmitry was killed during the Korean War when he and his mother left back to Russian in 1949. His mother died a year later in a car crash. Heartbroken and torn apart between his two lifestyles Arkard isn't sure if he wants to be Osborne or Arkard.

By December.13.1969 the new company is unable to find anyone wanting to take their work and Arkard tries branching out on his own. From the cartoon networks he finds and talks his way to allowing his show idea to be aired but isn't having much luck.

He prays to Lucifer asking for help again and when he reaches Miami on Dec. 25th he lied his way to head owner about his upcoming cartoon idea and is interested in it however this won't be the case as he died on that night in a car crash as the remaining diary pages are blank.

Hunter sighed and said, "This doesn't give us much to go on only his mother's house in New Orleans and an old cartoon studio and Arkard didn't say what the other company was!" I said, "Guessing it didn't have the funds or not enough people to get it going." Hunter finished his coffee and said, "So there was a chance that city hall might have a file on Osborne Louis or not." I said, "Maybe you're right. I guess we'll just relax for today and leave to New Orleans tomorrow but first I gotta call Harry and Trish and see if their alright."

Hunter asked, "You don't think the feds are taping their phone lines?" I shook my head and closed the diary set it down onto the table and said, "No they won't know about them and besides it would be a pain in the ass for them to tap into every phone line." I got up and walked over to the phone I picked it up and dialed Harry number first I placed the phone to my ear waiting for Harry or his wife to pick up but all I heard the same beeping noise. I gave it two minutes and hang up then tried Trish's number but the got the same thing I slammed the phone down and said, "Shit! Nothing from both of them!"

Suddenly the phone rang Hunter and I jumped as I thought, "Who the hell could be calling? Both Harry and Trish didn't have caller ID I looked over at Hunter again as he looked out the window but didn't see any cops or feds, I turned back to the phone picked it up and placed it to my ear. It was quite for a bit then heard Kane's voice say, "Evening Curtis." I asked, "Kane?" He replied, "Who else would be, and I know what you're thinking we can't reach you through other machines besides TV sets."

I asked, "Where's Manson?" Kane said, "He's busy doing his thing but has a lot in store for and your friend. He doesn't like the fact you been digging up graves as it isn't nice looking into something that has no relation to you." I said, "I'm reporter it's my job." Kane said, "Oh you humans are very strange bunch of people. Look why don't we save each some trouble by just giving yourselves up. Our ratings have skyrocketed which is enough and sure as hell can't stand you or your friend."

I raised my tone a bit and said, "We don't quit that easily. And I won't be defeated by a bunch of cartoon characters." Kane said, "Very well but be warned that there will be a nasty surprise for you two." Kane hanged up as I put the phone down as Hunter asked, "What did Kane want?" I turned over to Hunter and said, "Warning us about some nasty surprise in store for us but we're not going to quit." Hunter said, "Hell no. So, what's the plan driving to New Orleans or are going by boat." I thought about and knew the police and feds would be searching every street for us also the Mustang would most likely been reported stolen by now I looked back at Hunter and said, "By boat."

Hunter asked, "Should we try the docks here?" I said, "Nah we'll find a boat in Naples since it's facing the way we want to go." Hunter asked, "Wait doesn't Robert Ludlum live in Naples?" I said, "Yes he does but he won't be able to help us." Hunter said, "I bet his house there is nice." I looked outside as it was still pouring rain I said, "We'll leave after lunch as if we stay here too long things are going to heat up." Hunter said, "We still got enough ammo if we need to use it." I said, "Good. When we get a chance, we'll restock our weapons."

Suddenly a knock came at the door I took a peek out the window and saw it was hotel janitor. I scanned the street around us just in case it was a trap but saw nothing. I went over to the door but attached the chin as I unlocked the door opened it a bit and asked, "Yes?" The janitor said, "Room service." I said, "We're alright, thanks though." The janitor lightly nodded his head and began walking away I closed the door and locked it as Hunter looked out the window watching him going to the next room. Hunter said, "I hope the weather clears as it looks nasty outside." I took up at the sky seeing the dark grey storm clouds as thunder roared above us.

11:00-AM

We left the hotel and I double checked we didn't leave anything behind for the feds to track us. But as we drove through Miami the storm was getting worse, I knew our boat trip to New Orleans wasn't going to be well however this would work in our escape since the police and FBI won't believe that we would dumb enough to try but that's what we we're going to do. Wearing different clothes along with dark colored wigs and fake glasses and entered a bar. We sat in the face back corner and both ordered beers along with fresh fries and chicken wings. As we wait for our order to come from where we're sitting the raging storm outside could be heard over the loud talking and laughing.

When the busty waitress came, we thanked her and began eating our lunch. I took a quick look over at the other people sitting at the tables or bar as they we'll too busy talking about hot chicks, funny jokes, sports." I saw there were two large TV's showing football which almost everyone was staring at the TV's I thought, "Good nobody is going to bother looking at us."

Suddenly as I went back to eat, I noticed the football game had changed into a brutal and bloody sport with both teams killing each other I saw Hunter notice I whispered, "Don't look at the TV!" Hunter looked away as we kept eating but could hear the sounds of bones snapping, cracking and crushed. I tried not to think about it, so I won't puke all over the table.

We both finished our lunches as I didn't want to see what sick shit Manson was trying on us but hearing those disgusting sounds was giving us a headache. I finished my beer as the busty waitress came over asked, "Can I get you another beer?" I said, "No thanks we'll take our bill now." She lightly smiled and said, "Alright." She took out plates as I took my wallet ready to pay her when I notice Hunter was looking at the TV I whispered, "Hunter don't!" But when I took a quick glance, it was showing the news about the Tricksters and what I saw horrified me.

The news was talking about a school bombing along with city hall as the mayor of Miami has been killed in the blast. I felt my heart rate beating faster when we saw the TV screens showing the news anchorman talking at his desk an image popped up beside him and my jaw dropped open. Two sketches showed what the suspects and it was us in our disguises. Hunter whispered, "Quickly, let's leave." We both got up and quickly walked over to the front entrance and felt everyone was staring us down with anger and hatred.

Hunter and I quickly got into our Mustang as I was in the driver seat, I quickly took out the key and placed it into the ignition switch but just as I turned it, I looked to see an angry mob of people running toward us. Hunter said, "Oh shit!" I quickly shift the gear into Drive and press my foot down hard onto the gas pedal and sped off as the angry mob tried to grab onto the Mustang. I saw them pointing at the license plate I said, "Goddamn it! This place is going to be crawling with cops soon! Better get onto the highway."

Hunter took out the map of Florida as he told me where to go as I was speeding pass slow cars and went through a red light. Hunter looked around and said, "Don't see any cops yet." I said, "Good. Once we're on the highway we'll be safe." Suddenly the radio turned on as Kane voice was heard through the speakers, "Oh do you think it's going to be that easy?" Kane lightly laughed and asked, "Are you ready for my nasty surprise?" Raising my voice I said, "Try me!" Kane said, "I won't lie I like going fast on a motorcycle and seeing how you humans enjoy pushing your vehicles to their limits until you'll crash and burn, I thought it would be fun to watch to see if you keep your muscle car fast while I attached a bomb inside the trunk."

Me and Hunter's eyes opened wide as Hunter said, "Bullshit!" Kane said, "If you don't believe me why don't you pull over and... oh look here comes the men in black." I looked up in the view mirror and saw dark black Ford and Buick sedans with dark tinted windows speeding toward us. Kane laughed louder and said, "Have fun you two." Hunter yelled, "THAT MOTHERFUCKER!" I press my foot down and said, "Hunter keep the feds off us as they don't know that a bomb is in our car."

I saw an four way stop coming up and the lights ahead of me had turned red I gripped the steering wheel tightly and turned onto the wrong lane and nearly got hit by a car as it blew it's horn while Hunter took his Mossberg 500 Cruiser he flicked off the safety and pumped it as a metal slug shell was loaded into the chamber I made a hard right turn with an black Buick sedan catching up to us I could see the back passenger window roll down as an FBI agent holding a Uzi IMI with the stock folded down and an grip handle attached under the SMG.

Hunter rolled down his window and squeezed the trigger but missed hitting the windshield as the metal slug didn't break through. It was bullet proof glass. Hunter quickly pumped his shotgun, but the FBI agent fired his Uzi IMI but had it firing signal shot and nearly scored a shot on Hunter as the bullets tore through the rear window. Hunter aimed for his head and pulled the trigger. The FBI agent head exploded with splatter of blood. Hunter pumped his Mossberg 500 Cruiser and shot the front rear tire as it exploded, I rammed it off the road as it crashed head on into a van.

I saw a sign pointing to the highway I made a sharp left turn with more SMG gun fire hitting the Mustang. I felt one bullet zoomed passed my face as it broke my driver side window. I said under my breath, "FUCK!" Speeding along side was a Ford sedan both passenger and rear door windows row down I grabbed reached for my CZ-75 I had tucked into my pants. I pulled on the slid and quickly aimed at the passenger side and squeezed off a few rounds killing the FBI agent and other behind him fired his Uzi IMI. A few bullets zoomed by my face as the sedan got closer Hunter yelled, "DUCK!" I lowered my head, Hunter fired his shotgun killing the FBI agent as my ears were ringing.

I lifted my head up and nearly hit a taxi I turned to avoid and saw another red light coming I kept going and heard the loud horn blowing on my left side as I nearly got hit by a bus. However, three speeding FBI cars crashed into the bus I saw the highway coming up as I got onto it and kept going fast. Hunter reloaded his shotgun I took a quick look at the dashboard and saw we had half a tank of gas I said, "Shit!" Hunter asked, "What?" He looked and saw what I was talking about. He quickly turned his head back and said, "We really pissed off those feds their coming back!" I looked in the view mirror and saw the black sedans along with large SUVs with fog lights speeding towards us. Suddenly the leading SUV roof popped open a hatch as we saw an agent holding an M-16A2 with a scope and laser sight.

Hunter quickly grabbed the Ruger Mini-14 and loaded a magazine into the rifle and aimed at the agent and quickly squeezed off the trigger but the FBI agent was wearing a bullet proof vest. The agent fired back as bullets tore through the rear and front windshield and one bullet hitting the radio. Hunter quickly aimed for his head and pulled the trigger and killed him. As blacker SUV's and sedans were catching up Hunter fired off a few more rounds tiring to hit the tires.

The Ruger Mini-14 clicked empty Hunter yelled, "SHIT!" He quickly reloaded it then suddenly a spotlight was shined on us I looked up and saw a helicopter flying alongside the highway with an FBI agent holding a high-powered sniper rifle. I then saw the FBI agents were catching up with us I said, "I'll handle the chopper! Just keep those pricks off of us!" Hunter said, "Got it!" He armed his rifle and turned to FBI agents firing away I aimed my CZ-75 at the sniper and squeezed off the trigger quickly. A few shots hit the sliding door, but one bullet manage to hit an agent in the knee causing him to fall on his back I then aimed at the helicopter cockpit and fired off more rounds but saw the glass was bullet proof. My pistol clicked empty I quickly reloaded it and drove pass the slow-moving cars.

Then ahead of us was a semi-truck carrying gasoline trailer just as I went to pass the truck blocked our way, I only knew one way around it I drove onto the wrong side off the road as vehicles flashed their high beams and blew their horns. I dodged the oncoming traffic I turned to the semi-truck and had a bad idea, but it was only way we could lose the feds. I turned to Hunter and said, "Shoot the gas trailer!" Hunter looked at me for a bit but knew he had no choice he aimed it as the FBI was about to pass the semi-truck Hunter squeezed off a few rounds hitting it and within seconds it exploded. Bright orange flames lit up the dark stormy highway as the blast radius took out 2 FBI sedans and send the 2nd car into an SUV with such force it went onto the opposite lane crashing into a car. I quickly got back onto the right lane as traffic had come to full stop.

I blew air out as Hunter yelled, "GODDAMN IT! I SWEAR WE'LL MAKE THEM PAY FOR THIS!" We both hated the idea of killing innocent people but knew we had no choice. They would kill us first and not even ask why just following orders from Manson! I saw a sign showing we we're getting closer to Naples once there we would have to jump out this car as I wasn't going to take chances with these fucking psychopathic cartoon characters!

As we saw Naples coming up, I saw the gas gauge light was flashing bright red just head of us were the docks I said, "Hunter when I say jump. Do it!" Hunter put his two weapons into the duffel bag as I toss him my pistol knowing I wasn't going to be able to hang on to it. We both had our passenger doors open and just the Mustang drove onto the docks I yelled, "JUMP!"

We both landed into the cold water and the impact hurt our backs but at least we we're still breathing I watched as the Mustang crashed headfirst into the water and suddenly the car blew up, I coughed as I swam to the surface and said, "That son of a bitch!" I turned my head over to Hunter as he waved at me, we both swam back onto the docks and ran looking for a boat. We then found one as we got on board Hunter untied the rope as I went into the control room thinking I was going have to hot wire it but saw an start button I press it as the engine came to life I then heard sirens roaring far off in the distance I quickly pulled the lever full throttle as the boat speed off Hunter came inside carrying both duffel bags and sat down and said, "Shit! Too fucking close!"

I said, "No kidding!" Hunter asked, "So how the hell did Kane put a bomb in our car?" I said, "Magic...fucking magic!" Hunter said, "Alright we'll get to New Orleans ditch the boat find Arkard's house and see if there any clues for us to go on." I said, "If not then we can check out the paper he wrote those satire comics." Hunter asked, "What's the name of the paper?" I said, "South Sun Press." I turned my head back and saw the sirens flashing along with four more helicopters with their spotlights aimed where the

Mustang blew up I said, "Maybe we'll get lucky and they'll think we died." Hunter said, "I hope so."

Bright lightning strikes lit up the sky of darkness with heavy rain fall with rough waves making this trip very hard and uneasy. I had gone fishing many times with my father so I was used to being out on the sea however couldn't say the same for Hunter as his face had turn green. I knew if we tried reaching New Orleans by driving the police would have caught us as they would have made sure that we didn't escape them so easily. But since we did, I feared they would only step up their game as I thought, "If the FBI calls it quits then who else is going to come after us besides Manson? Would the US military get involve?"

I had sudden thoughts of things going bad to worse! With all this destruction, murder and mayhem that Manson was causing I thought, "Is he trying to start WWIII?" I couldn't get this nasty thought out of my mind and strongly felt that's what Manson was trying to cause nothing but chaos. I then heard Hunter come inside coughing a bit and said, "Fucking hell! Promise me we won't use boats again." I said, "If we'll able to keep a low profile we should be able to travel more on the road without the cops finding us."

Hunter said, "Say we lost our wigs when we jumped, and we don't have many left." I sighed and asked, "What do we have left?" Hunter said, "Just the dark hair wigs." I said, "When we get to New Orleans, we'll get some new clothes to wear and... Hunter asked, "What if Manson does that shit again on us. Showing what we look like with our disguise on?" I turned to Hunter rising my voice a bit and said, "It doesn't matter! Manson is just going to be a fucking prick to us! We'll do whatever it takes!"

New Orleans
9:00-PM

We felt very tried but made it at last! The storm was still raging on as me and Hunter carried our duffel bags and walked down the near empty streets with thick fog rolling in and roaring thunder. Me and Hunter stood under a bus stop stand to stop for a few moments. Hunter wiped off his wet face I did the same he asked, "Say what was Arkard's house address?" I said, "No way we're walking they're in this weather." Hunter said, "Think about it. The minute we step into any place that has an TV, radio or phone Manson and his gang will find out where we are and what we look like then plaster our faces all over the walls here and when these people see it, they won't rest until we're dead!" I realized Hunter had a point and after that steam ship bombing Manson did the people of New Orleans would be hellbent on killing us.

I said, "Good point. Let me check." I set the duffel bag down onto the bench and was glad these things were waterproof. I pulled on the zipper opened it then reached in. Didn't take me long to find it I pulled it out then flipped through the pages until I found what we we're looking for. Hunter moved in closer to look at the page I said, "It's on Rainbow Lane and the address is 1331." We both stared at the number as I thought, "13's and 31's? How can this be possible?" Hunter turned his head back and saw there wasn't any more else in the streets as more thunder roared, he turned back to me and said, "Let's get going."

Walking down the dark foggy streets felt creepy the air was warm as the rain was the only thing that was keeping us cool. When we reached Lakeview, we walked through the streets until we found Rainbow Lane, we took a good look at each house then found it. The house looked like it never saw another owner after Arkard's mother and brother left the place and couldn't believe it hadn't been torn down. However, we saw graffiti had been spray painted both on the outside and inside the house through the windows. But as we walked closer to it, I swear I felt a bad feeling about this place. The front door was unlocked, and we let ourselves in.

Hunter and I took out our flashlights turned them on I turned over to him and said, "I'll search around in the basement you'll start in the bedrooms." Hunter said, "Alright." I turned over to the left and saw the kitchen and the next room over was the basement. As I was about to enter it, I saw a spray painted message in red saying, "FREE SEX! DOWN HERE!" I rolled my eyes and aimed the flashlight downstairs and saw it was a very small basement I began walking downstairs and when I reached the bottom it was very cold.

I saw more graffiti all over the walls and lying on the dirty floor were broken beer bottles, used condoms, burned match sticks and some old clothing. I knew if Arkard wanted to hide anything from his mother and brother he would hide it in a place he would only know. I checked along the walls which were old brinks I felt them seeing if one of them was loose. I also listen closely outside but all I could hear the was raging storm however the brinks were all still in place I then tried looking under the stairs. I saw nothing but dust and cobwebs I looked at the floor, but nothing was there. I then looked down at the floor it was all stone. I lightly shook my head but stopped then looked up at the ceiling and saw wood boards I looked at them closely and saw one that looked out of place.

I walked over to it than using my left hand while aiming the flashlight with my right hand I removed the lose wood board and saw something hidden in darkness. I took out another part out of the ceiling and I was able to see what it was. Sketch books I pulled them out and blew off the dust saw they were dated when Arkard used them. I checked in the empty space in the ceiling but didn't see anything else I checked the other wood boards but none of them moved I thought, "Better go check on Hunter." I walked upstairs and placed the sketch books into my duffel bag I took a quick look outside and saw it was very foggy.

As I turned to see where the narrow staircase lead, I noticed how quite it was inside. I slowly walked upstairs as I switched flashlight to my left hand then reached with my right to my CZ-75. I slowly pulled on the side arming it then took a few steps up listening very carefully. When I reached the top, I saw there were only two bedrooms I looked at the floor to see where Hunter footprints went as they went into both bedrooms. I felt my heart beating faster I said, "Hunter! Hunter? Are you there?" Silence I quickly turn back but didn't see anyone behind me I turned my head back and began walking towards the first bedroom. My heart was beating faster gripping my pistol tightly and ready to use it if I had to.

When I reached the first bedroom, I shined the flashlight inside and didn't see anything but an empty room. I turned my head back to the next bedroom nobody was there. I raised my voice a bit and said, "Hunter!" I turned my head to the second bedroom and slowly walked towards it waiting for anything to happen. I swung my body facing the second bedroom and it was empty I took a few steps inside and saw nothing then suddenly I felt someone was behind me. I turned my body around to see Hunter. I jumped and said, "Goddamn it!"

Hunter said, "Sorry I had to take a leak so I went out in the backyard." I asked, "You couldn't just piss in here?" Hunter lightly shook his head and asked, "Find anything? Both bedrooms are empty." I said, "Yeah some sketch books in the basement ceiling." Just as Hunter went to talk, we heard cars pulling up me and Hunter went over to the first bedroom as it had a window and saw dark purple 57 Cadillac Eldorado Brougham with black tinted windows. 3 of them were parked in front of the house as bat men wearing dark purple or black suits looked up where we we're at then Kane got out of the Cadillac holding a big fuse bomb. He laughed loudly then we saw the others taking bombs. I said, "Shit!" We both ran as Kane threw the fuse bomb at 1ˢᵗ bedroom window it smashed as we went to the second bedroom, I kicked the window and we both jumped landed on the muddy ground and started running. Suddenly the house behind us exploded as the blast knocks us down onto the wet muddy ground.

We quickly got up and ran towards a wooden fence and climbed over it then onto the empty street. However, as we ran, we heard those Cadillac's coming I turned to Hunter and said, "Quickly hide!" As we went to climb over a fence suddenly two large dogs came out of the darkness barking at us then a headlight shined on us, I said, "SHIT!" We began running down the street as we heard the Cadillac coming after us. Turning left we jumped over a fence as the roaring engine of the Cadillac was getting closer to us. We both turned to a tall wooden fence and climbed over it as the Cadillac drove through the first fence then it turned to the wooden fence. By the time we hopped off of it, the car drove through, nearly running us over.

Hunter ran over to me suddenly the Cadillac backed up nearly hitting him as we climbed over another wall and ran out of the Lakeview Street. I felt my lungs were burning with my legs feeling tried. Hunter grabbed my shoulder and pulled me over to him as we ran inside a factory. As we got further inside the building, we could hear the Cadillac's pulling up and Manson's goons chasing us. Keeping low and trying not too much noise while looking for a way out I wasn't going to let my fear of this place get the better of me.

However, as we got further inside the factory, we won't seeing a back way out of this place. Suddenly we heard Kane laughing we turned our heads as he and Manson men were getting closer, I then saw stairs leading downstairs I whispered, "Quick, in there." Me and Hunter went downstairs however it was pitch black and we didn't realize we dropped our flashlights, so we had to feel our way out of here. But as we got deeper in the hallway, I swear I felt someone was following us.

Hunter stopped and said, "I found a door!" I turned to behind us and felt my heart beating very fast as the sound of footsteps grew louder Hunter then got the door opened but it was heavy, he said, "Quickly! Help me open it!" I grabbed the handle and pulled it open as we both ran inside then closed it as Hunter locked it, we turned around and began running through the darkness. Then just ahead of us were stairs leading towards outside I felt so revealed but just as I outside suddenly I heard Kane's voice beside me, "Hey Curtis!" When I turned my head over Kane punched me hard in the face as I landed on by back.

Hunter turned to Kane and went to punch him, but Kane dodged his attack and threw a hard blow to Hunter's face. As Hunter went to get back up Kane kicked him in the chest I aimed my CZ-75 at Kane's back and squeezed away at the trigger. Just then my pistol clicked empty as Kane slowly turned around as I saw the bullet holes in front of his chest, but he wasn't bleeding I said under my breath, "What the hell!?" Kane grinned and said, "Did you forget that were cartoons." The bullet holes disappeared as I tried to get up, but Kane grabbed me and rammed my back into the factory wall I felt his warm breath against my face as he stared back at me.

His right bright green leather glove gripped my neck tightly as I felt he could easily break my neck. Kane grinned and said, "I thought the real Tricksters would have been more of a challenge but I'm very disappointed how easy to beat you." I said, "Why don't you go fuck yourself then!" Kane rammed his left fist into my gut I growled in pain Kane eyes looked over at my duffel bag and said, "You have something that doesn't belong to you. I'm just going to give it back to Manson and... Suddenly I saw Hunter was standing behind Kane holding his Mossberg 500 Cruiser shotgun. I quickly kicked Kane in the groin causing him to drop me then Hunter blew his head off. I stood up we both ran as Kane's headless body turned to us and made a very loud demonic scream.

Running as fast as we could with heavy rain fall, we got far away from that factory and heard sirens roaring far in the distance. We came to a rundown abandon apartment and would spend the night here. Once we found a room, we had a door we could close our bodies gave out as I felt cold, tried and pain. I turned to Hunter and said, "Thanks, back there." Hunter said, "I won't leave you behind." I said, "Once it's morning we'll decided what to do next." Hunter lightly nodded his head as we both close our eyes and quickly fell asleep.

Feb.22
7:00-AM

I woke up by the loud roar of sirens I thought the police had found us as I opened my eyes, I saw that we we're still in the abandoned apartment I saw there was broken window with torn curtains I slowly stood up to see what was going on outside and my eyes open wide. The houses in Lakeview had burned all down with dozens of police cars, fire trucks and ambulances and helicopters flying above the destroyed houses I breathed, "That bastard!" Hunter woke up as I moved my hand away as he heard the sirens Hunter looked at me and asked, "How bad is it?" I sighed and said, "See for yourself." I moved away as Hunter took a peek out the window then said, "That fucking bat!"

I said, "Just what we fucking needed! The city is going to be crawling with cops and their going to search every inch of this place until they find us." Hunter sighed said, "Great...just fucking great!" Our clothes were damp, and we didn't have anything else to change into and hardly any energy left in me. I could tell Hunter was tired as I was, I now feared the worse if the police find us, they would just kill us, they will not bother taking us in alive.

Hunter asked, "So now what?" I said, "Let's wait a bit and see if they leave then try to find a house to sneak into and get us some clothes, food and wheels then leave New Orleans." Hunter rubbed his eyes then to our horror we heard dogs barking outside of the apartment I took a peek out the broken window and saw officers with dogs as they were pulling on their leashes I said under my breath, "Shit!" I turned to Hunter and said, "We gotta go now!" We both got up and heard the police officers yelling as they were making their way upstairs.

We ran through the fire exit and could hear the helicopters coming over. We ran through a small forest area and hoped by the time the police were done finishing looking in the apartment we would be long gone. But my fears were proven wrong when those dogs were barking and chasing us. Just as we got out of the small forest and onto a street without warning police cars drove in front of us with officers getting out aiming their pistols and shotguns at us. They yelled, "HANDS IN THE AIR! DROP THE BAGS NOW! GET ON THE GROUND!" Behind us were more officers as the dogs were barking wildly I knew they wanted to bite us. Me and Hunter toss our duffel bags down and had our hands up and slowly got onto the ground the officers came over handcuffed us as we we're force into the back of the squad car. I turned my head and saw they put the duffel bags into the trunk of the car. They got in drove off as I turned my head over to the small forest, I saw Manson standing there with his glowing red eyes and grinning his bright white teeth. I thought, "You haven't seen the last of me Manson!"

However, our ride to the station wasn't pleasant there was a mob of angry people yelling, screaming and showing their hate to us as I feared they would pull us out of the squad car let them beat us to death. But the police officers and SWAT teams kept them away from the squad car. The officer driving said, "You two are in a deep shit now." Hunter and I didn't say anything as we saw the police station coming up, I thought, "Ok, keep calm. We'll find a way out of this mess." As the squad car pulled into the underground parking lot waiting for us was heavily armed officers and FBI agents which didn't look happy at all.

As we we're taken out, I heard loud click noises and saw those standing by had flicked their gun safety off just in case they had to use them. I turned my head back to the trunk as the feds we're taking the duffel bags we would have to get those back as I had to see what was drawn on those sketch books. As I turned my head away, I heard one fed said, "Have them washed! They smell like shit!" Hunter said, "Fuck you, prick!" The fed punched him in the gut as I felt the barrel of an Uzi IMI pressed into my back I growled as we we're forced into the showers. They tore our clothes off and pushed us into the shower as hot steamy water poured onto our bodies. To keep us from fighting back they had their dogs barking at us.

When they done washing us they threw us towels to dry off and gave us bright orange prison outfits along with black shoes, and black socks. Hunter was taken to a different questioning room while I was placed into another one. I sat at the small table with a window on my left side knowing I couldn't see who was on the other side, but the officers could. I felt cool air blowing through the vents with only ceiling light above me making a light buzzing noise. I rubbed my eyes feeling more awake now.

I knew I tried attacking the FBI agent the officers would come charging in and use their guns if they had to. My mind was racing with ideas of how me and Hunter could escape out of alive. Fighting everyone in here was suicide and if the angry mob manage to break inside, they'll just keep coming until they can grab their hands on us. Sneaking out of here would be impossible with all the cops, feds and SWAT outside of this place. It seemed our only way out was by escaping prison but seeing how the whole world believed that we we're deadly terrorists they would throw into a maximum-security prison. I knew that once we escaped, they won't take a second chance on us they would kill us on sight. Then I heard door open with two FBI agents walking in then an officer sending up a video camera in front of me as the fed had a folder with a lot of paper inside of it. He had short black hair, dark green eyes and felt his burning anger inside of him. When the second fed finished setting up the camera and left a remote attached to the camera by a cable. The FBI agent asked, "Are you ready to talk Curtis?" I looked at him and said, "Yes."

Chapter 5

The FBI agent turned on the video camera but I didn't bother look at it I kept my eyes on him. He said, "Please state your full name." I said, "Curtis Parker." He then said, "Place of birth and age." I said, "January 20th,1964 in Black Creek near the state of New York. I'm 21 years old." FBI agent looked at me and said, "So from a small-time news reporter to a terrorist. Guess you won't getting enough of that frame you wanted hu?" I asked, "Do you really think I manage to pull off all these bombings in a short matter of time?"

The FBI agent said, "You tell me, Curtis. Tracking you and your friend down wasn't easy and left hardly a trail for us to follow so I'm wondering how you two did it." I said raising my voice a bit, "Cut the bullshit. I know nothing about making bombs and never been interest of being a terrorist." The FBI agent kept a calm face and asked, "Really? Then why did we find these?" Then the FBI agent opened the folder and placed pictures in front of me. On the photos were books along with guides of making bombs, military combat training, architecture, weapon manuals, lock picking & safe cracking, books about Nazism and The Turner Diaries.

FBI agent looked at me and said, "You were saying." I said, "Hold it! You think that all of this is enough evidence to pin these crimes on me." FBI agent didn't say anything as I felt my anger rising but I knew that's what he was trying to do to me trying to break me under pressure. He then asked, "If it wasn't you Curtis, then who was it?" I said, "Manson." FBI agent asked, "Charles Manson?" I said, "No, just Manson. He's worse than me or my friend." FBI agent said, "So you're telling me that it wasn't you or your friend Hunter Cunningham behind these racist attacks?" I said, "Yes." FBI agent asked, "What does Manson look like?" I knew if I said cartoon he won't buy it so I said, "Rumors. He likes wearing purple and has a thing for old style clothing such as a top hat." FBI agent asked, "Where did you hear this?" I said, "From what little information I could find on him after all I'm a reporter it's what I do."

FBI agent asked, "So from leaving a trail of dead bodies and destruction is your reason of going after Manson?" I could tell this question was personal I sighed and said, "Look. I didn't ask for this shit to happen. I was just following some leads and next thing I know I'm framed for murder, kidnapping, bombing, arson and terrorism. That's all-Manson's dirty work he'll do anything to keep anyone away from the truth and doesn't care who he kills after all Manson hates people." FBI agent stared at me with silence for a bit as I said, "And he's great for tricking and fooling anyone into believing his lies."

FBI agent asked, "Couldn't tell anyone this?" I said, "I tried but nobody believed me and...and what the hell was I supposed to do when the police came knocking on my apartment door? First off, the tape would I be dumb enough to send a snuff film to the police station then wait for them to show up? Second, I would have told someone about Manson and his gang, but it seemed those who were chasing us we're too trigger happy rather than asking us questions! And last...I didn't have a choice to do the things I did to get here." FBI agent lightly nodded his head and asked, "Why did you target the people you did?" I knew he didn't buy anything I said I thought, "Why did I bother saying what I knew he won't believe it." I said, "I am NOT a terrorist!"

FBI agent said, "You can deny it all you want Curtis we got the evidence against you and Hunter. After what you two did not even God will forgive you." I raised my voice a bit and said, "You didn't answer my questions! Why would I be fucking dumb enough to send the police a snuff film of me killing my parents and kidnapping my own brother!? Their no reason for it! I loved my family and would do anything to help them. I had the video cameras placed in their house to see what my little brother was hiding from me along with my parents." FBI agent took a slow breath and asked, "Hiding what, from you?"

I said, "Ok. Manson the person I was telling you about is from an TV show that only kids or young teens talk about. It's called The Manson & Barbara Show. That's what me and Hunter were looking into, and I know it sounds like I'm full of shit but it's the truth. Go to any school and see for yourself the kids all talk about and they are being brainwashed by Manson and his bullshit about our world! He wants kids to hate adults calming that they'll ruin the world and it's up to them to stop them. It's the goddamn truth and I can't believe most people are fucking blind to what they are seeing. Even you are blinded by Manson lies and those who do stick their noses into his matter he'll do anything to keep them away. Even killing people or children for that fact."

FBI agent sighed and said, "I heard enough. We'll see what the judge has to say about you and your friend but know this. Nobody will remember you for the things you did. And that I'm glad as a cocksucker like you desires to rot in hell!" He stopped recording as two officers came and took me away.

11:00-AM

Me and Hunter sat in a jail cell as the FBI would be taking us away to court where we would be facing our prison sentence, and both end up with the death penalty. Hunter said, "They didn't buy anything I said. I told them how it all happened, but they all thought I was full of shit." I said, "Same here." Hunter asked, "So what the hell are we going to do!? They'll kill us and Manson will get away with whatever he's planning." I shook my head and said, "No. We're not quitting." I looked at Hunter and said, "We'll find a way out of this mess. Sure, we lost the evidence we had on Arkard but I won't throw in the goddamn towel like Manson wants us to do." Hunter sighed and asked, "How many people have escaped maximum security prisons?"

I said, "The 3 guys who escaped from Alcatraz. Look Hunter it can be done don't lose your cool. We'll find a way out of this." Suddenly we heard heavy footsteps as it was FBI agent, I spoke with but behind him were US soldiers. We saw there heavily muscular bodies and were armed with M-16A2's FBI agent said, "Ok you two I hope you're ready to hear what the judge has to say about your crimes." Hunter asked, "Can we just skip all of it and be sent off to prison." FBI agent lightly grinned and said, "Oh you won't be going to any prison but a very special one." I had an idea what prison it would be and if it were true then me and Hunter would only have once chance to break free.

Our arms and legs were cuffed to short chains so we couldn't run fast. We walked into the underground parking lot and got inside an armored truck with more soldiers standing outside holding assault rifles and shotguns I thought, "They really think were that dangerous? I can't wait to get my hands on Manson and make him pay for everything he done to my life." Outside we could hear yelling and shouting of the angry mob with some stuff being thrown at the armor truck. I knew when we reached the courthouse there would be news crews waiting for us with their microphones, cameras and tape recorders shoving them in our faces asking us the questions like, "Why we did it? Do we feel sorry for your crimes against humanity? Do you think god will forgive us?" Me and Hunter won't going to say anything just keep our heads facing the courthouse get the whole thing over with then once we know what prison we're being sent plan our escape.

When we got to the courthouse the angry mob was waiting for us with soldiers and SWAT keeping them away from us while the reporters waiting for us. Me and Hunter walked up the steps with a few microphones nearly hitting us in the mouth. Once we got inside the feds followed us along with a few officers and the news reporters recording everything that was happening.

When the judge came out along with his court members, they all stared us down and when the judge read our crime sheet, he trashed-talked us like we we're low life and was looking forward us to rotting the rest of our lives in hell. When he was finished with his findings, we would be sentenced to Diablo Maximum Security

Prison that was on a man-made island out in the Gulf of Mexico. And we both would get the death penalty. I had a bad feeling that was the place they we're going to throw us in and our chances of escaping it were very slim as nobody has escaped Diablo Prison since it was opened back in the 40s.

We were taken back to the armored truck and would be taken to the airport where a military transport would be waiting for us. Hunter said, "I'm glad that's over. Holy shit, any longer of that judge trash-talking us and I might have gotten deaf." Hunter looked at me as I had my right hand under my chin as I was busy trying to think of an escape plan of Diablo Prison. Hunter sighed and said, "Diablo Prison. We are going to have a real challenge on our hands." I said, "No shit. I remember my father telling me his grandfather who surfed in WWII they sent Nazi war criminals along with some other sick bastards." Hunter said, "Even after we escaped, we still have to think what to do." I thought about it and said, "Maybe we might have a way to get the evidence we had on Arkard. If we do, then we head to Hollywood and see where Arkard's other house is." Hunter said, "We still need to find a way to stop Manson and his brainwashing signal."

I said, "If we can find where he's airing his show then we'll be able to stop him and wake everyone up." Hunter asked, "And when we do. Will everyone see that Manson forced us to do what we did, or will they still see us as the real villain?" I said, "We'll find a way. I won't quit until the truth prevails." Sitting in silence as the armor truck drove what felt like an endless drive until we reached the airport. When it stopped the back door opened up as US soldiers aimed their assault rifles at us as we both got out and walked on board a Lockheed C-130 Hercules.

Once on board the engines roared to life and felt the plane moving down the runaway as it lifted up into the air. The soldiers stared at us while we waited until we reached the prison. I was getting tired of it, so I turned to them and raised my voice and said, "You guys got anything better to do then fucking stare at us all day!? Some of the soldiers looked away while a few kept their eyes on us I turned my head away.

I did read about an escape attempt at Diablo Prison back in 79 but it quickly fell apart and after that the place got a full upgrade insuring nobody would escape Diablo Prison alive. But me and Hunter would proof the system wrong that we could escape it!"

D.M.S.P. 2:00-PM

The Lockheed C-130 Hercules transport touched down on the runway and when it came to a full stop the back hatch opened up as we walked out of it and when we saw Diablo Prison it was very tall and big building. Tall walls with guard towers covered the rest of the island with the only place with no steel walls was the hanger which had tall fence with electric bob-wire. The soldiers forced us to move as we went through air lock doors into an small guard outpost. The guards were heavily built and armed with the strongest fire power ever.

A guard wearing mirror sunglasses and had some scars on his face with short reddish-brown hair said with a Southern accent, "Welcome to Diablo Prison cocksuckers! It's been a while since I've seen someone came here." I said, "I can see why." He lightly grinned and said, "Heard what you two did and been looking forward to seeing rotten bastards like you get the chair. As a matter of fact, the other prisoners are looking forward to it as well. Interesting how everyone finds death so entertaining. Anyway, let's get you two into your cells and we already served lunch so if you haven't eaten yet, you'll have to wait for dinner at 7 clock."

The head guard which we learned his name was Clive took us through the outpost and into Diablo Prison. Once inside we saw there was a lot of video cameras, electric and air lock doors, heavily armed guards and lots of dangerous criminals. I saw the guards had card keys and used elevators which was the only way through this place as there wasn't any stairs to use. I thought, "If a fire broke out in this place everyone would be fighting to get out of here. However, the guards won't care about the prisoners they would flee the place and let everyone else die here. This might work."

Once we got on the highest floor Clive had us walk into our cell which had open bar walls on both sides with a thick electric door and in front of our cell was a video camera. There was one toilet and sink for us to use with two small beds for us. Clive said, "Enjoy your stay while it lasts." I asked, "Hey Clive when is our death sentence going to be?" Clive turned around to face me and said, "Got orders not to tell you yet but when the day comes I'll be happy to let you know. Now get in both of you cocksuckers!" We both got into our cell as the electric door closed behind us and the guards along with Clive walked away.

Me and Hunter looked out the small bar window with 4 bars in front of us. We could see far off in the distance where Texas was, but it was a long way. Even if we did find a way out of here, we would still have to reach land. Hunter turned to me and said, "I bet when it's dinner time the food is going to taste like shit." For some reason I lightly laughed.

Feb.28
11:00-AM

Me and Hunter we're eating lunch in the prison cafeteria and lucky for us nobody was sitting with us, but nobody here liked anyone. I saw a few video cameras above us in the ceiling we learned that the person watching everyone through the cameras could hear sound but not if we spoke quietly. Clive was going to have us both work in the kitchen by March and if we didn't get into any trouble, he would be nice enough to tell us when our death date was. But we didn't plan on waiting for that day me and Hunter had to find a way out of here before it was too late.

Hunter whispered, "Ok so we might be able to cause a fire in the kitchen but how are we going to get out?" I thought about it then whispered, "If one of us was able to knock out the power then we could climb through the elevator shafts since there are no air vents in this place." Hunter finished his lunch as I was already done with mine. Hunter whispered, "We could also try to sneak out an knife and hide it somewhere in our cell." I whispered, "We'll have to do it in a way the guards won't notice what we'll up to." Hunter whispered, "Also we'll need our hands on guns as we won't make it through here unarmed." I knew the showers were on lower floor and the guards would only take 5 of us at a time and watch us wash then have us sent back to our cells. The only time the guards won't be watching us is when we we're working that would be our only chance to do our escape however learning where the armory, power room or where the guards kept the trained soldiers, they won't allowed to talk about any of that.

Hunter whispered, "When we do escape, they'll be after us." I whispered, "And I won't allow them to capture or kill us." Hunter lightly nodded his head as he drank a bottle of water and so did I. While moving my eyes around, the guards had earpieces attached in their right ear so only they would hear what the camera men we're seeing, and they never went around anywhere without their sidearm and assault rifle or shotgun.

The guards also wore body armor which meant getting into a fire fight with them wasn't going to be easy to take out and to top it off the goddamn soldiers would be happy to join in since those guys will get trigger happy when they are ordered to shoot at the prisoners. I now had two choices to escape this hell hole. Cause enough trouble to make the guards and soldiers deal with the prisoners allowing us to escape or out smart everyone and sneak out under their noses. However, this was going to take time, planning and luck. Once we did get off this island the law and Manson would be after us again.

March.8
8:00-AM

Me and Hunter we're working away in the kitchen cooking all the prisoners' lunch. However, once we we're done cooking, we would only have 45 minutes to eat our lunch then be sent to do other chores Clive would have us do and won't allow us to be together until it was dinner and back to our cell. The other prisoners kept themselves and since they had no hope of gaining what they lost they won't care to drag someone down with them which meant we couldn't trust nobody else but that was fine by us. There was one guard that would check on us from time to time but won't come too close to us while we we're cooking. This would allow us to carry a knife or some kind of weapon for us to use but we would have to hide it in a good spot since the guards check our cell at the end of every week and force us to strip naked if we're hiding anything in our clothing.

Once we had a weapon to use, we only get one chance with it. If one of us were caught with a weapon or be in an a place we won't supposed to be, Clive would have us killed on sight. I overheard a few of the prisoners talking about other inmates that killed themselves as they couldn't stand it here and Clive and his guards didn't give a shit about anyone here only themselves. Another thing me and Hunter will need is those key cards. Without those we won't be able to go anywhere in this prison. If, however, we found out a way to shut off the power we could pry-open the elevator doors and climb through the shafts. I thought, "They must have boats here just in case the transport wasn't here or badly damaged. Only time would tell us when the time came."

I felt a guard watching me and Hunter along with two other prisoners cooking away then left us. While this food wasn't that good it was better than nothing. Me and Hunter have been working out in our cell which the guards didn't mind at all, but they were still stronger than us however what we lacked in strength we would beat them with our minds.

11:40-AM

Me and Hunter finished cooking lunch and were eating in a small room which had no camera or guard standing by which meant we could talk however once we heard that heavy door open it would only two guards a few steps to reach the room. Hunter said, "Ok so the knives we've been using there were like the ones you can buy at any hardware store however, I noticed the blades can be easily bent if too much pressure is put on them." I said, "So we would have to go for the neck with them not anywhere else on the body." Hunter nodded his head as he ate more of his lunch.

I said, "Only hiding spot is in our socks but the only place we could hide them is the ceiling above us." Hunter said, "Oh better tie one of our shoelaces around it and have it hanging out of the window after all they never bother looking out of it." I thought about it, and it seemed like a good idea I said, "Ok just getting it without the camera seeing it." Hunter said, "Ok now that we have two places, we can hide our knifes the question is which part of this prison has an weak spot we can use to escape?" I said, "The escape I remembered back in 79 a bunch of guys attacking a group of guards at once taking their weapons and key ring however when the soldiers were called in and they killed all them quickly as their isn't much to take cover in a fire fight in here. After that event all the stairs were destroyed and replaced with elevators and key rings were replaced with key cards."

Hunter said, "Hell if we're close enough to the shore we could just jump into the sea and swim all the way to Texas. After all there isn't any beaches or sallow water this whole island is surrendered by deep water." I said, "We would be better off using a boat as swimming all the way to Texas is long way and I think there are sharks out here as well." I finished my lunch and I said, "We'll think of something I know it." Just as we we're almost done, we heard the heavy door open as the guards were coming to get us.

I was sent to do laundry with a few other prisoners while the guards watched us. It was very hot in here I wiped off the sweat running down my forehead and carrying the same bright orange prison suits from one basket to another. As I was finishing another load of laundry standing behind a guard was an open doorway that had stairs leading down to it, I thought, "I wonder what's down their?" I turned my head away as I didn't want to stare at it too long or the guard know I was hatching an escape plan. Maybe Hunter will notice something out of place here and we can use to our advantage.

7:15-PM

It was pouring rain outside lightning flashed outside with roaring thunder that would keep any nearby guards hearing what me and Hunter we're talking about, but we still whispered. I asked, "So in the laundry I saw a stairway leading to downstairs with a guard blocking it so I couldn't see much but I bet that leads to somewhere." Hunter whispered, "Well the water and waste tanks won't be able any help to us. You were right they have boats that patrol the island and they're armed with machine guns. If we got on board one those boats, we could use it to escape."

I ate my dinner as I whispered, "Ok the only way we're getting out of here. First cause a fire to keep everyone busy, next we'll split up making it harder for the guards to find us and we'll regroup somewhere else here in the prison." Hunter whispered, "There isn't a machine shop so we can't make anything here we'll have to use what we can find." I whispered, "Ok the kitchen is small so we'll need to spread a big fire quickly as a riot may not work in our favor." Hunter whispered, "Yeah seeing how everyone keeps to themselves. If anyone is dumb enough to start a fight, they'll all join in and kill the person."

I whispered, "The stoves we use are gas powered so it won't take much to start a fire it's just getting out of there in time." Hunter looked over at the other prisoners and turned his eyes back to me and whispered, "What if we sabotaged one of the stoves that way if a guard happens to come in, he'll try to put the fire out and we can take him down." I nodded my head and whispered, "We'll get in early in there before the other two prisoners come in giving us enough time to find which stove would be the best one to cause a fire."

Hunter nodded his head I whispered, "Ok that's what we'll do, and we'll sneak out knives for us to use and tie them to the window bars and put some above the ceiling just in case. Once we have guards key cards and guns, we'll be able to get out of here." Hunter whispered, "I just need more time on what I can learn before we do anything as one of the guards might slip up."

I whispered, "I also notice something about the video cameras." Hunter asked, "What's that?" I whispered, "They don't have night vision. Meaning they can't see too well in the dark." Hunter lightly smiled and whispered, "Things are looking good for us." I whispered, "Got that right."

March.11
7:50-AM

Me and Hunter got up early and to our luck the guards came by to send us to the kitchen and it would be up to us since the other 2 prisoners were in the sick bay. Once we got into the kitchen there wasn't a guard watching us giving me and Hunter a chance to look at the stoves. They were old and showing signs of old age I thought, "Perfect!" Hunter whispered, "I see the pipeline that contacts to the gas line we'll just have to loosen for it to leak gas." I looked at where the open doorway was, making sure no guard was standing by. I then took a look at myself and said, "Or just damage it enough for it to leak." Hunter turned his back and whispered, "A guard is coming."

Me and Hunter turned on the stoves and began cooking lunch as I heard the guard stop at the doorway watching us then turned around and left. I took a quick glace and saw the kitchen knives I saw paper towel in front of us I grabbed it and took some then wrapped it around the blades, so we won't cut ourselves then passed two to Hunter. I placed mine into my socks and the prison pants covered up our socks nobody would notice it. We went back cooking I heard the guard came back but quickly left. I lightly grinned and couldn't wait to burst out of this shithole.

11:30-AM

Hunter found his stove was the oldest out of four and would damage the gas line allowing it to leak gas and we noticed that gas had no odor to it which no one would notice until it was too late. Hunter said, "Now if we could get our hands on a match or something to start a fire." I said, "I seen some prisoners have cigarettes which the guard don't care so one of them must have matches or a lighter." Hunter said, "See if you can find who does and get one off of them." I nodded my head and turned over to the door where we we're sitting and heard no guards coming.

I turned back at Hunter and said, "Wait until it's late then we'll hide our knifes since the cameras won't be able to see well what we're doing." Hunter nodded his head as we finished our lunches then asked, "When we get to Texas where should we go to lay low for a bit?" I thought about it and only one person came to mind I said, "I'm sure Harry won't mind if we stop by his place in Houston." Hunter said, "We won't be able to stay for long and if he isn't around someone might have moved in his house already." I didn't want to believe Harry was dead but Hunter might be right however we would only know once we got out of here. I sighed and said, "Let's make this Sunday our escape day as the prisoners who want to pray to god will give us the open window we need." Hunter said, "Alright."

March.17
6:00-AM

I woke up early while Hunter was still asleep. I felt my back was aching from this uncomfortable bed. I woke up Hunter as we both went over to the window and reached for the knives, we had tied with our shoelaces I couldn't believe none of the guards notice it. Outside the clouds were dark grey and felt a storm was coming which make it harder for the guards to chase after us. Hunter was able to get some matches from another prisoner that would allow us to set a fire for our escape plan. We slipped the knifes into our socks along with the matches. Once we had a key card we would hit to the top floor and go to the control room open all the cells and lock out the rest of the guards and soldiers and force them to go through only one way while we went out another way. By the time they got in to see what the hell was going on they would realize they fell into our trap and once everything was back under control we will be long gone.

As we both stretched our arms and legs, we heard the guards coming they opened our electric cell door as one said, "Alright, you two. You know the drill." We both walked out as they took us the kitchen and left us to work. Once in the kitchen Hunter went to work getting the gas line loosen or damaged enough to cause a fire while I tried doing the same with mine. Hunter got his lose while I mannish to cause the pipe to crack as we pushed the stoves back in place and turned them on as we began cooking. A few minutes later a guard came in with two prisoners as one guard, "Ok cocksuckers! Move over to the other stoves." We did as the prisoners took over while we started on the other ones however the guard was still standing there.

I could see gas fumes were starting to rise and the guard was still there I thought, "Shit! I won't be able to reach down for a match unless the guard leaves or looks away." I then saw the one prisoner having trouble with the stove he turned his head over and said, "Hey! I can't get this thing working!" The guard walked over and asked, "What the fuck did you do to it asshole?" This was my chance I kneel down took an match slowly stood up as the guard was too busy looking at the prisoner while the other was keeping to himself I turned to Hunter nodded my head as he slowly moved away a bit. I strike the match against the hard counter as it lit up I quickly toss it over to the stone and within seconds flames shot behind the stove and exploded.

The prisoner and guard were sent flying into the wall while the other prisoner burst into flames I quickly ran over as the guard went to get up, but I kicked him hard in the head then grabbed his pistol a Glock 17 I flicked off the safety and pulled back on the slid arming it then grabbed his key card I turned to Hunter and said, "Let's go!" We ran out of the kitchen and heard an alarm going off. Suddenly two guards came in front of us I quickly aimed the Glock 17 and capped a round into his eye while Hunter already drew out his knife ran into the 2nd guard and stabbed his knife into his throat and ripped it open as blood poured out.

Hunter quickly grabbed his Glock 17 and keycard we both went into to the elevator I swiped the card, but it didn't work Hunter said, "Here let me try mine." Hunter did the same thing as the elevator doors opened. We got inside as I pressed the control room button the doors closed as the elevator was moving quickly up. I said, "Stand over by the walls and couch down as they'll try to go for head shots." Hunter nodded his head as we both knelt down aiming our Glocks and when the elevator came to a full stop the doors swung open and standing there, we're five guards holding M-16A2 assault rifles they fired at the wall as we both squeezed away at the triggers shooting them in the head with one guard nearly hitting Hunter in his left shoulder.

We both stood up and ran over to them grabbed the M-16A2's and took the extra ammo and went inside the control room. There we saw a man hiding behind his desk with his arms up he said, "Please! Don't kill me! I'm just doing my job!" I went over grabbed him and lifted him up then press the barrel of the assault rifle against his chest and said, "Which button opens all the cell doors?!" He pointed and said, "That button over there!" Hunter went over to the computer keyboard as he pressed the button then checked the big TV screens showing the guards and soldiers trying to get into the prison, he turned over to him and asked, "Does this place have a fire exit?" The man said, "Yes! Yes! I know where it is." I said, "Tell us!"

The man told us everything we needed, and we saw on the screens the prisoners were going crazy trying to get out the as the fire we caused in the kitchen was getting bigger. For safety we tied up the man so he couldn't do anything to stop us, and we took his key card which said worked on all elevators and air lock doors. Running downstairs to an elevator that would take us to the back of Diablo Prison that would take us to the boats. Once we reached the elevator, I swiped the key card its doors opened we both got on I pressed the down button.

The elevator was going down quickly but we could hear a thunderstorm raging outside I said, "We picked the best day for this." Hunter grinned and said, "Got that right." Just the elevator came to a full stop and the doors opened suddenly I saw soldiers along with Clive waiting for us holding assault rifles and shotguns. Me and Hunter quickly moved away as they open fired on us, we both blind fired our M-16A2's at the soldiers when a hand grenade was thrown at us. I quickly grabbed it and threw it back at them. I pressed my back against the metal elevator wall with a row of bullets nearly hitting me then a loud bang went off followed by blood splatter. We both reloaded our assault rifles then stood up and saw we killed them all along with Clive.

We ran over grab more ammo as I looked at Clive's body covered in bullet holes and said, "Who the cocksucker now!" I saw a key ring on a guard's belt I took it and ran out to where the boats were. Hard pouring rain hit our bodies we reached the docks as I hopped on board and placed the key into the ignition switch. Hunter quickly cut the rope as I started up the boat then Hunter got onboard, I pulled the lever as we sped off. We both turned our heads to see Diablo Prison in flames we turned to each other and laughed.

Suddenly a spotlight shined on us as boats were chasing. The guards had M60 heavy machine guns on their boats. I said, "Hunter drive! I'll handle them!" Hunter took over and ran to the back window grabbed my assault rifle and press the stock firmly against my shoulder then squeezed the trigger. Bullets flew into the guard holding the M60 heavy machine gun as I took out the driver then aimed for the next boats chasing us as they fired their M60's but missed hitting the sea. I quickly took them out as I couldn't allow them to chase us to Texas and the storm seem to be in our favor as the remaining boats couldn't keep up. I blew some air out and turned back to Hunter and said, "Goddamn! We fucking did it!" Hunter and I laughed for a bit then he said, "Next stop! Texas!"

We drove through the rough waves and held on tightly as we almost fell over a few times but the closer we got to land we felt stronger. Hunter turned to me and said, "We're going have to ditch these prison suits." I said, "I know we'll break into someone's house and see what they got then we'll... Hunter stopped talking I quickly moved over thinking something bad was waiting for us on land and saw in the distance there was a parked vehicle, but it was just one. Hunter asked, "Who do you think it is?" I scanned the area but didn't see any police, SWAT, FBI or army vehicles or helicopters nearby I said, "Not sure."

When we reached the shore, we could see a better look at the vehicle it was a bright red 85 BMW E28 M5 with dark tinted windows. The head lights came on as we both got off the boat then heard a black woman yell, "Hey there! Need a lift?" We both ran over as the driver window had row down a bit, we saw her she said, "Get in unless you two want to walk in the rain." Me and Hunter got into the backseat as the black woman shifted gear into Drive and sped off. Once inside we could see what she looked like.

She had short jet-black hair, light green eyes, black lips. She had huge breasts, wide hips and thick bubble butt cheeks. She wore a short jacket with red shirt, black pants and cowgirl boots. I then saw attached to her radio was a police radio along with other gadgets attached to it. I asked, "Who are you?" She turned her head over to us and said, "I'm Melissa I'm a reporter for Houston." Hunter asked, "How did you know we escaped?" Melissa grinned turning her head back and said, "I was hoping to get an interview with you on the Manson & Barbara Show but I picked up a radio call about some prison break and I had an gut feeling it was you two." I asked, "So, you're looking into this cartoon too?" Melissa turned back to me and said, "Honey, we're both after the same bastard that killed our parents and took our children. Look I'll fill you in once we get back to my place as we got a lot of shit to get done."

I said, "Thanks." Melissa said, "No problem honey." Hunter leaned in and whispered into my ear, "Damn she's hot." I couldn't lie Melissa was and glad someone out there was looking into the Manson case and believed we won't the real villains. Hunter asked, "Say which part of Texas are we in?" Melissa said as she adjusted the radio knobs, "We're nearby Corpus Christi and we got a long drive back to Houston." Suddenly we heard a male voice on the radio speakers say, "Mayday! Mayday! This is Diablo Prison! We have a serious fire with half of the prisoners have escaped! We need backup now! We have lots of dead guards and soldiers here!"

Melissa said, "It's a good thing I was nearby or otherwise the US military would have gunned you down with choppers." We then heard a male Texas accent say, "Roger that we'll sending enforcement's now." Melissa got onto the highway and saw military helicopters heading towards Diablo Prison along with a transport. I said, "Damn we really pissed them off." Hunter said, "Won't mind eating something as I'm hungry." I said, "Same here." Melissa said, "I'll got us some lunch once we're far away Corpus Christi it's going to be crawling with military and police."

12:00-PM

Melissa got us McDonald's and it felt so much better to eat real food again. Hunter said, "It's been too long since I had a good cheeseburger." I said, "Much better than that shitty prison food they were feeding us." Melissa had stopped in the parking lot so we can eat while it poured rain outside, she asked, "So you two manage to escape only being there for 2 months?" I said, "Yes we won't planning to give up after getting caught." Hunter asked, "Melissa where are the documents you have on the show?" Melissa said, "My place but don't worry it's in my safe so nobody is going to find it." I said, "Good as we didn't get to look at Arkard sketch books."

Melissa asked, "Who's Arkard?" I said, "The creator of The Manson & Barbara show. Osborne Louis isn't his real name it's Arkard Glukhovsky. He's Russian not American. It's a pen name he used when he went to make racist cartoons in Hollywood and then was planning on making a cartoon but died before he could do it." Melissa said, "I didn't know that. From what I manage to find was his old cartoons he did, and that fucker is lucky he isn't breathing as I would beat the living shit out of him for what he did." I said, "I don't blame you Arkard was a real prick. You should see what he did in his life."

Melissa said, "I haven't read his diary

but read through what his show originally going to be about, and no way would Osbo...I mean Arkard won't be able to make something like that in the 60s." I said, "Arkard was part of a Satanic cult The Followers of Lucifer. He made a deal with the devil for his show to become a major success and just as things were going well for him in '69, he's killed in a car accident when he ran a red right as a dump truck crashed into his dark purple Ferrari Dino." Melissa asked, "Let me guess the same color as Manson suit?" I said, "Yes." Melissa said, "Wow I have so much to catch up on this case." I said, "We'll fill you everything we already know. So, what did you manage to dig up?"

Melissa said, "From I could get was that any kids or young teens who watched this show seem to act different and would end up gone or dead. I called over a dozen cartoon stations, and TV networks and they all give me the same bullshit. It seems nobody but the children know about it, and I can't find any of the VHS tapes of the show as well." I said, "Be thankful you haven't, Hunter and I have watched them and the more you watch, the more it fucks with your head." Melissa asked, "What do you mean by that?"

Hunter said, "Watching any of these episodes would give us nasty headaches which causes vomit and hallucinations like when you watch TV, and you'll see an ad for some product for the house or garden work then Manson and Barbara turn it into a snuff film. Other words really fucked up shit that they get a kick out of it." I said, "When I had these bad headaches and hallucinations, I felt I had bugs crawling around inside my brain. We avoid TV or radios as Manson and his friends listen to what we're doing. That's how we got busted in New Orleans when Manson showed what we looked like in disguise after we escaped Miami."

Melissa raised an eyebrow and asked, "Wait you mean the cartoon characters did this?" Hunter said, "Yes and they used bullshit magic against us. Kane put a bomb in our car which me and Curtis had to jump out and glad we we're able to reach Naples. I'm sure Manson and his friends are going to be pissed when they hear we escaped prison." I finished my lunch and said, "Before we get to your place, make sure to unplug the TV, and put it a room so he can't see us." Melissa said, "Ok but...do you think he already knows about me?" Me and Hunter looked at her as I said, "I'm afraid he already knows."

Melissa said, "Ok I want to know how this bastard does it!" I said, "Manson and his friends live in the cartoon world and through magic he's able to make things happen and I have seen him along with his friends enter into this world. Me and Hunter think he might be airing his show through somewhere and if we'll able to find it and shut it down it might wake everyone up from Manson's show." Melissa said, "I hope we do find it as I like to make him pay for what he did to me." I said, "Let me guess he killed your parents off and kidnapped someone from your family." Melissa said, "I guess the same thing happened to you?" I nodded my head and said, "I placed hidden video cameras in my parents' house as they were acting strange, and my little brother John won't talk to me anymore and changed. I watched him as he would watch that goddamn show non-stop. Manson found out about this and found a way to use my trick against me by framing me for brutally murdering my parents and taking John. He also framed me and Hunter as terrorists with that steam ship bombing."

Melissa said, "Damn that's fucked up. What Manson did to me was make my young sister kill my parents and killed our neighbors along with taking their two children with her. The police and the media stated it was you two, but I knew they we're lying as my little sister wouldn't stop talking about that show. So, I been working secretly on this case until I was fired from my job last week. But with the two of us here we'll be able to find more answers." We finished our lunch Melissa started up her BMW and drove back onto the highway.

Huston, Texas
7:00-PM

It was a very long stormy drive but reached Melissa big house she took out a remote opened her garage door and drove inside as it closed behind us. Melissa killed the engine as we got out carrying our weapons inside, we heard her say, "Here I'll get you some clothes you two can wear." It didn't take long Melissa to bring us some clothes we picked what we liked and went into two bathrooms to change. When we came out Melissa was waiting for us in the living room as she was holding the two leather bound books along with the sketch books. I said, "I'm glad you we're able to get these back." Melissa lightly smiled and said, "Oh the sheriff didn't mind if I just borrowed them for a while. I sneaked into his office and grabbed them as he wasn't giving me jack shit." I said, "Let's see the sketch books."

Melissa handed them over to me and Hunter looked through them and saw how good Arkard was at drawing along with what Manson and his gang was going to look like. Melissa asked, "So how did this Russian guy get into American." I said, "Have a look at his diary as it will tell you everything that's fucked up about Arkard's life." Melissa picked it up and began reading it while we heard thunder roaring outside. When me and Hunter we're done looking at the sketch books I turned over to Melissa and she was already halfway through Arkard's diary, and I could tell she was disgusted with what Arkard had done to get where he was.

When Melissa was finished reading the book, she closed it and said, "Damn that's some fucked up shit." I said, "It is." Melissa turned her head over to me and asked, "So where do we go from here?" I said, "Arkard had two houses one in Hollywood and one in Florida. I found both those leather books in his 2nd house in Fort Lauderdale and his sketch books in his mother house. However, when me and Hunter were about to leave Kane and Manson's bat men came after us and blew the house up." Melissa asked, "And the other house?" I said, "Someone was living in there, so either Arkard's house in Hollywood is still around or it's been taken down. We won't know until we get there."

Hunter turned to me and asked, "What about the President?" Melissa asked, "You think he'll believe this?" I said, "No it's a thing of Manson's version of Arkard's show. The White Order are the villains, and each member is based on real people which those who die on the show are killed the same way in real life. The latest episode we we're force to watch by Manson girlfriend Barbara showed us known as the Tricksters tried getting vice President to join us stating the King had killed his own men to gain more control over his kingdom. However, it didn't work as it showed us running off with the remaining crew members from the ship. And the captain who was killed was the President."

Hunter said, "My idea was to save the President's life and maybe they'll see that we're not the real villains as during these episodes a number is flashed which is 13 or 31." I said, "But if we got anywhere near the White House on that date we would be killed on sight. We'll better off going after Manson." Melissa said, "Well we got a long way to reach Hollywood." I sighed and said, "You know if it wasn't for you, I think me and Hunter would have ended up at Harry's place and...

Melissa said, "That's my neighbor who was killed!" My eyes open wide along with my jaw dropped open. Melissa asked, "You knew him?" I said, "He was from my father's side of the family. I...I can't believe it!" Hunter said, "We should leave quickly knowing how pissed the military is that we escaped they'll be searching every inch of Texas for us." I said, "We'll need more guns for later." Melissa said, "That won't be a problem since Texas is gun country." I said, "We'll need then to travel all the way to Hollywood." Melissa asked, "If his house doesn't have what we're looking for, then what?" Hunter said, "We could check out that Satanic cult and see if they have anything on Arkard."

Melissa and said, "We'll plan this out in the morning I'm going to have a shower. If one of you wants to use the shower next, I won't take long." Hunter said, "Alright, thanks Melissa." She walked away upstairs I felt tired and a nice hot shower would hit the spot. Hunter asked, "So, now that we escaped, is Manson going to frame us for the President death or have someone else do it?" I said, "We'll soon find out." Hunter said, "I hope the military won't be patrolling every state as we'll never reach Hollywood." I said, "I have a bad feeling they will."

March.18
10:30-AM

I woke up as I slept on living room couch while Hunter slept in a spare room, I rubbed my eyes while it was still raining outside. I yawned then slowly got up and felt good to be out of that shithole prison. I went over to the kitchen window to look outside and saw the street was empty with no cars passing by or houses with their blinds or curtains opened. I then saw which house was Harry's and saw no vehicles in the driveway. I then heard footsteps coming down I turned my head and saw Melissa wearing a housecoat she said, "Morning Curtis." I said, "Morning." She came over and saw it was still raining. Melissa asked, "Want some coffee?" I said, "Please, with extra sugar."

As Melissa started making the coffee, I rubbed my eyes then heard Melissa asked, "Did you sleep well?" I turned my head over to her and said, "Yes, I did." Melissa said, "I checked on Hunter, and he seems happy." I lightly smiled as she finished making the coffee and pass me a mug I said, "Thanks." Melissa said, "When Hunter wakes up, I'll get started on breakfast." I nodded my head and drank my coffee. When I lowered the mug I asked, "As anyone been in Harry's house after he was murdered?" Melissa turned her head to the window and said, "Yeah the police as they cleared everything out." I said, "Maybe they missed something?" Melissa said, "Are you thinking of going over their?" I said, "Yeah just to see if his children left anything behind the police have missed."

Hunter woke up near 11-AM and Melissa cooked us breakfast and damn it was better than my mom's cooking. I said, "Mmmm…it's been too long since I had bacon." Melissa lightly smiled as Hunter said, "This is really good. Thanks." Melissa said, "You're welcome, you two." I finished my breakfast Hunter asked, "So what's the plan for today?" I said, "I'm going to have a look around Harry's house to see if there any clues for us." Melissa said, "The books I got of Arkard's cartoons he started with don't have much to go on." I said, "I'll have a look-see."

Hunter said, "I wonder what the news is saying about us." I said, "You know if we get near any radio, TV or a video camera Manson and his friends will be after us and will be able to turn anyone against us." Melissa said, "We'll have to check if we want to know what they're doing."

I said, "Okay, but whatever you do Melissa don't say our names and make sure to turn off the radio and if you watch the TV pull the plug after you're done with it." Melissa said, "Alright I'll go check to see what the news has for us. And I'll get those books." Melissa got up and left the table I picked up a napkin whipping my face while Hunter went to make himself another coffee. I turned my head to where Harry's house wondering what I would find. A few minutes later, Melissa came down and had five sketch books in her arms. She placed them down onto the table then looked at us.

"I just saw what the local news showed of Diablo Prison. It's been destroyed."

Me and Hunter looked at Melissa as she continued, "They stated that all the prisoners and guards were killed during an assault on the prison." I asked, "And us?" Melissa said, "All the prisoners were a counted for expect you two." Hunter said, "I fucking knew they were going to say that." Melissa said, "They said that someone else is part of this terrorist group that helped busted you two out, but they didn't say how many did it." I said, "Good let's keep it that way. I don't need Manson giving us anymore trouble then we already got."

Melissa said, "However that was the good news. The bad news is that all of Texas is searching for you two and the National Guard is joining the army in the search of the escape prisoners and making sure they don't leave Texas alive. They also said they were searching Mexico as well." I said, "I guess we won't be going anywhere for a while then." Hunter said, "Alright let's see these sketch books then take a look in Harry's house." Melissa had a worried look on her face as she put down the sketch books and said, "I'll just head out and do some shopping."

Melissa left the kitchen and went upstairs to get changed I thought, "I have a feeling she doesn't have an job which means we won't be able to stay here long." When Melissa was dressed, she left the house and got into her BMW. Me and Hunter looked through Arkard's sketch books of his racist cartoons and I didn't find them funny. I sighed but kept looking through them to see if there was any hidden clues but after going through all five sketch books there wasn't anything.

I looked over at the clock it was now 12:30-PM I then turned my head over to the window the weather was overcast with no sign of sunlight and the street still looked empty. Hunter asked, "Should we do it or just wait for Melissa to get back?" I thought about it then said, "Let's go see if their anything for us to find." We both got changed and went out the front door and walked down the empty street. I could feel warm air blowing through my short hair. We got closer to Harry's house but the closer I got I had a bad feeling something nasty was waiting for us.

I quickly scanned the area around us, and it seemed we we're the only ones out as everyone was inside their homes. I hoped nobody was spying on us. Me and Hunter went through the backyard and saw the once beautiful garden that Harry's wife had made was now gone, I remembered how it use to look when I was shown a photo of it by his wife. However, I saw the rocks that were around the backyard were still here I turned to Hunter and said, "There's a a spare key hidden under one of these rocks. I'll start on this end you start on the other." Hunter nodded his head as we lifted up the rocks until I found it. I wiped off the dirt and went over to the back door Hunter came over.

I unlocked then enter inside the house I closed and locked the backdoor so nobody won't sneak inside. It was empty inside yet very warm I remembered Harry telling me how big his house was which meant we had a lot of rooms to search. I turned to Hunter and said, "We'll start on the first floor then work our way to the basement." Hunter said, "Ok." We started in the kitchen looking through the draws and cabinets but found nothing. We saw the living room was empty but could see the marks of where the furniture used to be. We went into the bedrooms first Harry and his wife's room. We looked closely at the floorboards and walls but saw nothing. Even the ceiling looked untouched as well.

We both went into his kids' room, and it looked like nothing was out of place. I opened the closet and saw it was empty inside I then looked up and saw a hidden panel which lead into the attic Hunter poked his head in to see what I was looking up he asked, "Want to search it now or after?" I listen closely for any sudden noises I felt my heart was beating a bit fast as if something was waiting to jump out at me around the corner. I said, "Let's search the rest of the rooms up here then we'll check it out." Hunter said, "Ok."

Walking out of the kids' room we searched through the guest room and bathroom and found nothing. Returning to the kids' room I opened the attic panel as Hunter would give me a boost to climb inside. Pulling myself I felt more heat and could see some light was breaking through small cracks above me. As I stood up but kept my head low so I won't hit the wood beams Hunter asked, "Can you see up there?" I said, "Yeah."

I coughed a bit from dust in the air I looked around while squinting my eyes while moving slowly I didn't want to miss anything. Then I noticed something square shaped in the far left corner I said, "I think I found something." I slowly walked towards it then reach for it with both of my arms. I picked it up and felt weight inside of the box I slowly turned around and checked the rest of the attic but didn't see anything else. I went over to the way I came through and got out.

Once I stood next the bedroom window which the blinds were closed but could see the box I was holding. I blew off the dust and saw written on the lead was Tom & Bill names which were Harry and Lisa's children. Hunter asked, "What do you think is inside?" I listen for any sudden noises as this silence was keeping me on edge. I said, "Feels like books. We'll see when we go back." Hunter asked, "So the basement next?" I felt the hairs on the back of my neck stand up after Hunter said that. I thought,

"Is there really something waiting for us down there? This house is empty and we're the first two people to send foot in here." I lightly nodded my head we walked down the hallway and where the front entrance was there was the stairs leading to the basement. We both stopped and looked down the steps and couldn't see anything it was pitch black down there and felt my heart was beating faster.

I saw a light switch on the wall I flicked it but no lights came on I suddenly felt something in the darkness staring at me I said under my breath, "Fuck this!" I quickly moved away Hunter did as well. We both went out the back door and locked it then walked back to Melissa house it was still quiet here I thought, "Something not fucking right and don't fucking like it!" Me and Hunter sat in the kitchen I placed the box onto the table then opened it and inside were drawing books. Hunter wiped off the sweat with a napkin and said, "Damn it! What the hell was down their?" I looked over to the kitchen window and saw nothing had changed since we left Harry's house, I turned back to Hunter said, "Not sure and I don't plan on going back there. For all we know there's a TV or something set up so Manson can see where we are."

Just then we heard Melissa's BMW pull into the driveway and entering the garage. It didn't take her long to carry two large paper bags filled with groceries. Melissa asked, "Hey could one of you two help me out here?" I said, "Sure thing." I stood up and helped Melissa with the paper backs and walked with her back into the garage and got more out. Once we got everything she bought and closed the trunk then locked her car and came inside as I helped put everything away for her. Hunter said, "We found some drawing books at Harry's house."

Melissa turned her head to see the box we bought over and asked, "Anything outs?" I said, "Yeah something nasty in the basement but we didn't bother going down." Hunter said, "We're not sure what it was but both me and Curtis had a gut feeling it wasn't good so we got the hell out of there." I said, "I even tried the light switch it didn't work." Melissa said, "Well better being safe than sorry." I looked at her as I couldn't help but look into her pretty light green eyes. Melissa then asked, "So what's on the drawing books?"

I had two drawing books out which one had Tom's name on it the other had Bill's name. I opened both books and turned each page while Hunter and Melissa looked at them. I know that both boys liked cowboys, wild west, science fiction and dark fantasy. I saw at the top they dated their pictures I remember seeing a few of these when Harry bought the kids over to my parents' house. As I flipped further through the drawing books reaching the time the Manson & Barbara Show came out, we now saw fan art of these characters along with the world of the show as well.

Getting further through both books the detail on the pictures was cleaner however the images started to look disturbing with an uneasy feeling looking at what was going on. On Tom's drawing book the image showed The Dark World however the forest of dead trees with thick fog and a full moon light shining down on dead adult bodies lying on the ground. On Bill's it showed a very graphic image of dead men and women being impaled upside down on sharp wooden poles with blood oozing on them. I heard Hunter said, "Christ!" I turn the pages with the images now showing each member of Manson gang including himself killing adults.

In Tom's book it showed Andrew posing with a pile of dead men while holding his cross bow. The pile of dead men lying in the open desert were shot in the head, arms, chest, backs and legs. I turned the page now showing Andrew lighting them on fire. On Bill's book it showed Andrew sitting in a old style leather chair and on the wall where women heads placed as trophies. I turned the page on Bill's drawing which showed women running through the hot blazing desert with Andrew shooting his crossbow at them. I lightly shook my head as Melissa asked, "Do you think Manson force them to draw this?"

I said, "No. I think it was a warning of what was really going behind his show and what his sick friends are really doing." I turned the pages of both drawing books now showing Hellen which on both drawing books showed air ships destroying cities with dead bodies lying in the war-torn streets. Turning both pages showed two different images. On Tom's it showed Hellen with adults tied up to the double cannons and blowing them in half. Melissa said, "That's an execution called blown from a gun." I sighed and looked at Bill's drawing which showed Hellen and her crew laughing while the adults were being hang from their air ship.

Turning the pages on both drawing books now showed Sydney the witch. On Tom's book it showed both men and women being boiled alive while inside her cauldron with a very big fire going. I could feel their pain just by looking on their faces and imagined hearing their screams. I suddenly notice Hunter's face went green and Melissa looked the same. I turned over to Bill's drawing book which showed Sydney grinning as she had an adult naked woman clapped down onto a wooden board while being skinned alive and her eyes had been torn out. I turn my head away along with Hunter gagging a bit. I said, "That fucking bat and his fucking sick friends!"

Hunter said, "I can't wait until we find him and beat the living shit out him!" I turned back to the drawing books and turned both pages now showing George the hammer hippo. In Tom's drawing it showed him standing in a large room with brinks and torches and lying on the floor were dead adults all crushed and smashed with his large hammer which was cover and dipping with flesh blood on it. George had blood on his muscular body while grinning. Looking over at Bill's drawing book showed George turning a creak on a wooden board with a man being ripped in half I could see on the man's face screaming in pain.

In the background I saw hanging on the brink wall were the upper half of adults both men and women with their guts hanging out and blood oozing from their torn bodies. Their arms were attached to chains which been bolted in place. I turned both drawing pages which now showed Kane the magic fox. On both drawings it showed Kane throw bombs at adults running for their lives with the blast radius blowing limbs off the others. I turned both pages and was shocked what I saw. On Tom's it showed Kane raping a woman while a man was tried and force to watch. On Bill's it showed Kane watching adults running with bombs tied to their backs to see who could make it the furthest before the bombs blew up. On the track were blown and dismember limbs along with a few dead bodies.

I turned both pages on the drawing books while Melissa rubbed her eyes and said, "I have seen some fucked up shit, but this takes the goddamn cake." I felt anger burning inside of me I thought of what Harry's poor boys felt when they were forced to draw this shit. Now on both drawing books was Barbara holding her dual daggers and lying on the floor were dead men with their eyes and throats sliced as blood covered the stone floor. I saw in the background it was inside of Manson's castle. On Bill's drawing it showed Barbara grinning while holding a double-bladed axe and standing naked with dismembered bodies around her. Her whole body was covered in blood and her right foot was resting on a dismembered head.

Reaching the next page on both drawing books now showed the villain we we're after Manson the bat. In Tom's picture it showed Manson holding his sword as he had sliced off women's heads and stabbed a few to death. In the background was inside his castle I notice that it matched Bill's drawing. Hunter asked, "Is it me or are both backgrounds are the same." I turned a page back on Bill's and Hunter was right. I turned the page forward and looked at Bill's drawing of Manson, but my eyes open wide as it showed me and Hunter lying on the floor in front of a fireplace dead with Manson and Barbara grinning at our deaths.

The remaining pages in both books were torn out. I closed them as I didn't wish to view them again. Hunter asked, "Melissa when you left this morning did you see anyone else?" Melissa said, "I couple people were out. But I didn't see any school bus and.... She stopped talking realizing that her neighborhood has been empty since this morning and nobody has come out of their houses. I quickly stood up and looked out the kitchen window and not a signal vehicle has driven by. I turned to Melissa and asked, "How many of your neighbors have children?" Melissa said, "Only here and your friend's house."

Looking at the empty street is didn't feel right at all I said, "Go check the news for us." Melissa went upstairs as I sat down back at the table rubbing my forehead I thought, "Ok we can't stand here for long but with the army and National Guard looking for us we're going have to find a way to sneak out of Texas." When we heard the footsteps coming downstairs Melissa came in and said, "Things aren't looking good for us. All the schools in Texas along with other states have been burned or blown-up including churches, city halls and foster homes. The governor of Texas has declared martial law and won't stop until he finds you two."

Hunter said, "Well we can't stay here forever." Melissa said, "Yes, you're right about this as I only have enough money for next month and after that the taxpayers and everyone else is going to be knocking on my front door." We we're all quiet for a bit then I asked, "How long will that food last us?" Melissa said, "Three weeks." I sighed and said, "Ok. We'll play the waiting game with the army while we'll busting their balls for trying to find us, we'll going to pull off master escape plan so we can reach Hollywood."

March.22
3:00-PM

Thunder roared outside with heavy rain fall as I sat in the living room reading over a newspaper which had been covering the madness and chaos that's been happening both in American and Europe. Children have been disappearing or killed themselves after burning down a targeted building by Manson along with killing their parents and yet no one was blaming the goddamn show for this as me and Hunter we're still being framed for these crimes which we haven't done. I bet Manson was pissed that we escaped and now that we've gone into hiding, he wasn't going to rest until he hunted us down. I feared if he did find us, he won't allow us to escape so easily.

As I read the next page on the newspaper, I saw an image which glued my eyes to the image of The Pope was lying in the Rome streets pumped with bullet holes with people looking at his corpse crying and in shock. I looked under the image and read,

"The Pope, was riding through the streets of Rome during an peace parade when suddenly the leading car was hit by a rocket launcher then 3 more rockets took out the other vehicles including damaging the Pope's armored limo. As guards went to help the Pope out a teenager wearing dark green camo clothing, black leather gloves, military boots. He had long blond hair and light blue eyes and a handsome face. However, he stepped towards The

Pope's limo now armed with a heavy machine gun as he killed all the guards then when the Pope begged his attacker to not kill him the man open fired filling the beloved Pope with bullet holes. When the Italian police showed up the attacker fought his way through them and went back to where he came out of. When more police followed by an angry mob the blond man was gone. Other reports of this mysterious blond assassin have been reported and linked to the terrorists in America, but Interpol and FBI have had no luck on tracking down this wanted murders."

I thought, "I have feeling this assassin is from Manson and this makes things even worse now." Suddenly I felt someone was watching me I turned my head and saw Melissa. I said, "Oh just you." Melissa said, "Sorry didn't mean to make you jump." I said, "It's ok. Ummm…we got more trouble." Melissa walked over as she sat down on the couch and looked at the newspaper, she saw the image of Pope John Paul II assassinate. Melissa said, "Oh my god!"

I said, "It seems Manson has a new weapon against us and is adding more fuel to the fire." Melissa sighed and said, "Great we don't ever find a way out of this place that blond assassin will turn this street into a war zone." I said, "That's only if Manson ever finds out where we are." Melissa turned her head and said, "I notice something when I went yesterday for some air. Wanted posters have been all over the place but it isn't the police." I knew who she was going to say Melissa said, "The text is the same ones on that cartoon show."

I asked, "Do the wanted posters showed what we looked in prison or now?" Melissa said, "Yes back in prison." I lightly nodded my head and asked, "What else?" Melissa said, "Military has gone through half of Mexico with the help of the Mexican army their ready to rule out that you and your friend haven't been there which means they'll start crawling through the rest of this country." I closed up the newspaper setting it down onto the coffee table and said, "Ok the army is going to be having roadblocks on every route and highway leading in and out of Texas." Melissa said, "Yes, and they'll search every vehicle making sure nobody sneaks in." I said, "Ok next the airports will be covered in soldiers with lots of guards and dogs."

Melissa asked, "Ok so how the hell do we get out of here?" I said, "That just leaves us the only thing left. A train ride." Melissa looked at me and asked, "A train?" I said, "Yes it's the only way out of Texas as it will take us through the desert until, we reach California then we'll be in Hollywood." Melissa asked, "That's your plan?" I said, "It's the only way besides if we tried using a plane to get out of here, I bet the Texas military and National Guard will be scanning the skies for anyone trying to fly in and out of Texas."

Melissa said, "I guess it's our only way out then." I looked over at Melissa as she looked at the newspaper for a bit then turned her eyes over to me, we stared at each other. I felt like saying something but couldn't find the words I was looking for. Melissa looked like she wanted to speak as well. I finally broke the silence and asked, "Where's Hunter?" Melissa said, "Upstairs, sleeping." We stared at each other as I suddenly felt hot under the collar, I turned my head and said, "Umm…I could use something to drink." I stood up and walked into the kitchen while I felt Melissa looking at me.

I opened the fridge and saw beer bottles, a case of milk and a few water bottles I reached for the beer bottle it felt very cold. Just as I went to turn around Melissa stood behind me and asked, "Mind grabbing me one?" I lightly smiled and said, "Sure." I turned back to the fridge and grabbed Melissa a beer bottle as she got a bottle opener from the draw opening her bottle then passing it to me. I said, "Thanks."

We both drank our bottles of beer I asked, "Should I go wake him?" Melissa said, "Nah, we'll wait until Hunter wakes up." I asked, "Alright. Say got a map of Texas?" Melissa said, "Yes I'll go get it." When she brought it out, we sat at the kitchen table looking at it. I saw where the train tracks ran and pointed to the one, we needed to get on. Melissa asked, "You'll think they'll have the train yards guarded?" I said, "Maybe but if we slip under their noses they won't know and can't double check the train once it's going." Melissa said, "Just hope the train we get on takes us to California as if it doesn't that, we got a long way to go." I said, "If so, we'll be able to get us some wheels and drive there. Besides they know we're somewhere in Texas and aren't bothering to guard the states that are further away from here. However, if we're spotted then they'll come after us and even that bastard Manson." I drank my beer as Melissa looked at me and asked, "So Curtis what else did you do besides being a reporter?" I said, "I would hang out with my friend, my family and my little brother. Use to take him the theatre to see action and horror films." Melissa lightly smiled and asked, "What else?" I said, "Umm I would spend 2- or 3-hours lifting weights at my apartment keeping in shape. I would also read or watch films." Melissa asked, "The same kind you and your little brother would go to see?"

I lightly smiled and said, "Well kind of. I would get other types of films for myself to enjoy." Melissa said, "Let me guess, porn, right?" I lightly laugh and said, "Yeah." She giggled as she drank her beer and said, "I would take my little sister out to the park and would go to the movies with her as well. Even shopping together." I asked, "Was she a big reader?" Melissa said, "Yes she was. There was this book series she would read a lot and told me everything that happened in it...until that goddamn show came." I said, "I know how you feel I bought my little brother John a typewriter he enjoyed writing stories and told me everything he wrote I could see him being an author. But when the Manson & Barbara Show came, he and all the children were brainwashed by it. I came to see him on Christmas and found it along with his stories thrown out in the trash bin."

Melissa asked, "What was it like in Black Creek?" I said, "Umm it was alright, but I planned on moving out of there. Always dreamed of working in a big news studio along with Hunter." Melissa asked, "You never had a girlfriend while in Black Creek?" I looked up at her feeling warm and said, "No I...I never found anyone while there. I did plan on finding a girl to fall in love with." Melissa asked, "And raise a child?" I looked into Melissa eyes and felt I couldn't speak all of a sudden. We both stared into each other then I manage to ask, "Would you want a child?" Melissa lightly laughed and said, "Yes." I suddenly felt my cheeks blush as she laughed more, I tried to hide it, but I began laughing. When we both stopped Melissa asked, "Would you?" I said, "I guess." Melissa looked at me as I didn't know what else to say she said, "You don't sound too sure about it." Drinking my beer I said, "I'm not sure if I would make a good father." Melissa put her bottle down then stood up and walked over to me as I looked at her, I suddenly felt my eyes locked onto her huge breasts then Melissa asked, "What would it take to convince you?"

I then lifted up my eyes at Melissa she then placed her hand onto my mine and said, "Come here." I stood up as Melissa wrapped her arms around my back then slowly moved her face towards mine, I did the same. Our lips touched. Then we slowly kissed. My hands rested on Melissa's sides as we kissed more, I really enjoyed her taste. Melissa broke away and asked with a smile, "Now, are you interested?" I said with a smile, "Proof it to me." She giggled as we went upstairs into her bedroom, she closed the door.

I never saw Melissa room before until now as it was very big with a queen size bed with an old-style dresser, a large round mirror, nightstand, lamp and grandfather clock. No windows as the walls were dark black with a black ceiling with a hardwood floor. I said, "Wow very dark in here." Melissa said, "Helps me sleep. Now let's get these off of you." Melissa placed her hands onto my shirt and pulled them off as she turned me around and saw how built I was. Melissa said, "My such a strong man." I lightly smiled as she began unbuckling my belt then removed the button and pulled down the zipper I felt my dick was getting hard. As Melissa pulled off my pants, she pushed me onto her bed, her very soft bed.

Melissa giggled while pulling off her pants and panties then she placed both her hands under her shirt and removed it now standing fully naked I saw how huge her breasts were. I saw her tits were thick, fat and dark black. Melissa giggled then crawled onto her bed and using her teeth pulled off my underwear as my big thick dick popped out Melissa giggled, she grabbed it and lightly stoke it and said, "Fucking big!" She crawled towards me as we kissed more, I placed my hands on her back working my way down to her thick soft yet bubble butt cheeks. I pressed my fingers firmly against her soft black skin.

She moaned as I broke away the kiss then lifted her up and licked her thick fat black tits and began sucking on her right nipple. Melissa moaned and said, "Yes please don't stop." I kept sucking while lightly pulling with my lips. I did this for a bit then did the same thing with her left tit. Sucking away while Melissa ran her hands along my muscular back.

Melissa placed her hands onto my face lifted it up as she moved towards my face and kissed some more with her huge soft breasts resting on top of my chest. I felt pre-cum leaking out of my dick and it was fully hard Melissa notice this as she crawled backwards back to my waist. I looked at her, she giggled then placed her hand onto my ball sack lightly grouping my big balls I moaned lightly Melissa began licking my long thick shaft it felt very nice. Melissa played with my big thick dick for a bit using her tongue she then kissed the tip of my dick and began sucking on it.

I moaned more with my hands gripping the edges of the bed. Melissa sucked harder while moving her mouth back and forth I thought, "Damn! This feels so good!" I held back until I couldn't hold it no longer and released my cum as Melissa sucked every drop of it. She moaned licking her lips and said, "Mmm...I want more of your sugar!" Melissa crawled towards me then she slid her pussy into my rock-hard dick I asked, "Wait! Don't you..." Melissa placed her hands onto my side and said, "Hush, I want to feel you inside me." Melissa began thrusting her waist up and down causing her bed to bounce I reached up to her sides holding onto Melissa and watched her huge breasts bouncing.

Melissa moaned louder and she was a lot to handle. I felt her pussy was getting tighter inside she picked up speed I moaned more I felt Melissa fingers gripping my shoulder tops as she was getting close of releasing her pussy juice. When I felt my dick release another hard burst of cum Melissa moaned in pleasure as I could feel her warm pussy juice running down my long thick shaft followed by my cum. Melissa rested on top of me and kissed away until we had enough. I rested my head on top of Melissa huge breasts as she had her arms around with me a smile on her face.

Melissa asked, "So did I convince you?" I said, "Yes you did," Melissa giggled as I looked at her face, but she pressed her huge breasts into my face and said, "Just relax handsome and enjoy my love pillows." I lightly laughed as I could hear the storm raging outside yet it felt louder. Melissa asked, "So we'll leave by the end of the mouth?" I said, "Yes and we'll need to get weapons, ammo, some clothes and extra cash." Melissa said, "Shouldn't be too hard to get in a place like this." I turned my head over to suddenly see the round shaped mirror facing us and on the other side was Manson and Barbara looking at us. Melissa notice as she gasped.

Manson and Barbara grinned as he said, "Don't you two make a fine couple." I suddenly saw the door was gone along with the walls replaced with pitch black darkness. Barbara giggled and said, "Yes they would make a good couple. But I like it better if they were dead!" Manson grinned and said, "Yes they would be better off dead."

I lifted up my head as I felt their eyes staring back into mine, I said, "How the hell did you.... Manson ask, "Find you Curtis? Haha magic of course." Barbara giggled and asked, "Did you really think you could hide from us forever?" Manson said, "You know I thought the last time I saw you and your friend back New Orleans would be the last time however you proofed me wrong again." Suddenly both of their eyes glowed bright red as Manson spoke with a demonic voice, "THIS IS GOING TO BE THE LAST TIME I WILL ALLOW THIS TO HAPPEN!"

Barbara spoke with her demonic voice was so loud it hurt my ears, "AND IF IT SHOULD HAPPEN AGAIN, I'M GOING TO ENJOY SLOWLY TEARING YOUR FUCKING FLESH OFF WHILE YOU SCREAM!" I growled showing I wasn't afraid of them and said, "I will stop you!" Manson and Barbara grinned and began laughing loudly suddenly I notice cracks were forming on the round mirror but as the cracks grew bigger, I could see blood oozing out of the mirror. Their laughter was getting louder, and the mirror was now vibrate I felt something was going to happen I quickly turned grabbed Melissa and pushed her off the bed. Just as I did this both Manson and Barbara screamed in their demonic voices, "DIE!" The mirror exploded sending sharp shards of the mirror flying passed my back nearly hitting us.

When we both landed on the floor, I turned my head to see the mirror was broken and the walls had turned back to normal along with the door. I turned to Melissa and asked, "You, ok?" She said, "Yeah I'm alright." We then heard knocking on the door and heard Hunter's voice, "Melissa! You alright in there!?" I said, "Yes Hunter we're ok." He was quiet for a bit I said, "We'll be out soon." Hunter said, "Alright." Slowly we both got up and turned to face the bed and saw the broken sharp shards of the mirror that went through the pillows and wooden bed frame like a hot knife through butter. Melissa placed her arms around me and asked, "Should we leave now?" I thought, "Goddamn it! Manson just couldn't leave us alone! Knowing he'll us that blond assassin or send the military here we better not take chances." I said, "Yes we're leaving."

We got dressed and told Hunter our plan and knew if we risked staying here tonight Manson or someone else would come for us and we didn't want to be here when that happens the only way we're going to win this was to be a step ahead of Manson. We took everything we needed. Melissa was driving through the near empty streets of Houston. I checked the time it was 4:40-PM. Hunter asked, "So what's first?" Melissa said, "I know where that gun shop is, and they close around 6-PM if we just wait a bit then we'll be able to bust in and get what we need." Hunter said, "Great now we have to watch for mirrors now. Melissa, please tell me that police radio of yours is on." She said, "Yes, it is."

The rain fall was coming down much harder with bight flashes of lightning and booming thunder. Looking around the city of Houston we suddenly heard on the police radio, "All units! All units! Curtis Parker and Hunter Cunningham have been spotted in a neighborhood area of McCloud Street please be advice that both suspects are armed and extreme dangerous." A lot of voices spoke on the radio and within seconds we heard sirens raging through the city followed by helicopters both police and military.

I was glad I made the right decision leaving when we had the chance but we we're going to have to be very careful. Hunter said,

"I hope that gun store is closed as we won't be able to wait with all this heat on us." Melissa stopped her BMW and pointed towards the gun store and said, "There it is." We both looked and to our luck it was closed.

Melissa parked around the back while me and Hunter went over to the back door which was older and had the hinges on the outside I said, "Perfect." Hunter grabbed a hammer and screwdriver from the BMW and got the back door opened. We ran inside grabbing ammo for the assault rifles and pistols we had we took two Remington 870 Marine Magnum shotguns with metal slug rounds. I then looked at the gun case in front of me and saw a Smith & Wesson Model 629 Snub I picked it up looked at it then said, "I'm so taking this." I then grabbed a box of .44 rounds loaded them into the cylinder I spun it with my hand that whacked my wrist as it closed inside. I tucked it down into my pants. Hunter grabbed a Colt 1911A1 taking a box of .45 rounds and loaded the pistol. I opened the cash register and there was a lot of money I took all of it along with duffel bags and we ran back into Melissa's BMW as she drove off.

As she drove, I saw helicopters with spotlights scanning the streets for us; however, our problems weren't over yet. Melissa sighed and said, "They just finished going through my house and now know what car they are looking for. So, we better reach the train tracks before it's too late." Melissa sped through the streets while we heard the police radio going crazy with every cop and helicopter pilot looking for us." Hunter said, "Here take this." Hunter passed Melissa his Glock 17 with the extra ammo. Melissa drove by a lot of big buildings so the helicopters won't be able to fly over to easily on them.

By 6:25-PM we we're now out of the city Melissa sped towards a train yard and it wasn't guarded. She hid her BMW in a ditch and carried everything we needed and saw a train moving with its box car opened. We ran towards it I throw my stuff inside first then jumped and grabbed on and pulled myself in. Hunter threw his stuff and got it. We both had our arms out as Melissa jumped and we grabbed them pulling her inside then closed the car door as the train picked up speed as we would be out of Texas in a few hours.

The storm raged outside Melissa lay besides me while Hunter was on the other side of the train car holding his M-16A2 I had placed both of my weapons into the duffel bag. Melissa asked, "So how much did you two get in there?" Hunter said, "Over $10 grand. We'll have enough to keep us going." Melissa yawned as she rested her head against my side, I placed my arm around her and said, "Get some rest, ok, sugar." Melissa said, "Alright. Wake me if anything happens." I said, "I will." I turned my head back to Hunter he grinned and whispered, "Right on, man." I lightly grinned and said, "This ride of ours will take us into New Mexico and if we're lucky if the train keeps going right into Arizona." Hunter said, "If not, then we're going to have one hell of a time walking through the blazing sun of the desert."

I said, "I'm starting to wonder what else can Manson do now he's glowing stronger." Hunter said, "Let's hope we don't bump into them again. We still haven't found out where Manson is airing his show." I thought about it and thought, "Arkard came from Russia but lived in America then how the hell could a bunch of cartoon characters air the show?" Then it hit me I sighed and said, "I think I know how Manson is doing it." Hunter asked, "How?" I looked up at him and said, "He's sending a signal from his world through our satellites then get send down to Earth through radar dishes and that signal makes it way through every TV across the world. The only way we could stop the broadcast is by shutting down."

Hunter set his assault rifle down and crossed his arms and said, "Shit. This sounds harder than it looks." I said, "There must be some way of doing this. NASA can't be the only space agency that controls this stuff." Hunter said, "Let's see we got weather, military and NASA satellites up in space. Who controls all of them?" I said, "The government." Hunter said, "Yes and the only place that I can think of is the Pentagon." I said, "Well we won't be able to set one foot in there with all the cameras, guards and a shit load of security." Hunter said, "However it would dumb to leave one place in charge of our satellites."

Thinking about it Hunter had a point I said, "If we can find what army base is capable of controlling the satellites we might be able to make it harder for Manson's signal to get through." Hunter said, "The question is where do we find this base? Their a dozen of them across this country but only one that controls them." I said, "Let's think about this later I'm tired." Hunter said, "Alright." We both closed our eyes, and it didn't take long for the sounds of the storm outside to slowly fade away.

March.23
New Mexico
7:00-AM

I woke up feeling my mouth felt very dry slowly opening my eyes the train had come to a full stop. I rubbed out the sleepy then turning towards the cracks in the train car to see what was going on but couldn't see anything as bright sun light was shining through. I listen closely and all I would hear was the blowing wind I thought, "Something not right here." Using my foot, I pushed Hunter's foot until he woke up. When he did, I put my finger over my lip, like the universal sign. My eyes were now adjusted to the bright light I was able to see through the cracks I didn't see anyone walking around nor any vehicles or helicopters. Hunter turned his head back to me and whispered, "What should we do?" I looked at my watch and saw it was 7 in the morning. After waiting five minutes I woke up Melissa and said, "Come on. We gotta go."

Opening the car's sliding door, we hopped out and felt the desert heat I said, "Damn it. Should have gotten sunglasses." I squinted my eyes and put my right hand over my forehead where the train was but didn't see any smoke nor anyone there. I looked down onto the sand nobody has walked by here. I held my M-16A2 tightly and flicked off the safety in case I had to use it. When we got closer to the train, we saw the small windows were covered in blood. Hunter said, "What the fuck?" I said, "Stand back." I climbed up the steps leading to the sliding door I grabbed the handle and opened it and inside was a dead conductor with his head blown off. The raw smell of blood hit me, but I was used to this sort of thing. Looking at the radio it was badly damaged like a bomb went off inside of it. I knew who did this I turned around got off the train and asked, "Who's got the map?"

Hunter took it out as we looked at it I said, "Ok if we follow these tracks it should take us to an nearby town where we can get something to eat, find some wheels and try reaching Hollywood." Hunter asked, "What about the army base." I said, "Oh right, that. Ummm.... Melissa asked, "What army base?" I said, "Hunter and I think we know how Manson is broadcasting his show through satellites. If we shut them down, then the signal won't be clear enough to be seen by everyone and could wake people up from Manson's brainwashing." Melissa was silent for a bit then said, "You know I heard a rumor when I was in collage back in the late 70s that US military built this underground base somewhere in the desert and had these huge radar dishes pointed up at the sky and use them to track any enemy aircraft or UFO's if you believe in that sort of thing."

I asked, "You won't know which state it was in?" Melissa thought about it then said, "Now I remember it's out in the Mojave Desert. They got it hidden within the mountains so nobody will see it." Hunter said, "That's close by where we're going. If we're lucky enough to find it and get someone to shut down the satellites, then that's our ticket." I said, "Alright let's get moving." We began walking down the long endless train tracks with the sun blazing above our heads with not a cloud in sight.

I wiped off sweat from my forehead as I lead the way with Melissa next to me and Hunter behind us. I would check around our area every 5 minutes making sure nobody was out watching us. After walking a couple miles my skin was starting to turn red, we found a small cave I said, "Let's rest up for a bit." We went inside and saw it was empty. Sitting down I could feel sweat running down my forehead. Hunter said, "Shit my legs are killing me." Melissa said, "Wish we grabbed some food and water before we left." I said, "We'll get some." A few minutes later we heard low thumping noise Hunter asked, "Hey! You hear that?" It got louder then saw Black Hawk helicopters flying by.

None of us said a word while watching these helicopters. Once they were far away, I said, "If they find that train, they'll know we we're on it." Hunter said, "I bet they have more people on board those things than just the pilots." I got up and went to the entrance to peek out using the shadows as cover. I saw the helicopters were in fact heading towards the train. I looked around the sky and didn't see any more nor other military or police vehicles. I went back inside the cave and said, "We better go before more of them show up."

Leaving the cave, we travel further down the tracks I had us pick up speed knowing how quickly the military would cover this area if they find us, I knew this open ground won't help us win a fight against them and they would be more determiner to kill us. After hours of walking, we came across a road and to our luck we saw a gas station and next to it was an used car dealer ship I checked the time it was now 10-AM. Hunter asked, "So what's the plan?" I turned over to Melissa she lightly smiled and knew what to do.

Melissa went inside the gas station to get what we needed while Hunter and I broke through the back door of the dealer ship which was closed. We took keys to a dark black 85 Oldsmobile Cutlass Supreme Coupe I got into the driver side started it up and pulled up alongside the gas station. Hunter asked, "How are we for fuel?" I said, "We're good." Melissa came out I popped the trunk she put everything inside of it closed then got inside as I sped off. I said, "It would be wise not to stay in the nearby town and go somewhere else further away." Hunter took out the map as he looked through and said, "Our only way out of here is through the highway. That well take us into Arizona." I said, "That's where we're going."

There was hardly any vehicle on the road and we didn't see any more helicopters. I kept going not slowing down as I wanted to put as much distance away from anyone who was after us. When we saw the sign showing we we're about to cross into Arizona I was glad to have made it this far. At 12:00-PM we found a hotel and we we're the only ones there. I pulled into the back parking lot so no passing by vehicles or police would see the black Oldsmobile we took. Melissa went to get us a room while we took everything into the hotel room. To our luck there wasn't a TV, so we didn't have to worry about Manson seeing us but now I was worried about mirrors. I had Melissa check and there was only a small mirror, but we won't taking chances with it she pulled it off the wall and placed it into the closet.

Taking the food, we got along with the bottles of cold water we ate and drank a lot which felt nice. Hunter turned on the AC and felt good having cool air blowing out of the vents. After lunch I went into the bathroom to take a hot shower. I had my Smith & Wesson Model 629 Snub resting on the sink in case I needed it. Once I finished my shower, I stepped out of the shower grabbed a towel to dry myself then got dressed and picked up my gun tucking it down into my pants and left as Hunter walked in next to use the shower.

I sat down beside Melissa she turned to me and said, "I booked us one night stay here since we have to keep moving." I said, "We'll leave around 6 in the morning and make our way towards Mojave Desert." Melissa asked, "So after we shut down the satellites we just head to Hollywood?" I said, "Yes." Melissa said, "Something bothering me about this. I feel their more to it just don't know." I said, "We got two leads to go after the satellites are shut down. We have Akard's house and the Satanic group to look into." Melissa said, "I'm also worried about that blonde assassin Manson has as well."

I said, "I know what you mean. The firing power he's packing I don't want to come face to face with him after what he did to the Pope." Melissa rested her head onto the sofa and said, "I just fear Manson has more in store for us then what we imagination." I said, "Once we get the satellites down his show will lose viewers and people will start waking up to what's going on and maybe those who have been after us will see we're not the real enemy." Melissa went to speak but didn't she sighed and asked, "Could you please get me another bottle of water?" I said, "Sure."

I needed one myself I went over into the small kitchen opened the fridge and grabbed two bottles of cold water I closed the fridge door walked over to the window looking outside and saw nothing.

No sign of helicopters or anything else. I sat down on the sofa and passed the water bottle to Melissa she said, "Thanks sugar." I lightly smiled and said, "You're welcome." We both drank our water then heard Hunter was finished in the shower. He came out dressed in his clothes he asked, "So anything going on out there?" I said, "No." Hunter said, "Good."

Laying the map out onto the coffee table looking all the routes leading to Mojave Desert and the only one was nearby a small town called Needles. Once we drove passed it, we would have to find the base quickly and get the hell out of there before anyone showed up. Hunter said, "There must be a road that leads to this base." Melissa said, "If we did find I'm sure it's patrolled so nobody gets near it." Looking at the map I found this search would take forever to find it and if anyone saw us then we won't have a 2nd chance to break in. Melissa said, "If we could find high ground and look for those satellite dishes then we would know where it is." I said, "That's good idea. If we find the base and see how the patrols work, then we can pick the right moment to make our move."

Hunter said, "Alright sounds good." I said, "Once we see the base then we'll plan it out. For now, let's just relax and get some rest as we'll need it for tomorrow." I folded the map and placed it into my duffel bag and relaxed in the hotel room. Near dinner Melissa took a shower as we ate half of our food and would try to save the rest for tomorrow. But I too was now wondering what else was in store for us. Once we shut down those satellites would things get better or worse?

March 24
6:00-AM

I could see the moon glowing bright in the dark tinted sky with no sight of the sun coming up yet. I drove while Hunter sat in the passenger seat and Melissa was in the back seat. We ate a small breakfast before we left but I wasn't hungry. I felt my eyes would check the radio as I wondered what the media was saying about us now or had Manson's blond assassin strike again but feared Mason would find us. Follow the route we had to take there was no traffic nor a squad car anyway it almost felt like we we're the only ones left alive on this planet.

I checked the gas gauge and saw we still had enough fuel to reach Mojave Desert. I rubbed my eyes feeling a bit sleepy but knew a few hours on the road keep me up. Hunter asked, "Mind turning the AC on?" I turned it on and felt the cool air blowing through the vents. Hunter rubbed his forehead and yawned I scanned the road around us and still nobody but us. By 9:30-AM we reached the town of Needles. I pulled over to refuel the Oldsmobile while Melissa went to get us some breakfast to eat. It didn't take me long to refuel it and when the man came to take the money, I handed him a $100 dollar bill he lightly smiled and looked at my face then turned around and went back inside the gas station. I thought,

"No TV just a radio so he won't know about us."

Melissa came back with our breakfast I pulled into a parking lot where we could eat. There wasn't a lot of people in the town, but we won't going to let our guard down if anyone tried anything with us. A lot of clouds in the sky and hardly any wind this would make it easy for us to find this base we we're looking for. We didn't waste time eating our breakfast since I didn't want to stay still a place for too long. Once we we're finished, I started up the Oldsmobile and sped off heading towards Mojave Desert.

As I drove down the empty road, I saw a sign that pointed to a trail that was coming up. Melissa said, "I wonder if we could that trail will lead us to a high enough hill." I said, "Maybe but we'll need binoculars if we're going to find that base." Just as the dirt road that led to the trail an RV turned in front of us Hunter said, "Maybe they'll have what we're looking for." I stopped the car and said, "And if they don't have it?" Hunter turned his head to watch it then back to me and said, "Nah, you're right. We're better off to find a store that has them as I'm not risking it." I drove on and hoped it won't rain when we got back here.

We reached a town around 1:00-PM and the sun had come out. I pulled into the gas station as a man came out, I rowed my window halfway down and said, "Full tank please." He went over to the gas pump and began refilling the Oldsmobile I turned over to Melissa and said, "Ok, get us dark sunglasses, some extra food, water and binoculars." I handed Melissa $300 dollars that should be enough she got out of the car and went inside a sporting store which was next to the gas station. Hunter said, "I bet that place as some guns in there." I said, "If we need more we know where to get it."

When the man was finished, I handed him a $100 dollar bill through the half-opened window and asked, "Want any change back?" I turned over to him and said, "No thanks you keep it." He looked at me for a bit then turned around I thought, "Shit! I hope he doesn't know we're wanted." I then saw Melissa coming out of the sporting goods store she got in. I started up the Oldsmobile and turned around heading back to the trail I looked up at the view mirror and saw the gas station had tinted windows I knew if that guy was calling the cops, they would be crawling all over this place looking for us. I press my foot down hard trying put enough distance so they won't interfere with our mission to stop Manson.

When we got back to the trail it was now 3:45-PM we had lunch then used a bathroom which the trail had. After we left, we saw the RV was still here. Looking at it we didn't see anyone in the driver seat however there was a TV, and it was very loud. We went back into the Oldsmobile to talk about our plan. Melissa said, "While I was inside the sporting store, I grabbed these." She pulled out Walkie-Talkies and said, "They're no radios so I don't think Manson will be able to hear what we're doing." I said, "It's worth a try." Hunter said, "Alright so we'll travel through the Mojave Desert and find the highest mountain and scan this place until we find those satellite dishes are." We put the sunglasses on and took our duffel bags in case we needed any of the weapons if something went wrong.

We got out of the Oldsmobile and suddenly we heard the noises from inside the RV. It was The Manson & Barbara Show I turned back as me, Hunter and Melissa didn't want to get near it, fearing that Manson or his friends might see us. Walking through the trail made us sweat as we drank cold bottles of water. The air felt very dry and blew lightly on our faces. I wiped off the sweat and kept moving I wasn't going to slow down knowing how far we came to reach this point if this was the way to stop Manson I would do it even if it killed me.

By 5:30-PM we found a mountain and went high as we could go with the sun slowly setting behind us. We sat down on the dry ground Hunter said, "Alright let's see what we can see." Taking out the binoculars and finishing my bottle of water I toss and wiped off the sweat from my forehead then rested the binoculars against my face I adjusted them while looking down at the desert landscape. I turned slowly until I saw more mountains, I lightly blew out air then looked over to the left side of the desert and it just seem the same, but I stopped I lowered the binoculars and saw large round satellite dishes that matched the color of the desert. I said, "Found it." I passed the binoculars to Hunter and pointed where it was.

Hunter looked and said, "I see it. However, it's hard to see if there are any guards." I said, "We'll have to get closer to find out." Melissa asked, "Say can you see where we parked our car?" Hunter looked where we came and said, "No it's too far away." I said, "Come on let's go." We got up and walked down the mountain carefully then began walking towards the base.

When we reached it, it was 7:00-PM the sun was halfway down and was glowing a dark tinted orange color with reddish and black clouds forming in the sky. Melissa said, "Wish I had my camera it's such a beautiful sunset." I said, "I know it is." I placed the binoculars against my face and looked at the satellite dishes and could see more detail on them. Below them we're guards wearing desert camo gear and armed with assault rifles and pistols. Hunter asked, "See any snipers?" I scanned the whole area and said, "No, they don't have any." Hunter said, "Good. What else does you see?" I saw the entrance to the base way which was an square shaped with two heavy duty doors with an light above it. I said, "I see the way inside. Thick door with what looks like thick armor on it. No keypads or outside locks." Hunter said, "That means it's locked from the inside then." I watched a guard walked up to it then took out a walkie-talkie and spoke then opened the door and went inside. I said, "Melissa I'm glad you bought those walkie-talkies as we should be able to jack-in on their channel." I set down the binoculars then picked up my walkie-talkie turning it on then turned the channel knob until I heard the guards talking.

Listening to the guards talked about their patrols and giving us every detail, we needed. When it came to 11-PM there would be only three guards out as there. I said, "That's when we'll make our move. We'll storm our way to the control room and find the person who controls the satellite and shut them down." Melissa asked, "I'm coming with you guys?" I turned my head over to her and said, "Yes I don't want to leave you alone where you can be easily captured or killed if anyone finds you." We waited and had all our weapons ready.

11:00-PM

It was almost pitch black with lots of clouds covering the sky giving us little moonlight, but it would help us sneak in. I had listened to the guards and there was one voice that almost sounded like mine so when I called it in with the guard's walkie-talkie, he won't know the difference. We hid behind large rocks where I poked my head over to see where the three guards were. Two of them standing nearby the satellite dishes while one was walking holding his assault rifle. I pulled out a knife I had taken from the hotel and pass another to Hunter. I turned my head and whispered, "When both guards are close enough, we'll take them out then sneak up on the last one." Hunter nodded his head I turned to Melissa and said, "If anything happens shoot the guards."

Melissa had her Glock 17 out I checked on the guards and saw now they were far away from each other I turned my head over to Hunter nodded my head as we slowly got up and crouched walk towards the guards. When I got close enough to the guard I stood up and wrapped my arm around him blocking his mouth; then slit his throat. Blood poured down and he was about to drop his assault rifle, but I grabbed it. Hunter took down the 2nd guard then saw the 3rd one heading towards the entrance I put the guard's body down and moved quickly without making a sound. By the time the guard when to make the call I slid his throat and slowly putting the body down onto the ground. Hunter and Melissa came over as I picked up the guard's walkie-talkie press talk and said, "It's Jim open up." We heard the door unlock I toss the walkie-talkie then opened the door as we entered inside.

Walking down the small stairs leading towards the bottom floor the walls and ceiling were bright white with lights along the walls while the stairs were black. Once I got to the bottom floor there was a guard check point. As two guards saw us, they went to draw their pistols but Hunter aimed his Remington 870 Marine Magnum shotgun and quickly pulled the trigger taking both of them out. We went through the guard check point and to our surprise no alarms went off. I said, "I guess the walls are thick enough to block out sounds." Looking at the computer and screens showing the video cameras we saw where the control room was then a map on the wall. I said, "Ok we're here and we need to get to this floor. It's marked so when we see it we'll know we found it." Taking extra ammo, we left the guard check point we ran through the hallways and going down more stairs until we got to the floor we we're looking for.

A large room with big screens and computers. People we're typing away. I nodded and opened the door holding the M-16A2, while Hunter aimed the shotgun at them. Melissa was guarding the door, also while holding a shotgun. I raised my voice and said, "Evening everyone!" When the workers turned their heads, they were shocked to see us Hunter yelled, "Nobody move!" I asked, "Who is in charge around here?" A man with light greyish hair and wearing glasses raised his arm I went over to him and asked, "What's your name?" He said, "Matthau but you can call me Matt." I said, "Alright Matt I'm going to be clear with you. I don't want to harm anybody but if I'm force to then I will."

Matt said, "I understand." I said, "Good now what I want is you to shut down all the satellites that are floating in space." Matt jaw opened a bit and asked, "All of them?" I said, "Yes every satellite that includes news, military, weather and network channels." Matt looked worried as he looked at the others, he turned to me and asked, "If I do it will you answer a question first?" I said, "Yes."

Matt asked, "How is doing this going to help people?" I said, "It's going to wake them up from their sleep and when they opened their eyes, they'll see the truth I'm trying to show them." Matt turned back to the computer sighed and said, "Alright you heard what he wanted. Do it." Matt along with everyone else was typing away then we heard an alarm going off I said, "Don't stop!"

Matt and the others continued then we saw on the screens showing the movement of the satellites had stopped Matt said, "This will shut them down for a couple hours. If you want me to shut them down fully, I'll have to cause an overload but it will... I press the barrel against his neck and said, "Just do it!" Matt typed away on the computer then we heard an auto voice on the speakers saying, "Warning! Lock down alert! Code red!" Hunter said, "Shit! That doesn't sound good!" On the computer screen that the satellites were disappearing I moved the barrel back as Matt asked, "Now that's done what do you.... Suddenly the screen exploded as the blast knocked me down onto the floor. Matt's head was blown off, but his headless body shot out blood and fell out of the chair.

The other workers were also killed when their screens exploded then we heard loud growling like static noises on the speakers I had to cover my ears it was painful to listen to. Hunter and Melissa did the same, but we could still hear it as it got louder. The growls turned into a demonic high pitch scream then we heard Manson scream in anger and heard more explosions going off in the base. Without warning the speakers exploded sending sparks flying into the air.

As I checked on Hunter and Melissa, I saw guards coming to the door I yelled, "GUARDS!" When one guard opened the door, I aimed at him and pulled the trigger shooting as Hunter fired his shotgun clearing the rest we got up and ran out of the control room.

Running down the hallways heading towards the back exit I saw a few of the lights were blown out with sparks shooting out of the empty sockets along with the speakers I thought, "Seeing how pissed Manson is, I bet he's lost a lot of viewers." More guards came out I fired my assault rifle as Hunter had switch to his assault rifle. Suddenly a guard came out from behind us he fired but missed

Melissa fired the shotgun shooting him in his chest with blood splatter onto the walls and sending his body violently to the floor.

Melissa pumped the shotgun running after us while both me and Hunter reloaded our assault rifles. Suddenly we felt the base floor was shaking as the alarms were getting louder. Another explosion went off and could hear the large satellite dishes outside crashing down onto the ground which made the ceiling crack with dust. Running upstairs and heard loud cracking noises behind us as I hoped the stairs didn't collapse. Once we got to the top a few workers running behind us screamed in horror when the stairs gave out. I opened the door and we're greeted by bright lights followed by police sirens and flashing lights. I yelled, "MELISSA GET DOWN!" Me and Hunter open fired with our M-16A2's as bullets flew both directions. I took cover just in time and heard loud smack noises outside as the thick armor doors were blocking out their shots. Hunter quickly got onto the floor lying on his chest and squeezed the trigger.

I aimed at more police officers then saw soldiers running alongside of them I pulled back on the trigger shooting at them before they could fire back. Blood splattered in the air with one soldier falling headfirst onto the hood of a squad car. Both our assault rifles clicked empty we took cover and reloaded then saw more of them coming. Melissa aimed the shotgun and fired at them giving us enough time we both turned and fired again finishing off the rest. We ran outside and reloaded our guns I then saw a dark black 85 Chevrolet Caprice Classic I opened the driver side door as Hunter and Melissa got in, I shifted the gear into Drive and drove down the dirt putting pressing my foot down hard onto the gas pedal.

Once I reached the road I turned right and sped down the dark empty road I blew air and wiped my forehead. I said, "Holy shit! I can't believe we made it out of there." Melissa asked, "So now that we're done here our next stop is Hollywood?" I said, "Yes but first we... Suddenly the police radio turned on. We heard loud static then other strange noises. I knew who it was. When the noises stopped, I was proven right.

With an angry tone Manson said, "First, I was amused watching you and your friends trying to stay alive but now I'M FUCKING TIRED OF IT AND YOUR FUCKING STUBBORNNESS!"

A loud bang came out of the speakers followed by more strange noises I checked the road quickly making sure no police or army vehicles were coming this way. When the noises stopped, we heard Manson breathing heavy then said, "When I find out where you three are going, I will make it my goal that none of you make it out alive! Your fucking interference hasn't stopped me at all! Just slowing me down but once I find a way around your fucking mess you won't be doing it AGAIN!" A loud noise came then it went died silent inside the squad car.

I then saw sign coming up when I looked it, it said, "Welcome To Las Vegas" I knew there was no other routes for us to take we had to keep going but feared what would be waiting for us once we got there. I then turned on the police radio and could hear men yelling about the sudden attack from the terrorists and most of American's satellites had been shut down causing a full panic in many major cities as radio and TV signals had been cut off. However, as I listen, I waited for someone to say The Manson & Barbara Show but not no one said it. I would check again later but I had to get the hell away from here as the FBI and military would be getting here quickly as they could. I also knew once we got into Las Vegas the city would be under lock down to keep us from getting out. I had bad feeling things were about get much worse.

Chapter 6

March.25
Las Vegas, Nevada
6:30-AM

My eyelids were feeling heavy and pulled over into a parking lot. I killed the engine then rubbed my eyes. It was still dark with little sun light coming up. I had so many thoughts running through my head. I was now worried if I went to any hotel we would be surrounded with FBI or army and they won't take us in a prisoners they would kill us and if it did happen we won't have enough weapons or ammo to fight back. I lifted up my eyes and could see the tall buildings and casinos with flashing bright neon lights I thought, "Where the hell am I going to go now?"

I checked on Hunter who had passed out in the back seat while Melissa is still awake. She turned her head and asked, "You alright?" I sighed and asked, "Where the hell do I go now?" Melissa rubbed her chin and said, "I say we ditch this car and find an RV and make our way towards Hollywood. We can't risk staying in hotels now." I said, "Ok then." Melissa said, "Here let me take over for you." I really could use some rest, so I got out and walked around to the passenger side while Melissa got into the driver side of the Chevrolet Caprice Classic she started it up and drove off while I let my eye leads close quickly falling asleep.

9:00-AM

I woke up as I felt Melissa touching my shoulder and calling my name when I opened my eyes, I saw we we're in a underground parking garage. I quickly looked around and only saw a few parked cars. I turned over to Melissa and saw Hunter was up, as well. I asked, "What's going on?" Melissa said, "Just listen to the radio and the police are looking for this car. We'll have to leave it here." I asked, "Anything else?" Melissa said, "I heard one of the officers saying that the highways and roads leading out of Las Vegas will be blocked until we're found." I sighed and said, "Shit!" Hunter said, "We better find a safe place as we'll be stuck here for a bit until we find a way out of here." We all got out of the Chevrolet Caprice Classic I rubbed my eyes and walked through the stairway leading to the outside.

Opening the door, we came out of alleyway with lots of trash cans, dumpsters, empty beer bottles lying on the ground. We saw some graffiti spray painted on the brink walls. It was pouring rain with roaring thunder above us. I looked up and saw dark grey storm clouds with bright flashes of lightning. Hunter said, "Might be able to find place around here we could stay." We walked down the alleyway and heard helicopters flying around in the air. Good thing the buildings were close by to each other, so they won't see us.

Then we saw a rundown apartment which had signs attached to it saying, "DO NOT ENTER" I took a good look at it then we went inside. Climbing up the stairs we reached the middle floor as the rest of the stairs were destroyed. Since none of the nearby buildings had windows, nobody would know we were hiding here. There was some furniture lying around so we didn't have to sit on the hard floor. We found 3 chairs and a table. Hunter took out the map and looked it I said, "We have lots of open land we can use to get out however walking out of here would take too long and might get spotted. If we're able find a way to sneak pass the roadblocks, then we could reach Hollywood."

I felt cool air blowing through the broken window beside me as look over and I checked down the alleyway nobody would be coming by here. Hunter said, "If the army is blocking all exits with the help of the police then this city is under martial law. Giving them full power to do what they want." Melissa said, "Just our fucking luck!" I sighed and felt hungry we would need to rest up before doing anything else along with getting more ammo. I said, "We'll have to stay here for a bit until the heat dies down. I'm going to look around the area we're in just see what's going on outside. I won't be gone long." I got up and left as they sat in silence.

I stayed close to the walls of the buildings I didn't bother to avoid the rain. Looking around I saw most of the nearby buildings had garage doors that could only be open from the inside. A few had lights above them while others were smashed. When I came to the end of alleyway, I suddenly saw a squad car I quickly moved back over to a brick wall and poked my head halfway and waited until it was gone. I slowly walked over but not too close to the alleyway. As I looked both ways down the street there was only few vehicles driving by. I thought, "If anything happens these streets would be suicide to run through there isn't any cover to take." I turned around and went down the other way. However, it only led to a dead end. I thought, "One of those garage doors must be able to open from the outside."

I went to all of the garage doors and couldn't open any of them I said under my breath, "Shit!" I saw an empty bottle I kicked it hard as it smashed into brink wall. I wasn't going to call it quits after making it this far I knew I had weakened Manson, but it wasn't enough to stop him. I knew how to stop him and his friends I would have strike harder than him. Suddenly I heard loud noise above me I lifted my head up thinking it was a helicopter but saw a big dark purple blimp flying above the buildings I thought, "What the hell?"

The dark purple blimp turned I saw along its sides were large screens with big speakers with text above the large screens was the name of the TV show. I suddenly heard Manson voice on the speakers as he said, "Evening everyone! This is Manson, The Bat!"

I suddenly heard the sound of cars slamming on their brakes I looked over to the alleyway entrance and notice a station wagon came to full stop a family looking out their windows looking at the big dark purple blimp. When I turn my head back to the one, I saw my jaw dropped open. On the large screen showed Hunter, Melissa and my face on the screens of what we looked like in full detail and color.

I saw two other blimps in the distance showing the same image then I heard Manson's voice again he said, "These three wanted criminals known as "The Tricksters" They have murdered dozens of people, caused mass destruction and last night have shut down all of America's satellites." I then heard loud yelling from children then Manson spoke and said, "And it breaks my heart that I can't bring smiles to the many fans who enjoy my show." The yelling got louder I looked back where the station wagon was as the parents were trying to control their children I thought, "Manson what the fuck are you planning now?!"

Manson spoke a little louder and said, "However, I can't do everything myself so I'm asking my fans to help in my quest to rid the world or evil. The evil that infected this once beautiful world is slowly being destroyed by adults! Everyday adults bring themselves closer and closer to self-destruction of wildlife, and their children's lives by waging war over energy, power and killing. I want all of you to turn against every adult! Stand strong together as the Tricksters won't be able to handle the power that every boy and girl that carries inside them. And if they use their weapons against you, you'll know who the real monsters are. Once you have the Tricksters, I'll take care of the rest for you and reward everyone who helps in my quest to rid the world of evil. Good luck to all of you."

I couldn't believe what I just saw and our chances of getting out of Las Vegas were about to turn into a real nightmare. The fighting I saw coming from the station wagon got worse. I looked over and saw a few younger kids and some teenagers running over to the station wagon they pulled out the father and mother and began beating them up to death. I heard loud screaming followed by sirens I thought, "Hunter and Melissa aren't going to like what I'm about to tell them."

I returned to the rundown apartment as they heard what Manson said and saw the purple blimps, but we could hear the sounds of gun fire followed by roaring sirens. Hunter said, "Just what we fucking needed! An army of children and teens hunting us down!" Melissa said, "I don't get it. How does Manson suddenly have blimps when before he didn't have any. It's like his getting more power from somewhere." I thought about and realized that each time an adult died Manson's show gained more viewers and when death toll rises he became stronger. And where was he and his friends getting their magic from? Adults."

I said, "I know how he's doing it now." Hunter and Melissa looked at me I said, "Each time an adult is killed Manson gains powers through their souls and is able to use it as magic. That's why he wasn't able to go after us earlier. Now that he and his friends have more power, they are able to brainwash, enter into our world and use our own technology against us. And the more children and teenagers Manson get the more followers giving him strength he needs to do whatever the fuck he wants. That's how he sees us through TV's, mirrors and able to hear us through radios because of his fucking magic."

Hunter had a dumbstruck look on his face while Melissa was shocked, I looked over at the window to see the dark purple blimps still flying around showing our faces on the screen. Melissa asked, "What if we knocked power out that won't allow Manson to... Hunter said, "He might have found a way around that if we tried." I sighed and said, "I think you're right about. The only way we'll going to stop this fucking bastard is by shutting his signal. Once it down Manson won't be do anything he wants."

Melissa said, "2nd thought if we did shut down power stations, we might cause more problems and some states use nuclear energy." I said, "Yeah if we tried shutting down one of those, we might cause a meltdown leading to a radiation leak or worse a nuclear explosion sending fallout into the air." Hunter said, "Wait. If Manson is having all children turning against adults does that mean the rest of American?" I said, "I don't think so as Manson knows we're hiding somewhere in here and is using all of his power to find us. If he had more magic, then he would be launching a full assault on the world." Hunter said, "Maybe that's what he's trying to do. Start World War III." I felt my eyes opened wide, I remembered the drawings of what Sam drew.

I said, "I hate to say it, but I think you're right about that." Hunter said, "Well shit! We better find a way out of this goddamn city!" I said, "We will but first we'll wait. Let the kids do their thing and once everyone has calmed down then we should have a better chance at night since all the children should be tired leaving a few out patrolling the streets." Melissa said, "Good point and we won't have to worry about them carrying guns." Hunter said, "Maybe the teenagers will but younger kid might get his hands on a pistol or a revolver. Which is better than going up heavier weapons." Suddenly we heard a woman screaming we turned our heads to the broken window and saw a gang of teens and children chasing after a woman. When she tripped and fell onto the hard wet pavement I whispered, "Get down."

As we couched down, we could hear the loud stumping sounds followed the woman bagging the children and teens to stop but they didn't stop. I knew if we tried to help her not only would those blimps be on us, but a gang of angry children would be after us as well. Then it ended by a loud crack with a young boy yelling, "DEATH TO ADULTS!" They cheered and ran down the alleyway we didn't stand up until we didn't hear them. Looking outside we saw the woman with her clothes torn and badly damaged and a pool of blood around her. Melissa was shocked while me and Hunter had a disgusted look on our faces. Manson was going to make it his mission to make our life's a living hell and he was doing a fucking good job at it.

1:00-Pm

The storm had stopped but it was still raining so we took this chance to leave the rundown apartment and see if we can find food, ammo and a vehicle of some kind to get us out of here. Once we walked down the empty streets, we saw a few cars smashed up with dead adults lying next to them or on the sidewalk. We saw an officer with his head busted open as a trail of blood poured out onto the wet street. I saw his pistol had been taken out of the holster along with the spare magazines.

Hunter said, "Shit, here comes a blimp!" I saw it coming we took cover beside a Ford Econoline van. It flew by and heard Manson's voice on the speakers, "Remember my children for each adult you hunt down I'll reward all of you. But the ones who find the Tricksters will be an even bigger reward!" Once it was far away, we moved on then came to a grocery store we ran inside. Grabbing a cart, we began taking what we needed. When we got back to the checkout, we took everything out of the cart putting it into bags. Melissa asked, "Should we stay here? We might get caught if we try going back to the apartment?" I said, "Nah we better go back to the apartment since those kids will most likely return here."

We went out the back exit and walked through the alleyway returning to the rundown apartment where we made sandwiches. Hunter found a portable burner and was cooking stew. I carried a cooler filling it with ice and placed Coke and water bottles inside it would take a while for the drinks to get cold. The rain poured harder with roaring thunder I saw more dark purple blimps flying around Las Vegas looking for us.

We ate in silence while one of us would look out the broken window. I checked the time on my watch it was now 2:45-PM I lightly yawned then rubbed my eyes. When I opened them, I turned my head over to the window to see a purple blimp flying by showing our faces I thought, "If I had a rocket launcher with a ton of rockets, I would shoot them down." I turned head away and finished eating. By 5:00-PM we we're planning a way out of the city I knew if we stayed here too long the children would find us. I planned on leaving tomorrow night since we needed to see how the blimps work during the night.

When nightfall came it stopped raining, but it was very foggy as the blimps flying low had their spotlights shining down onto the roads and any areas that were dark. Following them were the gangs of children and teenagers holding baseball bats, hammers, big wrenches, lead pipes or guns mostly pistols, revolvers. I saw a few older teenagers holding M-16's, HK-94A3's, bolt action rifles or shotguns. However, I notice something about the sky I asked, "Is it me or is the moon and the starts missing?"

Hunter and Melissa looked up and notice it I said, "It's almost like a shield is blocking out the sky." Melissa turned over to me and asked, "Will we still be able to escape?" I said, "Yes we will." Suddenly a loud horn was blowing which was coming from the blimps then we saw the spotlights shining down onto a squad car as it was trying to sped down the road with the teenagers shooting at it. The squad car drove into a wall and crashed, and it didn't take long for the gang of children and teenagers to surround the car within seconds like hungry swarm of piranhas. We watched a officer was pulled out while trying to fire his pistol but it was taken out and three other men were forced out and saw they were wearing prisoner suits. They yelled and swore at the gang of children but that didn't stop them as they were beaten to death.

A blimp got closer I said, "Get down." We got down as a blimp showed its light through the broken window then moved away while we heard the children and teens cheering and laughing of what they did. When I lifted my head up see what they doing I saw one teenager unzipping his fly and pissed on the corpse of the man he just killed. When he was finished, he pushed his dick back in zipped up his fly then picked up his shotgun resting against the squad car and walked away I knew it wasn't going to be easy getting out of here alive.

March.26
8:00-AM

I woke up when I heard a noise, I quickly grabbed my Smith & Wesson Model 629 and cocked the hammer hearing the noises of someone walking around below us I thought, "Shit! If it's a gang of children or teenagers, we'll need to get out of here fast." I woke up Hunter and Melissa and whispered, "Get your guns ready." Hunter picked up the M-16A2 as Melissa had her Glock

17. We listen closely I heard a young male voice say, "This should be a good place to do it." We then heard the sounds of a teen couple having sex I sighed but knew we had to be quiet as if we didn't want them knowing where we were. I checked the time on my watch then turned my head where the teen couple was. It wasn't until 9:40-AM when they left, I waited a bit then slowly got up and checked outside to see it was foggy but very warm yet wet outside.

We all ate breakfast as I said, "So driving out in the streets is suicide." Hunter said, "If we had a tank, we could drive through anything." Melissa asked, "What if those blimps have cannons on them?" I said, "From what I seen they don't have any weapons but maybe it's hidden somewhere on them." Hunter said, "You know I been thinking of another way we can get out of here." I asked, "What's that?" Hunter said, "My idea is why not try using the sewer system to get out of Vegas. Hell, we might even reach Hollywood." It sounded easy however, we would have to find the right way out, but I didn't think we would be able to reach Hollywood through the sewer system.

I said, "Well I guess their only one way to find out. Their a manhole we can try to go through but it's by the parking lot garage so here's what we'll do. I'll go down first and if I don't come up then you two will get in knowing we can go through it. However, if I come right back up that means we can't use it." I took a quick look outside and the purple blimps won't too close to this area I turned my head back and said, "If it doesn't work, we'll travel through the streets and try to find another way out."

Standing close by to the manhole with the duffel bags that had our weapons, food and other stuff I opened the manhole and climbed down the ladder it felt very cold as I lowered myself to the bottom. I looked down as there was some lighting but not much. When I got close enough to the bottom, I saw the dirty water running below me, but it was blocked by three bars as we won't be able to cut through it I said under my breath, Fuck!" I crawled back up and turned over to Hunter and Melissa knowing we would have to find another way out.

Walking down the sidewalk while holding my M-16A2 along with Hunter as Melissa was holding the Remington 870 Marine Magnum shotgun. We kept our eyes open for any patrols and blimps but saw the sky was a dark grey almost black in some areas. While some sunlight was shining through however the rest of it was being blocked out. Suddenly we saw a blimp coming we took cover behind dumpster in a short alleyway and waited for the blimp to fly by. As we waited, we then heard the sound of cars coming.

Speeding down the street were muscle cars with the teens racing each other. I thought, "I had a feeling they would do that." When it was quiet, I said, "Let me check first." I walked over to the alleyway and checked both ways and saw it was clear I turned my head back to the others and waved over to them as they came over to me and we began walking down the sidewalk again. We we're now in the heart of Las Vegas which we saw a few wrecked vehicles and some of the buildings have been badly damaged along with some casinos. And lying in the street were dead bodies both beaten and shot to death.

Suddenly we heard the sound of talking kids and teens coming we went to turn around but saw a blimp coming I thought, "Shit, we're going to have a fight on our hands." Then I heard someone behind us, "Hey! In here!" We turned our heads to see a black officer holding a Winchester Model 1300 I thought, "This better not be a trap." We went inside and moved away from the glass door following the officer as we we're inside a hotel. Taking the stairs to the manger office the black officer said, "You're lucky you came by here as if you went any further in this city you would have been tor apart by those children gone mad!"

He turned around and saw on his badge his name was Frank. He had short black hair with dark eyes. Frank was about the same height as me but heavily built then me. Frank said, "I tried to reach any other officers, but it seems most are dead or somewhere hiding out from whatever the hell has taken over this city. But seeing the crazy shit that's happening outside I know you three aren't the terrorists." I said, "Nice to see a friendly face for once." Frank lightly smiled and said, "I got food and cold drinks if you want any. We won't be able to leave for a while." I said, "Sure."

Frank brought them into the manger office as we sat and ate. Hunter asked, "So Frank do you know any way out of this city?" Frank looked at us and said, "Well since the streets are crawling with gangs and the skies with those blimps, we're not going have a easy time getting out of here." I asked, "Would be able to escape through the sewers?"

Frank turned to me and said, "That's not bad idea however the sewer system won't lead us out of Las Vegas it can lead us away from the city." I said, "We could try fly out of here but fear what's waiting on the other side is the army." Frank said, "You're right about that. While shit hit the fan yesterday, I watched in horror when an airliner was trying to escape was shot down by a fighter jet." Melissa was shocked as Frank added, "However I don't think the pilot was ordered to do it as a few seconds later he crashed into the ground killing himself. Now I'm not sure if the army is still their but we'll going have to make a choice drive or fly out of here, but I don't know how to fly a plane or helicopter."

Hunter said, "It can't be that hard. If we get something small and stay low to the ground, we should be able to... Suddenly we heard the glass doors being broken followed by sounds of footsteps I said, "Shit! We better get the hell out of here." We quickly got up and picked up our duffel bags Frank said, "I know way out the back." He pumped his Winchester Model 1300 shotgun and followed him as we went down the hallway leading to the back stairway. Moving quickly, we're outside in the back parking lot with a few cars we heard more children and teenagers coming.

Frank moved over to the concrete wall of the parking lot he whispered, "This way." We went over the wall and ran into alleyway of the nearby casino. We hid behind the casino hearing the children and teenagers walking around talking and knocking over stuff. Then we heard two blimps flying by but heard the sound of footsteps coming down the alleyway. Frank opened the back door as I turned my head, we all went inside quietly then locked the door and waited for the teenagers to leave. They tried the back door but saw it was locked. I heard one of them say, "We'll try going in through the front." We waited a bit as I turned over to Frank as he said, "We better get out of the city fast." We went out the back exit and walked through the alleyways until we were near the highway it was very hot, yet the sky was dark. Running across the highway now on the other side of Las Vegas which Frank told us the airport was here I knew we had two choices and once we picked a way out of Las Vegas we won't going be able get a 2nd chance if something went wrong.

We saw a police station which looked like it had been untouched Frank looked it and said, "We might find some ammo in there." Hunter asked, "Say is there a chance this place has a helicopter?" Frank said, "We'll have to find out." We entered inside the police station and saw no one. Frank walked over to the front desk he set down his shotgun onto the desk and typed on the computer and said, "It seems whoever was sitting here has left his or her report on unfinished." I asked, "Does that computer say if their anyone in the jail cell?" Frank said, "Let me check."

It didn't take Frank long to give us the answer he said, "Ok we got car thief, a drunk, and an arms dealer." I said, "If we bring them along with us it could double our chances of winning a fight if we'll force to." Frank sighed and said, "Alright but if they slow us down then they are on their own." I said, "Fair enough." Frank said, "Now let me check one last thing." He typed away at the keyboard while I looked over at the front doors. The windows didn't show anything, but the sky was still dark, and looked like it was going to rain again. Frank said, "Ok, let's get going."

We walked into the jail cell and saw the three men sitting on the beds. The car thief was a teenager with long dark brown hair while wearing a leather jacket, black shirt, dark green camo pants, running shoes with leather gloves that had finger openings. The arms dealer was the oldest but wore a sliver suit with a white shirt under it a black tie. Had short black hair and thin glasses with black dress shoes. The 3rd and last person had dirty clothes with long messy hair he turned to us and asked, "Say when I can eat something?" Frank said, "I am releasing you as there isn't law anymore." The car thief lifted up his head as he lightly grinned as

Frank added, "However this city has gone to shit as...as a mysterious person has caused the children and teens to turn against adults."

The arms dealer raised an eyebrow I said, "It's true. Look if we all want to get out of this city we have to work together. But if you rather go on your own it's up to you but be warned it's dangerous out there." The arms dealer asked, "What the hell is going on? Who this mysterious person? God?" I said, "Worse. It's Manson and his gang of... The car thief said, "The Manson & Barbara Show? No shit! That fucking show has fucked up my sister mind along with my best friend." Frank said, "Curtis is telling the truth. This bat man has turned the city into madness." Car thief said, "Hell you may be a pig but I don't want to end up with those crazed assholes. Let me out." I said, "Just do it." Frank opened the jail cells as arms dealer said, "Before we go I want my stuff back as I aren't leaving it for some punk to steal it." I saw the 3rd man raising his arms and yawned and said, "You're fucking crazy. I'm leaving this shithole." He walked past us but didn't bother stopping as it was his choice to come with us or go on his own.

Frank said, "Alright Tony we'll go get it." The car thief asked, "Please give me a gun as well." I said, "Of course you'll get one. But if you try anything on us... He said, "I won't as only an idiot would try that." I asked, "What's your name?" Car thief said, "It's Simon." We followed Frank upstairs he opened up the armory as Tony went over picked up his weapons. I saw Tony pick up a chrome AMT HardBaller Long Slide with a dark wooden handle and grip. He slapped a magazine into it then pulled back on it arming the pistol.

Next weapon Tony picked up was an assault rifle which I never saw before. Simon asked, "Cool rifle what is it?" Tony looked at Simon and said, "It's Beretta AR-70 I been selling these to many countries since Beretta came out with them in the 70s best goddamn assault rifle you can buy for $3 grand." Simon said, "Sick man." He looked at the guns and grabbed a Colt 1911 he loaded a magazine into it then tucked the pistol down his camo pants. Tony took a few other guns and ammo placed them into a big briefcase and asked, "Ok, so what's the next plan?" Frank said,

"I'm going to check if the police station here has a helicopter, we might be able to fly out of the city."

Tony said, "We should take my plane I left at the small airport. It's a few miles away from the city but it would be our best chance out of here." I said, "Alright then that's what we'll do. We'll grab a car from the parking garage and get out of here." Tony said, "I have a safe house in Beverly Hills we can lay low." Hunter said, "Perfect we'll be close by to Hollywood." Tony said, "Let's leave I hate this fucking place." Simon said, "Same here and I'm hungry for some burger and fries." We took the extra ammo as Frank took us downstairs into the parking garage and got a unmarked dark black Plymouth Gran Fury with dark tinted windows. Frank grabbed extra gas tank and placed it into the trunk for later he started up the Plymouth and drove out of the parking garage as Tony told him where to go.

I checked behind us and couldn't see the city of Las Vegas anymore I turned my head away as Frank said, "Before we reach this small airport, I won't mind getting something to eat." Tony said, "Same here." Simon turned his head over and asked, "So this Manson guy is real?" I said, "I'm afraid so. And we have a grudge against him along with his friends." Simon said, "Oh now I remember what the media said about you two. Thought it was crazy you two manage to escape a maximum-security prison." Hunter said, "Wasn't easy but we pulled it off." Simon asked, "So you saw Manson in person?" I looked at him and said, "A few times I also saw Kane." Hunter said, "I blew his head off which only pissed him off." Tony sitting up front turned his head over and asked, "So these cartoon characters I been hearing about they are really the ones causing all the mayhem?"

I said, "Yes and Manson used his dark magic to frame us and make every law enforcement believe that we we're terrorists." Tony said, "I did find some of the news I heard of you along with your friend hard to believe." I said, "Manson also had the power to brainwashed anyone who he wanted to fool and make them follow him. Those with minds strong enough to resist his bullshit won't be affected by his dark magic. Those he controls seems they'll regret it or join his cause."

Tony asked, "What's his goal? Rule the world?" I said, "Yes that's his plan rule the world and kill every adult." Tony, Simon and Frank had a disturbed look on their faces Hunter said, "Me and Curtis who were doing reports of these events that were happening in Black Creek back in 84 and early 85 Manson forced children to murder their own parents burn down churches, schools, government buildings along with killing anyone that stood as a threat to Mason. We've seen first-hand a young boy who felt so bad and broken inside. He killed himself while being I saw it, and nobody would believe me questioned." Simon said, "I knew this shit was bad the minute."

Tony asked, "What else is Manson planning?" I said, "We strongly believe he's going to start nuclear war since he needs souls of adults to gain his powers. I can't imagine what he'll do but I bet it isn't going to be good." Simon said, "You can't be serious." I said, "I afraid so. We learned Manson is sending his show through satellite and radio signals. We we'll able to shut down all the satellites when we broke into an underground base but Manson is now focusing all of his dark magic against us here so he can find a way to gain his strength back and I hope he doesn't; because if he does, I don't know what he'll be capable of doing next." Frank said, "I see a dinner coming up. Should be able to cook us some burgers and fries." Frank pulled into the parking lot I said, "Frank parked around the back in case anyone comes by." Frank parked in the back. Once he shifted the gear into Park and killed the engine, we all got out and went inside.

Hunter and Frank were cooking in the back while I grabbed cold sodas for the others. I opened the cold Coke can and drank it. I said, "Aww much better." Melissa said, "Same here sugar." I lightly smiled as Melissa bushed her hand against my crouch. Hunter came out with burgers and fries then asked, "Who's hungry?" We all ate at the front it felt good eating good grade meat again as it felt like ages since I had a good burger and hot fries. I turned my head looking outside with the sky was now pitch black with hardly any sunlight shining through I heard Simon asked, "What the hell is with the weather?" Everyone else turned their heads and saw it I said, "Manson blocking out the sunlight with some force field or something." Tony said, "I hope we'll be able to fly through it." Melissa asked, "We haven't seen anyone fly through it." Tony said,

"Well, we'll stay low to the ground so in case anything happens."

Melissa asked, "What kind of a plane is it?" Tony said, "It's one of those small two engine planes. If we ever make it out of this, I hope to save up for one of those small jet engine planes. I'll be able to bring my business to other places." I said, "I really hope the world goes back to normal after this is all over as I sure as hell don't want this happening again."

We left the dinner around 2:00-PM and nothing had changed since we left the sky was still dark with hardly any sunlight shining through which Frank had to put on the headlights. It was also very quiet inside the Plymouth as well with only Tony telling Frank where to go. I kept checking the sky and around us for anything. We haven't seen a single person, child or teen since we left Las Vegas. Then we saw a sign showing us that the small airport that Tony told us was coming up. I was glad to see it knowing we would be able to escape and hopefully Manson will just keep looking here until he finds out we're gone but if his power is growing stronger, I had a gut feeling he won't have any trouble finding us again.

Frank drove up the front booth with a gate he stopped and said, "Here I'll get it." He got out went inside the guard booth got the front gate opened then hopped back into the Plymouth and drove on Tony said, "Alright drive over that hanger right there." Tony pointed as Frank drove towards it, I looked up at the sky and could hear thunder roaring above us. Simon said, "Shit! Where the hell did this storm come from?" Tony said, "Relax we're getting out of here." Frank parked the car he turned his head back and asked, "Should I keep the engine running just in case anything happens?" I thought about it and said, "Alright." Tony said, "I'll need a hand getting the hanger doors open." Hunter said, "I'll help." Both Hunter and Tony got out of the Plymouth and ran over to the hanger. Tony took out keys from his silver suit pocket unlocked the door and he and Hunter went inside the hanger. As we waited, I checked the storm with the thunder roaring louder with bright flashes of lightning in the sky I felt something wasn't right about this. We then heard the hanger doors being pushed opened and with the headlights shining inside we saw Tony's plane. Once fully opened Tony ran over to the hatch door, he turned the handle and pulled as the hatch opened up with an small built in step ladder. It didn't take long for Tony to get the plane's engines fired up Frank said, "Alright let's go." Frank killed the engine I said, "Pop the trunk." Frank did the rest of us got out me and Melissa picked up our duffel bags and ran on board Tony's plane. Simon was the last one to get on board as Hunter closed the hatch Tony said, "Alright everyone put your seat belts and hang on." Tony got the plane moving down the runaway.

Just as the plane was picking up speed, I looked out the window and said, "You gotta be fucking kidding me!" Melissa turned her head and floating above the dark sky were the dark purple blimps as they shined their spotlights on us. Tony said, "So long, fuckers!" Tony lifted up his plane I noticed the ground below us spiting open with large cracks. We then heard Simon yell, "WHAT THE FUCK ARE THOSE THINGS!?"

Suddenly in front of us were large dark purple snake like worms with round shaped heads. Tony yelled, "OH FUCK OFF!" Simon said, "They look like dickheads!" One close by opened its mouth I could see dozens of sharp teeth. It tried to bite us, but Tony avoided it by going higher. However, the purple snake worms quickly rise higher Tony said, "What I won't give if my plane had weapons on it!" The snake worms moved their heads towards the plane trying to knock it down with one getting closer Tony saw some mountains coming up Tony yelled, "Hold on! I got idea!" Tony nosedived his plane towards the ground then quickly lifted it up with the snake worms chasing after us. Tony flew pass the Rocky Mountains but to our horror the snake worms could go through it. Without warning a snake worm rammed its head in the back of the tail of the plane causing it flip forwards as it was going towards the ground. Before it crashed, I held onto Melissa I shut my eyes and heard the plane crash into the hard ground.

6:00-PM

I slowly opened my eyes and felt my head was sore. My vision was blurry and d a light ringing in my ears. But as I tried to move, I felt my arms had been tied up with rope. Then my vision began to clear up I saw me, and the others were tied up in chairs while on a wooden platform inside a somewhat lit stage. I heard Hunter calling me, "Curtis? Curtis! You, ok?" I turned my head over and saw a cut mark alongside his forehead and said, "Yeah I'm ok." Hunter sighed and said, "Should have known it. Every time we think we're ahead of that bastard he was always ahead of us waiting for us to make our next move since he already made his move." I said, "We'll get out of this." Tony said, "Goddamn it! That plane I bought wasn't cheap! Shit my weapons were on their." Hunter said, "Curtis! The diary!" I said, "Damn it! We had it in our duffel bag! We'll have to get it back before Manson destroys it."

Simon asked, "Are we back in Vegas?" Frank said, "I believe so." Suddenly we felt cold air blowing as bright blood red curtains opened in front of us and outside the stage was children and teenagers as lights shined brightly on the stage. I could now see we we're inside a large dome shaped theatre. Then we heard heavy metal music playing on the speakers. However, it wasn't from any band I knew it was the theme song for The Manson & Barbara Show.

The children and teenagers cheered then we saw large screens placed all over the theatre turning on showing the logo of the show then it showed each character playing an instrument. Manson was playing a dark purple electric guitar wearing his dark purple suit and top head. Along Manson side his girlfriend Barbara wearing her red & black outfit playing a red electric guitar.

Then it showed Kane playing bass guitar and like his outfit his guitar was green on one side while the other was white. Then it showed George drumming away with a big drum set with thick drumsticks. On two of the bigger drums had the name of show on them. Then it showed Andrew blowing away on a harmonica but felt his eyes staring at us. Then it showed Hellen playing an organ which had a pirate theme to it. I thought, "I bet their all here." I didn't even want to think how we we're going to be killed but knowing how pissed Manson was, he was going to make all of us feel his wrath.

I looked up at the screens it then showed Manson and Barbara standing together as they finished the theme song with a guitar solo. When they done playing the crowd cheered so loudly then in the center of the theatre opened up with a platform rising from the floor with Manson and his gang standing together the crowd turned to them with the lights shining on them. Manson took off his top hat waved at the crowd along with other characters. Melissa whispered, "We need to get out of here!"

I tried moving my arms, but the rope was very tight I then looked down at the chairs and saw they were fused to the floor. I felt my heart beating fast I thought, "No! I won't give up!" Then Manson put his top head back on with Barbara holding his arm left arm while holding his cane in his right hand. As he and his friends began walking towards us the lights followed them with them getting closer, I said under my breath, "Oh shit!" My heart was beating faster I felt it was going to explode out of my chest I thought, "Stay calm! Must stay calm! If I don't calm down, I'll end up dying here! There's got to be a way out of here!"

They were a few feet away from us the cheering stopped as I felt Manson's bright red eyes looking at mine. He slowly grinned and lightly laugh then turned around with the others as he said, "My dear boys and girls I'm honored that all of you have helped me and my friends find and track down The Tricksters!" The children and teenagers cheered loudly I tried forcing one of my arms out of the rope, but it seemed to only get tighter." Suddenly the crowd quiet down Manson pulled the handle of his cane sword turned his body around quickly and felt the sharp blade pressing against my neck I stopped as my eyes were locked onto the blade it felt very sharp and was very shiny.

Then the edge of the cane sword slowly lifted up I looked up to see Manson looking at me while holding his cane sword tightly and could hear the sound of his purple leather grip gripping the handle. Manson said, "Now I have you and the others here!

This game of ours is now over!" I manage to speak up and said, "Dream on!"

Manson sighed and said, "Aren't you a stubborn one. I'll give you credit for making me and my friends working harder so we can find you and fix the mess you made. Come to think of it! I should have you and the others send into space and fix every satellite you DESTROYED!" Manson voice bombed loudly in the theatre I then felt the sword blade now pressing against the left side of my face and could hear his demonic growl then he said, "But you humans can't survive being in outer space! You'll all freeze to death, slowly suffocate without oxygen, float into the abyss as a dead empty corpse. Making all of you useless."

Manson moved his cane sword away from my face and said, "However, there is something you and the others can do for me and my friends." I felt Barbara, Kane, Andrew, George and Hellen staring at us along with the crowed and could feel their hatred towards us including Manson's hate. I then notice on the screens showed us sitting in the chairs. Manson's eyes glowed bright red and said, "I want to watch you and your friends...DIE FOR MY AMUSEMENT! DIE FOR OUR AMUSEMENT!" The crowd cheered loudly as Manson grinned, he looked at us and said, "Now put on a good show for everyone and don't make my audience bored. We all came here to watch you die!" The crowed started chanting, "DIE! DIE! DIE! DIE! DIE! DIE!" Suddenly I heard a strange noise behind us turning my head to see a pitch-black hole appeared then it began sucking in air I could hear the chairs making loud noises as the rope suddenly became so tight I growled in pain then I heard Frank scream in terror as he was sucked into the black hole. Next was Tony followed by Melissa. The pain was getting worse I couldn't fight it anymore.

Simon screamed as his arms were ripped apart from the rope I then watched as his legs were torn off next blood poured onto the stage floor and his head exploded into bits of flesh and brain matter. I yelled, "HUNTER! DON'T FIGHT THE PAIN!"

Hunter and I did then the chairs were sucked into the black hole. I could hear those who were falling through the darkness their loud screams. I shut my eyes closed while my body was spinning and falling faster dmy heart was racing. The screaming grew louder as I could hear other horrible noises around me. It suddenly felt colder the deeper I went. Too scared to open my eyes I just waited what felt like hours for this nightmare to end but I knew it was far from over.

I felt I had butterflies inside my stomach and my blood was rushing to my brain. My heart was causing my chest to feel sharp pain like knifes were stabbing me. I could then smell something burning it was the rope the hot flames licked my arms as my whole body burst into flames, I screamed loudly until I crashed into freezing cold water. The second my face hit the cold water I opened my eyes to see I wasn't falling anymore I was standing on soft ground.

I stood in a forest with bright green grass, tall trees, birds were flying above me and singing loudly as the sky was a nice shade of blue with white fluffy clouds, I felt the warm air blowing along my body when I looked down, I saw I wasn't wearing any clothes. I thought, "What the hell is going on?" I looked around but didn't see the others I began walking through the forest then I saw Melissa lying on a tree and she too was naked. I couldn't help but stare at her beautiful body then it hit me, "Wait, is Manson making us reenact scenes from the bible? But he hates religion."

Melissa woke up and saw me standing naked I slowly walked over to her and asked, "Melissa you alright?" She raised her arm up to me as I helped Melissa up she asked, "Where are we?" I looked around the forest but didn't see anyone else but had a feeling those screens back in the theatre, they're watching us, including Manson and his friends. I said, "Let's find the others." We walked together through the forest it seemed so beautiful and peaceful nothing seems to be a threat to us. Then we noticed a glowing almost golden tree. We walked towards it and saw a tall very thick golden tree with dark purple flower heads on with small black leaves on it. Then hanging on its branch were two large blood red fruit. It had the shape of an orange, but the skin texture looked almost like snakeskin.

I looked back at the fruit and had a bad feeling if we wanted out of this we would have to grab and eat it. Melissa said, "I don't like this." I said, "I'm afraid we don't have much of choice." We both reached up for the fruit and when we pulled it off from the branch the mysterious fruit had some weight to it, yet it felt very smooth and soft. I looked at the tree again and it was still glowing gold I looked back at the strange fruit. We both took a bite out of the mysterious fruit it had the sweetest taste I ever tasted yet it felt very warm. I took another bite out of it I looked at the fruit and stopped chewing.

The inside was like raw flesh and black blood was oozing out of it. Melissa gasped and dropped the fruit suddenly we felt the ground shacking violently as the golden tree wasn't glowing anymore it turned pitch-black and the dark purple flowers suddenly bust into white flames. The forest around us became very dark we both try to run away but thick dark purple vines with sharp black thorns blocked our way.

As we turned around the black tree branches turned into vines with razor sharp thorns. The vines reached towards the other nearby trees grabbing different birds they made noises then we're ripped apart with blood splattering all the pitch-black tree. Without warning the vines reached for us and wrapped around our legs and arms. I felt the sharp thorns tearing through our flesh. We tried fighting it, but the thorns only dug deeper.

We both screamed in pain I watched the pitch-black tree was now burning in white fire I could feel the blazing heat on our bodies. When it drew us closer to the vines wrapped tightly around our legs and arms forcing us to open up then more vines came towards our bodies, I felt the sharp thorns running along my dick and ball sack as it slowly drew closer to my chest. I saw the vines running around Melissa pussy and her huge breasts. I felt someone was watching us when I turned my eyes over to the left, I saw a man wearing a white rope with long golden hair with a handsome face and light blue eyes. I thought, "Wait! Is that supposed to be Jesus Christ!?"

He looked up at us and said with a powerful voice, "You have sinned by children. You must be punished!" I then felt a sharp pain as the vine's thorns tore off my ball sack and dick, I screamed loudly as my body being ripped apart, I wanted to shut my eyes but couldn't as Melissa's beautiful body was being destroyed by the pitch-black tree. Then her body burst into flames making her scream louder then I suddenly burst into flames, as well. I had never felt such horrible pain and when my eyes burned everything went black as my screams slowly faded out.

When I woke up again, I was lying on the ground and could still feel the pain all over my body. My sight slowly came back and lying, in front of me was Melissa I crawled towards her and said, "Melissa!" When she slowly opened her eyes said, "Oh...Curtis!" She began crying as I lifted her body up and hugged her. She placed her arms around me. I thought, "There has to be a way out of here!" Then I saw other people running towards something I said, "Melissa look!" She turned her head over then said, "I see Hunter and the other two!" We got up and ran towards them I could hear a storm raging towards us.

When we caught up with Hunter, Frank and Tony. They turned around and went over to us however they were still in their clothes while we we're both still naked. Hunter said, "Curtis? Why are you two naked?" I didn't answer his question as I could see a large wooden ship coming towards the shore I thought, "Noah's Ark? Is Manson retelling the bible but mocking it to show it's evil?" As the wooden ship came to a full stop an wooden staircase came out of the ship as everyone was getting on board.

Suddenly I notice the sea level was rising we tried to get on board but standing on the top of the wooden staircase was Jesus Christ. He pointed at us and said, "No sinners allowed on this holy ship." Tony yelled, "Fuck you, God!" The staircase lifted up as the wooden ship moved away then thunder roared above us as a tidal wave was coming towards us.

When it hit us, we were pulled towards the bottom. It quickly turned pitch-black. I didn't bother to hold my breath, knowing this nightmare would end faster. I felt the cold water going through inside my lungs however I didn't die right away as I thought I would. Instead, my body was slowly freezing then I could feel pressure and I sunk deeper into the abyss. The pain grew worse, and I couldn't fight it anymore. My eyes exploded, I screamed. I felt a sharp pain before my body blew up.

I woke up again and coughed up water then gagged a bit. I heard the others doing the same thing. I rubbed my eyes they itched and saw we we're lying in a field with fruit which looked like blood drops with a shiny red color to it. Frank, Tony and Hunter helped us up as Tony asked, "How the hell do we get out of this goddamn freak show?" I said, "Until Manson and the others get enough kicks of us dying." Tony looked at me and asked, "You gotta be fucking joking right!? There has to be some way out of this hell!"

Just as I went to speak Frank pulled off the blood drop shaped fruit it suddenly turned into a liquid along with the rest of the strange looking blood drop shaped fruit. Suddenly there was a loud, fapping sound when we turned our heads up into the sky, we saw a glowing blazing sun then Jesus Christ yelled, "NO SINNER SHALL EAT THE HOLY FRUIT!" Then flying by him were millions of locusts coming towards us. Tony yelled, "OH SHIT!" We turned around and ran but the field suddenly became longer with no end in sight. It didn't take long for the locusts to reach us. They began biting and eating away at our flesh it hurt I smacked a few off but more and more just came. I could hear the others screaming in pain while being eaten alive.

I yelled trying to get the locusts off of me, but it was pointless I fell on the ground feeling the sharp pain of every inch of my flesh being eaten away I looked up to see Jesus Christ watching us with an angry look. I went to shout at him, but the locusts reached my face chewing as I screamed loudly then felt my eyes being torn open. The pain didn't stop until they chewed away at my brain. Still screaming but I didn't have a tongue. *FUCKING MANSON! MAKE IT FUCKING STOP!"*

When I woke up I was now lying in the desert with the others my whole body was in pain I felt from every death was still there with my eyes getting watery I started to sob and couldn't help myself. I broke down and cried and heard the others crying as well. I wiped my eyes then opened them and now saw wooden crosses I thought, "I had enough of this bullshit!" When Jesus Christ appeared in front of us, I then heard movement behind me when I turned my head, I was picked up by a group of people Jesus

Christ say, "Place the sinners onto the crosses!" I tried fighting back as I threw a few punches but whacked hard in my face.

I felt my arms being held I tried using my legs kicking one man in his crouch which caused him to fall to the ground. A hard blow came to my face as I felt my nose was broken, I yelled in rage kicking the man who punched me in his face as blood splattered out of his mouth. Then a hand grabbed my face I bit into then tore away at the man's fingers as he yelled in pain. I saw Hunter, Tony, Frank and Melissa were fight back. Just as I was about to be lifted onto the cross, I grabbed a hammer out of a man's hand and smacked it across his face I heard a loud crack noise.

Another man went to grabbed me, but I smashed out his eye and kicked him hard in his face. The others manage to break free and we're fighting with hammers. Those that tried to stop us we smashed their skulls open as blood splattered everywhere. The rest of the people ran away and stayed back we all turned and face Jesus Christ but now looked very evil looking and yelled, "SINNERS! PUNISH THESE SINNERS!" I suddenly felt very angry towards this false god I went up to him and smashed the hammer into his face knocking him onto the desert ground. He tried to get up, but we all ganged up on him and smashed him to death with the hammers we we're all covered in blood. Our rage grew worse as I kept hitting Jesus Christ's head until it burst open, I saw his brain I felt the urge to rip it out and began eating it. The others tore off his limbs and we're eating them.

We ate more suddenly the hatred in us was gone and I puked out what I ate. Feeling the inside my body slowly burning. The others moaned and vomited up blood then the group of people came towards us and placed our bodies onto the wooden crosses and nailed us to them I felt the sharp pains of the large nails breaking through our bones. They all chanted, "DIE SINNERS! DIE SINNERS! DIE SINNERS!" The burning pain inside of me grew worse I began crying then the cross bust into white flames I screamed loudly as my body slowly burned away.

When I looked down at the group of people, they were eating the remains of the false god while the others were still chanting the same damn thing. I cried louder as my eyes felt very sore with my heart beating so fast, I surely believed it was going to exploded from my chest. I then heard the others nailed to the crosses give in to the pain and die I kept crying until my heart started to slow down I thought, "Just fucking end it already! I give up!" Then my sight started to fade out as the white fire burned my head away.

When I woke up again, I was now standing with a bunch of soldiers in dark grey uniforms and helmets. We we're all armed with bolt action rifles with bayonets attached under the barrels. Standing inside a bunker with dimly lit lights on the walls I saw poster which showed a hand pointing to a group of different people of race and text in bright red said, "KILL ALL WHO ARE NOT WHITE!" When I turned my head over, I saw another poster which showed a white man and a black woman being hang and red text said, "HANG THOSE WHO BETRAY THEIR RACE!"

I felt sick inside as I had nothing against difference races and this whole scene was ripped from the pages of The Turner Diaries. I won't be surprised if Manson had killed the author who wrote that terrible novel. Then we heard someone walking besides I moved my eyes to see what Hitler dreamed of creating the perfect pure white race. A tall very handsome and muscular man wearing a black leather outfit, thick heavy boots, black leather gloves and had a sword holster attached to his belt. When this man turned to face us his light blue eyes stared at us then said loudly, "My men! Go out there and find the scum of the earth! Hunt down and kill every color of the race that isn't white! Slaughter the faggots! Hang the traitors! And burn the lesbians!"

He then opened the door and yelled, "MOVE OUT!" I ran out with the soldiers as we went up a short flight of stairs to see a city in ruins with dark grey clouds above us with heavy rain fall.

Running through the streets were wrecked vehicles mostly covered in bullet holes and inside were dead people and blood splatter. The soldiers went in different directions as I followed a group moving towards a park. Lying on the grass were both dead adults and children of different race and color.

Suddenly I heard screaming and I knew who it was. We the soldiers in front of me moved out of the way I saw Hunter and Melissa. I heard the men pointing and yelling, "TRAITOR!

SCUM OF THE EARTH! FILTHY BLACK BITCH!" I watched in horror as they grabbed and taking over to a tree with Hunter and Melissa yelling for help. I wasn't taking part in this anymore I pulled on the bolt aimed at the soldier pulling Hunter and pulled the trigger. A loud bang went off as blood splattered out the side of the soldier's face, I quickly pulled the bolt back then slapped it forward fired off another shot freeing Melissa.

The soldiers around me went to aim their rifles at me I didn't have to time to act. I was shot from all sides and felt each bullet hitting my body, breaking my bones and tearing the uniform apart. I fell onto the ground as the soldiers ganged up on me and stumped me to death while calling me horrible names. I could hear Hunter and Melissa yelling and trying to escape. Everything went black when I felt my skull being crushed by a heavy boot, yet I could hear the sickening sound of bone breaking followed by my brain being pressed out.

I then heard Manson's voice inside my head, "The human race is cruel and hostile towards anything it sees as a threat or it strongly dislikes. Such a pathetic species and yet I was supposed to entertain your kind...Do you still think I'm worst then what the human race has done?"

I woke up again now I was in the seat of a bomber. Around me were the same people I saw now wearing dark grey and black leather outfits with some had helmets with black visors. I jumped when a voice came in my ear, "8 minutes until we reach target." I touched a headset on my head then noticed a screen which showed where the bomber was going and up ahead was an island I thought,

"Wait is this when US dropped the atomic bomb on Japan?"

I then heard that voice again, "Hey! Get ready to drop our present! I bet they'll have a blast with it." Sickening feeling hit me hard when the screen showed the island was in fact Japan. I thought, "I'm not pressing that button!" Suddenly I felt I couldn't stand up or speak my right arm was heavy I couldn't lift it as my hand was close by to the red button. I then heard the bomb doors opening up then the voice said, "Drop it!" I bit my lip and pressed the button then felt the bomber was climbing higher. I thought, "At least I don't get to see what happens next."

To my horror the screen suddenly changed showing a family having a nice picnic. A little boy was playing with his dog while the daughter was picking flowers as the husband and wife ate together. I could hear everything they were saying along with the background noises of birds signing, butterflies flying by the daughter and the dog barking while wagging his tail. Then the husband stopped what he was looking at with dog turning around looking up at the sky. They were quite as the daughter pointed to what I knew was the bomb suddenly the dog turned around ran away while whining the little boy went to go after it but it didn't get when a bright flash went off followed by the loud roar of atomic blast.

My eyes were glued to the screen I couldn't just watch in horror what was about to happen. I remember learning about the bombing of Hiroshima and Nagasaki back in history class and my teacher thought it was terrible what happened. What the textbooks lacked in the graphic images I knew this was going to be even worse.

The blast radius hit the family the daughter was first as the flowers she picked quickly burned away along with her hair. She screamed loudly as her skin was slowly melting away. Her parents held onto each other while their hair and clothes burned away as they screamed in pain. I saw the boy in the background getting knocked by the blast wave and could hear the dog crying out in pain as it slowly burned.

The flesh on the girl burned with muscle tissue now showing along with some bones sticking out. Her parents had fused together, and their moans sounded horrible. The area around them was covered in flames as dead birds and butterflies fell and burned around them. The howling wind blew dust into the little girl as she cried then fell onto the burned ground and called for her parents but had died.

I felt sick what I just saw and wanted to look away when suddenly I saw something crawling towards the family. It was the boy who was somehow still alive. His right arm was missing, his skin was badly burned. When I got a better look at his face, he didn't have eyes, his nose and ears had melted off. He screamed louder and louder by the minute, but nobody paid him any attention. Then he turned to the screen I could feel his hatred as he moved closer to me with my heart beating faster. He screamed at the screen I didn't speak Japanese but had a good idea what he was saying, "Why? Why did you do this to me?! Why did you murder my family? WHY!?"

I wanted to scream when suddenly the bomber shook violently when I heard the voice on the headset yell, "CONTACT!" I heard the sound of fighters flying by us and letting loose with their machine guns. When I was able to move my head again, I heard bullets piercing through the bomber as crew members were hit then heard other loud noises followed by alarms going off. Another voice yelled, "DAMN IT! THEY HIT THE ENGINES! WE WON'T MAKE IT BACK!" Suddenly the pilot turned his head over to us and lifted up visor and said, "Fuck returning back! We're going to die as heroes!"

The pilot then had the bomber returning back to Japan but was heading straight for Tokyo. I heard more machine gun fire behind us as more crew members were killed. The alarms grew louder and felt the g-forces I grabbed onto screen the only thing I could reach for then my jaw dropped open when I saw the city, we we're heading for. The pilot laughed loudly and yelled, "LET'S BURN IN HELL TOGETHER!" When the bomber crashed, everything was bright white. I couldn't see anything. When my eyes adjusted to the brightness, I saw what destruction the 2nd atomic bomb did – the whole city of Tokyo was destroyed.

I thought, "I don't get it? This never happened at all!" Then through the ruins I saw badly burned and wounded people walking while crying, moaning or screaming from losing a limb, their sight or a loved one. I couldn't move and felt I was stuck but as the people got closer to where I was, they all turned their heads. The horrible smell of burn flesh was all I could taste. They began walking towards me while all asking me the same question, "Why did you do this? WHY!?" Their hands reached for my face and screamed when my eyes were torn out.

When I woke up, I was lying on muddy ground I thought, "When will this end?!" I felt rain pouring on my body then heard a man yell, "GET THAT MAN UP AT ONCE!" I felt two hands grab my shoulder tops lifting me up. When I saw where I was now, I was standing in an open field with tall barb-ware fence on both sides, guard towers with spotlights shined on us. I could hear guard dogs barking behind us I looked over to see the others along with different people.

We we're all naked as the man who spoke was the racist leader who I saw earlier said, "Let's see how far these fucking Jews, blacks, faggots and other scum of this planet!" When a gunshot went off, we began running through the mud while the dogs behind us chased after us. I heard people slip and fell face first into the mud while the dogs were tearing them apart as they yelled for help. I turned my head back to see large black dogs were bright red glowing eyes, sharp teeth and spiked collars around their necks.

Then Melissa was running beside me as she turned her head and said, "Curtis!" I said, "Just keep running!" Suddenly Frank fell and he begged us to help but we couldn't. The dogs barked and tore him apart as he cried loudly. Thunder roared above us followed by flashes of lightning then we saw wooden signs coming up. At first, I wasn't sure what was next for us but when a lightning flash went of it showed a skull with cross bone which meant we we're about to go through a mine field.

I saw it was just me, Melissa and Hunter that made it as everyone else didn't but when we crossed onto the mine field the dogs stopped but kept barking and growling. Suddenly we heard the land mines going off as chucks of dirt along with mud fell on us. Loud explosions went off near us when I stepped on a land mind and within seconds it went off. I felt my legs were blown off followed by my left arm. When I landed back on the mud, I saw the damage and screamed in shock.

Hunter and Melissa stopped and turned to help me but as Hunter ran towards me, he stepped on a land mine and was blown into bits. I yelled, "HUNTER! NOOOOOOO!" Just as Melissa went to run towards me out of nowhere, she was grabbed by the soldiers then the racist leader walked over and said, "Aww the filthy black bitch made it!" Melissa yelled, "FUCK YOU PRICK!" He punched her hard in the gut as she coughed. He lifted her head up and threw a hard blow breaking her nose. Then all three men began taking turns beating Melissa up I yelled, "FUCKING STOP IT!" But they didn't listen I was forced to watch while the pain from my wounds grew worse.

When I heard the sickening sound of Melissa's neck snapping then they turned to me and finished me off until I was killed again. In darkness just waiting to see what I was going to be thrown into next or was Manson done with this bullshit!

I then heard Barbara voice say, "Why do adults feel the need to rage war for what purpose? Why is it that your kind see itself better than any other race and yet you buy and sell stuff to them? However, you slowly kill them off while trying to push people over to the edge. You called us monsters for the things we done and yet humans have done far worse than us. Who is the real monster now Curtis?"

I woke up sitting by myself while inside a theatre. In my right hand was a big soda and in my left a big paper bag of popcorn. The lights on the walls slowly dimmed down then the currents opened showing a blank screen. I heard the film projector turn on as it did the number count down but when it reached 1 it flashed the logo of Manson & Barbara on the screen. Then the lights went out and it was pitch-black, I couldn't see anything around me.

I then heard Manson's voice on the speakers, "Well Curtis you and your friends put on quite the show. A shame I won't miss your acting as you're not bad...haha! But relax and enjoy these pictures I made just for you!" When the projector showed the film onto the screen, I saw a tropical beach I thought, "Wait a minute! Is this my favorite porn film I used to watch back at my apartment?" Just like in the film the hot and sexy women ran out while their huge breasts bounced as they giggled, laughed and smiled while racing towards the shore. As their bras and bikinis were coming off suddenly Manson, Kane, Andrew and George came out while holding their weapons and ran after them.

The cheery music suddenly changed to horror when the screen showed close ups of Manson along with others stabbing, slicing and smashing their weapons into the women. The other women screamed and made to the shore while one tripped and fell into the sand. She went to get up, but Manson grabbed her hair pulled up as she begged, "Please! Please don't kill me!" Manson then stabbed his crane sword through her chest and forced the blade down then pulled it out as her guts spilled onto the sand.

I gagged while I turned my head away as this was fucking horrible! When I looked back at the screen showing the naked women swimming through the water. Then out of the darkness below them sharks swam towards I said, "NO! I DON'T WANT TO SEE THIS! MAKE IT FUCKING STOP!" The screen then showed each woman being attacked by sharks as they screamed underwater while the crystal-clear blue water quickly changed dark tinted red while the sharks chewed off their limbs.

A hammer head shark bit a woman on her head as it thrashed her body violently underwater then tore off her upper shoulder tops along with her. I turned my head away then saw John sitting behind and asked, "What's wrong Curtis? I thought you liked this sort of thing." I asked, "John?"

The theatre went dark for a few seconds then projector came back on, and John was gone. I looked around the theatre but didn't see him. Then on the screen it a woman walking out of a bar with long jet-black hair, mirror sunglasses, black lip stick. Wearing a leather jacket, short shirt, leather pants, black leather gloves, high heel boots. Had huge breasts, wide hips and very thick bubble butt. I remembered her from another porn film I liked watching I growled and said, "Is this what you're going to do to me!? Take my favorite films and turn them into goddamn snuff flicks!"

The woman in black walked towards a sliver 61 Porsche 356 B with its soft top down. She got in started up the car and drove off down the empty road. I knew she was supposed to have her boyfriend with her. As the screen showed a front view of her Porsche she turned her head over to the view mirror and adjusted it. A close up on the view mirror and she moved it back suddenly behind her was a big truck and grinning in the driver side was her boyfriend. He had an evil grin, and his eyes were open wider than normal.

It showed him ramming his truck into her Porsche as she tried going faster but he didn't slow down. Then it showed a cliff coming up as he sped up beside then rammed his truck into her car. She screamed while he laughed loudly as the Porsche was being pressed against the guard rail. When the car broke it, the screen showed a close up of the woman's face she screamed loudly, and it showed the Porsche crashing into the rocks below as the woman was thrown out of the sport car and heard the bones breaking along with the impact. Feeling sick in my stomach watching these fucked up films.

The woman moaned and was a mess then it showed a shadow outline of the man walking towards her. She lifted up her face as it showed the boyfriend but a close up on his face but now his eyes were glowing red and looked more disturbing. Grabbing her clothes and tearing them off then placing her against the rocks as the screen showed the boyfriend loosening his belt then pulling down his fly. I turned my head as I couldn't take this anymore. I went to stand up when suddenly rope wrapped around my arms, legs and chest and heard Manson's voice say, "Where do you think you're going? The show isn't over yet so sit back and relax."

Then hooks attached to my face forcing me to look at the screen and I couldn't close my eyes. On the screen it showed the man raping the woman as she screamed loudly while crying. When he was finished, he pulled a knife I thought, "Please just end it! I can't take it anymore!" A close up on the woman's throat as he slid it with blood pouring out then it was dark inside the theatre and felt it was getting cold.

I then heard Barbara voice on the speakers, "It hurts, doesn't it? Seeing you the things you love being abused and destroyed and yet why do you like it?" I yelled, "I DON'T LIKE IT! YOU DO!" Barbara said, "Oh is that how you feel about us? Do you really think we're trying to destroy the world?" I yelled, "WHAT ABOUT

THE CHILDREN WHO KILL THEMSELVES!? DO YOU FEEL FUCKING PROUD OF THAT!?" It suddenly got quiet, and it was getting colder. I moved my eyes around but didn't see anything.

Barbara voice came back but louder, "We would never harm them! They won't ready for the truth! And the truth is one answer you humans want to know about everything! Are you ready for the truth Curtis?" I yelled, "TRY ME, YOU SICK BITCH!" Suddenly Barbara's face came on the screen, but it was covered in bloody while her eyes glowed brightly. Barbara opened her mouth and saw razor sharp teeth as she screamed loudly hurting my ears then it got demonic. I could see my breath while it was freezing cold, I thought, "Does this mean of the end to this horrible nightmare?"

Suddenly it went dark then heard Barbara's voice beside me, "You wish it was a nightmare handsome." When the projector came back on, I looked but Barbara wasn't their suddenly I heard Hunter's voice on the speakers, "Curtis! Curtis, can you hear me?" I turned back to the screen to see Hunter tied down to a metal table while only in his pants and was looking at me I yelled, "HUNTER! CAN YOU HEAR ME!" He said, "Yes! I can hear you but...but oh man...I...I don't know if I can do this anymore! The fucking things these have forced me to go through and watch...I...I can't make it!"

Hunter started crying I yelled, "HANG IN THERE! WE'LL FIND A WAY OUT OF THIS!" Then Barbara walked onto the screen wearing a nurse outfit with a very short skirt and leather boots. Hunter turned his head over to Barbara and said, "Please...no more! I can't take anymore!" Barbara giggled and said, "Don't worry I'm here to make you feel better." She grinned then went over to a table as the screen showed a top-down view with different sharp blade weapons.

Barbara pointed to each one whole moving her arm and said, "Hmmm which one first?" Barbara then picked up a curve knife as she turned back to Hunter his eyes locked onto the sharp knife as Barbara giggled, I tried so hard to shut my eyes but couldn't nor turn my head with the hocks keeping my head locked in place.

Barbara teased Hunter with the curve knife while sweat was running down his forehead.

Then without warning Barbara stabbed the curve knife into his belly Hunter bit his lips so hard they were bleeding as she moved it up towards his chest, he tried to fight the pain, but he screamed when he couldn't fight it anymore. Blood was running down his body while Barbara grinned.

Barbara set down the curve knife and grabbed both sides of Hunter's chest and tore them open I never heard Hunter scream so loudly in his life. More blood was oozing out of his body and onto the table I could see his guts along with the rib cage with his lungs and heart beating very fast. I felt my face had turned green along with eyes getting watery.

Barbara then picked up a meat hock and stabbed it into Hunter's intestines and tore them out. I vomited all over my lab and onto the floor as Hunter screams grew louder. Barbara stabbed his stomach ripping it out with fluid and blood spilling all over the place. Barbara laughed as I yelled, "LEAVE MY FRIEND ALONE YOU FUCKING BITCH!" She grabbed a table saw and began cutting into his rib cage removing all his ribs. Barbara's eyes open wide as she grabbed Hunter's heart and tore it out killing him with his head resting against the table as blood poured out of his mouth with the look of terror on his face.

Barbara turned to face me while laughing then ate his heart. I yelled, "FUCK YOU!" She giggled then rubbed her bloody hands above her cleavage then the screen went blank. I felt lightheaded not knowing if they really killed Hunter or they were just fucking around with my mind. Then I heard Manson's voice on the speakers, "It seems your friend had enough and yet you still want to go. Let' see if you want to go on after what I do next." Had a bad feeling who I was going be forced to watch another painful death.

The projector came back on now showing Melissa wearing her clothes and holding a sword. She looked at me and said, "Curtis! Can you hear me?" I said, "Yes! Please don't give up, Melissa!" I saw she was standing inside Manson's castle then it showed Manson walking in as he pulled out his sword cane. He grinned as Melissa gripped her sword tightly, I yelled, "COME ON! KICK HIS ASS!" d ran towards Manson as the two clashed their swords at each other but Manson moved his cane sword back and slashed it at Melissa arm as blood oozed out, she grabbed where he slashed at her while Manson grinned with his red eyes staring back at her.

Melissa and Manson swung their swords with Melissa dodging a few of his attacks but he was too fast for her. Then Manson went to strike but Melissa blocked his attack he quickly moved and slashed at her back. Manson lightly laughed as Melissa yelled in anger trying even harder to hit him. As Melissa got Manson closer to a wall, she went to slice his head off, but Manson dodged it and sliced off Melissa arms.

Blood poured out as she screamed while Manson said, "What a shame you're not trying hard enough." Manson then rammed his cane sword up Melissa's crouch she screamed louder with more blood pouring out. I began to cry and just wanted all of this to end. Manson then pulled out his cane sword and sliced off her head.

Manson then turned to me and asked, "So, Curtis do you wish to continue? Or do you want to suffer more?" I said, "NO! I had enough!" Manson grinned and said, "Just as a thought but now let's be sure you have given up on this pointless quest to stop me." The projector shut off as it was pitch black and so cold, I thought I was going to freeze to death but then lights came back on and now I was tied to a tree with chains. Around me was hay and was in the middle of a forest. Then Manson and Barbara walked towards then I saw thousands of children following them.

When they got close enough Manson said, "It's time to end this. Fare well Curtis." The children holding touches tossed them at me with the hay being licked by the flames I could feel the heat it itched my skin then the pain grew worse. I tried ignoring it but as it got higher, I yelled in anger feeling flesh burning away the flames were reaching my face. I stared up at the dark sky screaming until everything faded into darkness.

Chapter 7

I woke up lying on the stage and thought I could hear someone calling me when I opened my eyes and saw Melissa, I wrapped my arms around her and cried. I swear I could still feel every painful death I went through then I felt another pair of hands hugging both me and Melissa when I looked to see who it was it was Hunter, I held tightly onto them and thought I really had died.

Manson said, "Please give them a round of applause to The Tricksters for their wonderful performance!" The crowd clapped and cheered while I looked at Manson and his gang with hatred. I saw Frank lying on his back and was white as a ghost while Tony lied on his side. I didn't see Simon and knew he didn't make it. Manson lifted up his arms walking over to us as the crowd was quiet. Manson stood over us and said, "See you cannot defeat us, Curtis. We are stronger because of the wonders of magic. We can do such much more with magic then what science can do."

I growled and said, "I still don't get it. Why are you doing this Manson?" He looked at me, but I wasn't afraid of him anymore. I said, "Barbara said I wasn't ready for the truth, so I want to hear it from you! No more bullshit just tell me, what it is your trying to accomplish!" Manson said, "Very well Curtis, I'll tell you." He walked away and said, "As you saw from my show, I have shown the dangerous of religion, science, power, war and what adults really are. You teach the children how to hate other people, harming your own planet with pollution while destroying it, to suffer and abuse the young so when they become older, they will do the same to their children."

Manson turned back to us and said, "I'm not trying to destroy the world Curtis I'm trying to save it." I raised eyebrow and asked, "By killing every adult you gain more powers through their souls. What about the children then? When they grow up they'll become adults too." Barbara wrapped her arm around Manson as he lightly smiled, she said, "Yes but we'll raise the way they should be forever. Learning the wonders of magic, love and peace. They shawl never learn hatred, war, suffering, pain and destruction."

Manson asked, "And once we have all the souls, we'll reshape this world and make it our world for future generation. They say when people die they will be reborn through the ashes of the old world." Hunter was right Manson was going to start WWIII by wiping the rest of the population with nuclear war.

Manson said, "You won't live to see the dawn of the new world, but you'll witness it's end." I lightly shook my head and said, "From a cartoon character to a god. You really believe that you're the hero of this despite everything you and your friends have done to reach this point." Manson said, "I knew you won't understand the truth when I told you." I stood up along with Hunter and Melissa then said, "No, I do understand. You're just full of shit!"

Manson and Barbara looked annoyed as I started moving towards them, I said, "After rejecting what your creator had planned for you, you all turned against him and used his magic to create your world then slowly over time began your plan of wiping out the human race to destroy the world." Manson walked closer to me ready to pull his cane sword out I locked into his eyes and said, "I guess when you have so much power you don't give a shit for anything else then yourself because when you're a god you can do whatever the fuck you want!"

Manson pulled out his sword pointing it at me. He lightly growled but I didn't flinch once. I asked, "Before you kill me Manson just answer this one question, I have left for you." Manson asked, "What is it?" I asked, "What is the devil getting out of this deal?" Manson asked, "Who?" I said, "The devil. After all, where did Osborne Louis get all his powers from?" Manson didn't speak I said, "I have a feeling you let him fuck your girlfriend for a deal to rule the world, huh?" Manson yelled in anger then went to swing his sword when Tony pulled out his AMT HardBaller pistol aimed at Manson and squeezed off a few rounds hitting him which caused him to miss allowing me to dodge his attack I threw a hard punch into his face then kicked Manson off stage.

Barbara pulled out her dual swords and yelled, "You bastard!" As she went to run over to us Frank pulled out his pistol and shot Barbara in the leg knocking her down. Frank went to fire another shot but was crushed my George's hammer. Tony yelled, "RUN! I'LL HOLD THEM OFF!" Me, Hunter and Melissa quickly turned around and ran Tony yelled, "BRING IT ON MOTHERFUCKERS!" As he capped off a few more shots Tony was hit by Sydney's magic beam turning him into ice then she kicked him breaking Tony into tiny pieces. Sydney turned to us and tried blocking our way out, but we escaped then heard Manson roar, "KILL THEM!"

Running down the hallway Melissa said, "Wait! We need to get back our stuff! We'll never find where Arkard house in Hollywood." Hunter said, "Not to worry." Hunter pulled out a notebook hidden in his pants and said, "I made a copy of it just in case anything happened." I lightly laughed and said, "Oh Hunter I can always count on you." He smiled suddenly the wall beside us smashed open as it was George he yelled running after us with his blood-stained hammer.

George went to swing his hammer at me I jumped out of the way and nearly got hit. The hammer smashed through the wall and was stuck Hunter said, "Here George let me give you a hand with that!" Hunter grabbed George's belt and pulled it down along with his black pants. George growled and yelled, "HEY!" This gave me time to get up and Hunter tucked the book back into his pants while George grabbed his belt pulling it up then pulled out the hammer turning to us and yelled, "I'M GOING TO CRUSH YOU INTO TINY PICESES!"

Running faster while hearing George's heavy foot stumps catching up to us. Then we saw 4 doors but none of them had the exit sign. Melissa said, "Shit! Which one!" I turned my head to see George's red glowing eyes out of the dark hallway getting closer I yelled, "SPLIT UP!" I ran through the door on my right while Hunter and Melissa went through the door on their left. When George reached the four doors, he looked at them and said, "Mmmm…which one to go through first?"

I ran down a long hallway with purple tinted bulbs in the ceiling suddenly I saw on both sides were mirrors and when I turned my head back the door was gone, I turned back and thought, "Great I'm in a fucking fun house! More like a nightmare house!" While running I bumped into a mirror which was a dead end I turned around and saw two hallways on both sides of me. My heart was beating fast I breath, "Fuck! Which way?" Suddenly I heard Manson say, "I can help you with that." When I turned my head, I saw Manson in front of me and went to stab his cane sword I ran left as the sword broke through the mirror and it was bleeding.

I turned my head back and saw him coming after me I turned my head away and breathed, "Shit! Shit! Shit!" I saw another dead end I went right but stopped when it was dead end I spun around and ran down the other way with Manson laughing then yelled, "Run all you want Curtis! You'll never escape me!" Suddenly the gravity shifted as I went up into the ceiling with mirrors now showing reversed images of myself. I got up and tried running but it was hard as I was upside down. While looking around for Manson when I turned to face forward, I stopped and gasped seeing him in front of him with his red glowing eyes.

Thinking quickly, I went to punch him but it was mirror and when it cracked blood was oozing out of the cracks. Then on the other mirrors it showed him laughing while grinning I saw movement in the corner of my eye I turned to my left and saw him. Manson swung his sword I used my arm to block and felt the blade leaving a gash I fell on my face hitting the ceiling. I quickly rolled and began crawling backwards while holding my left arm. Manson grinned with his red glowing eyes looking down at me and stepped closer to me with his sword dipping with flesh blood.

I turned my head back and saw hallway but couldn't see as it was pitch black. I quickly got up and ran for it while feeling gravity shift again now, I was running along the wall through the darkness hearing Manson laughs echo behind me. The purple tinted bulbs were flicking in the ceiling then gravity shifted again as I nearly fell but kept myself up now running around the ceiling.

I entered into a round shaped room with mirrors covering every side and surface of the room. When I turned my head the way I came was gone. My heart was beating faster I checked my left arm and was covered in my own blood. When I looked back at the mirrors, I saw none of them were showing my reflection. Manson said, "Oh, where could I be?" I jumped thinking he was behind me, but he wasn't I looked around and didn't see him but knew Manson was close by.

Manson said, "Oh Curtis, you got some blood on your shoe." I looked down and saw Manson standing under neath me he then waved at me. I lifted my head then without warning Manson came at my right side and threw a hard punch as I crashed into a mirror which hurt my back I growled. Manson then ran and went to swing his cane sword I rolled out of the way dodging his attack but was coming after me.

On the mirrors I saw Manson's reflection he swung his sword I dodged it but when I bumped back into a mirror, he went to stab me I grabbed the handle of the cane sword and held back. Manson grinned using all his strength while I fought back trying to keep the cane sword from stabbing me. Manson lightly laughed and asked, "Why do you fight it, Curtis? You know there isn't going to be anything left for you when this world is reshaped in my own image. John won't miss you and every inch of human history will be erased and forgotten. What's worth saving for this shitty world when it has no future."

I felt my grip was starting to slip with the blade slowly getting closer to my chest. Manson said, "It's such a shame you aren't younger Curtis as you could have joined your brother in the new world but you are part of the old world with ideas that don't work nor belong in my world so they must go." I moved my eyes around then saw purple light coming out under a mirror. Looking back at Manson he said, "And don't worry about your unborn child I'll take care of it." I yelled, "Like hell you will!" I then moved my arm over and let Manson stab the mirror behind me. I kicked him hard in his groin then threw a hard punch knocking Manson down.

I went to the mirror with the purple light and rammed my body weight smashing through it and ran down a long hallway. Manson growled loudly then slowly pulled himself up walked over and pulled his cane sword out and looked where I went.

Hunter and Melissa ran down a long hallway with red tinted bulbs in the ceiling. Melissa said, "I hope we find Curtis soon." Hunter said, "We will." They both came to a door Hunter opened it and stepped inside a room which had Halloween decorations with jack-o'-lanterns that had creepy faces and bright flames inside of them, dead trees with a few having cartoon versions of half-moons, witches and bats hanging from their branches. A thick fog suddenly rolled in Hunter said, "Stay close to me." Cool air was blowing with Hunter and Melissa scanning the room as it seemed to have no end to it, and it was like they were standing in a forest.

Suddenly they heard above them, "Such a fine night for a walk, isn't it?" Both Hunter and Melissa lifted up their heads to see Sydney flying above them and also saw her thick black butt cheeks. She lightly laughed then swung her arm at them shooting blue beams. Both Hunter and Melissa dodged the attack as the ground where they were standing turned into ice. Sydney landed in front of them while lightly laughing then said, "Alright you two play time is over. It's now time to DIE!"

Sydney lifted up both of her arms which glowed blue Hunter grabbed Melissa arm and said, "Run!" Both of them ran between the trees giving them cover as Sydney fired freezing ice shards at them which they went halfway through the dead trees. In front of them was a river they were about to jump across it when Sydney yelled, "No so fast!" Suddenly the river lifted up and turned into a frozen solid wall then spikes poked out of it.

Hunter and Melissa turned their heads back to see Sydney flying towards them. Melissa said, "We need to get out of here!" Hunter said, "Wait, I got an idea. Keep her busy." Melissa ran off as Sydney followed her Hunter ran off and grabbed a jack-o'-lantern and ran after them. Melissa ran through the dead forest while Sydney laughed and shot more ice shards at her. Melissa slipped on the mud and fell then Sydney froze it as Melissa couldn't get up. Sydney laughed and landed on the ground walking towards Melissa.

Sydney said, "Shouldn't have stuck your nose where it didn't belong." Melissa said, "You don't scare me you fucking witch!" As Sydney lifted up her arms glowing blue suddenly Hunter came out behind and smashed the jack-o'-lantern onto Sydney's face she screamed loudly and ran off as her head burst into flames. Hunter went over to Melissa and pulled her free getting some of the frozen mud off of her. When Sydney pulled off the burning pumpkin and put out the flames she turned around as they saw her face had melted off now a skull with bright red glowing eyes with blood oozing from burned fresh. Sydney had a demonic growl and yelled,

"I'M GOING TO TEAR OUT YOUR FUCKING EYES!"

Sydney ran towards them Hunter grabbed mud and threw it at her face then threw a hard punch into her face, but Sydney grabbed Hunter and threw him at a tree. Sydney wiped off the mud turning back to Melissa and felt her anger. Melissa asked, "What you're waiting for. Come and get me bitch!" Sydney growled then her arms bust into blue flames Melissa saw Hunter hasn't gotten back up, yet she ran towards Sydney as she pointed both arms at her. Melissa quickly took cover behind a dead tree as Sydney shot out blue bolts of lightning as the ground where Melissa was standing exploded sending her a few feet in the air and landed back on the ground.

Melissa felt pain in her side and slowly got up and breathed, "When the hell could she do that?" Melissa turned her and saw Sydney walking towards Hunter as he was slowly trying to get up. Melissa looked around for something to use as a weapon and saw the frozen wall with spikes. Melissa ran over grabbed a spike breaking it and ran towards Sydney. Hunter moaned feeling his back was sore but not broken he looked up to see Sydney with a pissed-off look on her face as muscle tissue had slowly healed on her skull and her red glowing eyes looking down at Hunter.

Sydney grabbed Hunter's neck squeezing it and said, "Your soul is now mine!" Hunter felt powerless as his eyes locked onto Sydney's eyes. But Melissa yelled, "Hey dumb bitch!" When Sydney turned her head over Melissa stabbed the frozen spike into Sydney's right eye, she screamed loudly covering her face as blood poured out. Melissa helped Hunter up as the two ran off getting further away but heard Sydney scream loudly. Running faster Melissa said, "Hunter! Look!" Ahead of them was a door they kept running when they both tripped over and were hanging upside down. They heard Andrew laugh and ask, "In a hurry?" Hunter turned his head and was shot in the right eye with an arrow. He yelled as blood poured onto his forehead. Melissa saw the wire was tied around her shoe she quickly reached for it and untied it and fell onto the ground. Hunter reached into his pants and said, "Melissa! Take it!" He tossed her the notebook and said, "Go! I'll only slow you down!" Melissa didn't want to leave Hunter but knew she had no choice she forced herself to turn around and run as Hunter yelled, "GO! JUST FUCKING GO!"

Andrew fired his cross bow but missed Melissa as she ran into the hallway. Sydney said, "Leave her. The others will deal with her! But let's deal with you." Andrew cut the wire dropping Hunter onto the ground as Sydney grabbed his should tops Hunter turned to face Sydney. She pulled out the arrow then tore out Hunter's left eye as he screamed with his soul being forcefully removed and felt his body was burning. When his soul had been removed it healed Sydney fully and looked down at his body that was now a rotten corpse. Sydney said, "Good riddance!" Sydney lifted up her foot and stump Hunter's head crushing his skull as it turned into dust.

Running down the hallway with purple tinted lights I reached another door I opened it and saw it was a room filled with different types of warriors from the past inside glass cases. Walking past each one they looked so life like I swear their dead cold eyes were watching me. I saw on my left side a big muscular man holding a large wooden hammer and wearing animal skin around his waist. I thought, "Wait a minute!" I turned my head to the right side seeing a mirror as it showed the same thing but when I looked back at the cave man it was George.

He roared and smashed his hammer through the glass case I jumped nearly getting crushed. Quickly pushed myself up and ran. I could hear George's heavy breathing and footsteps chasing after me suddenly the next room over changed into a brick wall I stopped and touched the wall feeling it was solid. George yelled,

"NOWHERE TO RUN NOW!" When I turned my head, I saw

George lifting both his arms up ready to throw his hammer I saw behind the models was a door. When George threw his hammer, I ran, and it crashed into the brink wall.

Running at full speed I rammed my body weight against the glass wall breaking through but tripped and fell onto of a warrior. George grabbed his hammer pulled it free then ran after me. I quickly got up and ran to the door as George swung his hammer hitting the models and their limbs smashed through the glass wall. When I reached the door and tried opening it, it was locked however I knew how to open it. George yelled lifting both his arms up again I jumped as the hammer came crashed down knocking down the door, but his hammer was stuck in the floor.

I climbed over him and hopped off his head and said, "Thanks." I ran downstairs as George glowed and pulled his hammer free and ran after me. When I reached the bottom floor, I opened the door in front of me and saw I was now on a casino floor I looked around and saw a shelf with glasses, mugs and different types of booze. I pushed the shelf to block the door and felt my lungs were burning with sweat running down my forehead along with the back of my shirt covered in sweat.

I walked away from the bar and thought I would hear George smashing through that door any second but maybe his big body had caused him to get stuck. I looked around but saw nobody I was sure that kids and teenagers we're searching every inch of this place looking for me, Hunter and Melissa. I looked at my left arm and saw the bleeding had stopped but I would have cleaned up the wound later.

I saw another bar coming up I ran over and went behind the desk and grabbed a cloth. I turned a sink on getting the cloth wet with cold water. I wiped my face with it then cleaned up the wound and took another cloth and tied it around my left arm then heard Kane say, "Mind getting me a milkshake sir."

Looking at the mirror in front of me with a glass shelf of empty wine, beer mugs and fancy glasses I saw Kane looking at me. He grinned then toss a fuse bomb over the bar. I quickly ran and jumped over the bar and landed on the floor as the fuse bomb exploded sending shards of broken mirror and glass everywhere. I looked where Kane was standing but was gone as I stood up and ran towards a row of slot machines with flashing lights going off, neon signs pointing to the different areas and fake plants and palm trees.

Suddenly I was kicked in the face by Kane as he hopped off a slot machine. I wiped my face and felt blood coming out of my nose. Kane grinned and said, The Tricksters from our show were more skilled and put up a real fight. You on the other hand are so easy to beat." I growled and said, "Here let give you a real fight!" I got up and threw a hard punch into Kane's face but as I went to throw another punch, he blocked my attack and whacked his arm into my gut then threw me at a slot machine.

I knocked it down and rolled on the floor. I saw Kane walking towards me he grinned then lifted up his right foot. I rolled out of the way as he nearly stumped on me, I got up and tried hitting him, but he dodged my attack. We threw a few punches then I rammed my fist under his muzzle then rammed his body against a slot machine and punched him in the gut. I asked, "Is that fucking better?!" Kane said, "Yeah it is." Without warning Kane kicked me knocking me down to the floor but threw a smoke bomb as I couldn't see.

I knew better not to stick around I left the slot machines and saw a neon sign pointing towards the exit. I was about to run pass a platform with a brand new 85 Lincoln sedan when suddenly George bust through the wall yelling loudly and smashed his hammer onto the sedan crushing it as the platform gave out and the tires popped off. I nearly fell but kept running then heard Kane yell above me, "Heads up, Curtis!"

I saw Kane standing on top of a sign and began throwing fuse bombs at me, I kept running, pushing myself as they exploded behind me with one hitting a slot machine and after it blew up coins were raining on me. Then I a fuse bomb smack me in the back of the head. I fell face first onto the floor and heard the fuse burning away I turned my head over to it and saw it along with George walking towards me. I grabbed the fuse bomb and threw it at George's feet then got up and ran. When George looked at it, it exploded and his legs were blown off, he yelled, "THAT FUCKING TRICKSTER!"

Kane hopped off the sign and used his powers to heal his friend as George's blown off legs attached back to his body. George said, "Thanks Kane." Kane said, "No problem that's what friends are for. Now, let's go hunt down this Trickster!"

I breathed, "Where the hell is the fucking exit!?" I suddenly heard teenager yell, "THERE HE IS! KILL HIM!" I saw a gang of children and teenagers looking at me and they were armed with guns I ran and heard bullets zooming by I ran towards a restaurant area hearing the sound of a thousand running shoes and boots behind me. When I reached the restaurant I heard the teenagers yell, "KILL THE TRICKSTER!" I saw a pool table in front of me I jumped rolled over it and landed on the floor as bullets hit the table along with taking out a pool ball. I wasn't going to get pass all of these children and their guns.

I quickly reached for the pool balls grabbed them and took cover and waited for the shooting to stop. One teenager with long blonde hair holding a shotgun ran over and fired at the pool table leg blowing it off I quickly stood up and threw the pool ball hitting him in the face. I turned and ran over to the tables as more bullets came zooming by I took cover nearly getting shot and breath, "Fucking hell!" I heard another teenager coming I turned around and said, "Think fast!" I threw it at his head knocking him down.

I was going to reach for his pistol, but more teenagers and children were coming I ran for the bar and jumped over it as bullets hit the glass shelf and glasses with shards of glass falling on my back. When the shooting stopped, I stood up and threw my remaining pool balls at them and saw door I spun around and ran out of it and down a long hallway. When I reached the end, I threw my body weight against the door, and it opened but I fell onto the floor. Breathing heavily, I slowly got up and saw I was back where I started when I went through the door. Just then a door opened, and it was Melissa holding onto the notebook.

Melissa said, "Curtis!" She ran towards me and hugged then started to cry it didn't take me long to realize that Hunter was dead. Melissa sopped a bit and said, "They...they got him, and I couldn't do anything to save him!" I said, "We're going to make them pay for this! Come on we need to get the hell out of here!" Melissa looked at me as I wiped the tears from her face as she said, "You're right." She gave me the notebook as I placed it into my pocket and asked, "What door should we try next?" Melissa looked at the doors we went through and said, "Let's try this one." We went through the last door on the left and ran through a round shaped hallway and felt the walls were moving which caused us to nearly lose our footing but kept moving.

Then a mixture of tinted lights flickered in a spiral as we ran further through the round shaped hallway then the floor and ceiling changed into mirrors. However, it seemed to go on forever we both felt very tired, and our energy was burning up fast. We then heard Barbara voice on speakers above us, "Aww are we getting tired already?"

We stopped and heard her giggling and said, "Well, one down and two to go. Judging what we put you two through you won't survive any longer." Manson spoke next, "It's time to end this game of ours as we have a lot of work to do. And thanks for Hunter's soul. Sydney really enjoyed its taste." I growled then saw mirrors on the walls open up with sharp spinning blades that were moving towards us. Melissa grabbed my arm and said, "Come on! Run!"

Using what energy, I had left we began running down the hallway and saw the mirrors moving the opposite way. I ignored it and forced my legs to move faster. We both heard Manson and Barbara taunting us to run while hearing the spinning blades getting closer. Suddenly the hallway in front of us changed into a dead end and saw blades opened up moving slowly towards us. I turned my head back to see the spinning blades were getting closer to us while Manson and Barbara's laughter roared. Looking for a way out then I noticed something. One of the mirrors I could see the outside I said, "Melissa look!"

I pointed and saw a way out we went over and grabbed the mirror and begin pulling on it I said, "Come on! Pull harder!" Melissa said, "I'm trying!" The spinning blades were getting closer I pulled harder then heard cracking noises I said, "We almost got it!" Then a chunk of the mirror came at me and Melissa kicked it breaking a hole for us to get out. Suddenly the spinning blades were about to reach us I pushed Melissa first then went out next but felt a sharp slice at my back I jumped out of the hole and landed on the hard pavement.

I breathed, "Fuck!" Melissa ran over to me and said, "Curtis!" She helped me up and we ran when he doutside of the building we we're in, "You won't escape me, Curtis! I WILL FIND YOU! Children hunt down the Tricksters and KILL THEM!" Melissa and I ran over to a parking lot and saw a row of muscle and sport cars. I saw it was still dark and there weren't any dark purple blimps knowing this would be our only chance to escape Las Vegas.

Melissa ran over to a dark blue and black 71 Ford Mustang Mach 1 and said, "Hey the keys are still in the ignition." I moaned as was in a lot of pain Melissa ran over and said, "Take your shirt off." I took it off and Melissa tied it around where I was bleeding then went into the Mustang as Melissa started up then heard a teenager yell, "HEY! THAT'S MY RIDE! NO! NO! DON'T FUCKING SHOOT IT!" Melissa turned the key then shifted the gearshift into Drive and slammed her foot down burning rubber while the teenagers ran to their cars to chase after us.

Melissa drove out of the city and was heading for the open desert I saw the headlights in the view mirror catching up. Melissa yelled, "Goddamn it! They just won't quit!" I opened the glove box and inside found my Smith & Wesson Model 629 along with a box of ammo. I quickly grabbed it and check to see if it was loaded. Melissa asked, "Can you take care of them?" I said, "Yeah! I ain't finished yet." I row down the passenger window then gripped the magnum tightly in my hands and aimed out the window.

Feeling warm air blowing through my hair the headlights grew brighter with the first car getting closer I saw teenager aiming a pistol while another was halfway out of the sunroof holding a shotgun, I squeezed the trigger taking out the teenager with the pistol I watch his head explode with blood and brain matter splattering all over the windshield and the teenager holding the shotgun. He yelled, "FUCK! I CAN'T SEE!" I aimed for the driver and pulled the trigger. I shot him in the chest which he turned his car violently and crashed into a van as both vehicles went off the road and crashed into the sand.

Then a black 63 Corvette Sting Ray with its soft top down as the passenger was holding an Uzi IMI he squeezed the trigger but missed hitting the truck and rear window of the Mustang. Melissa turned to dodge the bullets hitting the car I aimed at the driver and squeezed the trigger. I hit the driver in the head as the Corvette Sting Ray went off the road and flipped overthrowing the passenger out landing face first into the sand. I fired my remaining two bullets and went back inside the Mustang to reload.

A truck rammed us which nearly caused Melissa to lose control. I got all 6 bullets into the magnum then cocked the hammer. I went stick my head out of the passenger window but got rammed again and the passenger in the truck capped off a few rounds taking out the side mirror. I aimed out the broken rear window and pulled the trigger killing the passenger then shot the driver. I then saw a bright orange 71 Plymouth Road Runner drove round the truck with its high beams on. I quickly aimed for the driver and pulled the trigger but missed. Then shotgun shot went off hitting the trunk then driver side view mirror. I aimed at the teenager holding the shotgun and squeezed the trigger hitting him in the throat.

Suddenly a van drove beside us as the sliding door opened with teenagers holding shotguns, SMG's and assault rifles. Melissa slammed on the brakes as we nearly got shot but the Plymouth Road Runner rammed into us. Melissa drove around the van as I shot the driver in the head as it exploded with blood.

The Plymouth was quickly behind us with road leading higher up into a canyon I aimed for the driver and shot him and watch the Plymouth Road Runner drive through the barrier and crashed against the rocks.

Melissa saw a sign showing that we we're heading for California she pushed the Mustang harder trying to gain more speed. I fired off a few shots, but the teenagers won't giving up. I said, "What I won't give for a machine gun or a rocket launcher!" Melissa made sharp and hard turns with the muscle and spot cars still keeping up with us. I knew would need ammo for later I then had idea I aimed and waited for a car to get close enough. I said, "Come on you punks! Is this the best you got?" Melissa turned her head to me and asked, "Curtis what are you doing?" I said, "You'll see."

A dark green 79 Chevrolet Blazer getting closer I squeezed the trigger shooting at the right tire which caused the Blazer to make a sharp turn and crashed hard into the rocky wall then all the muscle and spot cars crashed into the Blazer creating a nasty pile up. Melissa looked up at the view mirror and said, "Good shooting." I reloaded the S&W Model 629 and went to see what time it was, but the radio wasn't working. Suddenly a spotlight shined on us I turned to the passenger window to see a dark purple blimp chasing after us I said, "Give us a fucking break already!"

Then cannons came out and fired at us with the large cannon balls hitting the rocky mountain walls and exploded causing the road to shake. I aimed at the blimp and took out the spotlight then fired another shot hitting its engine as smoke was coming out. It fired its cannons again with one cannon ball zoomed by the hood of the Mustang nearly hitting us. I capped off more shots taking out the engine as the blimp lost power and fell out of the sky crashing onto the ground.

Then ahead of us was a tunnel but as we got closer another blimp came out and its cannons were aimed at the tunnel. I yelled, "FLOOR IT!" Melissa pushed her foot down further on the gas pedal speeding through the tunnel as cannon balls tore through the thick concrete wall and nearly hitting us. When we sped out of the tunnel the walls collapsed, I aimed at the blimp and squeezed the trigger quickly with the blimp's tank leaking air as it fell out of the sky and crashed onto the hard solid ground.

Melissa blew air out and said, "Next stop California. I wonder what's waiting for us in Hollywood." I signed and said, "Whatever it is it won't be pretty." I passed out feeling tired and hoped Melissa didn't fall asleep behind the wheel. I wished I went with them and could have saved Hunter. I was going to make Manson pay for this and won't stop until I killed him and his friends!

March.27
10:00-AM

I woke up feeling my mouth was dry and slowly open my eyes to see I was still inside the Mustang. I yawned while rubbing my eyes. I turned my head over to see the driver side door was open and we we're still in the desert. I looked up at the sky to see the sun was shining brightly with not a signal cloud in the sky. I saw my S&W Model 629 was laying on my lap. I checked to see it was still loaded I looked around and didn't see Melissa I was about to get out when she came at the passenger door and said, "Morning Curtis."

I didn't jump as I looked at her and said, "Oh hey." Melissa said, "Sorry. Didn't mean to make you scare you." I said, "You didn't." She walked around the Mustang and got back inside and said, "Had to take a piss." Melissa started up the Mustang and asked, "Do you have to go?" I said, "No." She said, "Good." Melissa shifted the gear into "Drive" and pressed her foot down speeding down the road. I asked, "How are we on gas?" Melissa said, "About half a tank." I sighed and said, "Which means we'll have to walk the rest of way." Melissa said, "Maybe we'll get lucky and find a gas station."

I didn't say anything as I missed having my friend with me. I was too tired to cry and rested my head against the seat. I then remembered and asked, "Did you check the trunk?" Melissa said, "I did, it's empty." I said, "Guess whoever took our stuff left my gun here." I then pulled out the notebook from my pocket and flipped through the pages as Hunter copied every page from Arkard's diary. I closed it then put it back into my pocket knowing this was going to be a long drive.

Melissa asked, "How's your wounds?" I checked my left arm as it had stopped bleeding, I took off my shirt tied around my back and felt it. I said, "Sore but at least I'm not bleeding." Melissa asked, "So how do we kill Manson and his gang?" I said, "We need to infect enough damage or weaken them of their magic. Bullets don't work which means we'll have to use something else." Melissa said, "Fire! Hunter smashed jack-o'-lantern on that witch's head. It burned her flesh off, but she was able to heal herself." I lightly nodded my head and said, "Burning those fuckers sounds like a great idea." Melissa lightly smiled while I rested my fist against my check looking out the window watching the empty desert.

12:00-PM

We saw a gas station coming up and our timing couldn't have been any better with the Mustang nearly empty. Melissa pulled in and parked beside the gas pump as she shifted the gear into "Park" then killed the engine. I asked, "Want to rest before we hit out?" Melissa said, "Sure why not." Suddenly we heard movement I turned my head to see a big overweight man wearing a dirty tank top, pants, boots while holding a double barrel shotgun. Then another man much younger came at Melissa holding a Walther P38 with a short barrel.

The man holding the double barrel shotgun spoke with a Texas accent and his breath smelled awful, "You rotten son of a bitch! I never thought I see the most evil man on this planet! I guess god asked me to blow your fucking brains out!" I said, "Why don't you then, prick!" His face turned red as he yelled, I quickly whacked the shotgun behind me then moved my head away as he fired both barrels. Melissa grabbed the man's arm as he squeezed off a few shots as bullets went through the front windshield.

I then grabbed my S&W Model 629 rammed the barrel against the man's throat and squeezed the trigger. Blood splatter out the back of his big head and fell onto the pavement while Melissa pulled the Walther P38 out of the man's hand he tried to reach for another gun, but she shot him in the chest falling backwards onto the gas pump. Suddenly we heard a woman screaming we both looked and saw an older woman wearing a housecoat and holding a M1 Garand she was about to aim but I shot her first.

She yelled while holding her shoulder I swing the passenger door open and ran towards her and saw a puddle of blood was forming around her body. She growled and breathed, "Fuck you!" I aimed and squeezed the trigger blowing her head in half. I sighed and looked over at the gas station to see nobody else was coming out. I kneed down and picked up the M1 Garand as Melissa came over, I said, "Let's go inside."

Stepping inside the gas station we saw it was a mess inside. Most of the shelves were knocked down with a few cans on the floor. I said, "Guess they don't own it just living here while trashing up the place." Melissa said, "Let's eat, rest up for a while then we'll get going." I said, "Ok." I reloaded my S&W Model 629 and picked up food while Melissa was getting cold drinks and other supplies we would need for later.

In the back we found a makeshift home was made from those who came here, and they had killed the owner of the gas station a Indian which they hid his body in a dumpster. I took off my clothes while Melissa treated my wounds then put on a pair of clean clothes. Melissa did the same while we cooked lunch and sat together on the leather couch. There was a fan blowing cool air in front of us I rubbed my forehead while Melissa ate half her lunch but passed out on the couch. I still felt tired after what little sleep, I had and thought, "I swear Manson, or those followers better not come here!" I finished my lunch and rested beside Melissa and didn't take me long to fall asleep.

4:00-PM

I woke up to the sound of thunder I saw that me and Melissa were still in the same room together and nothing had changed.

As I slowly stood up, I could hear the sound of heavy rainfall outside. Then Melissa woke up and asked, "Is it raining again?" I said, "Yes, it is." When she stood up, she asked, "Do you want to spend the night here?" I said, "No we gotta keep going." We took everything we needed and found ammo and weapons in the garage along with a black and white 59 Chevrolet Bel Air with dark tinted windows and chrome rims. I said, "Damn nice ride." Melissa asked, "Do you feel you can drive?" I nodded my head and said, "Get all the jerry cans as we'll need them." I drove out of the garage with Melissa putting everything in the trunk then closed it and got into the passenger side I turned on the wipers and sped down the empty road.

Melissa turned on the AC and said, "Aww much better." She then unbuttoned her shirt allowing cool air to blow into her huge cleavage. We passed by a sign showing we still had a long way to go. I checked the view mirror to see nothing but the storm and lightning flashing in the sky. Melissa asked, "So those people we ran into. Do you think we'll run into more of them?" I said, "I won't be surprised if California is quickly turning into a war zone. If we're lucky enough and Arkard's house isn't destroyed, we might find something to help us against Manson, but he's got the diary too which means he'll be spending his followers to find it as well."

Melissa said, "Maybe not everyone will be under Manson control." I said, "I hope so and when this is over, I wonder if anyone will remember this event or forget about it." Melissa placed her hand onto my lap I looked at her and placed my hand onto hers while holding it for a bit as she said, "I'll always be with you sugar. Nothing is going to stop us." I said, "Yes nothing will stop us."

California
March.29
8:00-AM

It took us two days to reach California but our troubles were far from over. The President has declared martial law across America with children and teenagers turning against adults including Canada and Europe. We won't sure if the same thing was happening in South America, Africa, Russia, Australian or India. News stations had issued warnings of staying clear from big cities, but we had no choice. If kids and teenagers are causing mayhem and killing any adult in sight, then any adult would be smart enough to leave while they can.

We pulled over last night to get some sleep then continue the rest of the way to L.A. using the highway to reach the city. However, as we drew closer thick black smoke was rising high in the sky along with fire. A few news and police helicopters were flying by. Melissa turned to me and asked, "So where are we going to leave the car?" I said, "We can hide it under the highway then continue the rest of the way on foot knowing if any of Manson's followers spot us, they'll pump this thing full of bullet holes." I drove off the highway and went to the underpass then killed the engine.

We both got out taking everything we need then covered the Bel Air with a tarp then took out the diary. I flipped through it until I reached the book marker and said, "Ok let's find Arkard's house." Melissa asked, "It's in Beverly Hills, right?" I read through the diary and said, "Yes just need to find the address." I then saw it and placed my finger under it and said, "Got it." Melissa looked over I said, "It's on Crow Street address 1331." I stared at the number it was the same address from Arkard's mother house.

Melissa tugged on my arm I turned over to her as she asked, "Are you ready?" I said, "Yeah let's get going." I closed the notebook placed it into my pocket then held the M1 Garand while Melissa was holding a Ithaca 37 Stakeout with her Walther P38 tucked into her shorts. We left the highway and could hear gun shots going off followed by the helicopters flying by. Staying close to walls of taking cover behind wreck vehicles to avoid being spotted.

I knew Manson would send his forces here so we had to find any clues that we could get our hands before Manson or his followers. While running down a street Melissa gasped, I looked up to see dead adults being hung from street light poles a few were dipping blood with puddles under their dead bodies. I said under my breath, "Goddamn." Suddenly we heard a can being kicked we ran over to an alleyway and took cover behind a dumpster.

Walking down the street were teenagers with a few young children that looked to be 7, 8 and 10 years old. They were heavily armed with both guns, sharp and heavy weapons. When they came to a full stop one kid asked, "So what does Manson what us to do now?" A tall and muscular teenager wearing a black leather jacket with long hair holding a bloody baseball bat said, "We keep searching for the Tricksters."

Another teenager holding dual pistols said, "Let's head over to Hollywood next." The teenager with the baseball bat said, "Alright." They walked away and waited a bit then began making our way towards Beverly Hills. Halfway up the street we saw a dealer ship with teenagers trashing up the cars inside. Suddenly a loud crash was heard which made us jump and saw a group of young kids throwing furniture out of a high rise building. Going around the chaos we came to Beverly Hills and it too was in chaos. I said, "Stay close to me as I have a bad feeling shit is going to hit the fan soon."

A few of the houses were vandalized while some were burning. We then saw a black Bentley Mulsanne crashed into a wall. Lying on the street with the driver side door left open an old man beaten to death. Further up the street we heard thrash metal blasting loudly from a boom box followed by teenagers and children cheering and laughing. Suddenly we heard the sound of a car coming we both went over to the house and hid behind trash bins to see a dark blue 62 Ford Thunderbird driving with two teenagers then a sedan following them with a dead couple tied to the back bumper while their corpses were being dragged.

We went into the backyard of the house then heard the cheering and laughter was coming next door. Peeking over the wall we saw naked teenagers and children swimming in the pool. In the hot tub two teenage girls were giggling as they were letting a young boy playing with their huge breasts. One teenage girl with long brown hair asked, "Do you like how they feel?" The young boy chuckled and said, "Yeah! Very squishy!" They giggled then the 2ⁿᵈ teenage girl said, "It gets better." She turned to the other girl and began kissing her while the boy watched.

I said under my breath, "Lucky little bastard." Melissa whispered, "Come on. Let's go before they spot us." Lowering our heads, we walked backwards then back onto the street then we saw the address we we're looking for. Arkard's house was massive with a tall iron gate and had a very gothic look to it. The windows were tinted black and whole place was painted dark purple with a black roof. Just as we we're about move suddenly we heard the sound of a helicopter we turned our heads to see one being shot out of the sky and crashing onto the streets followed by loud cheering of kids and teenagers.

Running over to the gate I put the M1 Garand shoulder strap on as we climbed over it and went towards the front door but stopped when a video camera was moving, I breathed, "Shit!" Suddenly it jolted and turned to us while a red light was flashing beside then its lens zoomed in a bit. Suddenly we heard Manson voice above us, "Well, well, well. Look who finally showed up." Me and Melissa turned around and looked up to see a dark purple blimp facing sideways and its screen was showing Manson's face looking down at us.

Manson lightly grinned and said, "You should have known I would have taken everything you were carrying including that diary." Screen zoomed out a bit as it showed Manson holding the diary. Manson lightly laughed and said, "At first I felt like burning down this place but seeing how hard you two have come to reach it I came up with a better idea. Why not see if you can find anything useful while trying to avoid my lovely traps that await you two." Melissa said, "Fucking knew it." Manson said, "So what are you two waiting for. Please step inside."

The front door opened we both looked but couldn't see anything it was pitch black inside. Manson said, "Oh and in case you change your mind." Suddenly the iron fence burst into flames we won't be able to climb over it then the flames licked the grass which was moving towards us. I yelled, "Goddamn its Manson! I swear I'm going to get you for this!" We turned around and ran inside Arkard's house with the front door slamming shut behind us.

Inside Arkard's house was very gothic but as we entered the living room it had a disturbing setting to it as well. Knowing Manson and Barbara added their own sick touch to it. The walls were dark purple with black ceiling and hard flooring. On the walls were large gold picture frames however the images had stretched out faces with horrify expressions. Melissa screamed and got off the floor and when I looked where she was standing on it was a man laying naked but flatten like a bear skin rug.

I said, "Sick bastards!" Leaving the living room, we saw a spiral stairway on our left then a long hallway on the right. I saw a video camera looking down at us then hearing Manson voice on a speaker above us, "Which way to go? Why don't you two split up. It worked so well last time." Manson lightly laughed while I shot a look of anger at the camera. Melissa said, "I won't leave you." Just as we went to move Manson said, "I knew you say that." Suddenly a trap floor opened with Melissa falling through it.

I yelled, "MELISSA! NOOOO!" Then the hallway in front of me closed up I slammed my fits onto the solid wall. Manson said, "That way is blocked. Looks like you'll have to go upstairs Curtis." I turned to camera and said, "The next game we're going to play Manson is fuck off! You go first!" Walking up the spiral case I reached the top floor.

The walls were now black along with the ceiling and running along the walls were gothic style lights. The hard floor a dark yet shiny purple with black doors. I saw a video camera at the far corner watching me as I moved down the hallway. Gold picture frames hang on the walls but with disturbing paintings which I kept my eyes away from looking at.

I went to the first door when to turn the knob, but it was locked. Manson's voice came on the speakers, "Did you think I was going leave all the doors unlocked? You'll have to find the key for doors that are locked." I went over to the next door, but it was locked I sighed and kept walking until I came to round shaped hallway. Hanging from the ceiling were severed heads swinging on chains while dipping with blood. While walking under them I saw the eyes looking down at me. I stopped when saw a painting on my left side showing a face of a women screaming while on fire, I swear I could hear it inside my head.

I turned my head away and kept walking then saw a door that was halfway opened. Checking the other doors, they were closed I turned back to the door and slowly opened it I stepped inside to see a very roomy bathroom. The sink had an egg-shaped mirror, sink faucet was a skull with the two knobs that were arms both holding eyeballs. The toilet's bowl was a head with its mouth open wide while its lips were the seat. I thought, "I would never take a shit in that!"

I saw the bathtub that was filled with blood I thought, "I had a bad feeling about this. Hope Melissa is still alive." I placed my left arm into the tub filled with blood while feeling the bottom if there was anything in it while keeping my ears open for any sudden noises. When I touched a key, it felt very thick with a bit of weight to it. As I went to pull it up suddenly, I felt a hand grabbing my arm and was trying to pull me down. I went to grab whatever was pulling me down with my right hand when another arm came out of the tub.

It wrapped its long fingers around my neck squeezing tightly while I reached for my S&W Model 629 and rammed the barrel against the wrist and pulled the trigger. A loud bang ringed through the bathroom while chucks of rotten flesh were blown off of the arm, I squeeze the trigger again and snapped the arm off I pulled off the severed arm from my neck and stuck my right arm into the tub pulling my left arm free and saw the key.

I saw on the grip it had a logo of a purple heart I wiped off the blood and stood up reloading my S&W Model 629 then tucking it into my pants then leaving the bathroom and looked at the doors. The last one had the logo I walked over to it and stuck the key in. However, as I turned the key fully suddenly it was sucked out of my hand. I looked at the keyhole as it was covered up I grabbed the door knob turning it and swung the door open.

The dark purple hallway lead into the master bedroom I stepped inside to see a king size bed which had a large painting above it, it was Manson and Barbara posing together with their castle in the background with a glowing moon above them. I heard a ticking sound coming from an old grandfather clock which was next to a very big wooden desk. I walked towards it and began searching for it. Manson's voice spoke, "Find anything Curtis?" I jumped when I heard and saw a video camera looking at me with a speaker behind me.

I went back searching then found another key on the grip, it had a logo of a bat. I thought, "Better check the rest of the bedroom before I go." I went over to the bed and went to the nightstand which had a gothic style looking lamp with a red tinted bulb. I opened the drawn find a wooden box and a zippo lighter. Reaching in and taking out both items I tested the zippo lighter it worked. I flipped it closed then looked on the other side to see Manson's bat logo on it. I placed it into my pocket then opened up the wooden box to find a pack of cigars inside.

I brought the box up closer and checked each cigar and they all looked the same then under them I saw a hidden panel. I took them all out then lifted up the panel to find a handwritten notebook but it was in Russian. I set the box down on the nightstand then took out the notebook and folded it and placed it into the diary so I could read it later then closed it placing it back into my pocket. I turned to the bed but notice something was under it. Manson voice spoke behind me, "Do you really want to see what's under their?"

I had a bad feeling and choice not to look under it but Manson then said, "But maybe I hidden something for you...or did I?" It was hard trying to stay calm and keep my cool while this bastard is pulling my fucking chain whenever he gets the chance to do it. I pulled out my S&W Model 629 and cocked the hammer then grabbed the purple blanket with my left hand. I took a big breath and pulled it off and nearly screamed when I saw the corpses of my dead parents lying next to each other.

Covering my mouth and nose when a horrible stench that hit me, I turned my head away then ran out of the bedroom. Once I was out, I gagged a bit but kept myself from puking I breath, "Fucking hell!" I went to the one door I haven't opened but it was locked walked down the hallway back where I came up and looked at the doorknobs until I found one with the matching bat logo.

I placed the key into the keyhole and turned it and it was sucked out of my hand. When it was covered, I turned the knob and opened the door but saw nothing but darkness. Slowly moving inside, I couldn't see anything I went to turn around, but the door slapped shut behind me and was locked. When I tried opening it the knob won't turn, I said under my breath, "Shit!"

I reached into my pocket and took out the zippo lighter and flicked it on with the flame giving me enough light to see but my heart was beating faster while my eyes scanned the area around me. Still holding my magnum, I moved forward while feeling a chill run down my spine. I then felt something brush against my back I spun around and saw it was a swinging chain when I turned around there were more chains hanging from the ceiling. Scanning the area again I didn't see anything and kept moving until I came to a dead end.

I thought, "Damn it! Which way do I go?" I felt it was getting colder in here I went left following the wall but after a while I felt there was no end in sight. I stopped and turned around walking where I started. I stopped when I didn't see anything different, I thought, "The hell?" When I turned my head, I saw the same chains swinging back and forth. My heart was raising I took a few slow breaths and tried going into the areas I haven't gone yet. However, it seemed pointless no matter what I did.

I growled and yelled, "Goddamn it! Stop fucking around with me!" As I turned around, I felt the hairs on the back of neck stand up. I was now standing on the ceiling with the chains now having severed heads attached to the end of them while dripping blood on the floor. I wiped the sweat from my forehead with my arm and began walking to where I came in, but the door was gone. I thought, "Think damn it! Think! There has to be a way out of here!" Then it hit me the key or something was hidden in one of these heads and I would have to find it.

Tucking my S&W Model 629 back into my pants and walked towards the heads seeing if I could notice something on them but all I saw were eyes staring back at me. However, none of them had anything I could now see my breath with more sweat running down my forehead. While looking around I notice something

I moved closer and saw a severed hand holding a golden key. Suddenly I heard hissing above my head when I lifted up my eyes and saw snakes wrapped around chains.

I hated snakes since I was a kid and seeing this many, I felt my heart was going to explode out of my chest, but I had to keep calm if I was going to get out of this nightmare house! I took a big breath and ran towards the golden key while snakes hissed and fell onto the ceiling chasing after me. Suddenly a shiny spike shot out of the floor nearly hitting me as it hit the floor. I kept moving while more spikes were shooting out and snakes coming after me. I thought, "Please, they're not poisonous!" But I felt one land on my shoulder and bit me in the neck I grabbed the snake and threw it away as I went to grab the key but suddenly the fingers closed, I turned my head and saw dozens of snakes slithering towards me.

Turning back to the hand I grabbed the fingers and broke each one while hearing the severed heads screaming loudly. I yanked the golden key from the severed hand free and began running and felt snakes were at my feet. I went to turn my head when I notice the black walls were very close to me, I nearly bumped into them and turned my head back to see the door however the closer I got to it I noticed the floor was coming down. Without warning a hole in the ceiling came causing me to fall with snakes coming out of it. I could feel them biting at my leg I pushed myself up and ran towards the door.

I went to stick the key into the keyhole but saw it was upside down I said, "You gotta be fucking kidding me!" I tried putting it upside down, but they didn't work I then unscrewed the doorknob and screwed it back in then placed the key into the hole with the floor touching my head I unlocked and threw the door open and pulled the golden key out then jumped out as I landed on the floor.

I heard the door slamming shut behind me while I was breathing heavily. I rolled over to see the door was closed I slowly got up and flipped the zippo lighter closed putting it back into my pocket.

I thought, "Glad that's over now, where do I go next?" I was worried about Melissa as she hasn't come back yet I thought, "I better go find her!" I walked down the hallway and went down the spiral staircase but saw the hallway was still blocked and no other way around it. I sighed knowing I would have to find another way around. I went back upstairs then looked at the doors while thinking, "Which one do I pick?" I knew one of these rooms would take me downstairs while others would be traps.

I thought, "Which one? Would the last door lead me to the basement or is hidden entrance in one of these rooms?" My mind was racing while picturing what would happen if I tried one of the rooms. Manson voice spoke making me jump, "Tick, tick, tick Curtis. Time's a wasting." I saw the bat logo on the 2nd door, so I knew not to go in that one then looked at the 3rd door which had a heart logo on it. I turned and looked at the first door which had rabbit head logo I thought, "The first door. Is it the way or a trap?" I then walked a bit and went over to the last door, but it too had a bat logo I breathed, "Fuck it!" I walked back to the first door placed the golden key and unlocked the door.

It was sucked out of my hand as the keyhole was covered Manson said, "I hope you make the right choice Curtis." I opened the door and stepped inside the room which was a large dressing room. The door behind me slammed shut when I turned my head, I saw the doorknob was gone. I sighed and began searching through the fancy suits, pants, shirts, shelves with different shoes and socks. As I got closer to the end, I saw a large dresser I opened it to see nothing but darkness suddenly I felt gravity shift as I was flipped upside down then fell into the hole.

I screamed as the fall caught me off guard but landed on the stone-cold floor. Around me were tinted purple and red lights on both sides of the wall. I got up and checked my M1 Garand making sure it wasn't damaged. I put the strap back on and began walking down the long hallway and felt the air was getting colder. I then came to a hallway with different ways to go looking down each one I wasn't sure which way to go. In total it was 8 ways to go, 3 on both sides and other 2 in front and behind me.

Manson voice came on the speaker in front of me with a video camera watching me as well, "Alright Curtis I'm going to make this one easy for you since time is short and you could spend hours trying to find Melissa. I'm going tell you when you're getting closer to her or not. Now guess which hallway to go through." I rolled my eyes and thought, "Knew he was going to fucking say that!" Manson wasn't going to make this easy, so I knew going straight forward won't be right way I went left hallway. When I went to turn suddenly the ceiling in front of me came down nearly crushing me as a loud smack noise ringed my ears for a bit I yelled, "MOTHERFUCKER!"

I walked of the hallway then heard Manson say, "Try again, Curtis." When the ringing in my ears stopped, I tried the hallway on my right side; which was closest to the first hallway. When I went to around the corner nothing happened, I kept walking not sure if Manson was really going to guild me or just pulling my goddamn chain again. I then came to a set of stairs leading up. I slowly went halfway upstairs waiting for anything to happen while hearing my heart beating faster. Just as I got halfway up two blades popped out of the wall.

I moved my body back in time without falling and ran to the top as more blades popped out nearly hitting me. When I reached the top floor I stopped and said, "What the fuck?" In front of me was the same hallway that I saw. Manson chuckled and said, "Don't like it when I fuck around with your mind, huh, Curtis? Haha! I have to make it interesting, or I would just get bored watching you walking down empty hallways. But you are starting to get warm Curtis but be careful as the next set of traps might cost you a limb or two."

I said rising my tune a bit, "Thanks for the fucking heads up!" Looking at the hallways I haven't gone through yet I choice the last one on the right side. Just was I reached the corner and went to keep walking suddenly my foot fell through water I looked down at the floor to see it was acting like water. I pulled my foot back and watched the area I stepped waving like water until it was fully still again. I moved my foot and lightly pressed it until I found a solid area to step on. However, as I carefully moved from one step to another the space between them was becoming difficult to reach.

Halfway through the hallway I heard a loud clicking noise I thought, "Oh now what?" When I turned my head coming out of the walls were saw blades and began spinning while getting closer to me. I turned my head back making quick guesses where I had to step next. I hoped and nearly fell into the water but kept myself from falling and ran down the hallway reaching the end but when I came out, I was on the other side where I came.

Manson voice said, "You're getting cold now Curtis. Try another way." I went over to left hallway in front of other one. When I reached the corner, it was very long I knew something nasty was waiting for me and began running down it to reach the end. I could hear my footsteps echoing through the hallway with the tinted lights flicking a bit. I kept moving not wanting to slow down suddenly I heard something shot out behind me and hitting the wall I ran faster hearing what sounded like spikes being fired at me.

Just as I reached the end suddenly, I saw holes in front of me I quickly dove down to the floor and nearly got shot. I pushed myself and ran out and was back at the same hallway. Manson said, "That's it, Curtis! You're getting warmer now!" Breathing heavily, I wiped the sweat from my forehead trying to think which way to go now. I then looked at the back hallway and walked towards it. Reaching the corner were mirrors on both sides of the wall. I said under my breath, "Not this shit again!"

Walking past the mirrors as each one showed a different reflection of me with some moving backwards or upside down. Suddenly the lights went out I couldn't see then they came on and when I looked at the mirrors, I saw knights wearing dark purple and black armor holding long blade axes both behind and in front of me. I ran and dodged their attacks however the floor was coming narrower which I saw nothing but darkness and knew if I fell I would most likely be killed. A knight went to swing his axe I dodged the attack and rammed by body weight into the knight causing him to fall. I ran but the lights went out again then came on now I was standing on the ceiling.

It felt very cold then I heard glass cracking when I lifted up my head to see the mirrors was cracking and when they broke. Razor sharp shards of mirror came falling towards me I ran faster with a few of them brushing by my hair, but I felt one gash my cheek I didn't slow down until the lights went off again and when they came back on the floor with the mirrors back to normal. I felt my cheek and it had some blood oozing out of it I wiped it off my finger. When I went to move, I felt my foot was sinking when I looked it was a trap. Suddenly the mirrors on both sides exploded I jumped forward nearly getting stabbed by razor sharp shards of glass.

My heart was beating so hard against my chest I tried to calm myself I looked at the floor, but it was hard to tell which area would set off another trap. Once my heart rate slowed down a bit, I moved again making sure if I stepped on another trap floor to move away quickly. When I did, I jumped and landed on the hard floor with both mirrors exploded beside me but felt a sharp shard stab me in the leg. I growled and pulled it out then got back up and quickly reached the end and back where I started again.

Manson said, "Warmer Curtis. You're getting warmer!" I knew one of these times I would have go forward but felt that would be too easy. Looking down at my leg where I was hit, I could see blood dripping from the wound. I didn't have time to bleed lifting up the pant leg and using the zippo light I burned the wound stopping the bleeding, but it hurt. I lightly bit my lip and put the zippo lighter away and thought which way to go next. I went to the 3rd hallway on the right but as I reached the corner, I notice the hallway was going down I could feel it's steep edge just by looking at it.

I didn't like this one damn bit but had no choice I carefully went down but once both of my shoes were touching the floor I couldn't slow down. Suddenly poles shot up from the floor with sharp spikes I ran in between them nearly falling a few times. However, as I got halfway through it I slipped and landed on my side I was rolling towards a pole with spinning spikes I pushed myself up and moved by body out of the way feeling a spike nearly bush my nose and ran towards the end. When I got out back where I started. Manson said, "Very warm, Curtis! Very warm! You're nearly there but oh the traps that wait for you...Hahaha!"

I couldn't wait for the moment when I have my chance to burn this motherfucker! For all the sick and twisted shit, he has put me through and the death of my best friend and parents! Looking at the hallways I have went through most of them leaving the entrance and hallway in front of me. I went to the 3rd hallway in front of the entrance it was very dark with not many lights on. My heart was beating fast with my eyes moving everywhere for the next trap. Sweat ran down my forehead I wiped it but the further I walked I suddenly felt my head touching the ceiling when I looked up, I saw the hallway was shrinking down in size.

I lowered my body so I could keep moving but felt the walls were closing in too. I then had to crawl to reach the end of the hallway, but the space was starting to get tight. I suddenly found it hard to breath the further I crawled through the hallway but as I reached the end, I saw it was going to be a tight fit. I took off my M1 Garand and pushed it through the hole then put one arm through and pushed myself up. Using all my strength I squeezed out of the hole but went to stand up but bumped my head in the ceiling again.

I got back on my knees grabbed my M1 Garand and crawled out until I reached the ending I stood up putting the shoulder strap on back where I started. But this time they were only 4 hallways. One in front of me and 3 on the left side. Manson voice speak on the speaker with the video camera watching me, "Ok let's speed this up a little bit for each hallway you go through there will be less to pick from however each one has its own death trap which if you slip up it's over. No 2nd chance Curtis."

Taking a few breathes as my heart rate slowed down a bit, I looked at the hallways and walked towards the 1st one. Manson voice said, "You want to go through that one? Are you sure, Curtis?" My eyes moved over to the other 3 hallways then back at the one I was standing in front of. I entered it but I felt my foot pull on a wire suddenly I saw a big curve blade swinging down from the ceiling. I moved my head out of the way in time.

Walking further blades came out of the walls nearly slicing me in halfway then double axe shaped blades swinging back and forth from the ceilings. I jumped and ran past the sharp blades but just as I cleared them suddenly spiked shot out of the floor I stopped to look down and a chuck of my shoe and be tore out nearly losing a toe. Manson wasn't kidding that I might a limb or two." Carefully walking while I looked at the floor for anymore hidden traps.

I then heard a clicking noise and suddenly the walls on both sides bust open with saw blades I jumped through them and landed on the floor and quickly pushed myself up and got closer to the end. Then a hammer came out of the wall hitting me in the side it hurt like hell, and I was about to fall off the edge. I grabbed onto the hammer when it suddenly snapped off from the chain it was attached to. I grabbed onto the edge of the floor and pulled myself up ignoring the pain. Once I fully pulled myself up and left the hallway and was back where I started again but now were only 3 hallways left.

Manson spoke on the speaker, "You're starting to get hot Curtis, but if you choose that hallway last it would have made it easier for you. I guess you humans like making things difficult." Not looking at the camera I thought of which of the three hallways go through and picked last one and walked towards it but just as I entered suddenly my foot went to touch the floor but there was nothing. I fell but spun my body around in time to catch the edge suddenly I heard noises above me and when I lifted my head up the ceiling was coming down. I yelled, "FUCKING HELL! GIVE ME A FUCKING BREAK, FOR ONCE!" I looked over and saw pole sticking out. I quickly grabbed it and moved my left hand away in time before the ceiling came down blocking my way out, I looked down and saw I was going have to climb down to reach the bottom which was a very long way down.

There were only few lights in this tunnel which made it hard to see suddenly I felt the pole was moving in I quickly grabbed the next pole and started climbing my way down. My heart was racing with more sweat running down my forehead. As I went to grab the next pole my hand slipped, and I fell for a few seconds but grabbed onto the dark tinted purple light. It was hot to the touch, and I grabbed a pole beside me and pulled myself away.

Growling from the light burn I got my hands with my fingers gripping the pole so tightly while breathing heavily I reached for the next pole below me and felt my fingers were getting tried. I said, "Come on! I'm almost there!" Getting lower but as I did the poles were moving in quickly which made me rush. I thought, "Please I don't wanna fall again!" Just as I went to grab a pole my left hand slipped, and I nearly fell but grabbed onto it in time and pulled myself closer to the bottom.

With my head looking down at the floor I suddenly felt my right hand holding something soft when I looked to see what it was it was a snake it bit my hand, I tore it out of the hole and fell and landed on my back. I growled and yelled, "FUCKING SNAKES!" I stood up and threw it onto the floor then stumped on its head with my shoe. Breathing heavy I wiped the sweat and left the hallway and stood where I started but there were only two hallways left. One on the right side and the other on the left. Manson spoke, "Oh you're on-fire Curtis! Just one more hallway to go through and you're there!"

I choice the hallway on the right but stopped as I came to a dead end suddenly a gate shut behind me then gravity shifted again as I was floating up but saw spikes sticking out the of the ceiling. Poles popped out of the tunnel as I grabbed onto one but felt a lot of weight when hanging on. Looking where the next pole was, I let go and quickly floated up towards it but nearly missed it. I grabbed it with my left hand but felt my fingers were going to be crushed from the weight I growled from the pain and let go going up much faster.

Using my legs, I manage to change a pole with my feet and reached for a pole and pulled myself over it while climbing up. Sweating was running under my face and nearly went into my eyes as it dripped off from my head. But as I got closer to the top I saw how far away from where I had to go. I looked up at the sharp spikes I press my shoes against the wall and put as much energy I could into my legs then jumped. I floated forward for a bit until I was moving up again. I quickly swung my body around avoiding the spikes by a few inches I pulled myself up and saw I was now standing in a different room now...it was my apartment.

It looked just how I last saw it when shit hit the fan. I looked around and saw the tunnel I had to climb up was gone I thought, "What the hell? I don't get it." I notice the kitchen window was pitch black and couldn't see anything outside. Turning around I saw the front door wasn't there just a plain wall I looked at the living room to see it was the same. I went to walk pass it when suddenly the TV came on my head jolted towards the screen to see nothing but static. Walking closer to it the static began clearing up then I froze when I saw Melissa standing in front of the screen looking scared while standing in a white room.

Melissa said, "Curtis! Can you hear me?" I said, "Yes Melissa, I can hear you! Where are you?" Melissa said, "I'm trapped in some room and none of the other rooms lead a way out!" I said, "Hang in their Melissa, I'm going to find you! I'm... Suddenly the TV screen changed when I saw static, I grabbed my TV and yelled, "Melissa! Can you still hear me?" Then the screen showed a white background with happy music playing then red text that popped which read, "Operation Time with Dr. Manson & Barbara" The text slowly oozed looking like blood with the music slowing down sounding disturbing.

Then it showed Barbara wearing a sexy nurse outfit while posing she giggled and said, "Hi I'm Barbara and today on Operation Time my handsome husband and I are going to help a woman who is about to give birth to a child however she is unable to push it out so we're going have to.... My eyes open wide when it showed Barbara walking over to an operating table with a pile of sharp knives. Barbara turned to the screen with an evil looking grin and said, "Cut it out." I felt my heart had dropped when I realized where Melissa was. Then the screen showed Manson now wearing a doctor's outfit he looked at me and said, "I told you I would take care of your unborn child Curtis. And when we are finished with your girlfriend, we'll be coming for you next." I yelled, "NO! You're not laying your fucking hands on her!" Barbara came on the screen and said, "Relax Curtis, we won't hurt her...that much." She giggled as the screen went back to Manson and said, "Now why don't you sit down, relax and enjoy the show." I yelled, "FUCK YOU!" I looked where my bedroom and bathroom were but saw there wasn't any doors Manson laughed and asked, "So how are you going to stop us when I trapped you in your apartment. Might as well wait for us to come to you." I turned to the TV and had idea I said, "Oh, I think I know how I'm going to stop you, fucker!"

Manson and Barbara looked at me which it didn't take them long to realize what I was thinking I stepped back a bit then Barbara asked, "Do you think that's really going to work?" I said, "Why don't we find out." I ran towards the TV I yelled and jumped at the screen, and I was sucked through it I was going through a wormhole-like tunnel with different shows and films spinning around me then I saw an image of Manson and Barbara standing in front of which they looked shocked to see me coming.

I flew through the land and landed on the operating table while shards of glass littered the floor. I quickly got up as Manson ran towards me with his cane sword pulled out and ready to use it. Thinking quickly, I grabbed my M1 Garand and used it to black Manson sword attack. My back bumped into the wall while Manson cane sword went halfway through the rifle. Manson growled and asked, "How did you do that!?" I grinned and said, "Magic, isn't it wonderful, how it works?" I kicked Manson in his groin hard then pushed him away and went to use my M1 Garand, but it fell in half.

Just then a door opened, and it was Melissa she stopped when she saw Manson and Barbara. Manson went to get his sword, but I kicked it away then Barbara pulled out a long-curved knife and said, "I'll handle her." Melissa turned around and ran while Barbara went after her. Manson looked at me and asked, "You won't kill an unarmed man would you Curtis?" I said, "Yes I would." I stumped my foot on Manson's throat crushing it. Manson grabbed my leg trying to stop me as I added more pressure. Manson tried stabbing his claw nails into my leg I lightly bit my lip hearing the sound of his spine slowly cracking.

Manson's red eyes looked up at mine and said, "Wait! WAIT! I'll tell you where you can find John! Don't you want your brother back?" I said, "I'd rather kill you first!" Manson gasped for air while I pressed harder suddenly his eyes glowed bright red, and my clothes were on fire I tried to put the fire out, but it was too hot. Manson stood up growling loudly and could feel the flames quickly burning through my clothes and my flesh. Manson grinned I quickly pulled out my S&W Model 629 aimed at his head and pulled the trigger.

I shot Manson in the right eye as blood splattered out the back of his head. I screamed from the burning pain but squeezed the trigger again hitting Manson right between the eyes he fell backwards onto the floor. Suddenly the flames went away I walked over and saw he wasn't breathing I spit on his face and said, "That was for my parents and best friend you fucking, prick!" I turned where Melissa came out and ran through the doors hoping Barbara didn't get her hands on her. I swear if I find Melissa injured or dead, I'm going to beat the living shit out of Barbara and rape her just to add further insult to injury if Manson was still alive.

Running down an endless white hallway with lights on both sides of the walls while the ceiling and floor were dark black. I was looking for a door or another hallway to run through but didn't see any I pushed myself faster then I saw a door open but with a bloody hand print I ran towards it and forced my body weight on the door running down the hallway with my heart racing. I thought, "Please you're ok, Melissa! Please be alive!"

I stopped when I saw a pair of legs lying on the floor with blood puddle under it, I felt my eyes were watery I said, "Oh please no!" I walked closer then moved over to the hallway to see it wasn't Melissa but a different woman. Fully naked with her belly torn up and guts were hanging out. I nearly gagged from the smell but saw more dead women with their bellies having the same damage I thought, "Barbara is removing their unborn child so they can raise them!" Suddenly I heard Melissa scream, "CURTIS! HELP ME!" I ran where the scream came from pushing myself faster.

I saw double doors in front of me with heart shaped windows. I rammed my body against them, but it was locked. I yelled, "COME ON!" I saw through the window Melissa lying naked on an operating table and strapped down. I saw Barbara pushing a cart which I knew what was on it. I tried kicking open the door but that wasn't working either. I then saw another door above the operating room I just had to find it I turned my head and ran down the hallway then went left hoping to find the way to Melissa in time.

Melissa felt her heart racing while her eyes were locked on Barbara as she was pushing the cart closer to her. Barbara giggled and said, "There, now that we're alone; I'll be able to take care of your unborn child. Don't worry I'll take good care of it. Barbara reached for the long curve knife it was very shiny. Sweat ran down her hand while Barbara grinned then turned to Melissa belly while Barbara rubbed with it her left hand as the knife slowly got closer and Melissa suddenly felt a horrible pain as something was being forcefully moved through her body. Melissa saw a bugle pressing against her belly which looked like an infant's body while screaming in pain. Just as Barbara went to press the knife against Melissa's belly, they both heard the doors being flung open.

Barbara jumped and turned her head to where the door open then her eyes open wide followed by a loud bang went off. Melissa watched as Barbara was shot right between the eyes as blood splattered out the back of her head and fell onto the floor. Melissa lifted up her eyes to see Curtis had saved her she said, "Oh Curtis! I knew you would make it in time!" She heard Curtis running over to her then looked at her belly to see bugle was gone.

I reached Melissa and looked at Barbara's body as she wasn't breathing, I untied her then helped Melissa up and wrapped my arms around me. I said, "It's ok I'm here now." Melissa said, "Let's get the hell out of here." Then Melissa noticed my clothes and skin were a bit burned she asked, "What happened to you?" I said, "Manson tried burning me, but I blew out his fucking brains." Melissa lightly smiled turning her head over to Barbara and said, "And this bitch tore up my clothes." I said, "I'm sure we'll find something else to wear later." We both ran out the way I came in and found a hallway we haven't gone through yet.

Suddenly as we ran, I felt Melissa pull my arm and said, "Curtis! Look!" I stopped and noticed the walls were slowly oozing changing from black to dark purple. I at the floor and saw it was same flooring from Arkard's house. Then our hearts stopped when we heard the demonic screams of Manson and Barbara behind us. Melissa and I pushed ourselves through the oozing walls and we're back inside while feeling the wet yet sticky walls on our bodies. But as we broke through the demonic screams shook the house which caused all the video cameras to explode bursting into flames and the walls cracking along with the flooring.

Melissa yelled, "We better get the hell out of here!" We went to run for the front door, but the ceiling caved in blocking our way. Turning around and running through the large house with the demonic screams growling louder than we came to the kitchen with a big deck behind it with a glass sliding door. Suddenly the sliding door started to crack I quickly pushed Melissa and myself down to the floor within seconds the glass exploded sending razor sharp shards above us. We quickly got back up and ran through the backyard and climbed over the iron fence and Arkard's house exploded into a large fire ball.

Running over to a nearby house we hide behind a parked 82 Ford F-150 truck. A trail of thick black smoke quickly rising up in the sky. Then the dark purple blimp screen exploded, burnt remnants falling down. Melissa turned to me and asked, "Do you think we did it?" Suddenly we heard shouting and yelling coming from children and teenagers I said, "Come on let's get away from here as this place is going to be crawling with gang of angry children."

Running between houses till we we're back in the streets of L.A. we found a small apartment and went inside. I checked the time but saw my watch was damaged from the fighting, so I took it off while Melissa was looking for a new pair of clothes to put on. She came out wearing a short t-shirt and light blue jeans with cowgirl boots. I said, "Those look good on you." Melissa asked, "How are those burns?" I said, "It's ok. It doesn't hurt that much." Melissa looked at them and said, "They look bad. We better treat them!" I wasn't going to auger with her I followed Melissa into the bedroom as she got medicine and bandages to treat my burns. Sitting naked while Melissa got me some clear pair of clothes to wear. She said, "Here." I said, "Thanks." I happen to see an alarm clock, but it was flashing 12:00. I turned to the window to see the sun was setting with the sky a tinted orange and shades of pink and yellow. Melissa asked as I put the clothes on, "Did we kill them, Curtis?" I sighed knowing Melissa wasn't going to like what I was about to say.

I said, "No, we only wounded them. The only way we can fully kill them, is by burning those fuckers!" Melissa signed and said, "I knew you were going to say that." I said, "Seeing the damage I did to them it will be a while before we bump into them again. But I know they won't make it easy for us." Then we heard the sound of a blimp coming by. We moved over to the window and saw it floating above L.A. then on the screen we saw showing the US President standing inside the White House while a crowd was booing with security guards standing by.

The President adjusted the microphone and said, "Please! Listen to me! I never meant for this to happen!" The booing grew louder followed by people calling the President names and swearing at him. The President raised his voice and said, "Listen! We can fix this mess! Together we'll get out of this! If only we work together!" The crowd was getting out of control the President lowered his head and said, "Very well....I never meant for this happen. I pray that when this over it will be better place...for our children." Then the President reached into his suit and pulled out a pistol and placed the barrel against the side of his head and pulled the trigger.

Blood and brain matter splattered out the President head as his body fell backwards the crowd roared with anger then stormed the stage with the security guards pulling out their sidearms or Uzi IMI's shooting a few people before being overpowered by the angry mob. I said, "Holy shit!" Then the screen changed showing outside of the White House with film crews watching in horror as a full riot had broken out. People mostly adults were punching, beating and shooting each other to death. Melissa said, "This world has gone to hell." Then a shotgun went off as the camera man was shot with the video camera falling onto the ground with the news teaming running and getting shot.

The screen cut out with static as more dark purple blimps were floating above L.A. then on all the screens were Kane. He said, "Evening my boys and girls, I have some terrible news to tell you." We notice outside covering most streets were children and teenagers looking up at the blimps. Kane said, "Manson and Barbara have been badly injured by the Tricksters. We were able to save them from dying but it will be a while before they can continue with our plans. So, Manson asked in case of a event like this that I handle things until they fully heal. Now since everyone is busy which I won't be able to do everything myself. Lucky for us Manson has a helper to guild you on finding the Tricksters. He'll be coming soon to aid you. His name is Patrick Walker and he'll be bring supplies and gear to help you find the Tricksters. I'll keep you posted if anything else happens but don't worry Manson and Barbara will be back soon."

Chapter 8

March. 30
9:00-AM

We spend the night here since the streets were crawling with angry children and teenagers looking for blood. I woke up naked still holding Melissa with my left hand and my magnum in my right hand. She was only wearing panties I lightly shook her body and Melissa woke up she whispered, "Is anyone in here?" I said, "No, just waking you up." We slowly got out of bed and got dress. Melissa put the clothes on from yesterday while I wore a white shirt, a light jacket, black pants as we sat at the kitchen. Luckily the notebook wasn't burned nor the letter however none of us could translate the Russian to English. Melissa asked, "So how are we going to find out what's written on that latter?" I said, "Maybe we'll find a dictionary and can translate it, it's our only chance."

Melissa asked, "After that, then what?" I said, "I'm sure this note will have a clue for us to go on. Manson got cocky and because of his mistake we'll still alive." Melissa said, "Barely but after shit hit the fan yesterday in D.C. things aren't looking good for us. However, we don't have much choice." I said, "Melissa we're going to win this. I know we're tired and burned out, but we can't stop. I weaken their leaders which will mean less of their bullshit magic to worry about and only have Manson and Barbara's followers to deal with."

Melissa looked at me and said, "Maybe not all of the adults are under their control now as weakening them has snapped them out of their brainwashing." I said, "Yes however I had a feeling it won't last long. Let's have some breakfast and find a library with a Russian dictionary." Melissa lightly smiled as we cooked breakfast and ate quietly. I saw outside it was very sunny with few clouds in the sky. I knew we would have to arm ourselves with weapons since I was low on ammo and Melissa lost her pistol. I said, "We should visit a gun shop or police station for guns as we won't last long out there."

Melissa asked, "Don't you think most of the followers outside have cleared out every gun they can get their hands on?" I said, "Not all of them. I'm sure there is a few they left lying around." Melissa said, "I hope they don't find our car." I said, "I'm sure they won't find it." Melissa looked at me but lowered her head and went back to eating. When we finished, we left the apartment and walked through the alleyway and across the streets while dark purple blimps were flying above L.A.

The further we travelled through the city we saw how destroyed it was becoming more wrecked buildings with a few burned down to the ground, smashed up cars and other vehicles, dead adults shoot or beaten to death with a puddle of blood under them with flies buzzing around their corpses while we saw more hanging under street light poles. We came across a flipped over school bus resting on its side, it was burned, and spray painted on its roof was, "DEATH TO ADULTS! DEATH TO THE SYSTEM!"

We saw a gun shop with its windows smashed, and broken glass littered the sidewalk and road. Taking a few steps, we saw everything was taken I said under my breath, "Shit!" Melissa said, "Come on. We'll find another one." Moving on we came across a police station with smashed up and burned squad cars while dead officers laid in the streets covered in broken glass, bullet shells and blood. Entering inside it was a mess we made our way to the top floor and saw office area had been trashed with windows smashed open and destroyed furniture. Walking further we came to the captain's office and saw he had shot himself with his own Colt M1911. I said, "Take it."

Melissa walked over picking it up then searched through desk and found spare magazines along with ammo. I saw resting on a rack behind the police captain was a Winchester Model 1300 shotgun. I took it off the rack and asked, "Is there any shells in that desk?" Melissa said, "Yep. A full box of buckshot." I turned around and took the box and loaded the shotgun and put the rest of the shell into my light jacket. After searching for more ammo we we're about to leave when I saw a map of L.A. I said, "Hang on a minute Melissa."

She turned her head as we walked over to the map I pointed where the police station was, I said, "Ok if we go this way we'll reach the library." Melissa said, "Let's hope it isn't burned down." I said, "Only one way to find out." Leaving the police station, we stopped and ran for cover when a dark purple blimp flew above us which had our faces on the screen. Once it was far away, we ran away from it and made our way towards the library. I wiped the sweat from my forehead as the heat was rising.

When we saw the library, it looked to be built from '50s or '60s and was still standing with some damage to it. A light green VW Bug had crashed into a street light pole with an older dead woman hanging halfway out the front windshield with dry blood covered most of the hood. We saw the doors were halfway open I pumped the Winchester Model 1300 turning to Melissa and asked, "Ready?" She pulled the slid of her Colt M1911 and looked at me then said, "Yeah I'm ready." I nodded my head as we both entered inside the library.

Inside we saw front desk was a mess with notes, books and blood splatter all over the walls. A few shelves were knocked down with dozens of books torn up or burned. As a person who enjoys reading and with plans of writing my own novel ideas this was horrible sight to see. I said, "Fucking Manson! He's going to teach kids with his own sick written shit and yet has them destroy all of these books because he states they are evil. Fucking prick!" Melissa said, "Maybe we'll find some good titles that won't harmed."

I sighed and said, "Let's just find what we came for." There was enough sun light shining through the windows to allow us to see with some smashed. Looking up at the shelves that were still standing which had plats that said what books were on the shelf. I said, "We should find the dictionary in the far back." Melissa said, "I don't like the fact it's too quiet here." I notice she was right as there wasn't any noises both inside and outside. I said, "Maybe that's a good thing." Walking further through the library we suddenly heard the sounds of someone going through books.

I pointed to Melissa where the noise was coming from and had our guns ready. Slowly moving closer to it, we then heard a girl humming. We moved and we walked past the shelf, we saw a young teenage girl, looked to be about 15 years old. Wearing a dark blue shirt, black shorts, short socks with running shoes, a backpack filled with books. She had long black hair and light green eyes. I lowered my shotgun then the girl turned her head and gasped when she saw us.

We both saw she wasn't armed and was collecting a mixture of sci-fi and fantasy novels. Melissa lowered her Colt M1911 then the girl said, "Please don't hurt me. I'm just trying to save these titles from being destroyed." I said with a light smile, "We won't." The girl looked at us then asked, "Are you really the Tricksters?" I said, "That's what they call us but we have real names." The girl lightly smiled and said, "I thought you did. Found it silly if you ask me what those dumb kids call you." Melissa asked, "What's your name?" The girl said, "It's Suzie Streeter." I said, "Nice name. I'm Curtis and this is my girlfriend, Melissa."

Suzie was quiet for a bit then said, "You two look good together." Melissa lightly smiled I kneed down and asked, "What books you got there?" Suzie smiled turning back to the pile she had beside her. Suzie said, "I found the whole J.R.R. Tolkien series and Frank Herbert Dune series. When I tried reading it, I didn't understand but I want to save them so when I'm order I might understand it better. Oh, and my favorite science fiction author is Philip K. Dick. I was lucky enough to find all of his books here." I saw the novels she was talking about I said, "Hey I read Ubik, Do Androids Dream of Electric Sheep, Martian TimeSlip, The

Three Stigmata of Palmer Eldritch, Deus Iran and A Scanner Darkly." Suzie said, "I heard it's a good novel. Have you read Flow My Tears, The Policeman Said?" I said, "Yes I have." Suzie lightly smiled as she turned back to her novels putting them into her backpack then asked, "So what are you looking for Curtis? I know all the books in this library since I use to work here." I asked, "Do you know where the dictionaries are Suzie?" Suzie asked, "Why would you need a dictionary for?" I said, "I got a note that's written in Russian, and we need to translate what is said. We're trying to stop Manson & Barbara and this note might hold a clue we're looking for." Suzie said, "Could I see this note please." I pulled out the notebook and opened it up then handed the note to Suzie she looked at it and said, "Wow! I never seen what Russian text before. I heard they got some great writers too."

Suzie gave me back the note and said, "Yeah I know where the dictionaries are. Most of the dumb kids didn't touch them." Suzie stood up and zipped up her backpack putting it on as we followed her through the liberty. When we came to a long shelf Suzie said, "Here I'll get it for you." She pushed a ladder attached to the shelf then climbed up and got a very thick dictionary then climbed back down and said, "Here you good a English translation on every Russian word." Melissa said, "Thanks Suzie."

Suzie said, "I'm going to see if I can find any good novels before the dumb kids show up." I felt bad leaving her alone and knowing if the followers found her, they would kill her. I said, "You should come with us. It's very dangerous here." Suzie looked worried Melissa said, "Yes we won't want anything bad to happen to you Suzie." She sighed and said, "But I got some books at home. I can't just leave them here for those dumb kids to find them." I said, "We'll get them before we go, ok?" Suzie looked at me and asked, "You promise?" I said, "Yes, we promise."

Suzie lightly smiled and said, "Ok I'll come back shortly." She ran off as I turned to Melissa and said, "We don't have a choice as I don't want to leave here while this city is turning into chaos." Melissa lightly nodded her head and said, "Let's translate that note and get out of L.A." We found a table and cleared it as I had the note out while me and Melissa, we're looking through the dictionary. Slowly we began translating the handwritten note. We found out it wasn't written by Arkard but by his father Nikita Anton Lukyanenko, who was the Russian President.

It read,

"Arkard my son I know it's been years since I have last spoken to you. I'm writing to you because I have learned of the cartoons you have worked with talks of making a racist cartoon show. Arkard in the past I use to be like you I had a strong hatred towards Jews, Blacks and anyone that wasn't white but if it's one thing I learned during the after math with the Nazi's is that hatred is a poison. It slowly infects you and corrupts you and, in the end, you'll become nothing more than the person you hate the most, your own self. I wish for us to meet again and set things straight between us. I was very hard and rough on you and my actions have affected not only you but me. If you contact me back, then I'll make arrangements for us to meet and use your talent for better use. Please Arkard please I have heard what your mother and brother have said you've done, and it worries me the dark path you're on and trust me when you reach the end...it won't end the way you want it to."

We saw the note was written on Dec.13th.1969 a few days before Arkard was killed in the crash. The address was written down along with phone number. Melissa turned to me and asked, "So the President of Russia is Arkard's father. How can he help us?" I said, "Wait! If we get ahold of him and tell him what's going on maybe, we can stop this nuclear war from happening then make sure Manson can destroy the world." Melissa said, "Let's hope he can speak English." I wrote down the information on the other side of the note and said, "Ok let's get Suzie and we're leaving L.A." Suddenly we heard Suzie scream followed by the sound of dogs barking I packed up and saw the stairs leading to the 2nd level of the library Melissa said, "I'll take the 2nd floor."

I walked over to a shelf and pressed my back against the wall to see teenagers standing with a lot of German Sheppard's and Huskies standing next to a very tall, muscular and handsome looking teenager wearing all jungle camo outfit while holding M60E3 heavy magazine which had box magazine. I thought,

"That must be Patrick Walker! The guy who killed the Pope." Suzie was holding her backpack with a terrified look on her face.

Patrick with his blue piercing eyes and long blonde hair looked down at Suzie and asked a deep yet powerful voice, "My young child. Why are you collecting these books? Don't you know what harm it will bring to us." Suzie said angry, "It's a load of horse shit! Those damn cartoon characters are lying to us!" The German Sheppard's and Huskies growled with one teenager said, "Let's beat this little bitch up!" Patrick turned around aiming his M60E3 at the teenager wearing a cap facing backwards and holding a double barrel shotgun then asked, "Did I give you the order to speak soldier?" The teenager shook his head and said, "No...No you didn't it." Patrick said, "Then shut it!"

When Patrick turned around, he armed his heavy machine gun and said, "Now young child I'm not going to ask you again! Why are you collecting these... Suddenly the dogs notice me I aimed my shotgun at Patrick raising my voice and yelled, "DON'T MOVE!" A few of the teenagers behind Patrick said, "It's him!" Patrick lightly smiled and said, "So Curtis we finally meet in person. But where your girlfriend?" Melissa came aiming her Colt M1911 at the teenagers and capped off a few rounds taking them out Patrick spun around and fired his M60E3 nearly hitting Melissa as she ran.

Suzie grabbed her backpack and ran towards me, but the German Shepherd's and Huskies barked and went to chase her I aimed my shotgun and pulled the trigger. Buckshot tore through their bodies as chunks of flesh, fur and blood splattered in the air. I quickly pumped the shotgun as Suzie ran past me but with lightning speed Patrick spun to face me, I quickly shot him in the leg causing his aim to go off. I turned around and yelled, "RUN SUZIE! RUN!" I quickly reloaded my Winchester Model 1300 shotgun. I turned my head over to see Melissa running on the 2nd floor.

I heard Patrick yell, "GET THEM, YOU SOLDIERS! MOVE IT!" We heard more teenagers running after us followed by more dogs. I turned my head back to see them coming Suzie said, "Curtis! I know a secret way out of here. Follow me!" The teenagers were shooting off their pistols, shotguns, assault rifles or SMG's with bullets zooming by us and hitting the shelves and books which chucks of paper and bits of wood flying in the air. I then saw teenagers running nearby us I rammed my body weight into the shelf as they were crushed. Suzie said, "This way!"

She went left as Melissa ran down the stairs with bullets hitting the staircase along with the shelves beside her. I spun around and blasted off a few rounds taking more teenagers out. Then a big husky jumped knocking me down I quickly grabbed the dog by its neck and heard Melissa gun go off as blood splattered out of its head and went over my face I said, "FUCK!" I quickly got back up picking my shotgun whipping off the blood from my face and running down the hallway with Suzie and Melissa.

When Patrick caught up with us, he squeezed the trigger of M60E3 heavy machine gun as bullets tore through the walls. Suzie and Melissa ran over to a corner for cover as went crouched down by a corner on the left. Then a few of Patrick's bullets took out some hardcover books that were very thick and some of the books fell onto the floor. I looked down and saw resting by my feet was a hardcover of L. Ron Hubbard's Battlefield Earth.

Patrick was walking closer while still letting loose with his heavy machine gun trying to keep us from escaping. I grabbed Battlefield Earth and said, "I always thought Ron Hubbard was an asshole!" Patrick let go off the trigger I turned my body halfway out of the corner with lightning speed and threw Battlefield Earth hitting Patrick in the face I then stood up aiming the shotgun at him. I pulled the trigger and quickly pumped away hitting him in the chest and waist. But when my shotgun clicked empty to my horror Patrick was still standing, I thought, "Shit! He's wearing body armor!"

I ran over to Melissa and Suzie I open the door as Patrick angry yelled, "DIE MOTHERFUCKERS! DIE!" Bullets tore through the wall as I got the door open with both women going first, I then slammed the door shut locking it. Then Suzie pushed and Melissa pushed carts with more thick hardcover novels. Suzie said, "Don't worry about these! They're just boring math books!" We ran while Patrick was trying to open it, but it was locked.

Patrick turned his head to the teenagers and said, "Move back soldiers!" Patrick pulled out a hand grenade then ripped the pin out with his teeth and toss it at the lock door. Within seconds the door and the carts blocking it were blown out of the way.

We we're running through the back office of the library. Running up some stairs as Suzie took us to a fire exit door. But it was locked Melissa said, "Shit!" Suzie said, "Hang on I got the keys here!" I heard Patrick and the other teenagers coming I reloaded my shotgun Melissa asked, "How much ammo you got left?" I said, "A few shells." I looked over at Suzie to see her holding a key ring with a lot of keys. I said, "Give her cover." Melissa and I aimed where we came in and just as Patrick was about to step forward, we both pulled the trigger with Patrick and the others moving back.

I yelled, "TAKE ANOTHER STEP AND WE'LL BLOW OFF YOUR GODDAMN HEAD!" Patrick lightly laughed and said, "Not bad Curtis but you should have gone for a head shot when you had your chance." Suddenly we notice Patrick was changing weapons then heard something being loaded I knew it wasn't going to be good. Then I saw Patrick blind firing a M-79 grenade launcher. My eyes open wide I pushed Melissa and yelled, "GET DOWN!" As we fell onto the floor Patrick fired the M-79 with the grenade hitting the wall and when the explosion went off our ears were ringing.

Patrick grinned while most of the teenagers behind him were covering their ears. Patrick turned around raising his voice, "What the hell are you waiting for soldiers! Kill them!" One teenager said, "I can't hear a fucking thing!" Patrick grabbed the teenager by the throat raising his voice, "I SAID KILL THEM! MOVE YOUR GODDAMN ASS SOLDIER!"

Suzie screamed, "OOOW! I CAN'T HEAR!" Melissa quickly grabbed the key ring and found the key and jammed it into the keyhole unlocking the door. Melissa helped Suzie up I aimed my shotgun at the teenagers and blasted off a few shots then ran outside. I saw dark purple blimps were coming this way we quickly ran downstairs and onto the street with the teenagers shooting at us until Patrick came out and aimed his M-79 grenade launcher watching the Tricksters and the little girl running nearby a taxi. Patrick grinned and squeezed the trigger.

Just when I thought we escaped them a taxi close by to us exploded nearly knocking me down. Running towards an alleyway my hearing was coming back. We kept moving until we we're far away from them and the blimps. Melissa looked at Suzie and asked, "You ok Suzie?" She shook her head and said, "My ears still hurt!" I said, "Goddamn bastard! No regard for us or a little girl! Next time I see that punk I blow his fucking head off!"

Melissa turned to me and said, "Curtis!" I looked at Suzie and saw her ears were bleeding I went over to her and asked, "Suzie! Can you hear me?" She shook her head I felt angrier I slammed my fist against the wall and said under my breath, "Fucking prick!" Melissa said, "We have to treat her wounds." Just then Suzie pulled out a notepad from her pocket and flipped through the pages and pointed to an address. Looking at this we realized it was Suzie's house and it was close by here I said, "Ok let's go."

We reached Suzie's small house and went through the backdoor. I saw a clock on the kitchen wall that was still working. It was 12:30-PM I pulled a chair sitting down while Melissa treated Suzie's ears. When she came back a few minutes later she said, "I gave her some pain killers to help with the pain. She's resting now." I lightly shook my head and said, "If only we had with us earlier." Melissa said, "Curtis it's not your fault." I sighed and said, "I hope the damage isn't too bad." Melissa said, "It may take a while to fully heal but Suzie will be able to hear again. Let's eat and just relax here for a while." I nodded my head and that's what we did.

2:00-PM

I went to check on Suzie and she was still asleep with cotton buds placed into her ears while hugging a stuff teddy bear. I lightly smiled then heard Melissa come in she whispered, "How is she?" I turned my head over and said, "Ok." Melissa came over and carefully removed the cotton buds to see dried blood then slowly rubbed her forehead. Melissa turned her head over to me and asked, "How is it outside?" I said, "Blimps are everywhere, we'll never get past them during daylight." Melissa said, "Guess it's going to be tonight then." I nodded my head then said, "We can't bring her with us to Russia."

Melissa came over to me and sat down next to me and said, "She must have family still around that can look after her." I then felt Melissa looking at with a question in her mind and I knew what it was. I turned my head back to Suzie fearing if anything happened to us what would Manson's gang do to her or his damn followers. Looking back at Melissa I asked, "Did you see if Suzie's parents have anyone, we could reach in a phone book?" Melissa said, "I tried looking for one, but couldn't find any." I knew we won't get the answers still Suzie woke up and I really hoped she wasn't deaf.

6:00-PM

The sun set while blimps were flying over our area, we made sure not to get too close to the windows and keep the covered. Melissa took a gym bag she found and put all the food and drinks we could carry. I was looking out the kitchen window to see how far the highway and it would take us a while to reach. Just then we heard Suzie leaving her bedroom and walked into the kitchen. We both turned around I lightly smiled and said, "Hey, Suzie. How are you feeling?" She yawned and said, "A little better but I can hear a light ringing still." Melissa said, "That's good."

I asked, "Suzie do you have any family members that are still around?" Suzie looked at us and asked, "Why?" I said, "Where we're going, we can't have you come with us it's too dangerous." Suzie was quite for a bit then said, "Well, I do have my grandmother, who lives in Canada. But it's been a while since I last visit her." I said, "Then that's what we're going to do. We'll take you to your grandmother." Suzie said, "Alright just let me pack my things and could you help me with my books?" I said, "Sure thing."

Once it was dark enough, we made our way through the neighborhood with dark purple blimps shining spotlights down. We also heard the sounds of teenagers along with vehicles driving by. We got close to the highway I turned to Melissa and asked, "Do we have any more weapons back in the Bel Air?" She said, "No but we got more ammo." I sighed and said, "Better than nothing I guess." Moving on we reached the highway and ran over to where we left the 59 Bel Air. Removing the tarp then got inside.

I started up the Bel Air and drove onto the highway with the lights off. Driving across L.A. with the moon slowly rising up in the sky. Melissa looked at me and said, "So we're driving through San Francisco then?" I said, "Yeah and we'll be making our way to Vancouver." Suzie turned to us and said, "That's where my grandmother lives. She has a nice cottage there." I said, "Good you'll be safe there." Leaving L.A. behind us I said, "By the time they realize we're not there we'll be long gone."

11:00-PM

Driving down the dark empty with the headlights back on once far away from those blimps. Suzie hearing was now fully back as her and Melissa playing cards. I was glad to see Suzie was much better after encounter with Patrick. I was trying to think where he learned to use such heavy weapons. Were his parents survivalist types or was it the work of Manson? I looked at the radio wondering what else was going on in this world but already knew it was really bad.

The drive would take us 2 days to reach San Francisco and if it was like L.A. then it would take us longer to get into the Canadian border. I asked, "Hey Melissa when we get near San Francisco should try driving through or travel around the city on boat?" Melissa looked at me and said, "If it has children and teenagers running around causing mayhem and destruction then we try getting around them in a boat." I said, "Ok then but we'll have to find another set of wheels as we won't make it far on foot." I then checked the gas gauge and saw I was now halfway a tank. I would keep going until I was too tired to drive on and with any luck we might come across gas station to spend the rest of the night there.

March.31
8:00-AM

I woke up when I heard Melissa calling my name, I opened my eyes and had pulled over on the side of the road last night. I first thought we we're trouble but when I heard what was being said on the radio our situation has gone from bad to worse. Hearing a man speaking angry said, "To hell with our government! To hell with our rotten children! To hell with God! If this fucking world is going to shit, then we might as well end it with a goddamn bang! Send nukes to every fucking country so nothing will be left! Let's turn this planet into a goddamn war zone and kill everything in sight! And for those rotten little shits that are trashing up our towns! Our cities! Our way of life they'll be nothing more than mutated freaks of the nuclear wasteland!"

Melissa shut off the radio and said, "It's a recorded message as we can tell nobody is running this country anymore." I said, "Manson's goddamn plan! By killing every adult with nuclear weapons, he and his gang will use the souls to reshape this planet into whatever he wants." Suzie looking scared asked, "What about the children! Those followers of that damn show?"

I said, "They'll get to join Manson and whatever the hell is offering them." I shook my head and said, "Once they fire those warheads then everyone will be killing each other. Goddamn it!"

Gripping the steering wheel tightly while my mind raced of horrible images of what this planet would look like if those warheads went off. I remember back in the 50s & 60s how Americans feared a nuclear war would happen between US and the Soviet Union and the fear never left the 70s and got worse in the 80s. I never believed nuclear weapons would ever be used but after so much shit has hit the fan it might happen.

Suzie broke the silence, "Curtis? Melissa? You two are going to stop them and save the world, right?" For some reason I nor

Melissa couldn't answer that question knowing that any moment a warhead would be fired and within seconds the whole planet would turn into hell. Suzie placed her hand onto my shoulder and asked, "Please Curtis? I don't want to die; I don't want to lose my grandmother! She's all I got left! My...my mother is gone and... Suzie started to break down and cry while Melissa hugged her the horrible feeling of dread won't go away. I finally said, "I'm going to refuel this thing and we'll get going." I popped the trunk and got out of Bel Air walked over to the trunk.

I stopped and looked at the two women as they both were crying, I thought, "Could I really save the world from being destroyed?" I sighed grabbing the jerry can and stepped over to the gas lead. I opened it and checked around us and saw the empty road with no signs of life around us. I got the tank fully loaded then toss the empty jerry can back into the trunk closed it then got back inside started it up and sped off heading for San Francisco. The drive was quiet and not one of us spoke for a while.

1:00-PM

We reached a gas station I pulled over killed the engine and all three of us stepped out. Suzie said, "Damn after that I could use a shower." Melissa said, "Same here." I asked, "Is anyone hungry?" Both women said, "Yes." I said, "Alright I'll get cooking then." We ate inside the gas station while the weather looked clear. Eating sandwiches with a bowl of chips and drinking Coke. I did check from time to time making sure no blimps of any of Patrick Walker's soldiers would show up.

Halfway through Suzie asked, "So what did you two use to do?" I asked, "You mean work?" She nodded her head I said, "I use to be a reporter back in Black Creek along with my friend Hunter." Melissa said, "Same here but worked in Texas." Suzie asked, "Did you both like your jobs?" I said, "I didn't mind it as I didn't want to end up working in some fast-food joint." Melissa said, "Well, being a journalist wasn't my first job idea I always dreamed of being an artist. I enjoyed painting but sadly dreams don't pay for everything, so I took a job posting for journalism while...never mind you get the idea."

Suzie turned to me and asked, "What was your dream job Curtis?" I said, "I won't call it a dream job, but I always wanted to try out being an author." Suzie lightly smiled and asked, "Really? What kind of books would you write?" I said, "Mostly action, horror and some sci-fi." Suzie said, "Nice. Maybe I'll get to read them some time." I lightly nodded my head and said, "Sure. One day you'll will." Melissa said, "Let's finish up we got a lot of ground to cover." Finishing up lunch we all used the washroom then got back into the 59 Bel Air and sped off now this Melissa was driving while I rested in the back. Suzie was sitting in the front.

I was counting how many shotgun shells I left when suddenly I heard something coming behind us. Melissa looked up at the view mirror and said, "No! It can't be!" I turned my head looking out the rear window to see a few 84 AM General M998's behind us. They were all black but the one in the back had jungle camo on it which meant Patrick was in it. I turned my head halfway and said, "Floor it!" Melissa pressed her foot down hard pushing the 59 Bel Air faster while the AM General M998's were catching up with us. Then the two getting closer roof hatches popped open with teenagers holding shotguns and assault rifles.

I quickly rolled down the passenger window and aimed Winchester Model 1300 shotgun at them and pulled the trigger. I shot the first teenager holding an assault rifle hitting him in the arm but was still alive. I thought, "Goddamn it! That bastard has given them body armor!" I quickly pumped and shot the teenager in the head with chucks of flesh and blood splattered in the air. The 2nd AM General M998 rammed us with teenager letting loose with the shotgun taking out the rear window and shooting the taillight.

I quickly aimed at him and squeezed the trigger. I shot that bastard right between the eyes as his brains were blown out. The AM General M998 rammed us again I fired at the windshield but saw it was bullet proof glass. I quickly aimed at the tire blowing it out. Melissa said, "Hold on!" She made a hard sharp turn which the AM General M998 wasn't able to make the turn and drove off the road and crashed into a tree. I reloaded my shotgun but saw they won't going to get close enough now. I said, "Ok, assholes! Wanna play games? I'll fucking play them!"

I switched to my S&W Model 629 cocked the hammer then held tightly onto the magnum while Patrick's soldiers were shooting at us. I squeezed the trigger missing my first shot I quickly fired again taking out another teenager. A bullet hit the view mirror on the driver side door. Suzie kept her head down while covering her ears. I fired off a few more shoots then reloaded my magnum while Melissa was going faster.

But I saw Patrick's AM General M998 drive off into the forest I said, "Oh what the hell are you doing?!" Suzie and Melissa notice this and we're looking as well while the rest of his soldiers were staying behind. Suddenly we heard the roaring engine of Patrick's AM General M998 jump out from the forest flying over us and landed behind us. The hatch popped open as Patrick came out holding a flame thrower. My eyes open wide as Patrick armed the flame thrower he grinned then yelled, "LET ME WARM YOUR HEARTS UP!"

Hot flames licked the Bel Air as Melissa drove off the road and into the forest I growled and fired at Patrick hitting him. I tried to aim for his head but two of my shots were blocked by trees. I said, "Damn it!" I quickly reloaded then heard Patrick's soldiers were now behind us. Suzie said, "Here Curtis! I'll handle them!" She crawled into the back and picked up my shotgun aimed at the AM General M998 passenger side as a teenager popped his head out trying to shoot us with a pistol Suzie pulled the trigger blowing his brains out.

I turned back to Patrick and was getting closer to us Melissa said, "Here comes that prick! Remember go for a head shot!" I held tightly onto my magnum waiting until we we're clear from the trees. Suzie fired off a few more shots and took cover to reload then just as we we're about to get back onto the road suddenly Patrick smacked the roof of AM General M998 and it stopped causing me to miss my shot. I said, "You clever bastard!" Then he chased after us again Suzie reloaded the shotgun and said, "Guess going to the shooting range wasn't a waste of time at all."

I said, "We'll get him." As Patrick got closer, he let loose with the flame thrower with the flames nearly reaching the trunk I said, "Keep him away from us! If the trunk gets too hot, then we'll blow up!" Then two AM General M998's were speeding beside Patrick and getting closer to us I said, "There going to try and box us in!" Me and Suzie fired at both vehicles trying to take out their tires but rammed us. A teenager smashed out the passenger window with a crowbar then yelled, "LEARN HOW TO SHOOT YOU DUMB BITCH!" Suzie turned to face him then lifted up the barrel of the shotgun and pulled the trigger.

Blood and brain matter splattered inside the AM General M998's and Suzie quickly shot the driver in the back. Melissa rammed the vehicle as it drove off the road and crashed through a barrier and landed face first down a hill. I aimed at the passenger shot the teenager holding an assault rifle which I quickly reached out and grabbed it by its shoulder strap. I saw Patrick coming up again I quickly switched weapons and press the stock firmly against my shoulder and once I had Patrick in my sights, I squeezed the trigger.

I saw rounds tore through Patrick's body armor as blood splattered out his back which caused him to miss his shot. I and aimed for the flame thrower tank and shot it until it exploded. Flames bust out as Patrick quickly threw it off then took off his camo jacket and quickly padded his arms putting the fire. I said, "What the hell?" Suzie said, "I don't get it! You shot him!" I said, "Fucking Manson and his fucking magic! Must have taught Patrick how to use it!" We then drove through a tunnel with Patrick's remaining soldiers chased after us while Patrick was now behind them.

I pulled the magazine out of the assault rifle and saw I had fired all the bullets. Suzie said, "Ummm Curtis...I don't have much shells left." Melissa said, "We'll never outrun them in this thing!" I then had an idea I said, "Unless we steal one of those things for ourselves." Melissa turned her head to me I said, "It's our only chance." Melissa looked for a place we could stop and said, "Ok we'll run up there and have them chase us then get back down in time to steal one of those trucks."

I turned to Suzie and said, "Suzie once we get out lay low until they are gone and get our stuff into one of those trucks." She said, "Ok." Melissa turned back to me and asked, "Ready?" I nodded my head as Melissa pulled over and quickly shift the gear into Park and yelled, "RUN!" We got out and ran into the forest it didn't take long for the remaining AM General M998's to come to a full stop with all the doors opening with teenagers both men and women running after us. Suzie hid behind a rock still holding the shotgun as the others kept running. She turned around and ran back to our Bel Air and popped the trunk taking all the stuff and tossing it into the truck.

Me and Melissa split up but ran back the way we came but Patrick's soldiers caught on what we we're doing as they tried shooting us. Suzie was sitting in the driver side as she yelled, "GET IN!" I got into the back while Melissa ran around to the passenger side. I grabbed a fresh magazine for the assault rifle and reloaded it I aimed at the teenagers shooting at us I pulled back on the trigger taking a few out. Suzie pressed her foot down hard burning rubber with Patrick and his soldiers getting back in their AM General M998's I said, "There has to be something we can use here!"

I saw there were a few guns in the back with more ammo then Melissa said, "Hey Curtis." I turned my head to see her holding a few hand grenades. I chuckled and asked, "How many we got?" Melissa said, "Enough to take those fuckers out!" I said, "Then let's do it." I went over to the back passenger window and saw the trucks coming up I pulled the pin and toss a grenade out. Two AM General M998 exploded with another one driving off the road to avoid crashing into them but drove into a tree causing the teenager to be thrown off the roof.

Suzie pushed the truck faster while me and Melissa toss more hand grenades with bullets hitting us just glad this thing had thick armor. Then Patrick came back as it was just him driving now, I held onto a hand grenade I said, "Come on punk! Got a surprise for you!" Suddenly I saw Patrick holding the M-79 again but Melissa shot him in the shoulder with her Colt M1911 causing him to drop the grenade launcher. She capped off a few more shots but Patrick got back inside and was speeding towards us I pulled the pin and waited for the right moment to throw the grenade.

When Patrick was close enough, I threw it and the grenade landed on the hood of his AM General M998 but to my horror he was still speeding towards us. Suzie made a hard left turn which Patrick didn't make it and the grenade exploded with Patrick crashing his ride then hopped out. He screamed in anger while I replied back by giving him the finger. Melissa lightly laughed turning over to Suzie and said, "Nice driving." Suzie giggled and said, "Thanks. This is actually my first time behind the wheel. I've seen how people drive on movies but never driven a car before."

I turned around and asked, "Where did you learn to shoot Suzie?" She said, "Oh my mother. She was a cop and wanted to make sure that I would be ready for anything bad that I might face if she wasn't there." I said, "She taught you well." Suzie turned over to me as she smiled then looked back at the road and we saw a sign we we're getting closer to San Francisco. Melissa asked, "How much fuel we got?" Suzie looked at the gas gauge and said, "A full tank." I said, "Good we'll be able to reach where we're going."

6:45-PM

We stopped to rest and eat before we continue the long drive to Canada. I was glad that we didn't see any dark purple blimps or Patrick's soldiers which means Manson's gang isn't able to use their magic bullshit against us. The sky was turning a light peace color with dark red clouds as the sun was slowly setting. I was sitting beside Melissa while watching the sky. Suzie was reading a book in the back seat of the truck. I notice how quiet it was with a light breeze of air blowing against us. Not a signal sound of birds or bugs it was dead silent.

I looked over at Melissa and she too was looking at me with a disturbed look on her face like something wasn't right. Melissa asked, "Can you feel it?" I had a bad feeling what Melissa was asking me I sighed and said, "The horror that awaits us." Suddenly she hugged me and while lightly crying I wrapped my arms around her and said, "We'll stop them, Melissa. We can't fail." Melissa looked at me with watery eyes and asked, "How?" I turned over to Suzie and said, "I'm going to make sure that girl along with everyone else who isn't under Manson's control and give them a life. Even if we don't make it out alive, we can't let them win."

Melissa looked at Suzie then back at me I said, "We can't stop now. We must do this." She lightly nodded my head as I said, "Alright, let's get going." Stepping up I said, "Suzie we'll moving out." She placed book marker into her novel I stepped into the driver side of the truck as Melissa got in, I started it up and shifted the gear into Drive then press my foot down. While driving down the empty road it was quiet inside, I really hated the silence and wish to break it but I didn't feel like talking and their wasn't a radio to play some music.

11:00-PM

We reached the city of San Jose it was destroyed and no signs of life while it was pouring heavy rainfall. Melissa asked, "How much gas we got?" I checked and said, "Half a tank." Suzie had fallen asleep in the back with her teddy bear Melissa asked, "Should we stop here or keep going?" I shook my head and said, "No we'll keep going. Got to cover much ground as we can." Melissa yawned I said, "You got some rest, I'll be alright." She said, "Alright and... and sorry about earlier." I said, "It's alright we're both burned out." Melissa rested her head against the head rest and shut her eyes.

I press my foot down speeding through the empty city while roared in the pitch-black sky. Bright flashes of lightning would go off and each it time I hoped it wasn't a nuclear blast. I missed my heavy metal and thrash metal tapes I had back at my apartment. What I won't give to hear them again and see the movies I haven't watched in a long time. I swear this feeling of horror was the worst feeling I ever felt it truly was like the world was going to end. Blocking out these horrible thoughts I tried but couldn't.

I rubbed my eyes and kept driving hoping I wouldn't fall asleep behind the wheel. By one in the morning, I was getting tired I pulled over in an alleyway and killed the engine. I rested my head against the seat and closed by eyes. The sounds of the storm outside slowly faded away I tried to think of happy moments in my life but none of them came to me.

That night I dreamed I was standing with all the people I knew I saw my friends, family, those who knew me and others. I looked around to see where I was, but it was darkness surrendering us. I stopped when I heard Manson's voice behind me say, "Tick, tick, tick, tick Curtis. Time is almost up." When I turned around, I saw Manson grinning with his eyes glowing red. Without warning he grabbed me pulled me closer to him and bit into my throat. I felt his sharp fangs tear through my flesh and began sucking my blood. Then my body burst into flames and screamed while feeling my soul was being forcefully removed from my body. I woke up and saw it was morning.

San Francisco, California
April 1
7:00-AM

I grabbed the steering wheel and jolted from my seat. My heart was racing while I breathed heavy then grabbed my throat and rubbed where Manson bit me in the nightmare. I rubbed my eyes and breathed, "Fuck!" I moved my hand away then turned over to see that Melissa and Suzie were still sleep. I turn away then reached the key I turned it then shifted the gear into Drive and drove off. As I drove down the empty street, I notice on signs were spray painted messages saying, "TURN AROUND!" "DO NOT COME ANY CLOSER!" "DEATH TO CHILDREN!"

I didn't like this one bit but there was nowhere else to go now. Melissa woke up as she yawned then asked, "Have we reached San Francisco?" I stopped the truck and said with butterflies in my stomach, "Yeah...we did." When Melissa opened her eyes, she gasped at the sight. In front of us was a big welcome sign to San Francisco but attached to the sign were dismembered children attached to it with a few being hung from nearby streetlights that were both beaten and shot to death with some dipping blood.

One dead child hanging upside had a sign tied around his body which read, "DEATH TO THE CHILDREN OF SATAN!"

I hit the steering wheel and said, "Great! Just fucking great!" Melissa turned to me and said, "There has to be a way around this." Suddenly I heard someone jump on top of the truck we both and saw both men and women wearing torn clothing or not much running towards us while holding baseball bats, sledgehammers, meat clever, hammers, golf clubs and short swords. I pressed my foot down then a man on our roof tried breaking in, but I knocked him off. I heard yelling and screaming and said under my breath, "Oh shit!" Suzie woke up from the noise and saw what was going on she said, "Oh my! What are those people doing!?"

Then to our horror they were running towards us and throwing their body weight against the truck. A naked woman threw herself and landed on the hood while screaming I slammed on the brakes then pressed my foot down hard. She didn't move and heard the sound of the front tire running over hey body. The loud crushing noise of skull followed by her brain being pressed out hearing the other bones crush under us. Suzie held tightly onto her teddy bear as I sped closer to San Francisco.

Then beer bottles, rocks and anything these crazed people had were being thrown at us. Once in the city they won't be able to keep up but we we're far from safe. All of the buildings were badly damaged or burned down with more corpses of children and adults hanging on street light poles with. Suddenly I heard a noise at my left and when I turned my head everything went out.

12:00-PM

I woke up feeling very hard while hanging upside down while my head felt sore. My vision was a bit burly then heard loud chanting followed by heavy drumbeats. I then saw shadows moving around me and when my sight became clear again it was people covered in black paint while only wearing ripped pants or stood naked. I lifted up my head to see my legs were tied up with rope while being held by a hook along with my arms. I looked over to see Melissa, but I didn't see Suzie I thought, "Oh no! Please they didn't kill her! If they did, I'll make all these sick crazy fuckers pay!"

We we're inside what looked like a rundown church with the roof smashed open allowing sun light inside and hanging upside along the walls were more dead children. Chains attached to the ceiling had severed heads with a few missing their eyeballs. I then saw a group of older adults chopping limbs from dead adults with one man grabbing an arm and begin eating it.

Then I heard a woman say, "Aww…you're awake." I turned my head and was shocked what I saw. An old woman to be in her late 40s stood fully naked with a chain necklace that had severed baby heads attached by hooks, around her waist was a leather belt with a long knife holster and attached to the other side of it were two young severed girl's heads and sticking out their heads were hooks, the woman's finger and toenails were very long and smelled like she hasn't taken a shower in months. Her hair was very long light grey with light brown eyes and had red paint on her naked body. I gagged as Melissa woke up and asked, "What smells like fucking shit?" She turned to the woman and breathed, "Fuck!"

The woman looked at us and said, "You two were foolish to carry one of many Satan's daughters." I raised my voice and said, "SHE'S JUST A 15-YEAR-OLD GIRL, YOU STUPID

BITCH!" The woman looked at me and said, "Here suck on these until you learn your manners!" She turned over to the severed head of the girl attached to her leather belt and tore out both balls then two men grabbed my mouth trying to force it open. I tried biting them, but another man punched me in the gut causing me to gasp for air when the woman placed both eyeballs into my mouth then a man quickly attached a gag collar around my mouth.

The eyeballs tasted horrible and felt I was going to puke with these things. I tried breaking free, but the rope was on tight. The woman turned to Melissa and asked, "Now I will ask you the same question. Why were you carrying one of Satan's daughters with you?" Melissa eyes looked at me as bit into the gag collar. Melissa looked at the woman said, "She wanted a life. That's all." The woman then asked, "Who's idea was it to bring her?" Melissa said, "We both chose to let her come with us."

Suddenly the woman lightly nodded her head and said, "That was a foolish mistake." She then pulled out her long knife and said, "I mush punish those who had sinned and I'm going to make you learn your lesson." The woman walked over and pulled off Melissa's shirt allowing her huge breasts free as Melissa screamed in horror.

The woman chuckled and said, "I remember when I use to have breasts like these but as you seen they have shrunk. But yours would look good on me." I felt a hand grab me by the hair and turned my head forcing me to watch what was about to happen. As the woman was about to place her knife against Melissa huge breast and cut it off suddenly, I saw a laser sight on the woman's back. I moved my eyes to see Patrick holding a HK PSG-1 sniper rifle with a laser sight and high-powered scope.

Patrick then lifted up the sniper rifle and pulled the trigger shooting the rope above Melissa causing her to fall onto the platform we were hanging above. The woman turned around and Patrick shot her in the head. Within seconds her face was destroyed with large chucks of flesh, blood and skull bone splattered out the back of her head. The woman's headless body was forcefully sent backwards and smashed hard onto the platform. A man came over and was about to slit my throat but was shot by Patrick and with lightning speed he shot the other two men then shot the rope down.

Patrick took out more crazed people whole Melissa was able to break free from the ropes then ran over and quickly untied me and removed the gag collar as I spit out the eyeballs. Suddenly Patrick aimed his sniper rifle at us I thought he was going to shoot us. He then moved it away laughed loudly and said, "I'll catch you two later." He ran off as we heard shooting outside, I turned to Melissa and said, "We gotta find Suzie! I'm not leaving her behind!" Melissa said, "Alright." Melissa fixed her shirt while we ran across the platform and opened the door with a staircase leading downstairs.

Running down it quickly with the shooting and sounds of people dying outside grew louder. Just as we got near the stairs an overweight naked man came out holding a metal bat yelled, "HEY YOU!" I jumped off the steps and kicked the man in the face knocking him down I then stomped on his throat crushing it then picked up the metal bat. Mope crazed people came out I swung and smashed the bat hard into their faces while Melissa was punching and kicking against the others.

I killed a man holding a meat cleaver I quickly grabbed it and said, "Melissa! Catch!" I toss it and she caught it in time then swung at a woman's head slicing halfway through it. Melissa kicked the dead woman's body and hacked the meat clever at more crazed people.

Suddenly a muscular man holding a sledgehammer he yelled and went to swing it I ducked in time as he hit the wall above me and was stuck. I smashed the metal bat against his leg, breaking it. He screamed in pain I lifted the bat up with both arms and swung it down smashing the man's skull open. I heard the loud crush noise followed by blood pouring out his ear, nose and mouth. Melissa and I ran through a hallway calling out for Suzie, then we heard her voice.

Running over to a metal door I opened it and Suzie was sitting on the floor holding her teddy bear she smiled and said, "You two came for me!" Suzie ran and hugged us as we put our arms around. I said, "We won't leave without you." Suzie giggled and said, "Thank you!" Melissa said, "Alright let's get out of here." I said, "Wait we need to get the notebook back! It has the address to... Suddenly we heard Patrick's voice say, "For Nikita Anton Lukyanenko's place?"

We turned to see Patrick standing in front of us holding the HK PSG-1 in his right hand and in his left hand was the notebook with the note folded and sticking out. Patrick chuckled and said, "I have to hand it to you Curtis. You and your black girlfriend are quite the team. I heard Hunter was also good team player too bad he didn't make it." Melissa asked angry, "So, you're just going to kill us now?!" Patrick stared at us with those green eyes of his and said, "No. I have new orders. You three are to be taken in alive." I said, "You're bullshitting us."

Patrick said, "No sir, I'm not bullshitting you. Orders from Kane himself. Because of the damage you did to Manson and his girlfriend Barbara they need your souls to fully heal them and killing you two know would make their recovery take longer." I said, "Guess magic has its limits." Patrick lightly laughed and said, "Hey I'm bound to the same rules as they are. I can't push it like a junkie, or I'll die myself. You see in the real you can only use so much magic until you drain yourself of energy and it's risky to suck every drop out of you which can cause death. But in the Dark Kingdom you can do anything you want."

Melissa said a snarky tune, "Like making your dick bigger?" Patrick laughed and smacked the notebook against his leg then looked at her and said, "I like your girlfriend, Curtis. Got a fine ass, nice pair of huge tits and a good sense of humor. Now let's not keep Kane waiting as we're on a tight schedule." Suzie said, "Wait! What about my books! I'm not leaving without them!" Patrick said, "I don't have time for stupid literature! Now move your asses!" I said raising my voice, "We're not leaving until she gets her books back!" Patrick aimed the sniper rifle at me and said, "I'm not going to ask you again!"

I said, "You know what, fuck you. Go ahead and blow my brains out because I rather be dead than being taken in alive!" Patrick looked annoyed and had his finger on the trigger ready to pull it, but he sighed and lowered his sniper rifle. Patrick said, "Fine! If you want them, you carry them." Suzie said, "Suits me fine." He said, "Now move it! I won't fucking ask you three again! And drop your weapons!" Leaving behind the bat and meat clever as Patrick along with his soldiers took us outside then Patrick turned to one of the teenagers a cute looking girl with long black hair and said, "Hey Jackie! Bring the backpack full of books back!"

Jackie said, "Yes sir." She got the backpack which she dropped in front of Suzie as she picked up with Patrick looking at her and said, "Now what do you say little girl." Suzie said, "Thank you." He nodded his head and said, "Very good now get on the chopper." Patrick's soldiers got us on board a large camo helicopter and his soldiers were heavily armed. Once inside Patrick called all his soldiers back and got into the other camo helicopters. He closed the sliding door and said, "Takes up Billy." The engines roared to life and within minutes we we're flying out of San Francisco.

I looked down at the ruins then heard Patrick say, "It's amazing how fast people lose their shit within a few days." I turned him whole he was drinking can of Pepsi whole lightly smiling at us. Suzie was facing away while going through her books making sure she didn't lose any. I asked, "I'm guess that all happened after I wounded Manson and Barbara?" Patrick nodded his head and said, "Without Manson's brainwashing signal every adult snapped out of it and they saw what their children were doing they lost their shit. You two came close taking it out. If you have space shuttle with weapons you could have beaten them."

Patrick lightly laughed and drank his Pepsi I said, "There's something that's bothering me." Patrick looked at me and asked, "Of how I became such a badass?" I said, "Not just that but I saw Kane get his head blown off with a shotgun blast. How come that didn't weaken him?" Patrick chuckled and said, "Oh fuck it what difference is going to make you'll all be dead anyway." He wiped his lips and said, "Their like wizards as they been alive a lot longer than us since cartoon characters don't age. Manson and Barbara are the only ones that can do the more powerful stuff like changing a whole goddamn city into their playground, turning a loving mansion into a fun house and controlling people."

I said, "So they use too much magic." Patrick said, "Yes and because you two won't die so easily as you been making them bust their asses just trying to kill you. Now the other members of Manson's crew aren't the heavy weights like him or his girlfriend so they can't deal too much damage but keep enough of that magic of theirs so if anything does happen, they'll heal themselves up."

Melissa asked, "So what are you getting out of this Patrick?" He looked at her and said, "Well before I became Manson's personal soldier, I was slave to this system. For years my old man was trying to make me into him. Becoming a pure white American boy to destroy anything that wasn't white or American." Patrick shook his head then asked, "Do you like racist people Curtis?" I said, "No I hate them." Patrick nodded his head and said, "Good, that's good. I never wanted to be like my old man and felt like killing him and every motherfucker that just wanted to continue slaving us to be their slaves and force to fight their wars for their own pursuer. Then we reach their age it's our time to repeat what they did to us."

Patrick shook his head and said, "I will never raise my children to become like my old man or anyone else that wants nothing more than a dormant state. When Manson and Barbara came to me, they we're there to save me, help me and to bring their future plans to life and I could have anything I want. Like a bigger dick. Hell, I won't mind having two big dicks." Patrick and the others laughed with him for a bit then stopped as he finished his Pepsi then stood up and said, "I'll be right back. Have to make a phone call." He walked into the cockpit I turned to Melissa and whispered, "We have to find a way out of here." Melissa sighed and said, "That won't be easy."

6:00-PM

It's been quiet for a few hours and Patrick hasn't come back yet. This allowed me to start thinking of a plan of trying to get out of here. Looking at Patrick's soldiers they would shoot us if we tried anything and if we caused the pilot to crash the helicopter we would be killed. I looked out the window to see the water and thought, "Would we survive if we jumped out and landed in the water?" I've seen it on action movies and a few novels I read but would it really work?" Melissa turned to my ear and whispered, "What are you thinking?" I whispered, "What if we jumped out into the water." Melissa looked out the window of the sliding door and saw the ocean below us.

Melissa turned to me and whispered, "What about Suzie?" Suddenly we heard Patrick say, "Yes what about Suzie." We both jumped he had both arms holding onto the handlebars above him while leading in a bit he said, "You won't survive a fall from here. This isn't like Indiana Jones and not even a inflatable raft would be enough. Now if you had a boat that would do it. Sorry I don't mean to eavesdrop on you two just wanted to let you know if you tried jumping out you would most likely break your backs. Now onto the mission I have to complete."

Patrick moved his body back and said, "First order drop off the girl then take you two to Kane as he has a blimp waiting for us." I asked, "You can't just fly there in this thing?" Patrick lightly shook his and said, "Manson isn't a fan of machines that's why he lets me handle it. But I'll still have something like it in the Dark Kingdom." He turned his head over and said, "Billy! Land the helicopter! Tell the others to join us at the spot." Billy said, "Yes sir!"

The other helicopters flew on while Patrick's landed on the ground with him walking over to the sliding door and opening it. He turned to Suzie and said, "Alright little girl here's your stop." Suzie looked worried I said, "Wait! Let her have one our guns. Besides we won't be getting them back." Patrick lightly nodded his head and said, "You know what. That's great idea as I'm not giving her my gear but I'll pick for her." Patrick took Melissa's Colt M1911 and took out the magazine and reloaded it then slapped it in and said, "Ok get off first then I'll give you the gun."

Suzie looked at us and said, "Please be careful you two. I want to see you again." I nodded my head and said, "We'll be back one day Suzie." She came over hugged us and said, "Thanks again." I said, "Anything for you." Suzie let go of us then got out of the helicopter as Patrick said, "Keep walking." I looked at Patrick fearing he was going to do something. Then he cocked the hammer, and his finger was about to wrap around the trigger. I jumped and yelled, "NNNNOOOOO!" I landed on Patrick causing him to fall out of the helicopter with me which he pulled the trigger shooting the road.

One of Patrick's soldiers armed his HK-MP5 and went to shoot but Melissa manage to get a hold it and kick the teenager between his legs and aim the SMG at them and pull back on the trigger taking out Patrick's soldiers and shooting the pilot. Patrick and I were fighting over the gun and despite be being taller than him Patrick was very strong. Trying to pull the Colt M1911 free from his hand wasn't easy then Patrick reached for his knife holster on his belt and pulled it I grabbed it with my left hand.

Patrick had a lot of resistance, and I could barely get the knife to move away nor get the pistol out of his hand. Melissa grabbed a duffel bag of guns and magazine and reloaded the HK-MP5 running out of the helicopter and went to shoot Patrick suddenly two helicopters came back and sliding doors opened with teenagers shooting at us. Melissa fired back at them hitting one teenager as he fell out and landed on the spinning rotor blades chopping him up into chucks as blood splattered everywhere.

The two helicopters were coming in closer Melissa turned to me and ran towards Patrick, she quickly kicked him in the face knocking him out cold. She said, "RUN!" I quickly grabbed the notebook from Patrick's jacket along with the pistol and ran with Melissa towards the forest as Patrick's soldiers tried shooting us but missed. We kept running until we were out of breath. Just then we heard Suzie whisper, "Hey! Over here." We saw her hiding behind a tree we both smiled along with Suzie and walked towards her.

Thanks to the thick forest we we're able to avoid being spotted by Patrick's helicopters or their spotlights. Melissa said, "Hmm with all that hardware Patrick was packing you'll think he have a easier time finding us." I lightly laughed and said, "I guess he's in deep shit for screwing up big time." Melissa turned to me and asked, "If Patrick did give Suzie would have jumped him?" I looked at Melissa and said, "Oh course. I wasn't going to let him take us to Manson." She lightly smiled and said, "I knew you would say that." I chuckled as Suzie said, "We'll almost be in Canada." I said, "Yep almost there."

Vancouver, Canada
10:00-PM

It was very dark as me, Melissa and Suzie walk down the empty road into Vancouver. I asked, "So where does your grandmother live, Suzie?" She turned to me and said, "Near a town called Blue Lake. I know where to find it. Might take us a while but we'll get there." The air felt very cool while a light fog had rolled in and I could hear the sounds of the shore washing up on the nearby beaches. Further up the road we saw a few squad cars with bullet holes and some of their windows were shattered with broken glass lying on the pavement.

Walking past the squad cars we saw a few dead officers with flies buzzing around inside. Suzie asked, "You think we'll bump into any more of those dumb kids?" I said, "I don't think so. They all joined Manson and are somewhere else." We came to a town and felt very tired from walking Melissa turned to us and said, "I can't go anything further I need to rest." I said, "Alright we'll spend a night here then continue on in the following morning."

There was a nearby hotel, and we slept in the same room. It didn't take us long to fall asleep on the bed. I really hoped Patrick and his soldiers won't find us I didn't want to be captured by that prick again and if I did see him again, I would make sure I killed him.

April.2
9:00-AM

I woke up the next morning to see Melissa resting on top of me with her arms wrapped around me. I turned over to see Suzie was sleeping with her teddy bear. Suddenly Melissa screamed and woke up and nearly fell off the bed waking up Suzie. I held onto Melissa from falling as she said, "Oh shit!" Melissa rested her hand on my chest and said, "I had the most horrible dream." I knew what she was talking about. Melissa lifted up her head while lightly shaking her head then Suzie asked, "Are you ok Melissa?"

She got off me and said, "Yeah...I'm alright." Suzie could tell something was bothering her. Melissa turned to me and asked, "Would you mind getting started on breakfast?" I said, "Sure." Melissa said, "I'll be stepping out for some air." I said, "Alright." Melissa stepped outside while I began cooking breakfast and a few minutes later we heard the door open as Melissa stepped back inside. I turned my head over to her and said, "Almost done here."

Melissa asked, "You got coffee?" I said, "Yep. Here it's still fresh." Melissa walked over picked up a mug and said, "Thanks."

I wasn't going to ask about the nightmare as I didn't want to think about the one, I had. Suzie came over sitting at the small table as I bought the breakfast over. We all sat quietly and eat I checked outside to see it was very overcast. It didn't take us long to finish breakfast and we packed up. I checked what guns Melissa had gotten in the duffel bag and saw my magnum was inside. I pulled it put and loaded it then picked a Beretta 92F. Melissa said, "I got lots of 9MM in there." I nodded my head and said, "We should be good with this." I took a few spare magazines then tucked my magnum into my pants while holding the Beretta 92F pistol and flicked off the safety ready to use it.

Leaving the hotel, the air felt warm while grey clouds blew above us with hardly any sunlight shining through. Not a single sound of noise other than the wind, it truly felt like we we're the last beings on this planet. I saw a sign showing we we're heading for a place near Blue Lake I hoped Suzie's grandmother was still alive as I didn't want to drag her with us. We we're lucky enough to escape from Patrick and the other crazy people but if Manson and Barbara came back then we might not get another chance. Suzie pointed and said, "Look we're almost there."

It took us an hour to reach Blue Lake and when we saw it we all stopped to see a trailer park with people and children working and playing together. It felt like years since I've seen so much happiness in one place. Then we heard Suzie yell, "Grandma!" An old woman looked shocked to see her but smiled as Suzie ran towards her with the two hugging each other. We walked towards them as everyone stopped what they were doing and looked at us.

Suzie turned around and said, "Grandmother please meet my friends Curtis and Melissa. They saved my life and helped me get here." I lightly smiled and said, "Nice to see some friendly faces again." Suzie's grandmother chuckled and said, "I nearly lost hope that I won't see my granddaughter again, but I knew somehow I would. Please come in you must be hungry." Stepping inside Suzie's grandmother's trailer as it had candles lit while fans were blowing cool air. Suzie said, "I'm so glad to be here again as my back is killing me from carrying all these books."

Her grandmother lightly laughed and said, "Well you won't have to carry them anywhere else." She turned to us and asked, "What can I get you two?" I said, "We just ate a few hours ago so I'm not that hungry but a drink would be nice please." Melissa said, "Same here, I'll have a drink." She said, "Alright, coming up." Suzie went into her room dropping off the backpack and teddy bear and joined us. As we drank the weather showed no signs of clearing up. Suzie's grandmother asked, "So are you two staying long?" I said, "No. I'm afraid we have to leave soon."

She said, "Why don't you two stay for dinner." I said, "We can't. All I wanted to do was make sure that your granddaughter made it here safely. Where we're going, I can't say but if one of us does make it back alive then we'll come back." Suzie's grandmother stared at us for a bit then looked at her granddaughter. Melissa said, "Thank you for the drinks." We both stood up getting our stuff I turned my head over and said, "You know their one thing I want to ask before I go." Suzie's grandmother looked at us and asked, "Yes?" I said, "Would you know if there are any working vehicles we can find?" She said, "I'm afraid I won't know any." I said, "Alright, thanks again. Bye Suzie."

Suzie said, "Bye Curtis bye Melissa. I hope to see you two again." We left the trailer park with the clouds growing darker Melissa said, "I'm sure we'll find something that works around here." I said, "We will as we'll never reach Russia by foot." Melissa asked, "So are we going to try reach Russia by flying from Alaska?" I said, "Yes." Melissa said, "Wait. If we try finding the airport around here, we can just fly there and save us some time." I thought about it and said, "Good idea. Let's find some wheels first."

After walking for a bit, we came across Ford pickup truck I was able to hot wire it and drive through Vancouver. While driving I noticed how quiet Melissa was, I tried to think of something we could talk about but nothing came to my mind. We reached the city and saw a sign pointing to the airport I drove towards it and sure enough found a few planes left for us. Melissa asked, "Do you know how to fly?" I said, "No, but it can't be that hard."

I picked a two-engine plane as it would have enough fuel to reach Alaska then I'll land refuel and continue our journey to Russia. After reading over the manual Melissa and I got the plane running. I was getting ready to leave when I heard Melissa coming back in and closed the door. I turned my head and asked, "What did you bring back?" Melissa turned over to me and said, "Oh, just two pairs of parachutes. Just in case." I nodded my head and said, "Alright, we'll heading out then." I pulled the lever forward and got the plane moving down the runway and we we're flying up in the air.

Melissa sat up front beside me and said, "Hey you're flying well." I lightly smiled and said, "Thanks." Melissa lightly nodded her head and said, "Curtis. That nightmare I had." I looked over at her and said, "I had one too." She looked over at me and said, "I dreamed that I was standing with people I knew both from my past and those who I worked with. We we're all just standing in the darkness doing noting and nobody spoke. Then the sky lit up into bright flames and...and everything just burst into flames. Suddenly Manson grabbed me from behind and bit by neck sucking my blood and...my soul." I saw how disturbed Melissa was from this nightmare I said, "That's what Manson did to me as well."

Melissa asked, "Do you think he really did that to us?" I said, "He's only trying to scare us off. He knows we have weakened him badly and is going to try every dirty trick he has left. If we can stop this nuclear war from happening, then Manson and Barbara's plan is over as they won't have any power left." Melissa said, "And without their brainwashing everyone should snap out of their control." I lightly shook my head and said, "The whole world might be a big mess, but everything will be back to the way it was."

Looking out the cockpit we saw no signs of life nor anything else. Melissa asked, "Do you think there are others who are free from Manson's control?" I thought about it then said, "Maybe there is." It would take us 2 or 3 hours to reach Alaska and once we made it, I'll have to find airport refuel the plane and make the long trip to Russia. I heard stories of the Soviet Union having bombers flying over the American border to train them in the event of WWIII and scaring the shit out of us. I hoped that they didn't have any fighters patrolling their borders while we reach it as I have no idea where would have to go, once we set foot in Russia.

Alaska
1:00-PM

It was a long flight, but things won't looking good for us the weather to seem to get much worse with wind blowing harder and the clouds grew darker showing signs a storm may come soon. I touched down onto a airport with only half a tank left to go. I said, "Damn this weather might force us to wait until it clears." Melissa said, "I can use a hot shower after this." I said, "I won't mind one myself." I drove the plane into a hanger I killed the engine as we both got out and closed the hanger doors.

Taking our stuff with us we found the office close by to the hanger which had stocks of food, drinks and bathrooms, showers and bedroom. I said, "We'll be able to rest here tonight." Melissa turned to me and said, "And." I looked at her and asked, "And?" Melissa lightly smiled then said, "And we have to catch up where we left off." I chuckled as we left our stuff in the office bedroom and both got into the shower removing our clothes and stepping together. We wrapped our arms around each other and pressed our lips together kissing while feeling Melissa's huge breasts pressing against my chest.

It didn't take long for my dick to fully harden and damn I missed Melissa's sweet taste. The hot water poured onto our bodies. I placed my back against the shower wall Melissa held firmly onto my shoulder tops then lifted herself up while I held onto her, she giggled and said, "Oh, babe give it to me." I guided my big thick dick into Melissa's pussy as she began thrusting her body up and down. I lightly moaned and said, "Aww yes!"

Melissa thrust her body faster while feeling her pussy walls were getting tighter. I watched as the hot water poured onto Melissa head making her hair wet and onto her body. When I felt I couldn't hold it any longer I released a hard burst of cum Melissa held tightly onto me while moaning loudly. I slowly sit down on the shower floor with Melissa. She said, "Oh, that felt fucking good." I chuckled and kissed for a bit then stop to catch our breath. While staring at each other we suddenly heard a loud roar of thunder above us.

April.3
6:00-AM

After a good night sleep and not getting any fucked-up nightmares from Manson or Barbara. We we're getting the plane ready as the weather had cleared up which might be our only chance. I asked, "Melissa. Do we have everything we need?" She looked at me and said, "Yep. Made sure we won't forget anything." I said, "Good." We both got hanger doors opened and into the plane I fired up its engines and pulled the lever forward. Melissa joined me in the cockpit as I sped down the runaway.

Once at full power I lifted up the plane and was heading for Russia. I said, "Once we get there, we have to find Nikita before Patrick or Kane does." Melissa said, "I hope that little punk is dead." I said, "If we do bump into him again, I'll sure it will be the last time." After flying across nothing but land we we're now flying over the open sea. I bet the water was freezing cold and if we we're shot down and left in the middle of the ocean we won't survive for every long time.

Melissa asked, "So how long do you think it will take?" I said, "3 or 4 hours I say. As long the weather says like this." It remained quiet inside the cockpit while Melissa was holding a pair of binoculars if she spotted anything. I rubbed my eyes and turned my head over to Melissa and asked, "Could you please get a can of Coke?" Melissa said, "Sure thing I could use a drink myself." Melissa stood up and walked into the back to get the drinks.

9:00-AM

Halfway through our fuel tanks which meant no turning back from this point on now. Melissa yawned and said, "At least we didn't have to wait in line for this flight." I lightly laughed when suddenly out of nowhere two fighter jets zoomed by us. We both jumped then heard them coming back for us. I said, "Shit! Russian fighters!" Once they were behind us Melissa said, "I think they're going to shoot us down!" I said, "Hold on!" I pulled the joystick forward going down I gained a little more speed and saw land up ahead. I said, "There it is! We're almost there!" Suddenly we heard the fighters shooting at us with bullets hitting the wings.

I said, "Fuck! We're going to lose power!" Then alarms were going off as the left engine had thick black smoke coming out it. Melissa said, "We'll have to jump!" I said, "Alright." I set the plane into auto pilot as we ran got our stuff and put on the parachutes then the Russian fighters shot at the 2nd engine taking it out. I ran towards the door with Melissa holding my hand I turned to her and asked, "Ready?" She nodded her head I turn back to the door opened the hatch as we both jumped out.

Loud wind rushed through us as we fell through the sky I couldn't see since the air was blowing into my face, but I heard the plane we we're flying in crashed towards the ground. I lifted my head up see Melissa staying close by to me. She covered her eyes and moved her fingers a bit to see me I yelled loud as I could, "PULL THE CORD!" We both did and our parachutes opened we slowed down and we're able to open our eyes fully.

Suddenly we heard those Russian fighter jets coming back I said, "Oh hell no!" I grabbed my Beretta 92F pistol and Melissa took out her Colt M1911 we both hold tightly onto our pistols and squeezed the trigger away. I managed to hit the pilot and so did Melissa. Both jets flew by us and crashed into the ground while our ears ringed a bit. However, I saw driving toward us were trucks and black sedans. Melissa raised her voice and asked, "Do you think they are going to kill us?" When the trucks came to a full stop the doors swung open with fully armed soldiers running out armed with Ak-74's, SKS's or PPSH-41's.

I saw there wasn't anywhere to take cover or run we we're both out in the open. When our feet touch the ground the sounds of weapons being armed and aimed at us with a man shouting in Russian. Melissa looked at me fearing this was the end for us when suddenly we heard a sound behind us. I noticed the Russian soldiers were looking up I turned my head to see a swarm of helicopters flying towards us and attached to their short wings were heavy machine guns and rocket launchers. It was Patrick!

They open fired on the Russian soldiers as blood and chucks of flesh splattered into the air while the soldiers were trying to shoot back. We helped get the parachutes off I said, "This might be our only chance to escape." We went to run when the helicopters fired rockets at the vehicles blowing them all up I signed and said, "Or not." When all the Russian soldiers were killed we went to run but bullets hit the ground forcing us to stop then in the camo helicopter Patrick's voice was heard on loud speaker, "DON'T FUCKING MOVE!"

Patrick's helicopter touched down on the ground with his soldiers getting out including him. Patrick walked towards us now wearing white camo and holding his M60E3 heavy machine gun. Patrick looked at us with annoyed look and said, "I swear this is going to be the last time I save your goddamn asses again! Now drop the weapons as we don't have much fucking time left." Knowing we had no choice we toss our weapons down Patrick moved his heavy machine gun and said, "Get on board."

Patrick followed behind us once we we're on board then the helicopters were heading towards Russia and see how much fire power they were packing I knew Manson & Barbara were desperate to stop us.

Chapter 9

Patrick was sitting in front of us with his heavy machine gun pointed at us and beside us were his soldiers having their weapons ready as well. I heard pilot turn his head over and said, "We'll be entering Moscow in 10 minutes." Patrick grinned and asked, "Isn't magic cool? You see, in a normal flight, it would take us hours to reach it; and we'll never get past all their fighter jets and anti-aircraft weapons." I said, "I thought you would have gone ahead of us." Patrick lightly shook his head and said, "Getting Nikita is the 2nd task of the mission. You two, are the first task." I said, "I already know what the 3rd task is going to be." Patrick said, "Yes, and goddamn! I wish I could have some video cameras set up and watch those nukes go off. You don't get to see that every day! Say Curtis ever saw footage of the nuclear tests?" I said, "Not much." Patrick chuckled and said, "I have it on a VHS tape I ordered with unseen footage and goddamn some of the best fucking nuke footage of all time!" Melissa went to speak but Patrick raised his voice and said, "Don't say a fucking word! I'm still pissed with you. But you Curtis, I'm fine with." I said, "Can't say the same with you."

Patrick lightly shook his head and said, "Yeah, I know. I should have tossed the pistol out, but I learned my lesson after that." The pilot said, "Ok, Patrick we're all set here." He turned his head back and said, "Alright, tell the others to stay close as we can NOT fuck this up!" The pilot said, "Yes sir." We saw the other helicopters getting close to each other then we saw a large golden ring come out of the clouds above us. Inside of the golden ring was nothing but darkness but then a dark purple ring opened, and we could see a tunnel. Patrick said, "Alright! Everyone, hold on as it's going to be a bumpy ride."

When we flew through the purple tunnel suddenly everything went faster while the helicopter did shake a bit. Around us was electric rings while the tunnel walls moved like water. I turned to Patrick and asked, "So, this is how you caught up to us so fast?" Patrick said, "No, we just followed you, after you left Vancouver for Alaska. Just be glad I caught up with you, before the Reds got you first." The pilot said, "Five minutes to Moscow!" Patrick put on a headset and told his soldiers to get ready once they reached the Kremlin Palace they would move in and get Nikita and a few others to ensure that the warheads would be fired at every target that Manson told him. I knew somehow that we had to stop Patrick and Manson from accomplishing their plans.

At the end of the tunnel the helicopters flew out another hole and we we're flying above Moscow. Patrick said, "Alright soldiers! Head for the Palace and only kill those whom we don't need!" Patrick turned to and lifted his headset up and said, "And as for you two." He armed his heavy machine gun and said, "You're not leaving my sight again." I thought, "Shit! We'll never be able to grab a gun or do something to stop him. Patrick lightly laughed and said, "Sucks to be you, guys."

As the helicopters were flying towards the Kremlin Palace me and Melissa watched as Patrick's soldiers landed inside the palace then storming out and shooting at the guards while the rest of helicopters flew around the city block attacking those down below. Patrick said, "Gotta let my soldiers have a little fun." He grinned while I shot him an angry look then suddenly, I heard the pilot yell, "RPG!" Patrick turned his head, and the side of the helicopter was hit by a rocket which caused the helicopter to turn sideways and spin out of control and crash into the palace wall and smack hard into the ground.

We saw most of Patrick's soldiers were killed in the crash while he was knocked out. Melissa said, "Now's our chance!" I looked at Patrick, but the flames were getting worse I thought, "Burn in hell!" We ran outside and ran towards the Kremlin

Palace and saw some dead guards me and Melissa picked up their AK-74's and taking a few spare magazines then ran inside and heard shooting. We saw walls covered in blood holes and blood splatter along with dead bodies but not one of Patrick's soldiers was down. Melissa said, "I hope we find this guy in time!"

Just as we went to run out of the hallway, there was heavy machine gun fire, we both moved back. It was one of Patrick's soldiers keeping us from stopping their mission. I looked at Melissa and said, "I got a plan. I'm going to run out and when I do kill that fucker!" She said, "Got it." I ran out and bullets zoomed by me as Melissa quickly aimed at Patrick's soldier and pulled back on the trigger. She held tightly onto AK-74 while firing full auto shooting him in the chest, neck and head and fell backwards.

I then saw more of Patrick's soldiers coming out I aimed at them pressing the stock firmly against my shoulder and held back on the trigger. Bright muzzle flashes went off as bullet shells flew out the side I watch as Patrick's soldiers didn't have time to react and were all hit. I let go off the trigger as we ran where they came out taking more ammo and following where they went.

Following where the shooting it led up going upstairs then reached the 3rd floor as we one of Patrick's helicopters let loose with the rocket launcher blowing chucks out of the Kremlin Palace. A few guards came out and went to shoot back but were killed. When the helicopter stopped firing me and Melissa quickly aimed at the pilot and pulled back on the trigger taking him out. Quickly, we reloaded our AK-74's then we heard shouting. Melissa and I both turned over and saw the double doors blown up. Out came Patrick's soldiers holding Nikita, along with other Soviet Union leaders held at gun point.

Nikita was wearing a white suit while the other members had grey or black suits on. One of Patrick's soldiers holding a Remington 870 Marine Magnum Shotgun said, "Alright, you Red bastards! You're coming with us, and if anyone tries anything! You'll end up like your dead comrades." Nikita spoke angrily in English, "You're making a big mistake! Your country will suffer for this!" The soldier chuckled and said, "Oh it will, along with everyone else as that's our goal." Melissa whispered, "We'll never take them out like that. Let's wait until they come out."

I nodded my head and we moved back and waited for them to come out while Patrick's soldiers were leading Nikita and the other Soviet leaders. One solider said, "Hey Patrick! We got your guy along with his staff." We heard on Patrick's headsets, "Good. Now, find those two fucking Tricksters! They manage to escape again!" I turned to Melissa nodded my head as we popped out and aimed at Patrick's soldiers taking them out while more of them came out and fired at us but killed some of the staff members. Me and Melissa took them out as Nikita and the others went to grab their weapons and aim them at us.

I said, "Wait! Don't shoot! We're not on their side!" Nikita and the remaining staff members still held their weapons on us I said, "We came here to stop Manson and Barbara's plan from causing total nuclear Armageddon! He's going to kill everyone so he can change the world with every adult soul! We have to stop him before... Suddenly Patrick popped out and fired his M60E3 heavy machine gun killing all of Nikita and staff while I fired at Patrick hitting him in the arm which forced him to take cover Nikita ran towards us and said, "Follow me!"

Following him as we heard Patrick yelled, "YOU FUCKERS ARE GOING TO FUCKING GET IT!" Storming towards us were heavily armed Russian soldiers Nikita spoke in Russian and they didn't stop us, we kept moving but heard lots of machine gun fire behind us. Nikita took us to the stairway running downstairs Melissa asked, "Where are we going?" Nikita said, "The parking garage to my car!"

When we reached it, we saw a lot of fancy high-end cars. Nikita pointed to a dark blue 83 Porsche 911 SC Cabrio with the soft top down. When we got near it, Nikita took out his car keys and unlocked the door then got inside while we ran to the passenger door. I got in first and went in the back while Melissa sat in the passenger seat. Nikita started up his Porsche then turned his head to me and asked, "Where the hell am I going?" I said, "To where the warheads are! We can't allow Manson to fire them." As he went to drive suddenly, we saw Patrick running towards us while holding his M60E3. I aimed and fired shooting at him while he fired back, we both missed each as Nikita sped out of the parking garage.

Nikita drove fast and it didn't take us long to get out of their and sped down the road avoid hitting a truck with soldiers on the back. Suddenly chasing after us was Patrick in a black sport car. I said, "Son of bitch just won't give up!" I aimed at him while Nikita drove around the other cars. Once Patrick was close enough, I squeezed back on the trigger. Bullets hit the black sport car, but Patrick wasn't backing off. When the AK-74 clicked empty Patrick pulled out a Colt Python .357 and fired at us. Nikita made a hard right turn avoiding Patrick's shots then made a left turn while I was reloading.

Then Melissa said, "Oh shit!" I looked up at the sky to see dark purple blimps in the sky but attached to both sides were large speakers. I thought, "Great! What's Manson going to do to us next?! Make us go deaf?" Then ahead of us the road was blocked by police cars with officers getting out then shooting at us. Melissa quickly fired back as a few bullets hit the windshield but none of bullets came close to us. Melissa took out the officers as Nikita drove around the roadblock and made a hard right turn. Nikita asked while we reloaded out AK-74's, "What the hell is going on?! Why would they shoot at us!?" I said, "It's fucking Manson! He's brainwashing everyone to fight against us!"

Nikita had a shocked expression on his face and said, "I can't believe this is happening!" Patrick caught up and fired a few more shots but missed I fired back and hit him a few times but wasn't backing off. Then a police car came out and rammed Patrick he quickly aimed at the officer and pulled the trigger. The officer's face exploded, blood splattered inside the squad car. I went to fire, but Nikita made a hard left turn to avoid hitting a truck. Nikita raised his voice and said, "You know, there are a lot of bases that control warheads!?" Melissa asked, "Isn't there a main base that controls all of them?" Nikita was quiet for a bit then said, "Wait! Green Spring of course!"

Melissa looked at me with shock as that was the town that Arkard was born in. Patrick caught up and was about to fire but I aimed and fired first. I hit Patrick above his chest and arm causing him to make a hard turn and crash into a parked car flying through the front windshield and smack into a building. I knew he wasn't coming back this time.

Nikita drove away from Moscow and said, "It will take us a few miles to reach Green Spring. It..it used to be a town until Stalin destroyed it in '79 and rebuilt it into the main control base for all our warheads." Nikita turned to us and asked, "So how did you find me?" I said, "We found your note in Arkard's house in Hollywood." Nikita lightly shook his head and said, "The things I have done. I wish I could have undone every bad thing I have caused towards my family." I said, "We'll stop Arkard's creations from completing their mission."

Nikita was silent and didn't say anything else other then look up at the sky to see more dark purple blimps popping up. I thought one of them would start shooting at us but remembered what Patrick said about Manson and Barbara needing our souls to fully heal. Melissa turned to me and asked, "Should we try shooting those blimps down?" I said, "Don't. Save the ammo we'll need it for later." Nikita said, "He's right." Suddenly we saw Mil Mi-24 Hind gunships flying above us. Nikita said, "They're sending soldiers to stop us and arm the warheads! Once they do, we won't have much time to stop them."

Nikita pushed his Porsche faster trying to reach Green Spring. But chasing after us were black sedans then Russian soldiers were shooting at us. Me and Melissa were firing back at them as some bullets hit the Porsche. Nikita kept his head low to avoid getting shot at. Melissa fired at the grill of the black sedan until thick smoke to come out then the engine exploded taking out the two sedans beside it.

One black sedan tried to drive around the burning cars but crashed in the ditch with the others stopping. Nikita said, "You two better get down as we'll be getting close to Green Spring soon!" We did what he said knowing these Russian soldiers under Manson's control won't stop until we we're dead. A big sign showed that Green Spring was up ahead along with warnings of nuclear warheads. We saw the front gate coming up, two guards came out and were both aiming their pistols at us. Nikita pressed his foot down as they both fired at us.

Nikita drove through the front gate and ran over the guards he made a hard left turn and saw the gunships have landed in the parking lot with the soldiers getting out me and Melissa stood up and fired away taking them out while Nikita kept his head down. Not stopping, we took out all the soldiers we saw before they could fire back at us. When it was over, both our AK's clicked empty. Nikita got out and pulled out a Walther P5 Compact pistol armed it while we reloaded and said, "Stay close to me. It's easy to get lose in the base." We followed Nikita inside the base. We ran down the long set of stairs leading us deep underground while lights were on both sides of the walls. An alarm was also going off followed by speakers blasting words in Russian which I knew wasn't good.

We came to the elevator but was blown out. Nikita turned to us and said, "Keep moving! We only got 7 minutes left!" Pushing ourselves faster downstairs the alarms were getting louder. Just when I felt it would be endless, we reached the bottom with Nikita ran towards a guard booth. The door opened but Nikita shot the guard before he could shoot him. Then Russian soldiers blocking a heavy-duty door went to aim their AK's I quickly shot them taking them out as Nikita said, "I hope they didn't cancel my code!" Nikita ran over to a heavy duty's keypad and typed his code in a green light flash.

Me and Melissa went over and aimed our AK-74's ready to pull the trigger as Nikita opened the door. We stepped inside but stopped. Soldiers had killed all Soviet leaders, along with the workers there. Nikita said something in Russian then ran over to a computer and began typing away then I saw a digital clock showing we had 2 minutes left. Nikita had sweat running down his forehead while moving his fingers quickly trying to stop the countdown. I knew there wasn't anything for us to do but to wait.

My eyes would move back and forth to Nikita typing away on the keyboard while watching the countdown getting closer to. Then on the digital clock showed 1 minute left. Nikita yelled and slammed his down fist on the desk. He wiped the sweat off his forehead and pressed harder on the keyboard cursing in Russian.

Unable to speak, I just stared at the countdown. Melissa wrapped her arms around while I held onto her, hoping Nikita could stop the launch.

Then just as the countdown reached 10 seconds it suddenly stopped along with the alarm. Nikita's jaw dropped open with his hands stacking and asked, "I did it?" Nothing happened we both laughed then Nikita stood up from the chair and came over to us and said, "Holy shit! I can't believe I fucking did it!" I said, "Well, I guess Manson and Barbara can kiss those plans of theirs go bye." Suddenly all the computer screens went dark purple then heard Manson laughing loudly on the speakers.

Then on all the computer screens we saw Manson's face looking at us with red glowing eyes and said, "Haha nice try Curtis! You thought by killing Patrick, stopping a countdown would halt my plans of making this world a better place. Oh Curtis, you should have known I would have a backup plan, in case something like this happened." We were all shocked I said, "No! No fucking way! You and your girlfriend are supposed to be... Manson said, "Healing? Well, we we're but if case Patrick failed his mission, we used him as back up. You see by giving a person enough magic powers that makes them stronger which allows us to use his soul to fully heal. And I didn't want his kind around after anyway, so you save me some trouble of dealing with him."

Manson then turned to Nikita and said, "Aww the father of Arkard Glukhovsky or better known by his allies as Osborne Louis. Despite the pain and abuse he treated us if it wasn't for your actions of killing our creator, we won't be able to use his magic to gain life." Nikita turned white as a ghost Manson turned back to me and said, "You know Curtis when you asked me about making some deal with the devil, I didn't know who this person was until I asked one of the teenagers and told me the lies you people have created. So, two places where good and bad people go, called heaven and hell. Well Curtis here's the truth there is no heaven, there is no hell. Your world wasn't created by gods or aliens it as all made by big bang and magic. And only those who know how to harvest it can truly have the power!"

Manson lightly laughed and said, "I find it funny how humans will make themselves worship anything just for the sake of ensuring that when their time comes, they'll go to a place that isn't real and fool everyone. Today, that all ends." Suddenly the countdown continued where it left off as Manson looked at us and said, "No more song, no more love, no more joy. The sun has been out too long it's time for it to go to sleep." When the countdown reached zero, we felt the ground shake then heard the sound of the warheads being fired from their silos.

Then on the computer screen Nikita had been typing on showed a map where all the warheads were going. Manson said, "In a few minutes every inch of human history will be erased from this planet and all the souls will reshape it into my own image." Nikita broke down and cried while Manson turned over to him and said, "Before the warheads each Green Spring why don't you tell them how this whole event happened." Nikita stood up pulled a chair while looking at us and said, "I...I was the one who ordered a hit on my own son! I feared his cartoon show would being harm and would inspire those to start what Hitler and Stalin did in the past. I used all my power to cover up his creations thinking it would keep anyone from bring that cartoon show back to alive... yet I was the one who did."

Then without warning Nikita pressed his Walther P5 Compact pistol against the side of his head and squeezed the trigger. Blood splattered out the side of his head and his lifeless body fell off the chair and onto the floor. Manson then asked, "So Curtis what's it going to be? Do you rather be done with this world or still want to keep going?" I looked at Melissa and lightly nodded her head I knew she wasn't going to give up yet. I turned to Manson and said, "Bring it on you motherfucker!" Manson grinned and said, "Very well then." Suddenly the computer screen opened up a portal I held tightly onto Melissa as we ran towards it and jumped through it.

While traveling through the tunnel around us were screens with different images from around the world while seeing cities, towns and historian places being destroyed by the nukes going off. I saw city hall from Black Creek blown to bits while people screamed until they were burned into ashes. I felt we we're going faster while Manson and Barbara laughed as the world we once knew was destroyed. Their laughter grew louder than all the screens around the tunnel changed to close ups of their mouths.

Suddenly below us was a large screen with Manson's mouth grinning then he said, "Well, what are you two waiting for? Come right in." Me and Melissa watched as Manson open his mouth wide and we fell through the screen which felt wet yet sticky. The liquid like screen was on our bodies then we we're pulled through and heard strange noises we fell into darkness while we screamed until everything was silent.

When I woke up, I was lying inside a dark forest with thick fog. Above me was a dark sky with a large glowing moon. I slowly lifted my head up then I saw Melissa lying a few feet from me I got up and said, "Melissa! Melissa! You alright?" When I went over to her Melissa open her eyes and asked, "Where are we?" I said, "We're in the Dark Kingdom." Melissa opened her eyes to see where we we're she asked, "So we just find Manson and his gang then kill them?" I said, "Yes and after that...maybe everything will change." Melissa said, "Guess there only one way to find out."

Cool air blew through the thick forest as it was very quiet. I scanned the forest for anything that might come at us, and we didn't have our guns with us. I said, "Remember we have to burn them or cause so much damage they won't be able to heal in time." While walking we could see Manson & Barbara's castle far off in the distance. Suddenly I heard movement behind us when I turned my head back, I saw Andrew holding his crossbow I turned my head back then grabbed Melissa's arm and said, "Run!"

Andrew fired his crossbow but missed us but was running after us. I knew he would have traps set up for us which we'll have to watch out for. Andrew aimed his crossbow and fired it hitting me in the shoulder. I broke the arrow and snapped it then pulled it while Andrew ran off. Melissa asked, "Where's he going?" I said, "He's playing with us." Just we went to run further we stopped and saw the patches of the ground have been disturbed and could see trip wire. I said under my breath, "Goddamn bastard!" Melissa said, "Let's try to find a way around it." Just as we went to turn around an arrow zoomed passed our faces as Andrew yelled, "RUN WHILE YOU CAN!"

We took cover behind the tress as I said, "Oh I'm so not in the mood for this bullshit!" Suddenly an arrow went halfway through the tree above my head I turned my head and heard Andrew lightly laughing and said, "Come on! I waited all night for this! Don't make me bored!" I growled knowing we had no choice me and Melissa ran and carefully hopped over the trip wire not to see it off nor step on whatever traps Andrew had left for us.

Andrew aimed with his crossbow going back and forth between the two Tricksters until he chose which one to shoot next. Melissa was hit in the back with the arrow and nearly fell but caught herself on a tree. Andrew was reloading his crossbow I found a rock and threw it at him causing him to drop it. We ran while Andrew quickly picked up the arrow loaded his crossbow and ran after us. I pulled the arrow out of Melissa's back she asked, "I'm not bleeding too bad, am I?" I said, "No." I looked back to see Andrew was following us I saw a few more rocks I said, "We have to get rid of him." Melissa looked at me and said, "I keep that bastard busy." I said, "Alright, but don't run too far."

Melissa said, "Got it." As Andrew was aiming with his crossbow I said, "Go." She ran and within seconds he aimed and fired but missed just as he went to reload, I threw a rock hitting him in the head. I ran towards him while he saw me coming. Andrew then tossed his crossbow and pulled out a machete and went to swing it, but I dodged his attack. He chuckled and said, "Not bloody bad but not good enough!" He ran towards me swinging his machete at me. When my back bumped against a tree, he went to chop my head off I ducked as it went halfway through the tree.

I threw a hard punch into his gut as he growled and kicked his boot into my chest. He went to grab his machete, but I threw my body weight onto his causing him down onto the ground. I threw more hard punches but he kicked me off and landed on the ground. Andrew growled as he went to pull his machete out and said, "Damn humans! You're never easy too... Suddenly an arrow hit Andrew in his hand he yelled and saw Melissa had shot him. He yelled, "You clever bitch!" Andrew went to reach for his pistol with his hand, but Melissa ran towards him and smashed his crossbow into his head causing it to break. But he grabbed her by the neck lifting her body up and squeezed hard.

I got up and ran over I grabbed the machete pulled it then stabbed it into Andrew's neck. Blood poured out as he gasped for air. I pressed the machete harder and sliced off Andrew's head as blood shot up from his headless body and fell onto the ground along with letting Melissa go. She rubbed her throat and said, "Thanks." I looked at Andrew's head I picked up and said, "Just to be sure." I toss at one of the patches which exploded into bits.

I turned back to Melissa and said, "One down six to go." Leaving the forest, we saw ruins of the old town. The fog rolled in while a few gothic-looking streetlamps were lit while a few flickered as moths flew around the lights. While walking we heard Kane say above us, "Such a fine night, isn't it?" Turning our heads around to see Kane grinning. Kane moved both of his arms behind his back and said, "Such a shame this will be the last time we meet again." I said, "I'm fine with that!" Kane chuckled then pulled out two lit fuse bombs.

When he went to throw them, we ran and within seconds they exploded then threw a smoke bomb in front of him. When the smoke cleared, he was gone I thought, "I really hate it when he does that!" Me and Melissa were looking from to pop up then I heard something move behind me and when I turned my head, I got punched hard in the face knocking me flat off my feet. I landed on the brick road while Melissa went to punch but Kane pulled her towards him spun her body around while holding her in a headlock. Kane said, "After I'm finish with Curtis here, we will have some fun later."

Kane reached for Melissa's groin as she rammed her elbow into his gut hard enough to make him let go. I got up and picked up the machete running towards him, but Kane threw another smoke bomb. I yelled, "Cut the chicken shit and fucking fight me!" Melissa yelled, "Curtis! Behind you!" I heard Kane coming behind me I spun around as she went to throw another punch but grabbed his arm and rammed the machete through. He yelled as

I pulled it out then slashed across his face. Blood splattered in the air while Kane growled then kicked me in the chest knocking me down.

Kane held onto his face then moved his paw hand away as it was covered in blood. I saw Kane went to grab a fuse bomb as he lit it. But just as he went to toss it, I threw the machete into his chest which caused him to drop it. Once the fuse bomb fell onto the brink road it went off blowing Kane to pieces as his limbs went flying in the air. Melissa ran over to me and asked, "You alright?" I nodded my head as she pulled me up. I said, "Two down five to go." Walking further through the town a cool breeze blew at us as thunder flashed in the sky.

Suddenly a wall of ice blocked our way we turned around to see Sydney flying towards us and shooting ice beams. Running for cover while she laughed more ice walls popped up while running through town. We we're now trapped as Sydney yelled, "Play time is over! It's now time to die!" Just as she was about to fly towards us Melissa yelled, "RUN!" We ran down a brink street with Sydney getting closer but as a ice beam hit the ground close by to be which exploded knocking me down. Lying on my back I saw Sydney about to fire another beam when Melissa grabbed the dlamp pole and spun her body around and kicked Sydney in the neck as she flew through the air a bit and landed hard on the brick road.

Me and Melissa ran towards Sydney as she tried to get up while growling, we both kicked and stumped her to death. Sydney screamed trying to get up, but we won't let her I felt the anger rise inside of me I stumped harder hearing her bones break. I said, "This is for my friend Hunter!" I kicked Sydney's beak causing it to snap in half she screamed louder. Melissa crushed her rib cage as she coughed up blood then tried crawling away, I stumped on her back then crushed her head. Blood and brain matter pressed out the sides of Sydney's head.

Breathing heavy I spat on Sydney's corpse as the ice walls melted allowing us to move further on. While walking Melissa said, "I hated that bitch. So, fucking annoying." I lightly nodded my head and said, "Just four left to kill!" Thunder roared in the sky while lightning flashed brightly. We then saw the docks coming up with air ships we ran behind a tree for cover to see Manson's guards fully armed and looking for us. Melissa said, "If we use one of those airships, we can reach Manson's castle." I said, "Yes but how are we getting past all of those guards."

Watching the patrols, we might be able to sneak pass them I said, "If we time it right, we can sneak onto one of those air ships." Melissa said, "Alright." Getting closer to the docks we waited until the guards had moved away from each other and moved pass them. Wooden buildings with dark tinted windows, streetlamp poles lit up brightly and crates placed. We hid behind them for cover then ran out when with one guard spotting us and yelled, "It's the Tricksters! Kill them!" They fired their rifles nearly hitting us.

We ran aboard a air ship when I got to the top I turned around and kicked the ramp knocking down the guards as they fell onto each other. Melissa got the rope untied then we ran to the bridge as I pulled a lever which bright the engines to life then filled the sacks filled with hot air lifting the air ship. The guards were shooting at us but stopped when we we're out of their range. I turned the air ship towards Manson & Barbara's castle and moved forward while heavy rain poured onto the air ship.

I said, "When we get to Manson's castle let's trash it up." Melissa said, "I go load the cannons." She ran off while thinking about my little brother and hoped he won't be under Manson's control when I found him. I looked over and saw a radio I thought, "Should turn it on to see how Melissa is coming along." When I did, I heard Hellen's voice say, "Well, well if it isn't the Tricksters!" Flying beside us was another air ship with Hellen on it.

Hellen said, "Seeing how the others failed on stopping you two I'll make sure to avenge their deaths!" I saw the double cannons sticking out of Hellen's ship I press the radio and said, "Melissa! Get the cannons on the right side ready! Hellen is about to fire!" Without warning Hellen fired her double cannons with a few shots hitting the air ship. I then heard the door open behind me I turned around to see Melissa looking shocked as she said, "Curtis! There aren't any goddamn cannons on this ship!"

I said, "Damn it!" Hellen fired her cannons again and this airship was taking hits. I said, "I got an idea!" I turned the air ship towards Hellen's air ship I looked at Melissa and said, "When we get close enough jump on board their ship, so we'll have something against Mason." Melissa asked, "What will fight with?" I said, "There has to be some weapons lying around here somewhere!" Melissa said, "I'll go check." I said, "Hurry up!" The closer I got Hellen fired more cannon shots as this air ship wasn't going to last much longer.

Hellen spoke on the speaker, "Hey! What do you think you're doing?" I press the talk button and said, "You'll about to find out." I ran out of the bridge and was greeted by heavy rain fall I heard Melissa call my name I turned around and she ran over to me holding two axes. I took one as we ran towards Hellen's ship as another cannon shot went off. We both jumped off and landed on board while the air ship burned towards the ground.

We heard Hellen's voice on the speakers yelling, "Attention! We have the Tricksters on board on our ship! Do whatever it takes! KILL THEM!" I said, "Damn we really pissed her off." Suddenly bear men came out running toward us armed with clubs, axes and spiked maces. Me and Melissa fought our way through them as thunder roared above us with lightning flashes lighting up the deck. I whacked the axe into a bear man's neck and quickly pulled it out and kicked his body down while Melissa blocked a spiked mace from hitting her as she kicked the bear man in the groin then whacked the axe into his head with blood splatter.

A bear man yelled and went to swing his axe into Melissa back I ran over to him and chopped off his arm he screamed in pain as I whacked my axe into his back knocking him down. Me and Melissa swung, chop and hacked our way through the remaining Hellen's crew while breathing heavy. We went inside the air ship making our way towards the bridge to find Hellen when suddenly the door exploded. We both jumped out of the way in time nearly getting hit by mini cannon balls.

Hellen kicked down her door holding a large rifle that fired mini cannon balls in her right hand while holding a long curve sword in her left hand. Hellen growled and said, "You'll be paying blood for my crew along with damaging my ship!" Hellen ran towards us as we went to swing our axes, but she blocked my attack and whacked Melissa with her rifle. I went to swing my axe again, but she swung her sword leaving a gash across my nose. I didn't stop and swung my axe, but she blocked it with both weapons.

I could feel how strong Hellen was while she grinned showing off her sharp teeth. Melissa yelled and whacked her axe into Hellen's back she screamed in pain she headbutt me hard knocking me down to the floor she dropped her rifle grabbing Melissa and smashed her head against the wooden wall squeezing her neck. I quickly grabbed Hellen's rifle and rammed the barrel against the back of her head and squeezed the trigger. I loud bang went off followed by Hellen's head exploding into chucks of blood, brain matter and skull blood.

Hellen's fingers let go of Melissa as she coughed for a bit as Hellen's headless body fell onto the floor. I ran over and helped Melissa up she looked at me and said, "Let's finish this shit!" I went to the bridge flying towards Manson's castle while Melissa got the double cannons ready. Lightning flashed in the sky then heard Manson's voice on the speaker, "Hellen have you taken care of the Tricksters?" I pressed the talk button and said, "Four down and only three left to go." Manson growled raising his voice and said, "I should have never let you into my world!"

I press the talk button as I laughed and said, "I think you like it when I come to play with you." Once I was close enough to Manson's castle, I turned the air ship and cut the power I heard Manson say, "Curtis! What are you doing?!" I pressed the talk button and said, "You ruined my life, so I'll ruin yours!" I changed the channel pressing the talk button and said, "Let him have it!" Melissa fired the double cannons I watched as his castle was hit with big explosions going off and some of the guard towers going down.

I laughed watching half of the castle go down I changed the channel make to Manson press talk and yelled, "HOW DO YOU FUCKING LIKE THAT! MOTHERFUCKER!" Suddenly cannon shots were going off hitting the airship and it was heading straight for the ground I couldn't control it with nowhere to go I held on until the air ship crashed into Manson's castle it didn't take long for the crash to be over.

I pulled myself up and could smell smoke I thought, "Melissa! I better find her before Manson's guards do." I ran out of the bridge and pulled the axe out of Hellen's back and ran to where the cannons were but saw the lower deck was destroyed. I yelled, "MELISSA!" I didn't hear anything I yelled louder, "MELISSA!" The smoke was getting thicker making it harder to breath I had no choice but to leave. Running towards outside I heard shouting and when I got out, I went over behind destroyed wall of the castle for cover.

Manson's guards looked pissed as they were looking for us I wasn't sure if Melissa survived the crash or not but if she didn't I had to continue on. I saw a basement door was open I ran over to it and when I got inside, I slowly closed the door and locked it. Turning around and walked down the steps slowly as there wasn't much light so I was careful not to slip. Once I reached the bottom floor it felt very cold down here with a few torches lit up my heart was beating fast, but I wasn't scared of Manson or anyone else I was going to end this now!

I made my way through the basement and started climbing upstairs with more torches lit up and guiding my way to the upper level of Manson's castle. Just as I was about to open a door suddenly, I heard guards coming I turned over to see a metal door I quickly opened it and went behind it. I had it open enough to see the guards running down the hallway. As I waited for them to be gone suddenly, I heard loud breathing and knew George was behind me. Before I could move, he grabbed me and spun me around and slammed my back into the brick wall.

Pulling the axe away from my hand and tossing it away he growled and said, "First, you murder my friends! Then attack my home! Now I'm going to tear you from limb to limb!" George's grip felt impossible to break free from with his fingers squeezing my neck tightly I couldn't breathe. George grabbed my leg while lightly laughing and said, "You know what they say? Break a leg." I could feel my bone being pulled along with the pain but before George could pull any further, he screamed in pain as Melissa whacked the axe into his back.

Pressing the blade further into his skin as blood ran down his back George yelled and threw me across the room as I rolled on the hard solid floor. Melissa avoided being grabbed by him and ran over to help me. George pulled out the axe then snapped it in half tossing the two pieces away then grabbed his hammer running after us. As Melissa pulled me up, we ran however George was catching up quickly. In front of us was a metal door we opened it got inside then locked it to see we had trapped ourselves inside George's tool room and gym.

Suddenly his hammer was slamming against the door, and it wasn't going to hold for long. I turned to Melissa and said, "We'll never win in a fair fight with him." Melissa looked at the torches and said, "Quick! I have idea." We pulled the torches from the wall and put of the fire making it dark enough then grabbed a weapon.

George burst through the door breathing heavily. It was dark inside his tool room and gym. Looking around as he slowly walked closer, he said, "You can't hide from me!" Then he noticed a torch had fallen onto the floor showing a shadow outline of the Tricksters. George grinned while laughing then swung his hammer to where they were hiding but only heard the sound of stone being crushed not flesh or bone. Before George could react both of his knees were smashed with weights he howled in pain and fell onto the floor.

We ran away before George could try to grab us and I picked up the torches which had pointed bottoms and stab out his eyes. Blood gushed out as he screamed louder. We pressed harder until the torches reached his brain with blood now pouring out his nose and ears. Slowly we stood up Melissa said, "There are two left now." I said, "Let's find them and kill them." On George's tool rack we took two swords and left his room and continued further through the castle until we reached the dining hall.

Looking around we didn't see anyone with a few chairs knocked down and some cracks on the walls. Then walking in front of us was Manson holding his cane sword and his eyes were glowing bright red. Melissa turned around and Barbara was behind her holding her curve sword with glowing red eyes. I said, "It's time to end this! Once and for fucking all!" Manson and Barbara laughed loudly as they slowly walked closer to us, I said, "Your friends are dead! And soon you too will be joining them!"

I ran towards Manson yelling along with Melissa. I swung my sword, but Manson blocked my attack I quickly pulled back and went to strike but Manson dodged my attack.

I heard Melissa and Barbara whacking and hitting each other with swords. Feeling my anger rising I swung faster and whacked harder trying to break through Manson's block. With the storm raging outside I noticed that me and Melissa were walked back into each other. Quickly I went to swing as Manson blocked my attack then I kicked him in the knee and went to stab him, but Manson grabbed me by the neck and threw me across the dining hall. As I landed on the floor Melissa was thrown above the fireplace. I stood up with Manson quickly coming back I yelled and went to swing my sword but with lightning speed Manson stabbed in the heart with his cane sword.

I couldn't move and felt my fingers lose grip with the sword falling out of my hand. Melissa's jaw dropped open and screamed, "CURTIS! NNNNOOOO!" She went to stand but Barbara sliced off her right arm she screamed then Barbara stabbed her sword into Melissa hard while pressing the blade firmly against the soft flesh as blood poured out of Melissa mouth.

I gasped for air with my heart slowing down and felt blood pouring out of my mouth Manson laughed louder then kicked me towards the wall. Slowly I fell to the floor as Barbara walked over to Manson grinning at me. I manage to speak, "How? How can you do this!?" They both laughed as Manson rested his cane sword onto the floor while leading on it with his hands looking at me and said, "Curtis, Curtis, Curtis. How many times do I have to tell you? You can't beat us as we are stronger than any other living creature." Suddenly the remains of Andrew, Kane, Sydney, Hellen, and George appeared in front of me while grinning.

Manson said, "Now that you and your girlfriend are finished, we will use your souls to reshape your world into our own!" I suddenly felt everything was being sucked out of me in the most painful way ever. I screamed loudly until there was nothing left of me as everything faded to darkness. My last thoughts were, "Please that John will never forget me."

Chapter 10

It took a few weeks but Manson and Barbara had their castle fully rebuilt. The Dark Kingdom merged itself with the planet, once called Earth. Now, renamed Dark World. Every inch of human history was gone, and the children shall not repeat the failures that they were taught in the past. However, it would take many years 'til the whole planet will be reshaped in Manson and Barbara's image. It means putting up walls to keep the children from exploring the forbidden places. Anyone who dared went out where they shouldn't be, were punished.

The children and teenagers have been fitting well. Each one given a task to do around the castle and helping the town's people. They were taught how to use magic. Sydney has been very busy, but the kids learn quickly.

Manson and Barbara stood in their bedroom looking over their town.

"In the months to come we'll have bigger towns for our people and children to grow up in." Barbara looked up at Manson's face with adoration. Manson began undoing Barbara's suit.

"Yes, the time will come when the whole planet will be ours. We'll travel to outer space and spread our great plans anywhere we want."

Barbara moaned as her clothes dropped the floor. Manson played with her huge breasts. Barbara giggled.

"While we wait for that future. There are other things we have to do."

Manson turned Barbara around. She unbuttoned his suit and loosen his pants.

"Yes, we'll need a family to raise, as well." They went to bed naked and spent hours having sex. Moonlight glowed above them. Manson was thrusting his big dick. Barbara was moaning louder. She was holding onto the edges of the bed begging.

"YES! YES! FUCK ME HARDER!"

John's magic class with Sydney was done for the day. They would learn more next week. At first, John enjoyed living in the Dark Kingdom. It was always night, there was never any sunlight. He had lots of friends to play and learn magic with. George teaches them black smith stuff. He learned card tricks from Kane, survival skills from Andrew, and he even get to ride on Hellen's air ship. But for the longest time John felt something was missing in his life. He couldn't put his finger on it, but no matter how hard he tried he couldn't push the thought out of his mind. John wasn't sure if he was missing a sister or a brother. This made him uneasy at times, and he would prefer to be alone.

When everyone is done with their tasks, they return to Manson & Barbara's castle for dinner. John jumped when he felt a hand touch his shoulder.

"Damn it, Danny! Don't do that!" Danny was sort of his friend. He had long blonde hair, light blue eyes and was one year older than him.

"Relax John, besides you know I'm the only one who does that."

"What's up?"

"After dinner a few of us want to go swimming at the lake. Want to come?" John thought about it for a bit.

"No thanks. I don't feel like swimming, maybe next time."

"Is something wrong, John?"

"No, Danny, I'm alright just tired from Sydney's class today. I swear learning magic makes me feel tired." He smiled for Danny's benefit.

"I wonder if we'll learn a trick that will show us Sydney's lovely butt." John rolled his eyes and Danny laughed.

"You'll get in trouble for that."

"They'll have to catch me first."

Inside the castle the children went to the dining hall and waited for dinner to be served.

John rested his fist against his cheek while tapping the table with his right hand. *Why won't this thought go away? I can get rid of it for a few days or weeks, but they always come. Did I really have a sister or brother? If so then why won't Manson or anyone tell me? I feel like something is missing from me."*

The waitress came in bringing large dishes of everyone's favorite food. When all the dishes were brought out Manson, Barbara and the others would join them at the table. They would each ask the children what they learned today. Or ask if they made any new friends. Or what they liked best about the Dark Kingdom.

John's turn never came. He liked it that way. He didn't feel like talking. He ate what was needed by his body. He checked and half of them are done with their dinner. John finished his glass of milk, left the dining hall, and went to his bedroom. They shared rooms with the other children. Others would spend time reading books, writing, playing card games or talking. John wanted to go somewhere quiet to clear his head. He waited until everyone was asleep, then he sneaked out of the castle. This wasn't the first time John had done this. He never told anyone, and he's scared someone might tell on him.

John went to a spot he liked, where he could think. Sitting behind an old tree, he could see far off in the distance, the wall that Manson and Barbara have told everyone not to go near. Apparently, it was dangerous. If anyone was caught, they would be punished. John wasn't sure if he should ask Manson, Barbara or one of the others about this strange feeling he was having. Most of the time they were busy, but they would listen to anyone if they needed to talk.

John looked up at the sky to see the large glowing moon along with the flashing stars. Suddenly he felt someone was watching him. He looked around and saw a girl standing near the wall. It seemed like she was holding a teddy bear. *Did she sneak out too? How would she do that? With dread, John stood and walked towards the wall. Please, don't get me in trouble.* As John got closer, he noticed the girl looked nervous.

"Hey there. How did you get out of the castle?" John smiled in an attempt to be less intimidating.

John noticed behind the girl, was a hole in the wall. He could see a tunnel that led to somewhere else. When John looked back at the girl, she looked upset.

"Are you ok? My name is John Curtis. What's yours?"

"It's...it's Suzie. Suzie Streeter. I can't find my grandmother! I can't find anyone back at Blue Lake! Their all gone!" The girl wiped her eyes. John went closer to hug her, and Suzie pressed her head onto his shoulder. She held her while she cried.

"Suzie, where did you come from?"

"The world that I once knew. It's all gone. It's..." She started and stopped. She stared at him. "Did you say your name was John Curtis?"

"Yes, I did. Why?"

"You look a lot like a man I met a long time ago. His name was Curtis Parker." He could feel the of hairs on his back standing on end. Then, it came back to him. Curtis Parker was his older brother's name.

"Do you know what happened to my brother?" John can barely speak. Emotions clogged his throat.

"He and his girlfriend Melissa were on a quest to stop these two cartoon villains, Manson and Barbara, from taking over the world...they never came back!"

The words hit John hard. He just realized his older brother was dead. Now, he knew why he felt something was missing from him. John wrapped his arms around Suzie as they cried together. They do not what world they should be in or even who to trust.

The End

www.ingramcontent.com/pod-product-compliance
Lightning Source LLC
Chambersburg PA
CBHW060758210726
48292CB00013B/222